ALSO BY MILA KANE

Mafia

Vicious Vengeance Duet

WICKED HEIR

SAVAGE THRONE

Made of Mayhem Duet

MALEVOLENT KING

RUNAWAY QUEEN

Devil's Own Series

KING OF THE CAGE

Original Sin Series

UNHOLY VOWS

BRUTAL LEGACY

SACRED RUIN

Bully

Hellions of Hade Harbor

BAD INTENTIONS

DARK DELIGHTS

TWISTED DEEDS

WICKED ENDS

UNHOLY VOWS

MILA KANE

DELL • NEW YORK

UNHOLY VOWS

A NOVEL

Dell
An imprint of Random House
A division of Penguin Random House LLC
1745 Broadway, New York, NY 10019
randomhousebooks.com
penguinrandomhouse.com

2026 Dell Trade Paperback Edition

This work was originally self-published by the author in 2023.

ISBN 979-8-217-29967-6

Printed in the United States of America on acid-free paper

1st Printing

Cover design: Angela Haddon
Cover photograph: Wander Aguiar

BOOK TEAM: Production editor: Dennis Ambrose • Managing editor: Saige Francis • Production manager: Linnea Knollmueller • Copy editor: Shannon Barr • Proofreaders: Nicole Ramirez, Andrea Gordon, Caryl Weintraub

The authorized representative in the EU for product safety and compliance is Penguin Random House Ireland, Morrison Chambers, 32 Nassau Street, Dublin D02 YH68, Ireland. https://eu-contact.penguin.ie

Welcome to Mila Kane's New York. It's not the city you know, and here the Kings and Queens of the Underworld reign supreme. Along with life-or-death love, darkness and mayhem rule this corner of the book world. If that's your thing, read on. This book contains themes of kidnapping, stalking, forced marriage, birth control tampering, and breeding. If you're not sure, check out my website for a full list of content warnings.

UNHOLY VOWS

1

CHARLIE

When you were single, twenty-six, and living in a party town like Atlantic City, there was a buffet of options for an evening's entertainment. You could go out on a date, eat something nice, maybe even get lucky. Or you could get lucky another way, high-rolling in one of the opulent casinos that lined the boardwalk. Maybe you'd prefer a quiet night, spending time with friends at home.

There was something for everyone, and yet, I was pretty sure *nobody's* idea of a good time was sneaking into a dilapidated warehouse on the Jersey Shore in the dead of night. Well, no one I knew, anyway.

Yet, here I was, and embarrassingly enough, it wasn't even the first time I'd spied on my little sister with my trusty tracker app and followed her somewhere I shouldn't. Next time, though, I'd prefer a frat party I was too old for to a warehouse that smelled like rotten fish and old sweat.

Man, this was bad. But not bad enough to turn back.

My baby sister, at nineteen years old, was in this hazardous shack somewhere, and I wasn't leaving without her, even if I had to drag her out by the ear.

I ignored the gnawing worry in my gut that the trouble Lucy was getting into was only escalating. It had started with fights at school. Then there was the shoplifting. Then the underage drinking. And most recently, dating losers on a one-way ticket to nowhere.

Now, I had no idea what she was getting into. She didn't talk to me, even though we were the only family we had left. Growing up in Mercy House, a group home run by nuns, had turned me into a shame-ridden rule follower, but it'd had the opposite effect on Lucy.

A firm talking-to was clearly in order. Hanging out at an abandoned property that looked like the set of a horror movie wasn't a great idea. What was next? I shuddered to think.

My sneaker pressed on a shard of broken glass and made a loud crunching sound. I froze. I was still in the large room I'd first snuck into. Old crates and other shipping equipment were stacked haphazardly along one wall, leaving plenty of shadowy nooks and crannies for eyes to watch me unseen.

Broken windows lined one side of the long room, and an upper catwalk ringed the entire floor. Metal creaked, and the wind whistled through the gaping window frames.

Get Lucy and get out of here, a voice inside me urged. *Nothing good happens in places like this*. Well, that was pretty damn obvious, but I couldn't see a single sign of my wayward sister, despite that blinking dot on the tracker app assuring me she was here somewhere.

It was tough to brush aside my highly attuned survival instincts and creep farther into the warehouse. I had spent my life trying to stay out of trouble, but growing up in Mercy House hadn't made that easy. I was thirteen when we'd ended up there, and all the social worker said as she'd patted me on the hand was how lucky I was not to be separated from my sister. Sure, our Da had just passed, mowed down in a random drive-by shooting while waiting in line to buy takeout. Sure, we had to sleep in a dorm with ten other girls, one of whom liked to set her pillow on fire, and another who hid and tortured small animals. A dorm where the nuns grilled us about our shameful thoughts and performed random middle-of-the-night bed checks for "impurity."

Okay, Sue Granger from Social Work. We were the luckiest girls in all of New Jersey.

"Lucy?" I hissed, breaking the oppressive silence in the dark room. She had to be here somewhere.

I pushed on, heading toward the next room over. I had to hand it to my baby sister. If they gave awards to people with the most talent for getting themselves in a pickle, Lucy would win, hands down. Technically, she wasn't a baby anymore. I knew that. But at nineteen, she was at that weird age where she was old enough to get herself in serious trouble, and yet young enough to ignore the possible consequences. I didn't think I'd ever be able to cut the cord between us.

For the last thirteen years, I'd been the only parent she had.

Look after her, Charlie. You're the only one who can.

My Da's ghostly voice drifted through my mind. That night, he'd given me the most important responsibility of my life, one that still sat heavily on my shoulders.

Some nights it was harder than others to honor his dying wish.

A shuffle sounded to my left. "Charlie?" a voice I knew better than my own whispered.

"Lucy," I muttered and dropped to a crouch. My hands landed on broken shards of glass in the dark, but I didn't flinch. When it came to protecting Lucy, nothing would ever be too painful or inconvenient to stop me.

My sister was sitting on the floor with her back against the wall, a wild look in her huge eyes. She was scared. Considering she hadn't been scared of anything at all lately—treating her "bad girl" status like a badge of honor—her sudden fear was worrying. She had to be in a tight spot if she was dropping her tough-girl act.

I maneuvered myself into the tiny space beside her. "What are you doing here?"

"Did you follow me?" she asked without anger.

I elbowed her gently. "Of course I did. That's what big sisters do, right?"

"How?"

"Phone tracker app." There was no point in lying to her; she'd figure it out eventually.

She nodded. Something was wrong. She was too subdued. I made out the sound of distant conversation. We weren't alone here.

"What's going on? Tell me," I urged and wrapped my hand around hers. Her skin was cold.

"Miguel. You know Miguel, right?" she started nervously.

She knew I didn't approve of her new boyfriend. He had trouble written all over him. I'd been hoping that it was just a passing thing, and the intrigue of dating someone so volatile and dangerous would fade. It seemed that hadn't happened yet.

I nodded. "I know him."

"Well, he had the idea that we could make some money on the side, you know, doing odd jobs and stuff."

"And an odd job brought you here? This doesn't look like the kind of place people order takeout to."

Lucy's eyes slid from mine. She was lying. I could always tell. But now wasn't the time to pester her for the truth.

"We just had to come in here and get something, something he could show his new boss, and then we'd get a full-time gig."

"I'm not following," I confessed. There was too much she was trying to hide, and her story was quickly falling apart. "Where is 'here,' for starters?"

We were whispering so quietly, the murmur of the men talking in the next room was easy to make out. I kept one ear on that noise, a guarantee that we hadn't been discovered.

Lucy swallowed, her face pale. "A De Sanctis drop point."

I took a moment to process this information. "De Sanctis. As in the criminal enterprise, Italian royalty of Atlantic City . . . that De Sanctis?" I managed in a controlled tone, even though I was sweating bullets.

Lucy nodded.

"And by drop point you mean . . ." I trailed off, unwilling to finish the obvious sentence. It would make it too real.

"This is one of the places where they drop their products and have dealers pick them up for distribution."

Well, at least she knew exactly what she was getting herself into. There was a cold comfort in the fact that she hadn't been misled in the slightest.

"Products, dealers, De Sanctis," I muttered, shocked. Maybe it made me naïve, but I'd clearly underestimated the level of criminal activity my sister had become comfortable with. "Who are you right now?" I huffed angrily.

I was angry at her for dragging her life to new lows every day.

I was angry at myself for not watching closely enough and allowing her to fall.

I was mad at my Da for going and leaving us when we'd needed him.

I was even mad at Social Worker Sue and her brittle positivity. *Yeah, Sue, we're really lucky. Totally unscathed by our terrible childhoods.*

I didn't need to point out the danger we were in. Lucy knew;

her tearstained cheeks gave that away. She was in over her head, and I was the only one who could get her out of this mess.

Lucy had gone big when she'd broken into this warehouse and tried to steal from a vicious mob syndicate. She'd skipped right over the low-hanging fruit of gangs and the smaller cartels that sprang up and disappeared frequently. She'd gone right to the top of the food chain. The apex predator of the state.

New Jersey was riddled with crime. During my clinical rotations in big Atlantic City hospitals, I'd seen firsthand the damage that the criminal syndicates wreaked as they sank their claws into the city. If it wasn't gunshot wounds from rival families fighting for turf, it was drug overdoses caused by their products. It didn't matter which family it was—Irish, Italian, Russian—the aftermath was bloody and lethal.

New Jersey and mafia were as intertwined as the Fourth of July and apple pie. And Lucy had gone straight for the De Sanctis family. Theirs was no fly-by-night organization. The De Sanctis family ran a serious operation. They called the capo of the family the King of A.C., because he ruled the casino scene with an iron fist and crushed opposition with ease. Renato De Sanctis was notorious, and no one in their right mind would cross him.

I stared at my sister, seeing her in a different light for a moment, before the murmur of approaching voices jolted me out of my thoughts.

Things were about to get even worse.

Sharp shouts and protests bounced off the warehouse walls. Lucy tried to get up beside me, but I quickly pulled her down, fear coating my mouth. It tasted like metal. I fumbled for my necklace. A small, simple gold pendant that my Da had given me. It bore the image of St. Anthony, patron saint of lost things and people. I'd always been a lost person; even Da had seen it.

"I'll look," I told her in a nearly inaudible whisper.

I rose on my knees, the cold cement floor digging through my cheap polyester trousers. Two men entered the room from a side door. One seemed to be dragging a smaller man by the hair. I gripped Lucy's hand hard, preventing her from kneeling up and looking. I'd gag her, if I had to.

The sound of cruelly amused laughter echoed around the space.

"You thought you could wiggle in here like a snake and win points for the Castillos? Brave, but dumb, and now it's the last thing you'll ever do," one of the men grunted, throwing the shadowy figure he was hauling down on the concrete floor.

He landed with a harsh slapping sound, the two men towering over him ominously. I could tell immediately that he was smaller than them. Younger.

Miguel, Lucy's piece-of-shit boyfriend.

One of the attackers kicked Miguel hard in the side three times. My nursing instincts kicked into gear, and I mentally assessed the damage that might have just been inflicted and how to treat it. I continued to hold Lucy down in a death grip. I couldn't let her see her boyfriend getting beaten. As for trying to help him, I didn't even consider it. He was the reason we were here, and Lucy was my priority. I had no illusions about how our combined strength would stack up against these mobsters.

"Did the Castillos put you up to this? Did they say they'd let you into the cartel if you stole from us? You stupid boy. Those fuckers don't let anyone in except blood relations. You had a better chance with us . . . instead, you disrespected the De Sanctis name, and I have to make an example out of you. It's not personal. It's about optics, kid. By the look of you, it's no great loss to society."

The men laughed cruelly between themselves.

A sense of foreboding slithered in my gut. This wasn't just a beating. They were going to kill him, and I was in the position of trying to stop it, and risking my own life, or letting it happen. I was a nurse. Saving life was my calling. And yet, as I glanced down at the shiny strands of Lucy's head below mine, I knew I wouldn't. Maybe if I'd been alone, I might have tried something, but I wouldn't risk her safety.

"Wait! I'm not here on my own," Miguel cried out.

Fuck. I knew that kid was a rat.

"No? Who did you come with?"

"My girlfriend—well, the girl I'm fucking around with. She has some stuff on her. You can have her. Take your time. Have a party, go nuts."

I held my tongue, fear and guilt creating a toxic mixture inside me, fear and guilt giving way to the rising fury in my veins. This kid thought he could hand Lucy over to save his own sorry ass? Lucy's fingers bit into mine. It was a reminder that she, too, could hear every word.

I peeked again when silence fell. I had to know what they were doing. Were they considering Miguel's offer?

One of the men laughed and pulled a gun from his jacket. "What makes you think we won't just do both? End you, the useless, pussy boyfriend, and have all the fun we want with your girl?"

He straightened his arm and took the safety off the gun, laughing at Miguel's attempt to roll away. "Looks like the end of the line, kid. Not a very impressive way to go out. I'm doing you a favor really." He pointed the gun at Miguel's balled-up body.

The other goon stepped in. "Shit, wait a minute, Tony. Just scare the kid and beat him up a little . . . don't piss off the boss again. We're on thin ice with Ren, and we both know it."

Ren. Renato De Sanctis. I found myself glancing over my

shoulder, as if just thinking his name might invoke the man. A Bloody Mary chant.

"What Ren doesn't know won't hurt him," the man with the gun said. I could hear in his voice that he was eager to deliver rough justice. He wanted to kill the guy lying in a bloodied heap in front of him.

His buddy once again intervened, and they argued quietly for a second. My heart pounded so hard I could barely think over it. I should call the cops. I should do *something*.

"We have to run," I whispered. "They know you're here. We have to get out of here while they're distracted."

"The cops—" Lucy started.

I nodded. I'd call once we were out. They weren't going to come in the next thirty seconds, so they couldn't save Miguel. After he'd bargained for his life by offering my sister, I wasn't sure I cared so much. I certainly wasn't putting myself in danger to help him. He'd chosen his path.

We never reached the door.

A bang sounded, and I shoved a fist into my mouth to muffle my scream.

Smoke and the stench of metal filled the air.

"Christ, man, you shouldn't have done that. Ren's not going to like it."

"Whatever. Stop trying to crawl up the boss's ass." The deep voice of the one who had shot Miguel was full of mirth and amusement. "Shall we look for the girl?"

"What girl? That little punk was just trying to buy himself some time. What girl would agree to follow him in here? Let's get out of here."

"Yeah, whatever."

Lucy shook in my arms, crying soundlessly. She knew what

had happened to her troublemaking new boyfriend. We were frozen there in our guilt and fear for precious long minutes before the sound of the men talking faded away.

This was it. Our chance to go. We had to do it now, before they changed their minds about searching for the girlfriend.

We were only a few feet from the side door I'd used to sneak in. If we could creep out, we could make a run for it or hide in one of the abandoned buildings that lined this seedy end of the shore.

"Lucy, we have to get out of here now, run and never look back."

"They killed Miguel, didn't they? They killed him," Lucy mumbled, the shock sending her gaze hazy with shock.

"Yes, and they'll kill us, too, if they find us. That's why we have to leave before they hear us," I explained as patiently as I could, trying to navigate through her shock.

She nodded, her big, teary eyes staring into mine. My heart clenched at how incredibly young she seemed at that moment. She looked like my baby sister again.

"Let's go," I whispered.

Together, we crept out of our hiding place. Shadows seemed to move, pouncing at us. Lucy whimpered, trying her hardest to stifle her tears. Every step through the dilapidated warehouse felt like a target was pinned to my back. My skin crawled, my heart pounded.

Finally, we shuffled our way toward a side door and out into the dark, cool night.

It wasn't until we were in a cab home, speeding away from the warehouse, that I realized I'd been holding my breath. My head hurt, and my lungs ached. Straightening my hands from claws took effort, but I managed it. I cradled Lucy's head on my lap and stroked her hair. "It's okay. Everything is going to be okay."

For the first time in a long time, I had no idea if those words would turn out to be true.

Da's voice spoke in my head, his old catchphrase turning in circles and holding me in a warm embrace. *Worry about that later, kid. Tomorrow, you could be dead.*

Oh, Da. You have no idea.

I jolted awake to the sound of sobs.

I was up and shuffling out of my messy bedroom before I could blink the sleep from my eyes.

Reality rushed in on the beams of fall light flooding the small kitchen of the apartment I shared with Lucy. The sound of taxis honking and the hubbub of the city filled my senses, but even that couldn't drown out the sounds of anguish.

Our southside neighborhood wasn't glamorous, or even safe for that matter, but it was near the casino I worked at, and the hospital that I did my clinical rotations in—part of my student experience—wasn't too far, either. With our limited budget, I couldn't afford to live closer, and I also didn't have time for a longer commute, so we were stuck in this grim apartment by the highway. If you stood on the roof and leaned over the broken safety barrier, you could almost see the shore.

I knocked softly on Lucy's door and waited. I traced a finger over the old wooden plaque on the door, the one she'd made and held on to since our time at the group home. Glittery pink polish spelled out her name. A few faded, peeling stickers dotted the corners, but that had been the extent of the craft supplies she'd been given to carve a little place of her own.

"Lucy, I'm coming in," I called when she failed to open the door.

My sister was curled in a ball on the bed, her face red and puffy with tears. I hadn't heard her crying last night. I'd fallen into a kind of deathly deep sleep that I'd learned how to do as a nursing student for the last five years. The idea was to sleep when you could, no matter what was going on around you.

I sat on the bed and reached for her hand. "Hey, have you been up all night?"

"I can't stop hearing that awful sound over and over," Lucy sniffled.

I grabbed a tissue and handed it to her, watching as she roughly blew her nose. She was right, after all. The last twenty-four hours had been a living nightmare. She'd seen her boyfriend get killed. She'd been there when it happened. It could have been her, too. It was terrifying.

No, Lucy was reacting appropriately. It was me who wasn't. I was reacting out of shock and carefully honed survival skills that demanded I power through this. But deep down, a gaping chasm of panic threatened to engulf me.

"And now he's gone . . ." Lucy whispered, her tears starting up again.

I leaned in and hugged her. Sure, I hadn't liked Miguel for Lucy at all, and I'd never forgive him for trying to sell her out to save his own skin. But still, I didn't like to see Lucy hurting, and I wanted to help her through this.

"I know, it's so hard. I'm sorry," I said softly.

As I held my heartbroken little sister, I realized that I'd become a bit hardened to death. Going through nursing school and doing rotations in the ER could do that to you. I'd felt the fragility of life, and I'd seen that barrier break so often that it rarely caught me off guard anymore. Last night had been different, though. It wasn't slipping away in a hospital bed or flatlining on a surgeon's table while medical professionals worked to save you. Last night had been violent. I couldn't get the horror out of my head.

A phone vibrated on the bedside. I didn't recognize the case. "Whose phone is that?"

Lucy sniffed and reached for it. "Miguel's. He gave it to me to carry since I had a pocket in my hoodie."

She looked so young for a second that it stole my breath away. Everything I'd done, the countless crappy jobs I'd worked, the sacrifices I'd made—all of it had been to keep her safe and protected from the horrible reality of the world we lived in.

Last night I'd failed.

"You have his phone? Lucy, what if the police are looking for him? They might be able to trace it," I chastised, fresh fear running through me, waking me up more effectively than any jolt of caffeine could.

"So what? I'm not going to hide what they did to him," Lucy said defiantly.

I was distracted from arguing with that ridiculous statement by the phone. A number had called nearly twenty times. As I stared at it, a message popped up: *Kid. I said I'd give you a chance, and I did. 25K worth of chances. The boss wants to know where the cash is. Give back the product or the proceeds. Clock's ticking.*

I dropped the phone like it was a viper trying to sink its fangs into my wrist. I looked at Lucy. "Did Miguel have drugs on him? Had he been dealing?"

Her watery eyes met mine and then slid to the side. *Goddamn it.*

"Are you serious right now? You were dating some dealer? Some wannabe gang member? Are you out of your mind?" I shouted.

"I liked him! I wouldn't expect you to understand what that's like," Lucy shot back.

I flinched, her unexpected barb hitting me in sensitive spots. "Meaning?"

"Meaning not everyone wants to live like a robot and just work, study, work, study, then work some more. Some of us want to live."

I swallowed my words of disagreement. Hurt spread through

my chest. The only reason I worked all the damn time was to keep me and Lucy in relative comfort. Out of habit, my eyes moved to the small alarm clock on Lucy's nightstand.

"I have to go. I have work," I muttered, aware I was playing right into her accusation but unable to do a damn thing about it. I needed my job, and I loved it. It was my dream, and every day I single-handedly supported us was a triumph for me.

"Stay here. Don't talk to anyone. Don't even think about going to the police. Those men we saw, the De Sanctis family, they aren't playing around. They're dangerous, and I don't want us on their radar. Miguel is dead, nothing we do now can change that. You wanna risk joining him?"

My words sounded cold. Lucy stared at me in shock, looking like she'd just discovered that her sister was part demon. It was true, in a way. As her caregiver, I had a single-minded purpose that I'd always prioritize above everything else: Stay alive and keep Lucy alive. It was simple, really. Our survival was what it always boiled down to. I suspected it was the same for everyone, once everything else was stripped away. We were all just rats in a maze, desperately trying to survive.

I left Lucy, taking the damn phone with me. It was a smoking gun, and I didn't want to leave it with her. I didn't have time to worry about it right now. I'd worry about it later. It was my usual coping mechanism for things that I had no solution for.

So, it sounded like Miguel had already been working for some higher-up distributor. I wondered where the hell the drugs were, and how far this guy texting Miguel would go to find them.

A shiver of worry moved through me as I left the house and headed toward the bus stop.

2

RENATO

At forty-two, and as the leader of New Jersey's most influential and profitable Mafia syndicate, I found that life could get pretty dull sometimes. For that reason, I liked to switch things up a little here and there.

My business flourished when I employed a personal touch to keep my clients in line, and it worked well for my men, too. Whether that was torturing information out of someone myself, showing up at a christening to bestow my blessing, or carrying out the odd assassination personally, it paid to be unpredictable in this game.

I was expecting to drop by the warehouse on Clements Drive and see my busy worker bees getting my product ready for distribution. Imagine my surprise at seeing a group of rival cartel members on their knees, surrounded by my armed guards.

Today was turning out to be more fun than I'd expected.

"Atlantic City is a place where you can be whoever you want to be, or so people say." I perched a hip against a beat-up vintage Chevy sitting in the dark parking lot behind the warehouse. On paper, Renato De Sanctis didn't own a single thing in A.C. In reality, I was closing in on half the Boardwalk. The other half was owned by a bunch of billionaires who needed me to clean their money. The casinos I didn't own, I ran. Making money had always been my talent. Well, that and keeping order.

The man cowering before me worked for the Castillo Cartel, a group who was determined to pump illicit chemicals into the casino scene. *My* casino scene. Nobody sold to my clientele except me.

Behind the man, about twenty of his lackeys waited to see what would go down. We'd cornered them along the north shore, far too close to the warehouse where we received some of our shipments. The cartel cockroaches were growing bolder all the time. I'd diligently stamped out every single one I'd uncovered, but I was far from finding the head.

The man before me was sweating. I could smell him. He shifted in his shiny white sneakers that probably cost as much as his rent. Sneakers, at his age. Alas, the old adage was true. Money couldn't buy class. Or brains, for that matter.

"Who says that?" he asked, stalling for time.

I waved my hand in the air. "People. People say it." They certainly hadn't handed out spare IQ points when this guy had been born.

"I don't know people," he muttered, his eyes shifting to the side. He was trying to work out how to walk away from this alive. He didn't realize that was a futile hope.

"Of course you don't. The real question is, if you could be anything you wanted to be here, in this great, neon mecca for human greed and gluttony, what would you be?"

He licked his lips. "Look, man, we weren't touching your stuff. We were searching for someone, a kid—"

"The older generation ushering in the new. While I love traditions, I wouldn't lie to me, unless you want me to make it hurt."

He blinked at me, trying in vain to decipher my meaning. It

seemed clear as fucking day to me, but much like idiots who smoked and then were surprised when they got cancer, no one expected death to be imminent. If we truly understood the risk we took leaving the house every single day, we'd never cross the threshold. The truth was that humans were very breakable creatures, and this world was full of danger.

"I'm not lying. One of the new recruits, Miguel—he went missing. Last we heard, he was hanging out here, Clements Drive. We just want to know what happened to him."

"Skipped out with some product, did he?" I asked.

I didn't give a shit what had happened to a young wannabe cartel cretin, but a subtle glance at my second-in-command ordered him to check it out. We couldn't have the Castillos sniffing around our drop sites. The police were all over the new cartel, trying to root them out of the state. Unlike me, they had no connections in law enforcement who could look the other way, destroy evidence, and even make the odd body disappear now and again, and that was just the way I liked it.

I was the King of Atlantic City, and the *capo dei capi* of New Jersey, and no one would take that title from me. No one.

I stood, having gotten what I wanted from the conversation. My men shifted around me.

"Regardless, Castillos don't come around my property. I trust you'll give that message to your *patrón*."

The sucker actually looked relieved. "I will, I promise, man. No problem."

I loomed over the man. "I misspoke. I meant your worthless body and those of your men will send the message nicely."

After that, all hell broke loose.

I ended the man I'd been questioning, the head of his little group, with a sharp slice to the jugular. I almost always carried a knife, and my thin stiletto blade was like an extension of my hand.

The only thing I disliked about this method of killing was the gush of warm blood that hit my hand afterward. For that reason, I wore black leather gloves.

His face was frozen in a comically shocked expression. Once his body hit the ground, his men jumped into action. Some of them swung for me. Elio—my second, my bodyguard, and my most trusted man—intercepted, snapping necks and kicking out knees as he went.

My men were so well trained, I didn't have to slow my pace as I strode from the parking lot. They cut down every attack without a single blow landing on the target. Me.

As the son of one of the richest, most vicious mafiosos in the country, I'd been a target my entire life. I was used to it, and my men acted accordingly. If you had an ounce of survival instinct, you didn't dare come close.

Just the way I liked it.

In my office in La Leonora, my favorite casino—one of the oldest in the De Sanctis portfolio and named after my mother—the other member of my inner circle, Giada, waited behind my desk. She had her feet up, her shitkicker boots on the dark wood, and chewed bubble gum. She blew a perfect pink bubble just as we walked through the doors.

"Move," I snapped at her.

Sometimes she felt more like my younger sister than my real sibling did. Sofia Chernova, formerly De Sanctis, lived in Maine with a crazy Russian and their two children. As much as I'd struggled to trust Nikolai Chernov—the Russian *Bratva* gangster who'd become obsessed with my younger sister—we'd come to respect each other over the years. Besides, his bloodthirsty nature and talent for violence had earned him a reputation that ensured Sofia's life remained unthreatened. Nikolai was known as the

Palach, the executioner, and he was a powerful player to have in the family.

Giada, on the other hand—my *sottocapo* Elio's mouthy, hot-tempered younger sister—was sometimes more of a liability than anything else. Despite that, she was family, and one of the few people who wasn't scared to talk back to me. She had bigger balls than the rest of the made men in the family in that regard, and I respected that. She was also a tech genius.

She grinned at me and poked a hole in the bubble so it sagged against her chin.

"Say please," she laughed.

I headed around the table toward her. She shot up, planting her boots on the carpet with a wink before sashaying away. I'd yet to find a subject that Giada took seriously.

Elio glowered at his younger sister. "Giada," he muttered in warning.

"Oh, please, stop being boring! So," she sat down on the couch and leaned back, holding her face in her hands, "who did you kill?"

Elio snorted. "How do you know we killed anyone?"

"Ren is wearing his killing gloves, and I just have an instinct for these things. The real question is, why didn't you invite me?" Giada sighed and sank into the leather. She turned to stare at the huge picture window that overlooked the Boardwalk. "I never get to do fun things. If I'd known there was a glass ceiling in the mob, I would have just worked for a bank or something."

"Feel free to go and do that," I deadpanned.

She rolled her eyes. "Maybe I will. Though, it won't pay well, and do banks really need hackers? On second thought, I'll just rent out my services to the highest bidder. Freelance hacking for criminals, that's a thing, right?"

"Yeah, a thing that'll get you killed. Did you eat?" Elio asked, falling into his usual dynamic with his little sister.

It was funny to think of Giada as "little" anything, considering how dangerous she was. I'd seen her torture men and laugh when they cried. They were bad men, sure, but still. Very few could find humor in human suffering. Besides being slightly unhinged, she was brilliant. Technology came to life under her talented fingertips, and there was nothing she couldn't achieve with Wi-Fi, a laptop, and a steady supply of energy drinks.

"Of course, I ate. You think I don't know how to take care of myself?"

"Last time you were working hard on something, you forgot to eat for four days and fainted in the shower," Elio reminded his sister. "It took two men to get your wet, naked ass downstairs."

"So what? It was probably the best day of their lives. Think of it as a charitable donation, helping ugly fuckers see some real tits and ass, instead of all the crap they watch online or at a club." Giada grinned at her brother's impassive face. Only a ticking muscle in his jaw showed his irritation.

"As entertaining as this is, I presume you're here to update me on the Castillo situation?" I interrupted and stripped off my black gloves, finger by finger, before dropping them in the trash can beneath my desk. Taking a cigarette out, I lit up and inhaled the nicotine. It felt good crashing into my bloodstream. I only allowed myself to smoke after killing someone. A fucked-up version of a postcoital smoke.

Giada nodded and pulled her laptop out of her bag. "Here're the people they're paying off to look the other way."

"Make me a list of their names . . . call it Who to Kill for Being a Fucking Idiot," I sighed.

How anyone, no matter how much power they had in the normal world or how many billions they had in the bank, thought they could get their drugs from someone else at a cheaper rate in *my* city was baffling. Undercutting me was tantamount to suicide.

Clearly, they were too dumb to live anyway, so I was really doing the planet a favor by wiping them out, hopefully before they procreated. Survival of the fittest in action.

"Your title is a little clunky . . . Let's call it the Kill List," Giada said thoughtfully.

"Whatever." I clamped my cigarette between my teeth, picked up the small bottle of lighter fluid I kept on my desk, and squirted it into the fireproof trash can.

"Also, I prefer Excel," Giada continued.

I gave her a dark look and flicked my lit cigarette into the trash can, watching my bloodstained gloves go up in flames.

"Giada," I warned quietly.

She simply laughed. "Okay, boss, don't get your boxers in a bunch. One Kill List spreadsheet coming right up." She pushed herself to her feet, making sure to fix her tight black T-shirt where it had ridden up. Giada liked to dress her curvaceous body in skintight clothes. Those clothes on a body like hers pulled men's eyes wherever she strutted, and it stressed Elio out. Causing her older brother anxiety was one of Giada's favorite hobbies, so it worked out well for her.

After she left, Elio approached. He'd had his head buried in a tablet, and now, his lips had become a thin line of worry.

"What is it?" I asked, reading his mood immediately.

"I pulled up the CCTV of the warehouse on Clements Drive. The kid was there, and he wasn't alone."

Elio placed the tablet before me, and we both watched. The dumb Castillo goon wandered into the warehouse, and a little shadow followed him. In the grainy night-vision glow, I made out a girl, probably in her teens.

We watched the girl hide, and then saw two De Sanctis men, Tony Guardini and Aldo Vasi, move into the frame. They'd been there to make sure there weren't any problems with the shipment.

I'd recently taken them off the more face-to-face tasks that my men carried out, because lately they'd been getting a little too trigger happy. The video then showed them dragging the boy into the room. The shot was loud, even on the recording.

I didn't have an opinion about killing the boy. He worked for the Castillos, and he was on *my* property, trying to take *my* product. But still, Tony Guardini was on thin ice. He'd been explicitly told not to kill anyone without my say-so. The most dangerous thing to have on your books was an armed man you couldn't control. It was bad for the De Sanctis reputation, and worse, it came off like I couldn't rein in my men.

They left the body there, probably calling on our family cleaners to take care of it. I stared at the video a long time, until a small movement caught my attention.

Ah, that's right. *The girl.*

She crept out from underneath a crate. She had been off-camera for so long, I'd nearly forgotten about her. Just when I expected her to turn tail and run, another figure appeared.

A woman. She was older than the first one, but not by much. She gripped the younger girl's hand tightly, her body curving around her like a protective shield. A sister?

"Call in Guardini and Vasi and let them know they fucked up. They need to answer for it."

"And the women?"

In the video, they crept toward the door, the elder one's face becoming clearer as she moved right under the camera. I reached out and paused the video just as she looked to her right, her face beautifully framed by the darkness around her. The classical lines of her face pleased the art lover in me. I stabbed a finger at her graceful profile.

"Bring her to me."

3

CHARLIE

My classes started after lunch. First, I had to get through an ER rotation at Camden Community Hospital.

My shift dragged while my thoughts swirled obsessively around Miguel's phone and the missing drugs. I could recall every word uttered by the two men in the warehouse the previous night.

They talked about the Castillo Cartel. I've never heard the name before, but it sounded like Miguel had been trying to get in with them through some dumb initiation, and he'd also been given product to sell? Where the hell was it? The cartel wouldn't come after Lucy for it, right? She had nothing to do with it. I'd spent all day repeating my internal arguments to an unforgiving jury in my head.

"Burke, are you listening?" a deeply irritated voice snapped at me.

I blinked up at the speaker. Right. I was in the staff room, and Dr. Daniel Worthington, asshole extraordinaire, was deigning to speak to me. I knew I had better listen. He seemed to think that all students were just waiting around for him to bestow some of his greatness upon them. He had no idea that every single one of us thought he was a jerk.

"I'm sorry, what?"

A deep frown lined his overly tanned brow. Doctor Dan was one of those guys who'd be as white as me, with my Irish genes, if not for regular tanning sessions and monthly trips to tropical locales. He was privileged, rich, arrogant as fuck, and by far my least favorite person in the hospital.

"I said that the spina bifida benefit is tomorrow and asked if you're attending." His smirk revealed that he knew I wasn't invited but wanted me to confirm it. These kinds of benefits involved buying a table for an astronomical fee and then selling off the seats, or giving them away to your friends, if you were rich like Doctor Dan.

I gave him a tight smile. "Not this time, I'm afraid."

He nodded, expecting my answer. "Well, don't be disappointed. My date pulled out at the last minute. Her husband is coming home early from his business trip. You'll come with me instead."

There was a lot to unpack in that sentence. I took my time sorting through it before giving him a strained smile. "Thanks for thinking of me, but I'm afraid I'm busy tomorrow."

Doctor Dan snorted like he couldn't believe someone lowly like me wouldn't immediately cancel my plans for the chance to hang on his arm. "Exactly what kind of plans do you have that you can't support a charity?"

I laughed; I couldn't help it. I was too exhausted from the stresses of last night. "I wasn't aware that being your date was an act of charity."

His expression hardened at my flippant words.

Crap! Get it together, Charlie. Pissing off the resident doctors was never a good idea.

"I mean—I'm busy with my sister, and I also have work. She's going through a hard breakup, so I have to be with her. You understand, right?" My placating tone was flimsy at best, and we both knew it.

"Your sister? You act more like a mother to that girl," Dan sneered, his curled lip conveying just how trashy he found this idea.

"Anyway, I'm sure there're about thirty women at this very hospital who'd be thrilled to take you up on that offer." A little ego stroke was usually enough to get Dan to ignore the occasional jab I aimed his way.

"Hmm, probably, and no doubt ones who'd fit in better at such an event," Dan said, turning away dismissively.

His casual put-down stung, but there was nothing I could do about it. The truth was that he was the doctor, and I was the nurse. He was rich, and I was poor. He'd gone to Princeton, and I was struggling my way through community college on a roller coaster of student loans that I couldn't imagine ever being able to pay off.

We were not the same. It might hurt my pride to admit that, but it was true, and being resentful of men like Daniel Worthington would only cause me stress and make my life more difficult.

Life was already hard enough without that kind of complication.

I finished my shift and headed home, Doctor Dan and his unsubtle insults melting into the miasma of anxiety swarming inside my head.

By the time I got home after three back-to-back classes that had thoroughly exhausted my brain, I'd decided that Lucy and I needed to get rid of the phone. Smash it up and drop it in the sea or something. No good could come of having it, and hopefully it was the only thing tying Lucy to Miguel.

"Lucy?" I called as I went in. The kitchen was dark. It looked like there'd be no hot dinner waiting for me before I started my waitressing shift, but then I couldn't blame my little sister. She was young and grieving. If I were in her shoes, I had no idea how I'd react.

Yes, you do. You'd get on with life. You've never had an alternative.

I pushed that voice of treacherous resentment down inside my chest until I couldn't hear it anymore. Another voice reminded me that Lucy had been drifting aimlessly since graduation and making no moves to figure out what she wanted to do with her life. But now wasn't the time to bring up all my grievances with my only sibling. Put out the fires first.

"Lucy?" Silence met my call, so undisturbed that I immediately knew no one was home. She'd gone out? *Where?* I had barely begun to consider the possibilities when my phone rang. A terrible sense of foreboding filled me as I answered.

"Hello, I'm calling for a Charlotte Burke?"

I swallowed, my throat painfully dry. "This is she."

"Ma'am, this is the Atlantic City Police Department. I'm calling from Precinct Fifty-eight. We have your sister here, and she seems very upset. I think it would be best if you came down and sat with her while the detective in charge prepares to take her statement."

The precinct stank like stale coffee and vomit wafting from the direction of the drunk tank. I hurried through security, dropping everything I had into a box to go through the scanner.

"Two phones, huh? Are you a dealer or an escort?" a drily amused voice spoke from behind me.

I whirled around to take in a petite lady with short, steely cropped hair and even steelier eyes.

"Dolores, don't be rude." A lanky younger man stood beside

her. His leather jacket and plaid shirt appeared well worn, and he had a badge clipped on to his pocket.

Wait, two phones? I whirled back to my bag just as the security officer finished checking it. In my panic to come down here, I'd brought both my phone and Miguel's. *Great.* The Burke sisters were really winning today.

I grabbed both phones and stuffed them into my bag. "It's for work emergencies," I muttered, turning to meet the two cops.

"Sure it is," the woman said.

"Don't mind Dolores, she's grumpy in the afternoons, and in the evenings. She's pretty much grumpy all around. I'm Mark, Detective Mark Whitely. This is Detective Dolores Vane. You're Charlie, Lucy's sister?"

I nodded, my face on fire. How was I going to make it through this? Lying to the police? My life had gone to shit in the last day, and I had no idea what was going to happen next.

"Come through here and see her. She was quite upset when we left her earlier," Detective Vane said, her tone making it sound like being *quite upset* in her presence was a crime in and of itself.

They buzzed me in to another section of the building, one that was crawling with cops. Nerves clawed at my throat, threatening to steal my voice. I'd never felt comfortable around cops. My Da had been a hustler, and he'd always taught me to keep my head down, avoid eye contact, and take care of things myself. *The cops don't help people like us, Charlie. They just use 'em. Steer clear, my girl.* It was a shame Lucy had been too young to get that message before he'd died.

"Do you know why your sister is so upset?" Detective Whitely asked me.

I shook my head, my voice still stuck in my throat. I hated lying. My face always glowed a fiery red, and my eyes were guilty as sin, giving me away.

The detectives looked at each other and then opened the door to a small room.

"She's in an interrogation room?" I rasped.

"Well, there aren't that many places to put a distraught young woman whose story changes every few seconds."

With a hot panic enveloping my entire body, I headed into the room. Lucy sat in a metal chair, her arms wrapped around her drawn-up knees.

"Lucy?" I murmured, getting close enough to put my arms around her. She looked up at me, her tearstained face all red and blotchy.

"Now, Lucy, can you please confirm your name?" Detective Whitely had settled into the chair across from us, while Vane leaned against the wall and watched us with an inscrutable expression.

"Why? This is all a mistake," I said. "We don't need to make a complaint or a statement or whatever it is. We should just go and stop wasting your time."

"We'll decide if our time is being wasted, Miss Burke. Now, your sister was telling us her boyfriend is missing?"

Shock poured over me like a bucket of ice water. *What the hell?* This was a complication we didn't need.

I turned to Lucy and pasted on my best patient older sister look. "Now, Lucy, just because someone ghosts you, it doesn't mean that they've gone missing." I forced a laugh and smiled at the cops. "Teens."

Did it feel good to gaslight my own sister? Hell, no. But what she was doing right now was the equivalent of juggling flaming chainsaws, and she seemed to have no idea.

"Ghosted you, eh? Give us a name and we can run it through the system for you, check if he's been hospitalized or anything like that."

"Surely that's a misuse of police resources," I argued. Thank fuck I had no social life and watched court shows at night. "He has a right to ghost someone if he wants."

"Let us worry about police resources, Miss Burke. We were just offering to make sure a young man hasn't been hurt or gone missing. That's a just cause."

"Still, I'm sure it's fine. We really have to get going now. I'm so sorry for wasting your time."

Detective Whitely stared at me for a long moment before shifting his focus to Lucy. "What did you say his name was?"

I shot to my feet. "Okay, like I said, this is all ridiculous. I'm so sorry to be a bother."

"Why are you so upset, Lucy, if all that happened was your boyfriend, *Miguel*, ghosted you?"

Shit. She'd already given them his name. Now if his body showed up . . . I swallowed down a sudden bout of nausea.

"Don't you remember being a teen? This stuff is life or death at nineteen years old," I quipped before cringing guiltily at my words. *For fuck's sake, Charlie, get a grip*. Taking my own advice, I took a deep breath and let it go, smoothing a pleasantly bland expression over my features. "Now, we'll just be going," I muttered and yanked Lucy to her feet.

She stumbled into me. She was subdued, like someone had snuffed out the light inside her. She came willingly enough when I pulled her toward the door. Neither of the detectives made to open it, and I stared at them.

"Are you holding us here in an official capacity? Are we being charged with something?"

Detective Vane raised her eyebrow as she approached us, taking her sweet time. "Do you think you should be charged with something?"

"I love armchair psychology as much as the next person, but

we need to be going," I said firmly, refusing to participate in her little game of chicken.

The detectives watched us closely the entire way out of the precinct. I dragged Lucy three blocks away before stopping.

"What the hell, Lucy Burke?" I demanded. Yikes. I never called her by her full name. I was madder than I thought. "What was the point in creeping out of that place last night when you're determined to put a target on our backs?!"

"I didn't know what to do," Lucy muttered, scrubbing a hand over her pale face. "I got a call while you were at work, on my cell."

"What call? From who?" I didn't want to hear the answer. Dread had drop-kicked me in the belly, and I struggled to breathe.

"I think it was Miguel's boss. The one who sent the message to his phone." Lucy's lips were bloodless. "I think they know about me."

"Shh, it's okay." I reached out and pulled her close, hugging her petite body hard. "It's going to be okay. I'll take care of everything."

I had no clue how, but the words just flowed. I'd always taken care of my sister and I always would. She was still and unyielding in my arms. Lucy always pulled away when she was upset and shutting me out. It was her coping mechanism.

"Why did you go to the cops? You could have waited until I got home," I gently reminded her. The service sucked in the hospital's locker room, where I had to leave my phone during shifts.

"I thought maybe if I reported Miguel missing, the cops would find him themselves, and then their investigation would find the drugs and the killers . . ." She sighed and rubbed her temples, drawing back from my embrace. "The police would get the killers, and the drugs would get confiscated, and the dealers would drop it."

I smoothed my hand down her hair. I got it. Lucy was sheltered, despite having only an older sister as a parental figure. I'd made sure that the worst of the life we'd lived in sketchy neighborhoods and group homes hadn't touched her. She still believed in the system. In Lucy's unspoiled mind, the cops had power and caught the bad guys. I'd lived long enough to know that wasn't always the case.

"It's okay, I understand. It makes sense," I reassured her. Once her shoulders stopped shaking, I leaned back and looked her in the eye. "But remember this. We have no one but each other. The police can't help us; in fact, they might even think you were involved. They aren't on our side. Worst of all, if we tell them what happened and they investigate, do you think the De Sanctis family will just sit back and let the police build a case for murder against one of their men? Of course they won't. They'll eliminate the problem, which is us. You think the cartel will be cool knowing that we saw what happened to Miguel? They might want the money for the drugs from *you*."

I touched her hand. Her skin was cold. "We have no one but each other. We need to get rid of the phone, now, before I have to go to La Leonora," I told her.

She looked at me for a long moment, biting her lip. Finally, seeming to win a war with herself in her head, she nodded.

"Let's go to the shore," she suggested.

I tightened my grip on her hand. The Burke sisters might have shit luck, but we also had each other. We'd survive another day. I wouldn't allow anything else.

4

CHARLIE

After an endless twenty-four hours, I moved around La Leonora like a zombie. For the most part, I didn't mind my waitressing job at the high-end casino. Sure, the clientele could get handsy, but the tips were great, and security was pretty good about throwing the offenders out.

Growing up at Mercy House, we'd been taught the dangers of gambling and drinking and how that path could lead to a life of sin and burning in hell. The reality was far less dramatic: Rich people having fun, and poor people trying desperately to catch a lucky break. There were no saints or sinners on the floor tonight. Just ordinary people, as good or as terrible as any people could be.

Tonight, I bustled about the tables in the Atrium Bar mindlessly, handing over drinks and checks for more money than Lucy and I spent all week, distracted and exhausted.

There were a few big shots drinking at the bar, and ignoring their loud, braying laughter was nearly impossible.

"Does anyone really need to laugh that loud? Is anyone ever that happy about anything?" I complained to the bartender halfway through my shift.

His name was Alec, and he was an aspiring dancer. Like all the staff at La Leonora, he was just paying the bills and hustling on the side as he worked toward his dream. A.C. was full of dreamers trying to become something else. Someone else.

"But how would everyone know they're having a great time if they aren't broadcasting it? Though, I think in their case, it's just the coke talking, or laughing," Alec deadpanned and sighed. "And just think, that's our justice system right there."

"Meaning?"

"That's Commissioner Reynolds and Judge Ellens. Look how annoying they are, and they're the good guys."

I stared at the two bloated older men, laughing, drinking, and winking at the waitresses passing by. Linchpins of the New Jersey justice system. I shuddered at the thought. Any mention of the police had me sweating. Waking nightmares of the cops appearing to arrest me and Lucy filled my head. They didn't seem like they'd bought anything I'd said.

Even scarier was the thought of the missing drugs and the phone. The cartel had Lucy's number. Would they come and get her? Would she be on the hook for the drugs or the proceeds? Maybe we should have told the police everything. *No.* I might be scared, but that would still never be my go-to instinct.

I'd learned how the police could mess up. I'd seen it firsthand. When I'd started nursing school, one of my nurse friends had reported her violent boyfriend for smacking her around at home. The police had barely investigated. Then, after he'd put her in the hospital, they'd taken him in for questioning and charged him with assault. A month later, after a judge had gone easy on him since it was his first offense, he'd come after her and hit her with his car. There wasn't any evidence to connect him to the hit-and-run, but everyone knew it was him. That was the legacy of the police in my head.

Or take my father's death. A poor Irish immigrant who had worked a couple of side hustles and hardly been a huge contributor to society. They'd never found the perp who'd gunned him down. They'd barely bothered to look. Our neighborhood wasn't exactly high up on the cops' priority list. They didn't care what the people there did.

I was a person from that neighborhood, and so was Lucy. At the end of the day, the cops wouldn't care unless we had something they could use against someone important. The De Sanctis family was important. In a clash between them and the police, we would be the casualties. I knew it without question. No one could take care of you except you.

I'd never had any reason to doubt the truth of that depressing statement.

I left work on a cloud of distraction. Soon, I'd have exams coming up, and I had to find time to study. Typical that my head felt like it was filled with swarming wasps. Worries zoomed around inside, vicious and mean.

I waited at the bus stop outside the casino and sank down in a rare seat once it came. The sky was brightening. I'd worked an overnight shift, and my feet throbbed, like I was walking on the bare bones. I was on them for so many hours, it didn't matter what shoes I wore; they ached all the time.

I dozed off a little and only woke when I realized somewhere in my brain that the bus had stopped for longer than usual. Damn, had I reached the end of the route while I was asleep? It wouldn't be the first time.

I peered around. It was dark inside the bus, though the sky was shifting from dishwater gray to pale white, tinged with pink. It looked like blood spilling across a new canvas. I wiped my mouth and eyes. They were gritty and heavy. I would wash off my dried-up makeup as soon as I got home. It was always a highlight of my night.

I grabbed my bag and pushed myself up.

The bus had pulled into a place I didn't recognize. It appeared to be a rest stop. I glanced out the window, wondering why the hell we'd stopped here. In the distance, a few people hustled across the parking lot. I thought I recognized one of them from being on the bus earlier. Did we have to get off here?

The quiet sound of male voices drifted to me. The driver was talking to someone. I peered forward, a trickle of unease working through me, chasing away any remnants of sleep.

Ahead of the bus, a huge black SUV was parked at an odd angle, like it had forced the bus to stop. The bus driver was speaking with someone outside. As the conversation went on, the driver went pale, then turned and barked what felt like an order over his shoulder. There were two others with him.

My blood turned to ice. I recognized them.

The De Sanctis men from the warehouse. The killers whose crime we'd witnessed.

Swallowing my cry of panic, I backed up the aisle. There was a door at the back, and it stood open right now. The men moved toward the front entrance; I could just make them out. I reached the back stairs and started down them silently.

My sneakers barely made a sound when I stepped onto the hard dirt of the rest stop, but it didn't matter. Someone was there waiting for me.

A man dressed head to toe in black stood at the foot of the steps. He wasn't one of the men from the warehouse. This man was clearly in charge.

"Miss Burke? I'm Elio Santori. There's someone who'd like to meet you." His deep voice sent claws of fear raking across my nerves.

In the growing light of dawn, I could make out his blunt features and oddly pale eyes. He held himself like ex-military and had little in common with the other two. This man was tall and powerful looking. His all-black attire gave off a deadly vibe the other men would never manage.

It was abundantly clear that his request was an order, but I still pretended like my life wasn't about to end. *Miss Burke?* He even knew my name. I could bet everything I had in the world, which really wasn't much, that he already knew everything about me, down to my pantie size. Which meant his boss did, too.

Renato De Sanctis. King of A.C. In Atlantic City, just the name was enough to get people to drop their eyes and keep their heads down. He was like a specter you could invoke, but you really didn't want to. People died when they did.

They say an organization is its leadership. If that were the case, then Renato De Sanctis had to be one of the most terrifyingly powerful, brutally vicious men on the East Coast—and now, he knew everything about me.

"I'm afraid it isn't a good time. I have to get home." My voice barely shook. It wasn't much to be proud of, but I needed to hold on to all the wins I could get right now.

Elio wasn't holding a weapon, but I knew instinctively that it didn't matter. He *was* the weapon. He stood lightly, like he could spring in any direction at a moment's notice. He wouldn't let me past him.

He was quiet for a second and then sighed. "My boss doesn't take no for an answer."

"I just want to go home," I said again, panic edging my voice.

"It's too late for that, and you know it. Don't make me force you," Elio said quietly. His hands were huge and scarred. If he had to, he'd make me, and it would probably hurt. He could have just killed me here. He didn't have to take me to his boss.

And maybe this was a good opportunity. If the boss wanted to speak to me, maybe I could change his mind about killing me and Lucy. It was a long shot, but it was all I had left.

Then, my decision was made for me. One of the men opened the back door of the SUV, and I saw her.

"Charlie? What's going on?"

They had Lucy.

We drove out of the city and along the shore. The sunrise reflected off the water, a gentle pink and blue. The scenery was far too pretty for a death march. I watched the sea and prayed I could live.

My focus soon shifted to Elio. I watched him like he was a bomb that might go off at any moment. His eerie eyes gave nothing away as he watched me right back. In the light of the car when we'd first gotten in, I'd seen they were a light jade green, and unsettling as hell. The other two men were there, too. Sneering and sullen, they glared at me like it was my fault they'd killed a teenager the other night.

"You haven't covered our eyes," I pointed out quietly. It felt like my heart was breaking.

"This isn't the movies," one of the men mocked.

"Meaning?"

"There's no need," Elio said in a tone that brooked no further questions.

I reached out for Lucy's hand, but she folded in on herself, her arms snaking around her middle, her face blank.

After about an hour, we reached a set of huge metal gates with a guard station outside. I couldn't make out the inside of the compound. Dense trees and vegetation crowded up against the boundaries of the massive property. The metal gates slid open, and we drove up a long, winding driveway. It felt like we were entering another world. The veil had slipped on this one, and now, I had one foot on the other side.

"What is this place?"

"Casa Nera, girlie. The last place you'll ever see," one of the goons in front snapped. He was the trigger-happy one. He turned a dark look at me. "Serves you right for causing trouble."

"*Basta,*" Elio said. The word was quiet but somehow held the weight of a gunshot.

I turned to peer out the window and tried to stop myself from hyperventilating. The compound was filled to the brim with armed men, patrolling despite the early hour. High walls surrounded the entire property, from what I could see in the dark, and the tops of them bristled with cameras.

There were buildings of all shapes and sizes grouped in clusters. It was more like a village than a single property. *Casa Nera.* The Black House. It seemed fairly obvious that the name had been inspired by the Gothic mansion, perched like a crown jewel in the middle of the site, reigning over everything around it.

The center of the maze. The heart of the labyrinth.

And, of course, our destination.

The king's castle itself.

"Out," Elio ordered when the car pulled to a stop. I got out carefully, shivering in my waitress uniform. Elio eyed the crest of La Leonora on my shirt, his face devoid of emotion.

He turned toward the entrance, the imposing stone steps leading in a graceful curve toward huge doors. The kind someone could ride a horse through if they were so inclined. There was no sneaking in the back here. Whatever the De Sanctis family did to people like me, witnesses, they did it in plain sight. That wasn't nearly as reassuring as it should have been.

"Watch the steps, they get slippery."

A humorless laugh left me at Elio's warning. He was warning me about falling when his boss was about to kill me?

"Something funny?" he asked flatly, shooting me a curious look.

I shook my head, but my mind was already spinning. *Get a grip, Charlie. If not for yourself, for Lucy.*

Lucy, that's right. I had to protect Lucy. I had to do something to save Lucy. Lucy was the only one who mattered.

Inside, the house was silent as a tomb. Lucy's hand gripped mine so tight I could feel the blood leaving my fingers. Only the ticking of an intimidating grandfather clock broke the silence. Dark red wallpaper lined the walls, and black-and-white tiles covered the floor. The farther we moved into the maze of the building, the more opulent the surroundings became. This wasn't a place of business; it was an inner sanctum.

Home of the boss.

The boss.

We arrived at a huge door, ornate, but somehow also fortified. Elio knocked with a distinctive rap and opened it. The door opened soundlessly and swung inward. Fear worked through me, firing adrenaline through my blood. As a nursing student, I was trained to focus and get the job done in tense, high-stress situations. But this was different. It was personal. It was about Lucy.

Elio touched my lower back to move me forward when I failed to take a step over the threshold. The wallpaper around the door was a rich red brocade, scrolling vines adorned with apples and leaves. The door was old-fashioned, wooden with studs and metal reinforcements.

For a second, I had the thought that if I moved over this threshold, I'd be taking a step into another realm. A world where the rules as I knew them didn't exist . . . I didn't want to go inside.

I wanted to hide. But then Lucy's slight weight pressed into me, and I knew I had no choice.

I inched forward, shooting Elio a frown so forbidding, he dropped his hand from my back. I took it as a win, even though his subsequent smirk ruined my illusions of power.

"Stay behind me. Let me do the talking," I muttered to Lucy. The thugs who had started it all crowded into the room behind us.

Inside the office, the feeling of otherworldliness continued. It wasn't an office from this time, that was certain. A huge leather-bound desk dominated the middle, and oil paintings were mounted at intervals around the room. A real fire burned in a hearth, and one of the walls was packed with bookcases that reached right to the high ceiling, crammed with hardbacks.

A wooden cross was nailed above a portrait of a beautiful woman. The portrait was an oil painting, and the subject was serene, staring at the painter with a wistfulness that drew the eye. The sight of the crucifix was jarring. I wouldn't have expected something religious from a man who had so much blood on his hands. Maybe he was the type to believe that as long as he confessed to his numerous sins, he was absolved. As a woman who'd knelt before such a crucifix many times at Mercy House and waited for judgment, I had come full circle.

"Boss," Elio said quietly, once again pushing me forward when I froze. I had no choice but to focus on the person in front of me. Renato De Sanctis. In the flesh.

It was dimly lit, but that didn't hide the man who sat behind the desk at all. If anything, he seemed like a creature who thrived in the darkness.

"Well, if it isn't the woman we've been looking for. Welcome to Casa Nera, Miss Burke." His voice was deep, holding a hint of smoke that brushed through my mind and fogged my throat.

I'd never thought of a voice as intoxicating before, but now I knew that one could be. There was a tinge of an Italian accent, just a touch, and a drily amused undertone that told me it wasn't anything unusual to have two people dragged before him this early in the day.

"She was finishing her shift at La Leonora," Elio said coolly.

"Was she? Nurse by day and waitress by night. You certainly are a busy little lamb, aren't you?" The boss's voice was deep and warm, reminding me of the expensive cognac I served at work. His words elegantly communicated volumes. He knew everything about me.

The lamb comparison didn't fill me with confidence, considering how wolfish these men were, but when I locked eyes with the man behind the desk, I had no room in my mind to dwell on it.

He pushed all other thoughts out.

Growing up dirt-poor, the child of well-meaning Irish immigrants who had gotten in with the wrong people and died in poverty and unnoticed, I'd learned important lessons about power. My parents had never had any, and no one had cared when they died, except Lucy and me. The remnants they'd left behind. In the group home, I'd never had any power either. In my hospital work, the doctors held the power, and I'd planned that someday, somehow, I'd work my way up there and be just like them. One day, I'd have power, too. People would listen when I spoke. People would respect me.

Standing there in the inner sanctum of the capo of the De Sanctis family, I realized I'd never known true power until now.

True power was tangible. It radiated off this man in waves as he watched me with dark eyes. It was present in every line of his body, the arrogant tilt of his regal head, and the curve of his beautiful mouth. It emanated from him as he inclined his head toward Elio.

"Bring her closer." It wasn't a request.

Elio firmly prodded me toward the desk, and I twisted away from his touch. If I was going to die here, I wanted to walk toward that fate with my head held high and not stumbling.

He chuckled softly and gestured me onward with mock politeness. I stepped forward and crossed the distance between the door and the desk. A thick Persian rug muffled my steps. The fire warmed me on my right side. A clock ticked, perhaps the antique one on the mantelpiece. Counting down the last seconds of my life.

Tick-tock. Tick-tock. Do something, Charlie. Tick-tock. Save Lucy. Tick-tock.

Renato observed my approach. *The boss.* There was no denying that was who he was. No one gave off power like that and served another. It just didn't happen.

He wore a black suit with a red shirt beneath. Red like the wallpaper. Red like blood. If he weren't about to kill me, I could have appreciated his foreboding good looks. He looked like he'd just stepped off a runway. He looked sharp, like the lines of his cuffs could give you a paper cut. His olive skin glowed in the firelight like burnished gold. Dark chocolate waves of hair softened his powerful face, dominated by an aquiline nose and slashes of black eyebrows. His mouth was beautiful, but mournful somehow. He was a man more used to frowning than smiling. A hint of silver worked through the dark strands on his head, making him even more intimidating, though his face was unlined.

He studied me just as closely as I did him. His gaze burned hot on my skin.

"Sit," he commanded.

I swallowed a lump of terror and the annoying urge to comply. I didn't want to be lower than this man. He was already intimidating enough. "I'd rather stand."

Silence ensued at my refusal. Slowly, one of those imposing

black eyebrows rose. His eyes were beautiful, chestnut-colored and dreamy, fringed with lashes that were too pretty to belong on such a masculine face, but somehow, they worked.

"And I'd rather you sat."

A hand landed on my shoulder and pushed me down into the seat. I shot a glare at Elio over my shoulder, and then turned back to the boss.

"Now, isn't that more comfortable?"

There was something so unbearably arrogant about his confidence that my roiling emotions got the better of me, and my mouth was moving before I could stop it. "Get off on ordering people around, do you?"

Oh my God. Well done, Charlie. Now you're really dead.

The boss merely stared at me. "You have no idea. Do you know who I am?"

I held my tongue, suddenly afraid to admit it. There was no doubt that if this freaky, otherworldly office was a step into another realm, then this man here was the dark prince who ruled it. Admitting that I knew exactly who he was, and what he was capable of, felt like suicide. My mind whirled over possible answers before discarding each one.

He tutted. "I don't ask things twice. You should remember that, Miss Burke." His tone was mild enough, but the tension in the room warned me that pissing this man off wasn't a wise idea.

I found my voice and forced it to work. "It's just Charlie." That response was a force of habit. I hated my real name. It sounded too fancy for the reality of my life.

"Charlie? That's a boy's name," Renato said. His gaze slid down my fall of wavy brown hair. "You don't look like a boy to me."

"It's a nickname, but I prefer it."

"*Charlie.*" He mused on it for a moment. "I don't care for it."

I blinked at him, feeling far out of my depth in this conversation. He was dangerously unpredictable. The meandering confidence of his speech and his slow perusal of me made my skin feel like it was two sizes too tight. There was no way I could handle this man. I had no idea where to start. All I could do was plead my case. Plead Lucy's case.

"I'm Renato De Sanctis, just in case you weren't aware." He paused, letting my mind conjure the specter that his reputation painted.

He didn't have to try to inspire fear; just his name evoked it. I got the impression that Renato De Sanctis wasn't the kind of man to go out of his way to scare his enemies. He just killed them. I watched him, and he watched me right back.

"So, what did you see, Miss Burke?" he finally asked.

I shook my head. "I didn't see anything. Neither of us did," I began.

A loud snort came from the two men who had started all this. One of them sneered. "They must have seen everything, boss, she's just lying to stay alive."

A reluctant laugh left me at his accusing tone. All eyes turned back to me. Renato raised a lazy brow at the sound of my derision.

"It doesn't take a rocket scientist to figure that out. Isn't that what everyone wants?" I muttered.

The man behind me scoffed again, this time annoyed that I'd embarrassed him in front of his boss. He stepped forward, hitching his trousers up in a way that felt obscene. "Let me clean up the mess. I'll put her down, and her little sis, too, get rid of the problem. It's my mess, so I'll clean it up . . . Maybe have a little fun while I'm at it."

His voice was conspiratorial, like he was expecting all the men to agree with him. *Sure, go on and have your fun with the dead-girls-walking, and then get rid of the leftovers.* They'd probably all agree. This was it, the end of the line. Our deaths would boil down to inconvenient messes to be cleaned up, then forgiven and forgotten. Our lives meant less to them than the custom paint jobs on their fancy cars.

Renato held up a single finger, and his man snapped his mouth shut so hard his teeth rattled. The boss reached into a drawer beside him and took out a pair of black leather gloves. The sight of them sent a chill through me. He pulled them on slowly, carefully adjusting them so they were a perfect fit.

"Again, I don't like to repeat myself, but seeing as we were so rudely interrupted, I'll give you another chance to answer. What did you see, Charlotte?" the boss continued.

I shook my head. "I didn't see anything. Neither of us did," I repeated.

"You killed Miguel! Your men shot my boyfriend dead, right in front of us!" Lucy's violent outburst hit the air like a gunshot. She'd been standing behind me, her arm gripped in Elio's huge palm. Now, she fought to step forward.

I shot a silencing look at my sister, but she was too determined. She glared at Renato, while he watched her with faint amusement, not so much as flinching when she lunged forward. He almost looked bored by the display, like normal human emotion couldn't break through his jaded shell. He was a man who had seen the full spectrum of dark and desperate human emotions and found it monotonous.

He flicked a look over her shoulder at his henchman, and Elio reached out and wound a muscle-bound forearm around Lucy's neck. She was a doll in his brutal grip.

"No!" I shot up and ran toward Elio. He had already lowered

Lucy to a velvet settee sitting along one wall, efficiently cutting off her air supply in seconds. "Don't hurt her!"

I lunged at Elio, scratching and kicking at him. The other men hauled me off, their harsh fingers digging into my arms and chest, pulling at my waist, wrenching me away from my sister. Sobs of terror shook me, and I couldn't breathe. The sight of Lucy in a killer's hands, her face turning red as she slowly went under, was more than I could stand.

"Fuck this," one of the men snarled and wrenched a gun from his waistband. It was the same man who had killed Miguel. He aimed his gun toward Lucy. "Calm the fuck down, or—"

"Or what, Tony?" Renato's granite tone sliced through the escalating tension like a knife through silk.

Everyone paused, and I took advantage of that moment to break free from the hands that held me and step in front of the gun. Standing on the other end of a point-blank shot was terrifying, but not as terrifying as seeing that black muzzle aimed toward my little sister.

"Don't hurt her. Hurt me if you need to hurt someone. Kill me if that's what you need, but let her go. She's just a kid." My voice faded away to a whispered plea. My forehead pressed against the end of the gun, the metal cold as ice. As freezing as impending death.

The man holding the gun on me seemed frozen, too, unable to move, as the boss stood slowly from his chair. Everyone seemed spellbound for a long, silent moment.

"*She's* just a kid? How much older can *you* be?" Renato broke the silence.

"I'm twenty-six, and she just turned nineteen. That's just a kid. She doesn't understand . . ." I trailed off.

Renato came into view, standing just behind the man who held the gun on me. Now that he was standing, I could see how tall and broad he was.

"She doesn't understand what?" He prodded me when I lost myself in staring, fear dragging my mind into lingering pauses.

"Men like you." The words left me before I could decide if they were a mistake or not.

Renato came closer, and the man holding the gun trembled. He wanted to move, I could tell, but he didn't know if that was a wise call.

"And you do? Tell me, what do you know about *men like me*?"

"Can you—can he put the gun down first?" I attempted, wetting my lips twice to get the words out.

Renato raised an eyebrow. "But you're doing so well. Most men would have pissed themselves by now or pleaded for their lives. Most never would have stepped in front of it in the first place." He stepped closer to me, passing behind me. "Why do you want it moved now?"

"I don't trust the man pointing it at me. He looks like a coward," I ground out. The man's eyes widened, and his grip slid on the metal. "He's shaking," I added.

Renato turned to look at the man. His man. He nodded slightly. "Yes, he is, isn't he? Not a very reliable man after all, are you, Tony? First, you make your own judgment calls, and then, you're too weak to stand by them. It's not behavior worthy of the De Sanctis name. Maybe under my father such weakness was tolerated, but that family isn't this one, as you know."

Renato took Tony's shaking hand and slowly pulled his fingers from the grip, prying the gun away from him. The entire time he did, the pistol was turned toward his chest. He wasn't afraid of being shot by the terrified man. That was power.

He gripped the gun and looked at me, holding the butt of the pistol out. "Do you want to, or shall I?"

"What?" I asked numbly, my brain too shocked and scared to keep up.

"He pulled a gun in my presence without permission . . . and he decided the fate of a kid without my input. He's a dead man. Do you want to do it, avenge your sister's friend, or should I?"

"I-I could never . . ." I stuttered.

The hot spray of blood against my face registered before the bang. I brought a hand slowly to my cheek and wiped, barely noticing the blood dripping from my fingers. The man who'd been holding the gun, the one who'd killed Miguel, slumped dead to the floor.

The other guy from the warehouse, the one who'd tried to stop his friend, scrambled back, bringing his hands up like it could stop what was coming. The bullet entering his head sounded wet. It blew out the back like his skull was an overripe fig, and he fell to the side. My head spun, and the room tilted. I couldn't catch my breath.

"Never say never, *bambina*. It makes me want to prove you wrong."

Renato stripped off the gloves and handed them and the gun to Elio, the shadow at his side. Elio handed him a small towel in return, like wiping up blood from a shot to the head was just a regular Thursday morning in this family. It probably was. Then Renato took the gun back, and I knew in my bones, it was my turn.

"It's a shame that you ended up where you did the other night, Charlotte. You seemed like a good person, and good people have consciences that bother them. It's a loose end, and I don't like those."

Seemed? I was already dead to this man. *Fight, Charlie. Fight!*

"I don't have a conscience. I don't care that you just shot that guy, he deserved it. I only care about my sister," I burst out. I was dizzy. I could have fainted, if not for the urgency beating through me.

"And she has proven herself to be a liability, I'm afraid," Renato continued. He looked totally unmoved, blood drying on his cuffs where the gloves hadn't covered. There was a light spray across one of his high cheekbones. With the light from the fire and his dramatic coloring, he really did seem like a king of the underworld at that moment. A monster wearing a man suit.

"I'll keep her quiet. She'll do what I tell her. I'll make her understand."

"I'm afraid your word isn't enough," Renato continued.

I was panicking, scrabbling like that rat in the maze that I so empathized with. Trying to find an exit, only to keep coming up against obstacles.

Tears rolled down my face, burning hot and desperate. Before I could overthink it, I grabbed his arm. It was taut beneath his jacket sleeve. I held on and met his dark eyes. Behind his head, the portrait of the serene woman beckoned, and the light glanced off the cross on the wall. Without another thought, I lowered myself to my knees and knelt before him, head bowed.

"Dear God, who art in heaven . . ." I started, the words of the Lord's Prayer deserting me when I needed them most. I grasped for the next phrase before changing tack. "Do you believe in God?" My voice shook. I was really scraping the bottom of the barrel expecting this monster to fear heavenly retribution, but I'd leave no stone unturned.

Renato was silent for a long moment. I could tell that the swerve in tone had thrown him. This might be futile, but he hadn't shot me yet. My time left on Earth had narrowed down to heartbeats. Every single one I could win was a victory.

His voice was mildly curious. "And if I said yes?" he mused.

"Then, I'll swear on everything in this world and the next, on heaven and hell and all the worlds in between, we will keep this night a secret and never speak of it again. I swear to God."

I held that pose. When I was a child, my parents had taken me to the small Catholic church in our neighborhood. I hadn't understood much, but I'd gotten that when you wanted something or needed help, you asked God. When my Ma died giving birth to Lucy, we'd had a small funeral at that church. I'd prayed for God to make her welcome in heaven and to help my Da. He was so sad.

Then, my Da had died, and I'd prayed for him to return every night for a year from my narrow bunk at Mercy House. I'd prayed for him to return when the nuns had disciplined us for impure thoughts, with cold showers or hours of Bible study. It had taken me a while to understand that he was never coming back. I hadn't prayed since the night I'd realized that if anyone was listening, He didn't care about the Burke sisters.

But I prayed now, before the man who held both Lucy's and my lives in his bloodstained hands.

My new god.

He stilled, seeming fascinated by my approach. I had my eyes closed; I couldn't look at him as he stood over me, gun in hand, and decided our fate.

Slowly, he crouched before me. "What would you do to save your sister?"

"Whatever I have to," I said without hesitation.

Renato's dark eyes stared down at me for a long moment before he spoke again. "I'm afraid I'm not really a believer, Miss Burke. That was my mother's domain."

His mother. That had to be the beautiful woman in the painting. I could see a strong family resemblance now that I knew their relationship.

Straightening up, he towered over me, his judgment cast.

"Then I'll pray to you," I implored. "Worship you instead . . .

accept your word as my gospel . . . if you'll give us a chance to live. Please . . . *please*. I'll do anything, whatever I have to, please."

Renato was silent. I steeled myself as I raised my eyes to his. He was so close that I could see the sparkling variation of browns in his warm eyes. Really, those eyes were far too soulful and real to belong to a monster. It wasn't fair at all. His mouth was slightly upturned, like he was amused somehow by my prostrating myself and begging him for mercy. I had no pride; I had no dignity. I couldn't even pretend to have any. There was nothing I wouldn't do, for *her*.

That was my truth, and I let him see it. Something passed between us in that moment. Something intimate and born from darkness and desperation. It was a second where you could take the measure of a person's soul and know its worth. It was the most intimate moment I'd ever experienced with another human being, and it was terrifying. I didn't want to see what he hid in the dark recesses of his black soul, but I couldn't look away. To flinch meant certain death.

Renato swallowed. I suddenly realized he was as unsettled by my unerring inspection as I was by his. Maybe I wasn't the only one who kept people at a distance.

His eyes fell to the shining pendant on my necklace. "Saint Anthony. Saint of the lost."

I didn't trust myself to speak, so I simply nodded.

"Are you lost, *bambina?*" His voice was rich.

"I've always been a lost thing," I admitted, letting this man see right inside me, to the deepest, darkest corners of my soul.

He took his time measuring my worth and deciding my fate. I held his gaze and didn't dare to blink.

Finally, he delivered his verdict. "Then, Miss Burke, we have a deal. You keep your sister quiet, and in return . . ."

"Yes?"

"You'll do whatever you have to. Whatever I want you to." He held out a hand to me.

A devil's bargain.

I had no idea what he'd ask me to do. It might be illegal. It would probably be dangerous. It could be anything. I shouldn't take that deal. Maybe I was only putting off dying for another day.

Still, another day was another chance to live a little more.

I took his hand and shook it.

5

RENATO

Charlotte rose slowly, her hand cool in mine. It was so slender I could have crushed it with a wrong move, yet she made no attempt to pull away. Much like a misguided little lamb, thinking the wolf might save it from the farmer, she looked at me as though my mercy might just save her from the unfortunate derailment of her life.

Tonight, she had joined an exclusive list of people who had looked to me for mercy, ones who'd put their fate in my hands and trusted me to save them. In fact, she didn't just make the list. She *was* the list. She was distracting to look at. Petite with an hourglass shape, smooth velvet skin, and doe-like eyes. Her thick eyebrows and pretty bow lips were straight from an eighteenth-century painting. She wasn't trying to look beautiful, but nonetheless, she did. I suspected it was impossible for her not to.

No one in her position had ever gotten down on their knees and offered to make me their god. Especially since she'd just seen me kill two men in cold blood. She was an intriguing mix of contradictions. Good, pure, and apparently mercenary. It seemed there was nothing she wouldn't do to keep herself and her sister safe, and that was interesting. Life had been stale lately, uneventful. Charlotte Burke was a burst of color against a black-and-white background. She was too tantalizing a prospect to pass on.

For now.

Elio's phone rang as I forced myself to drop Charlotte's hand. He listened to the caller, nodding, and then hung up.

"Incident in the kitchen. Angelo was burned on the stove," Elio said.

The code was pretty obvious if you were a De Sanctis man, but Charlotte was just confused. We often spoke in code, even in the halls of Casa Nera. There were spies everywhere these days, just waiting for a good sound bite they could sell to the highest bidder.

I looked at Charlotte. *Charlie.* "You're studying nursing?" She jumped, her leftover adrenaline making her edgy. She nodded.

"Then come with me. You can start our bargain right now." Without waiting for an answer, I turned and walked out of the study. I knew Charlotte would follow, or Elio would make her.

"W-wait. My sister," Charlotte stuttered.

Lucy lay soundly unconscious between two dead men. "Don't worry. They can't touch her now."

I headed down to the basement level of the property. It housed cells and a makeshift medical room at one end. Many a man had been held down here to be tortured or killed. A few made it back to ground level, but not many. It had seen more use under my father, but I still found it useful at times.

The air grew stale as we descended the cold stone staircase leading to the basement, one of the features of the original house.

Grunts of pain and snippets of conversation could be heard as soon as we reached the lowest level. Charlotte peered curiously in the direction of slurred Italian, peppered liberally with curses.

"This way. I want to see what you can do, *bambina*," I murmured to her, putting my hand on the small of her back when she failed to move.

She leapt forward, escaping my touch, and I allowed her. Now wasn't the time to demonstrate what it meant to be mine. Soon, she'd understand that her fate was mine to decide, she was my property, and I'd touch my things whenever I damn well pleased.

But since I'd decided not to kill her just yet, and to give her a week or so to see if she could live up to her promises, there wasn't any point in scaring her now. That could come later. It always did. No matter how driven a woman was to get close to me, or how far they thought they'd climb socially by being with me, there was always a moment when their mask would slip, and I'd see their fear.

I didn't have time to play those games with Charlotte Burke right now, and besides, her courage upstairs had been such a fucking turn-on. I didn't want to ruin it already.

We reached the cell at the end, which we'd set up with a hospital bed and a cabinet of supplies. A man sat in the middle of the bed. His name was Angelo, and he was one of the longest-serving made men in the family. He groaned as he held his face in one hand, a bottle of liquor in the other. The smell of metal and booze was thick in the air.

"Renato! They just came out of nowhere. Castillos, right there at the diner. They jumped me, but I got a few good hits in," the older man panted.

I liked Angelo, as much as I liked anyone who wasn't blood. He was a good man and a loyal soldier.

I clamped a hand on his shoulder and squeezed. "Bravo. You protected our name well. Let the nurse see your face. We don't want to let it become uglier, for your wife's sake."

He chuckled at my teasing and relaxed a little, looking at Charlotte. She stood rooted to the spot, staring at him.

"Come on, Miss Burke, this is your chance to shine. Show me what you've got."

"I'm just a student. I've never done anything like this without supervision," she hedged.

"I'll supervise you, how's that?" I offered.

She shot me an annoyed glance, a flash of her true feelings.

"I might mess it up," she said flatly.

"While I'm sure your confidence is really setting the patient at ease, don't worry about it. There'll be no complaints here to the hospital board. If you weren't here, we'd duct tape it closed until our family doc comes out tomorrow. You can't do worse than that," I pointed out. "Stop the bleeding and get a move on."

I settled against a nearby wall and watched her. Her hands curled into little fists and then released. I wondered if it pissed her off to be ordered around. It would be more fun if it did. Maybe that way, I'd get to see more of those fiery sparks she'd shot at me earlier; little glimpses of her true self.

Instead of arguing, she took off her leather jacket. The emblem of La Leonora, favorite of my casinos, winked at me as she rolled up her sleeves and doused her hands with sanitizer. This woman had been right under my nose, and I'd never seen her before. I'd have remembered her. I was sure of that.

"Good girl," I murmured.

She scowled at me, and the look was an aphrodisiac. This woman was more than fiery, she was the entire bonfire. And I liked it, I realized dimly as I watched her prepare her workspace. She was the most interesting person I'd met in a very long time. I settled back to enjoy observing her.

"First of all, no drinking. It makes the bleeding worse," she said firmly, prying the bottle of hooch away from Angelo. She ignored his protests and started to clean the long slash on his face.

He hissed when the cotton ball touched the cut.

"This might sting," she said after a long pause.

"Bit late for the warning, Doc," Angelo grumbled.

"Yeah, well, ask for forgiveness, not permission," she muttered, her eyes lifting and catching mine for a moment before shooting away.

I wondered if she was half as affected by my presence as I was by hers. No, I doubted it. I was the one living in monochrome, not her. The one whose world had become unbearably dull.

After one last dab with the cotton ball, she straightened and looked at Angelo. "I have to stitch your cut now. It's going to hurt, and I'm sorry," she said evenly.

Angelo sighed, resigned, but obligingly held still. After a moment, he spoke. "You're right, it's worse to be warned, but I can take it."

I shifted, wishing they would finish up and I could have Charlotte's undivided attention again. "Of course, you can," I said. "You have no choice," I added, more for her sake than Angelo's.

Her mouth formed a firm line, and she focused on her task. Painful moments ticked by, and then, suddenly she was done. I moved closer to take stock of her handiwork. It was lovely. Just as neat and tidy as if it had been done by a surgeon.

"Leave us," I tossed to Angelo, who thanked Charlotte profusely and made for the door, swiping the bottle on his way past.

"So, what else do I need to do to prove to you that I'll keep my word? You really didn't have to bring me to this kind of place to make your point." She had her arms folded, like that fragile barrier of bone and flesh could keep me from her.

"This kind of place? This is my home," I added.

She turned critical eyes around the basement cell. "Well, it looks like it was ripped straight out of a *Medieval Torture Chambers Monthly*, special edition."

That outrageous, unexpected statement nearly pulled a laugh from me.

"Since the décor isn't to your liking, I'd recommend doing everything you can not to end up as a guest here. That means keeping your smart little mouth shut, and your sister's, too."

She swallowed hard, and my eyes tracked the movement. "I know. I get it. Don't worry. I know what I agreed to."

No, bambina, you're wrong. You have no idea.

"You offered to make me your god, Charlotte. A man like me doesn't forget a promise like that."

"A man like you? What kind of man is that?" she asked, her soft voice failing to hide the undercurrent of challenge in her tone.

"A man who gets whatever he wants," I clarified.

"You mean takes it, right?" she added.

The sass on this woman would be the death of her.

I shrugged. "Either way, it ends up mine." I reached up and rubbed a dirty smudge from one of her plump apple cheeks. "You've started out as mine. Don't forget that."

She stared at me for a long moment, her gaze reminding me of the long look we'd shared upstairs. The one that had shown into her soul, and I'd been able to see how it glowed.

"You can go, for now. But remember, Miss Burke, I'll be watching. I'll always be watching, so behave accordingly, and be a good fucking girl, or we'll be right back to where we started."

The bodies had been taken care of, and my study was once again undisturbed. But the stink of death remained, and my handwoven Persian rug was gone.

"What do you want on them?" Elio asked as soon as our guests left, driven home by the two men I'd be using to tail them from this point forward.

We ran several different levels of surveillance on our targets. Most often, our targets were politicians or important public figures. We used the information we gathered to curate a nice leverage folder (blackmail was such a dirty word). This was the first time I'd be using my invisible eyes for a pet project. We never watched potential problems or witnesses. They ended up fertilizing the Black Baccara roses that grew in abundance on the Casa Nera grounds. The burgundy velvet blooms were splendid this year; they'd been fed so well.

"Eyes on them round the clock." I sat back in my chair. This was the highest level of invisible eyes. I wanted to see what Charlotte was going to do with her hard-won chance to impress me. Men my age often took up new hobbies. I already read voraciously and played chess. That left golf, and I'd beaten too many people to death with golf clubs to take the sport seriously. Maybe stalking the little nurse could be my new hobby, at least until I grew bored of it. As I inevitably would.

Elio nodded and left. My *sottocapo* didn't question my reasoning, even though leaving the sisters alive would require a lot of effort on our part. This was uncharacteristic of me. I wasn't a man known for mercy.

And yet, when that beautiful, brave young woman had sunk to her knees in front of me, she had blown something inside me wide open. When she had prayed to me . . . the darkness lurking in my soul had become hungry for more. Sure, I was no saint, but people used to worship demons, too.

For all the religious education I'd had as a child, beaten into me by uncaring or downright evil-intentioned men, there was a twisted kind of curiosity in me toward this girl. Besides, my mother had always worn a St. Anthony pendant. My mother, who had never deserved her terrible life. A woman who had prayed for my father's soul every single day, until she'd died too young. A light stolen from the world.

Charlotte shared her goodness; I could feel it radiating off her. Innocence and compassion. Things I had little experience with but felt curious about. I was a man who could buy anything he wanted, do anything he dreamed of, and had long since realized how tedious that kind of life became.

Charlotte pressing her forehead into a loaded gun and asking to die in place of her sister was a fucking turn-on. It was brave in a way I'd never seen. As pale and innocent as a Caravaggio angel, a nurse who would step in front of a gun to save her sister, she shone with goodness. While I'd long ago accepted what I was, I was intrigued by how much darkness and temptation it would take to sully her angelic aura.

How much sin could turn a heavenly creature to the dark?

I looked forward to finding out.

6

CHARLIE

I was late for my rotation Friday, but considering that I was running on fumes, it was a miracle I'd made it at all. At this stage in my nursing program, I couldn't afford to miss work shifts. It looked unprofessional, and besides, I needed good references to get a job afterward. I didn't want to waitress at La Leonora any longer than necessary. I was born to be a nurse. At certain points over my five years of part-time study, it'd felt like an impossible mountain to climb, but I was so close now.

Now, when everything else in my life was threatened.

I hurried around my tasks, keeping my head down and hoping that no one noticed I was late. Doctor Dan's smirk told me he had certainly noticed. I was three hours into an endless day, gulping down a bottle of water near the department reception's desk, when I heard my name.

"Burke? Are they a patient?"

A man leaned on the counter. He was young but had the confidence of a life lived recklessly. His low jeans were nearly falling off his butt, and his T-shirt looked like a designer knockoff. Everything about him reminded me of Miguel, Lucy's recently departed ex.

"Nah, I think she's a nurse. Nurse Burke or some shit," the stranger said.

The person behind the desk shook her head. "I'm afraid I can't give you any information on staff. If you know her, give her a call."

"Seriously, bitch, that's how you're going to play it?" The guy sneered.

I stepped back and hid behind the doorway as he glanced around.

The receptionist had had enough. She pressed a buzzer. "I'm calling security, since you're just here to make trouble."

The guy glowered at her and then leaned on the counter, jumping up a little to get right in her face. Why wasn't there safety glass there?

"Listen, mama, I'll show you trouble. I'll show you how trouble feels when it rips a hole in your pretty chest. Bang," he whispered, laughing as the receptionist turned pale.

After that, security appeared and grabbed the guy, dragging him away down the hall. I sagged in my hiding place. Miguel's boss had found me, which meant that they'd figured out who Lucy was and somehow me, too. How? I guessed if they had Lucy's number, then finding out her name and who her family was wouldn't be too much of a stretch.

You need to go to the police, pleaded the voice of reason inside my head. Okay, great, go to the police and then what? Would they put us in a safe house? Would we go into witness protection? If we went to the police, we'd be forced to tell them the whole sorry story, and then I'd become a witness pointing a finger at Renato De Sanctis and his family.

We wouldn't survive that. He'd promised as much.

I had to ask Lucy if Miguel's cartel connections had contacted her again. I should have gotten rid of both of our phones, not just Miguel's. *What had I been thinking?*

I'd been making mistake after mistake since that night, and I couldn't seem to stop.

To top it all off, I had a long waitressing shift tonight, and I'd just found out I'd be working in the banquet room that was hosting the spina bifida charity benefit—a benefit that half the hospital was attending. But having to serve the people I wanted to take me seriously as a medical professional was the least of my worries.

Outside, the early-evening air was cool. Even if it was full of exhaust fumes, it was better than the sterile, recycled air of the hospital.

I set out toward the bus stop, making a list of things I had to get done when I got home. Check in on Lucy, dodge that random gang member looking for us and the missing drugs, stay out of jail, and avoid being murdered by the Italian mob.

If I hadn't been so tired, I might have cried. Instead, I dragged myself toward the bus stop. I had just reached the crosswalk when my name was called. In the evening gloom, I could only make out their outlines as they crossed the street toward me, but that was enough.

Detectives Whitely and Vane. Pure panic flooded my chest, and I had to lock my legs in place to stop myself from bolting. These were the police; I couldn't run from them without looking suspicious. Swallowing my panic as best as I could, I tried to subtly glance around the busy street. Renato had warned me he'd be watching. How long would it be until he found out that I'd talked to the cops?

"Miss Burke? Can we have a moment of your time?" Detective Whitely asked as they approached.

I stepped back, my head shaking. "I'm afraid not. I'm late for work. I'm waitressing a charity benefit. I have to go."

"Have you ever heard the expression 'Charity begins at home'?" Detective Vane said, falling back into her bad cop role.

"Meaning?"

"Meaning your little sister was very upset the other night. A caring older sister would want to ease her burden, surely."

A ragged laugh left me at the detective's callous words. I gathered myself and stopped backing away. I was acting guilty, and I had to get a grip. "Excuse me, Detective, but you don't know anything about my family. Are you here in an official capacity?"

Both the cops watched me for a long moment before Detective Whitely spoke gruffly. "No. Just concerned."

"Well, I don't have any obligation to talk to you and be late for my shift. This isn't a good time, so I'm leaving."

"Don't forget, Miss Burke—we're supposed to be on your side . . . if your side is the right one," Detective Vane called to my departing back.

She had no idea that I'd already promised my silence to the devil, and his was the deal I couldn't break.

When I got home, Lucy was in her room, loud, angry music seeping around the closed door. I couldn't deal with her oscillating emotions right now.

I dragged myself to the shower and stood underneath the spray for far too long. Hot tendrils of steam rose around me, and I focused on the feeling of the water running over my body to drown out my worries. What could I do about the drug dealer? *If you can't tell the cops, tell Renato De Sanctis.* The thought alone was bananas enough to make me worried for my sanity.

I shut the water off and stepped out of the shower onto the faded bath mat.

My reflection in the mirror was exhausted. Dark circles ringed my eyes, the whites bloodshot. I looked scared. There was a haunted quality to my expression that I couldn't shake.

Darkness and danger. Trouble with the cops and criminals. This was the life I'd strived to avoid for me and Lucy. This had been our legacy, from our parents' deaths to growing up in a group home, poor and unwanted. I'd fought tooth and nail to set us on a different path, to walk in a different world, and now, we were right back where we'd started.

Maybe you couldn't fight destiny after all. Maybe you could only ever put it off for a while. Fate would always find you and claim you.

Renato's darkly handsome face flashed through my mind.

We have a deal. You keep your sister quiet, and in return . . . You'll do whatever you have to.

The reminder of his words sent a full-body shiver through me. I couldn't believe I'd knelt there, before the most dangerous man I'd ever met, and vowed to worship him like he was my new god, to take his orders like they were heaven-sent. I had no idea what he would ask of me, but I'd already agreed, anyway. It felt like I had the sword of Damocles hanging over my head.

I brushed my teeth while turning my mind to work, which rapidly approached. I wasn't excited for this shift. I'd been dreading the possibility of being scheduled to work the charity event all month, and yet, given what else I was dealing with, it had lost its ability to scare me. Maybe there was a silver lining to learning new levels of fear. It certainly put the small daily struggles I dealt with into perspective.

I'd just left the bathroom when I caught the soft murmur of voices in the kitchen. Who the hell was that? Lucy and I didn't get visitors. Our apartment couldn't really accommodate more than two people at a time.

I headed down the hall toward the kitchen. A familiar tone

struck me cold with terror. I turned the corner and stepped into the kitchen, hoping against all odds that I wouldn't see who I feared I would.

Detective Vane sat at the table across from Lucy, and Detective Whitely stood at the sink, filling the kettle.

"What the hell are you doing here?" I demanded, panic making me abrasive.

Detective Vane raised an eyebrow at me, her overly plucked arch mocking my undressed state. "Miss Burke, good evening to you, too. We won't get in the way of you getting ready for work. Please, go and get ready. Lucy was just having a little chat with us." She turned back to my sister, who perched in a miserable ball on the edge of her chair.

Her long hair was strewn around her shoulders, her eyes red. She glanced at me, her expression torn. She wanted to talk to the cops. She wanted justice for Miguel, but she didn't want to go against me. While we might fight sometimes, we were all each other had.

"And you think it's appropriate to just barge into someone's private residence?" I attempted to gather my wits.

"Lucy let us in," Whitely pointed out, flipping on the kettle and settling against the counter, crossing his arms.

"And it's also appropriate to sit and speak alone to a teenager without her guardian's supervision?" I began but didn't get far before Detective Vane interrupted.

"Lucy is over eighteen, I believe? If she wants us to stay, I think we need to honor that."

I blew out a frustrated breath. *Fuck*. I turned to my sister. "Tell them to leave, Lucy. We don't need anything from them, and the whole thing is a misunderstanding."

She stared at me, biting her lip. I could see her confession building. I couldn't let her say it.

"Lucy Burke! Stop wasting police time and tell them to go. *Deirfiúr*," I muttered the magic word.

What the detectives thought about the Irish Gaelic word, I had no idea. I only had eyes for Lucy's reaction. The word had become a mantra between us. Before Da had died, he'd peppered Irish Gaelic words into his speech, and *deirfiúr* became our code word for when she needed to listen to me, no matter what. *Deirfiúr. Sister.*

A tear fell from Lucy's eye as she looked at the detectives. "My sister's right. I'm going to bed, and she's going out. It's not a good time for tea. Sorry for the fuss. I was confused, tired, I don't even know what I'm saying . . ." She stood and shrugged her thin shoulders. "I just don't know."

Her pajamas had cats on them, and at that second, she looked so young and helpless, my heart broke. Both our lives as we knew them had ended in the last forty-eight hours.

"You heard her. Please go and don't bother either of us again," I said briskly and opened the front door expectantly.

The detectives exchanged long looks. They had their own language, too, it seemed. Annoyingly slowly, they gathered their things.

"If you're sure, Lucy. But don't forget to call if you change your mind," Detective Vane said, eyeing me as she passed by. "I'm sure we'll be seeing you soon, Miss Burke."

"I'm not." I closed the door behind them and locked it, then peered through the peephole at the detectives standing in the hall outside. They lingered, speaking so quietly between themselves I couldn't hear their words. Finally, they moved away, and I sank against the door, my heart pounding.

"What are you thinking?" I whirled to Lucy.

Instead of dissolving into a tearful mess, she glared back at me. "I'm thinking of telling the truth—you should try it sometime!"

"Are you serious right now? Do you have any idea what will happen?"

Lucy shrugged with the arrogance of youth that I'd never had the luxury of enjoying. For as long as I could remember, I hadn't had the privilege of being childish or irresponsible. I'd been Lucy's caretaker since I was thirteen, and suddenly, I was so tired.

"The police will arrest those killers and protect us," Lucy said.

A ragged laugh left me. "Right. Because the police always manage to protect witnesses and bad guys are always caught, right? Don't be such a child. You have to be stronger than this."

Lucy's glare only heated up. "Strong like you? I never want to be like you."

Her words stung, and her anger sparked my own. "And what the hell does that mean?"

"Joyless, alone, a workaholic, a worrier. You never do anything fun, you never laugh, you never take a break from being a fucking nag!"

I flinched back from that verbal slap. Tears warred with fury inside me.

"Whatever you might think about me, the police won't protect us. Neither you nor I have the power to take down Renato De Sanctis, and he'll kill you. He promised me he would if we go to the cops, and I'll bet he's a man of his word."

Lucy swallowed hard and shook her head. "You're just scared of him, and everyone—"

"You're the reason this is all happening," I interrupted silkily. It was a horrible thing to say, but her cruel outburst of honesty had ripped something inside me. "This danger, this threat . . . it's all because of you."

I stepped closer to my little sister. My greatest love and my greatest burden all at once. Taking care of her had always been both a privilege and duty. Tonight, the resentments of a lifetime bubbled out.

"Because you couldn't stay out of trouble. Because you let a loser wannabe drug dealer gangster into our lives, we're in this mess. Because you have no idea what the real world is like—and maybe that's my fault. If you want to know why I work all the time, why I'm always worried—look in the mirror. I have a child I never asked for, and she can't even be grateful.

"I've protected you my entire life, even when I was just a kid. So, I never got to be one. Maybe I should be done with that. Provide for yourself, go to the police if you want . . . let's see how long you last—but don't call me when the police take a statement and send you away to watch out for yourself while they investigate. And certainly, don't call me when the De Sanctis family takes you to a warehouse by the docks and presses a gun to your head."

Lucy's face had drained of color as I spat my vitriol at her. I spun on my heel even as her hurt expression etched itself into my memory. I'd never forget that look.

I headed back to my room, my righteous anger quickly running out of steam. I slammed the door and sank down to the floor, curling into a ball.

For the first time in longer than I could remember, I cried.

I sobbed my fucking heart out.

I had a pounding headache by the time I made it to work. I was scared of leaving Lucy on her own in case she decided to go back to the cops, but I didn't know what else to do. We needed money, and the tips from my job saved us every month. I couldn't miss this shift on such short notice. I just had to hope that my uncharacteristic outburst had slapped some sense into her.

So, I'd pulled my hair back, washed my puffy eyes with cool water, slapped on some makeup, and went out to be an adult. So far, it sucked.

I'd already seen five doctors I knew from the hospital, and

they'd seen me, too. To their credit, every single one had been friendly and greeted me, but I still felt small.

"Charlotte!" a jovial voice shouted at me across the room as I circled with water refills.

Gritting my teeth, I approached him. Doctor Dan and his fucking punchable grin. His table was full of his Princeton pals.

He patted the seat beside him. "Sure you don't want to join us?" He gave me what he clearly thought was a charming grin.

"I'm working, as you can probably tell." I lifted the heavy water carafe. "I don't just carry this around as an accessory."

Some of his friends sniggered, and Dan's smile turned brittle.

"Yes, I see. Well, when you have a chance, I'll take the cocktail menu," he said to me and then turned back to his friends. "She's an intern at the hospital, you know the type. Never going to finish her degree, trashy family situation . . ."

I gripped the water carafe and seriously considered dumping it over Dan's head. The urge was so strong, I couldn't make my feet move away for a minute. Instead, like a glutton for punishment, I stood there and listened to him talk horribly about me, before I tore myself away, his words ringing in my ears. I couldn't afford to make a scene and lose my job or damage my reputation among the hospital staff in attendance.

There was nothing I could do but walk away. My tattered pride ripped a little more with every step in the opposite direction. Pretty soon, I wouldn't have any dignity left at all.

I tried to rally. *Hey, I could still spit in Dan's food.* My attempt to comfort myself fell flat. I'd never do that. I was the type of person who could take a punch and keep on going. It was a claim I hated to be able to make. I'd been taught early on to turn the other cheek. Lately, it felt like both my cheeks had tread marks on them, considering the number of people who had walked over me.

Self-critical, dark thoughts circled my head as I made my way across the empty dance floor, then abruptly died at the sight of a couple of latecomers, strolling through the banquet doors like they owned the place.

I stopped dead in my tracks, feeling like I'd accidentally hit my head or passed out and was hallucinating. There was no way that Renato De Sanctis had just walked in the door, in a tux and drawing all eyes.

He surveyed the crowd, his classically handsome features looking as regal as ever, and seemed to find it lacking. He had an innate aloofness that rich people like Daniel tried to cultivate, but never came close to.

His tux had the luxury bespoke style I saw on high rollers, and his dark waves, with that streak of steel, caught the lights and shone. His olive skin glowed, too. He was a man born to wear formal wear and look like a god doing it. He was also a man who had just threatened my life and shot two men dead in cold blood—perfect, precise shots to the head, right beside me. My ears still rang from the bangs.

The water carafe was sweating in my hands and nearly slipped. I grabbed at it and started off the dance floor. I couldn't wander around all night. My line manager would wonder why I hadn't come back to the kitchen. As I headed toward the edge of the tables, I finally registered the woman beside Renato.

She was stunning. About the same age as me, with a soft cloud of inky curls, a black dress that seemed like she was paying homage to the Black Swan, and blood-red lipstick. She looked right at Renato's side. A dangerous man, with an equally dangerous woman. I'd never felt frumpier in my ill-fitting waitressing uniform and my low ponytail.

The moment Renato's eyes met mine was like I'd put my hand in an electrical socket. A full-body shock lit up my nerves when his gaze rested on me. There was no surprise in his expression. He simply stared at me, and I stared right back.

"Excuse me, could I have a water refill?" someone asked beside my elbow, startling me.

"Of course," I muttered, messily pouring a refill. My hands shook.

"Did you see that Renato De Sanctis is here? He'll sometimes make an appearance at these types of things." A group of women gossiped amongst themselves.

I moved around the table, refilling water and shamelessly eavesdropping.

"And what an appearance it is. I wonder who the chick is?"

"I'm not sure, but he's been seen with her before."

"Well, she's certainly pretty enough to be his armpiece. I can't believe he owns this hotel," one of them said wistfully.

He owns this hotel? Sickness surged through me, and I stepped away and forced deep breaths. I'd been skulking around all day, wondering how we'd stay off Renato De Sanctis's radar, when I literally worked in one of his casinos? It was just my kind of luck.

A deep voice interrupted my spiraling. "Miss Burke. What a coincidence."

Holy crap. Renato had come over to speak to me. Right here in front of everyone.

I held my carafe in a death grip and turned around. There he was, looking like the powerful god I'd promised to believe in, staring down at me with that intense expression I'd come to associate with him.

"Is it really a coincidence?" I asked immediately. "I'd have expected a man like you to do your due diligence. You probably know everything about me, down to whether I prefer tampons or pads."

What the hell, Charlie? Okay, well, I'd clearly lost my mind.

Renato was unruffled. He picked a speck of invisible dirt from his cuff. "I must say, I might have overlooked that one. I'll have to add it to the list."

A scoff left me. This guy was equal parts terrifying and smart-ass, and I didn't know how to handle that. He was utterly undisturbed by whatever I threw at him. "So, you knew I'd be here?"

"In this ballroom, no. In my hotel, of course. That said, I don't believe in coincidences, Miss Burke. I believe in fate."

Over his shoulder, the stunning woman headed toward us, her black ball gown rippling like ink as she approached.

"Ren. You lied. There are exactly zero fuckable men here, and I got waxed for this," she accused Renato as soon as she got close. She wrapped one hand around his biceps and inspected me, tilting her head to the side.

"You're Charlotte Burke. *Charlie*. Aren't you?"

I swallowed hard. "And you are?"

She laughed and gave me a wicked look. "I'm the IT guy. Nice to meet you, Charlie." She stuck out a black-nailed hand.

I took it after a moment, giving it a limp shake.

"You too. I have to get back to work," I muttered, my eyes darting to Renato's and away.

"Of course, the boss at this dump is a real dragon, or so I've heard. You do *not* want to get on his bad side." The mystery woman laughed and whirled away from me, just in time to intercept the benefit organizers who were making a beeline for Renato.

Of course they were. The man oozed wealth and power. He was a magnet, and eyes were drawn to him from all over the room.

Renato didn't turn when the organizers spoke to him. Instead, he stared at me. I backed away, shooting a polite smile across the group, and then swiveled on my heel and hightailed it to the kitchen.

I could feel his eyes on me the entire time.

7

RENATO

I had no desire to make an appearance at the benefit tonight, but it usually paid off to show my face. Everyone of power and wealth in this city knew who I was. I showed up at these things to remind them that I was real, not just some fairy-tale monster people told their kids about. People needed incentives to stick to the rules, and fear was the best motivator.

Running into Charlotte Burke was just an unexpected benefit.

She tried hard not to stare at me as she worked. Her waitressing uniform was unflattering, yet it didn't hide the classical hourglass proportions of her body. I wondered if she picked out clothes that were purposefully large for her, disliking the attention that something formfitting would bring her. It was possible. Charlotte was smart. She didn't exaggerate the largeness of the uniform. It was only just big enough to make her look unshapely, with a hint of sloppy. Hiding in plain sight from the clientele of the casino, who could err on the side of handsy.

"So, when can we leave?" Giada asked, six cocktails deep and still bored. "You said ten minutes, in and out."

"Ten more." I sipped my scotch, my attention on Charlotte as she moved efficiently around the room, clearing empty glasses.

"You know, I spoke to *Zio* Sal this morning." Giada's change of subject was enough for me to lose my focus.

I turned to her. "And what did Salvatore have to say?"

The De Sanctis family wasn't only a powerhouse of organized crime in the States, but in Italy, as well. My uncle Salvatore ran the *famiglia* in Naples like a well-oiled machine, and I'd learned far more from him than I had from my actual father. He was my mother's brother and had never fully gotten over her death. There had been no tears shed in Naples when my father had died.

"You know, the usual. He wants to know what time the christening is."

I sighed, familiar with this routine by now. "The christening for his imaginary godchild? Any day now."

Giada laughed. "You have to hand it to the old guy. Give him one book on manifesting and he's all in. He's not going to stop until he's holding the heir of the De Sanctis family's U.S. operations in his arms and cooing over them. You have to give in at some point, Ren. You're not getting any younger. Clock's ticking."

"I'm not sure it works that way with men."

"I mean *Zio* Sal's clock. It's only a matter of time before he pushes someone on you, if you can't rise to the challenge to finding a wife yourself and knocking her up."

The image of *Zio* Sal's sweet, quiet-as-a-church-mouse wife filled my mind. Meek, silent, and far too breakable for my liking. At my age, I was set in my lifestyle and my routines. I wouldn't be making space for some Mafia princess who had to be coddled, or a fragile leaf of a girl who'd snap at the first harsh word or the strain of motherhood. I needed someone resilient. A woman with grit.

"Tell Uncle Sal I don't require his help."

"You can tell him yourself. He's coming to visit, that's why I called."

"When?" I wasn't displeased to hear that my Italian family was visiting, but I wasn't looking forward to more pushing on the wife-and-heir subject. It wasn't something I'd accept being forced into. I wouldn't be marrying someone *Zio* Sal suggested just to check having an heir off the list. I'd choose the woman who would be the mother of my children with the same precision I chose everything in my life.

"In the new year. If I were you, I'd find someone to show off to him before then. For fuck's sake, Ren. You're annoyingly gorgeous, rich as Croesus, and powerful as hell. Women throw themselves at you wherever we go, but sure, it's hard to scare up a few candidates."

My grin stretched wider. "So, you still have that pesky little crush on me, do you? 'Annoyingly gorgeous'?"

"Fuck off," Giada grumbled at me and turned on her heel. "I'm going to find the tequila."

She strode off, leaving me alone to consider the prospect of a visit from the Neapolitan side of the family.

Sal would push me about taking a wife and securing an heir, and he wasn't wrong. The problem was, he thought it was easy to find a woman I could stomach being the mother to my children, and I knew it wasn't.

The scars of my parents' ill-fated relationship ran deep in both me and my sister, Sofia. When my mother was alive, Casa Nera had been a simmering pot of tension, resentments, and tears. I wouldn't live like that again. I wouldn't bring children into it, either. I had my habits and ways of living, and at my age, I didn't see those changing. There was only a certain kind of woman I'd accept as mother to my children.

My eyes found Charlotte as she crossed the floor. Her fierce protectiveness of her younger sibling showed a strong maternal instinct. She'd make a good mother one day. Nurturing, loyal, fearless.

I studied her while she approached a table of guests who were well on their way to being drunk. One of the men said something to her that sent her shoulders up around her ears.

After the other night and her absolute bravery in the face of death, it seemed wrong to see the live wire that was Charlotte Burke flinching away from some loser's attention.

The man caught her wrist, and I found myself striding toward them.

"Be polite, Nurse Burke. We're the customers here tonight," the man slurred at Charlotte, just before my hand landed on his shoulder.

His weak bones creaked as I squeezed hard enough to make him release her wrist. "Is there a problem here, gentlemen?" I asked in a silky tone. Velvet-covered violence.

A couple of people around the table went pale, clearly knowing me for more than just owning a casino.

Charlotte rubbed her wrist and blinked up at me, a frown marring her creamy brow. Her pulse fluttered in her neck. I wondered if I'd upset her even more by intervening.

"No, no problem," the man under my hand panted, trying to loosen my grip. I only squeezed harder, barely exerting a quarter of my strength, though judging by the man's sweating brow, it was more than enough.

"Happy to hear it. If you need something, come to me. Directly." It was an order, not a request.

I turned away before they could agree and went after Charlotte, who was moving away quickly in the opposite direction.

"Miss Burke." My voice lashed out like a whip. She came to a reluctant stop. "A word."

I walked past her and continued to the hallway outside the restrooms, where the noise of clanking tableware and conversation wasn't so loud.

"Yes, sir?" Charlotte shifted her feet, her eyes intently trained on a distant point. It immediately irritated me that she wouldn't look me in the eye.

"Do you make it a habit to let the clientele here push you around and grab you?" Where exactly that question had come from, I had no idea. All I knew was that this timid woman in front of me wasn't the same one as the other day, and I didn't like it.

She swallowed. "I'm sorry. It won't happen again, Mr. De Sanctis." Even her deferential tone pissed me off.

"That's all you have to say? Was your defiance last night an act, or are you someone who needs to be held at gunpoint to grow a spine?" My words were mocking and cruel, but deep down, I was disappointed. It was an odd thing to realize. I generally expected nothing from people and it didn't bother me when they proved me right in this regard. Somehow, this woman, with her unfailing courage and loyalty, had sparked my interest.

But just when I lost hope that she was anything different, her hands curved into tight little fists, and she met my eyes.

To be precise, she glared at me.

"Am I supposed to be grateful you protected me from a drunk co-worker? Should I get down on my knees and kiss your feet in front of the whole room? Is that what you expect after the other night?" Her eyes flashed fire at me.

A grin tugged at my lips. *Ah, there she was.* "I'd prefer it in private, *bambina,* but your mind really is a fascinating place."

Her cheeks flushed prettily. "I don't need you to protect me, especially considering you're my biggest threat. I can take care of myself."

"Hmm." I realized dimly that I'd stepped closer to her, and she'd stepped back. A dance neither of us was aware of. But now the wall had trapped her, and she had nowhere to go. I rested my hand on one side, caging her in. She straightened her shoulders and glared at me. She really was intriguing when those rich brown pools flashed amber fire at me. I could get addicted to the challenge held there.

No one looked at me like that.

"Do you think you're doing a good job so far? Seems to me like you could use someone to take care of you."

She curled her lip, her contempt clear. "I've been taking care of myself and my sister since I was thirteen years old. I don't need or want a white knight to sweep in and take care of me."

A chuckle left me at that comparison. "I'm no white knight, Miss Burke, as I'm sure you realized last night. I'm the dragon who guards the maiden in the keep and will swallow you whole if you try to escape me. You put me in control over your life, don't forget that."

She was quiet, that damn alluring pulse in her neck pounding harder.

"I didn't realize that the promise I made extended to every single part of my life," she said finally.

I nodded lazily. Someone passed behind us in the hall, reminding me that we weren't alone. Not yet anyway. But soon.

"And if you had, would you have chosen differently? Would you have died instead?" My casual question was met with a pink blush, her eyes widening and chest rising more rapidly. She shook her head slowly, like the admission cost her deeply.

"Just remember that, and behave accordingly," I finished in a murmur. A long strand of hair had escaped her ponytail. I reached for it before I could stop myself. She turned her head to the side, contorting her body to avoid my touch.

I didn't like that. She didn't get to avoid my touch.

I tugged her wrist and pushed open the door to the bathroom beside us. It was the ladies' room, and it was blessedly empty. Charlotte's eyes were wide, her pulse thumping. She was scared. She met my gaze steadily, regardless. *Good girl.*

Inside, I pressed her against the wall, shedding the mask of civility I'd worn in the hall. I finally had her alone, and I'd do what I damn well pleased.

"Let's get something straight, right here and now, Miss Burke. You promised to make me your new higher power. Like any cruel and terrible god, when I want something, I take it."

I wanted to taste that pulse point and feel the blood rushing beneath the surface of her skin. I needed to, to make sure she was real.

She stiffened when I pressed her head back against the tile and lowered my lips to her throat. "What are you doing?" she whispered.

"Tasting my property, because you *are* mine, aren't you, *bambina*? My devoted disciple?"

My lips moved across her skin, and goose bumps spread out from the point of contact. She was so responsive, her body hummed with energy beneath mine. It was a connection unlike any other, and I knew in that moment that fucking Charlotte would be the highlight of my life. Our bodies communicated on a cellular level. A primitive part of me that was pure biology and hormones pushed me forward, urging me to take her. *Yes,* whispered the devil on my shoulder, *take her, keep her, breed her, pump her full of your seed, and then, your children. She's supposed to be ours.*

Her hands pressed against my chest, but she didn't shove me away as I sucked on her thrumming pulse point. Her skin was hot and soft. I licked up her throat; a long, wet stripe.

Playground taunts circled my head. *I've licked it, so now it's mine. Mine.*

I found her ear and bit the lobe, making her jerk against me. Her breath was coming in short pants, and every single one pushed her tits more firmly into my chest. Her damn too-large uniform made it impossible to feel more than the general shape of the soft mounds. I needed more.

I kissed and nipped the side of her ear, enjoying her shivers. A gasp escaped her as I traced my tongue along the delicate shell, and I made a note of her sensitivity there.

"Is this part of it?" Charlotte whispered. Her words swept through my lust-fogged brain, digging in icy talons. "Is this part of what you want from me?"

I pulled back, my hand sliding across Charlotte's mouth before I could stop myself. I didn't want her to speak and damn me more.

What the hell was I doing? Giving in to temptation in a public bathroom, where anyone could walk in? I was measured, precise, and coolheaded. I wasn't someone who lost control. Ever.

"And if it was?" I wondered quietly. My other hand dropped to the shining necklace around her throat. "You seem like a very good girl, Miss Burke. Will you give me everything I want from you?"

I held her there, my hand clamped over her lips, my body pinning her to the tile wall. I was dangerously close to losing control again. I had to get out of here. I never felt like this, and it was unsettling.

She held my gaze and nodded compliantly in response to my question. She wasn't angry now. Her eyes weren't spitting fire.

She likes this, I suddenly realized. *She likes being ordered around and manhandled. She wants me to take control.*

Just like that, I lost all self-control again. My hard-on ached at the new knowledge about my little nurse. I wanted to see just how far I could push her.

I unclamped my hand from her mouth, relishing its soft feel against my skin, and held my bunched fingertips to her lips. She parted them reluctantly, her color burning in red circles on her cheeks. I let my fingers invade the hot cavern of her mouth. I could fit all four fingers, and they were anything but small. She'd be able to take me deep when the time came.

I gripped her chin with my thumb, keeping the other four fingers inside her mouth as I held her there, open and vulnerable as hell. She stared up at me, unflinching. Brave and so fucking sexy. It was all I could do not to bend her over a sink then and there and fuck her, over and over again, until she could barely walk, and every step would send cum dripping down her legs.

Then no one would question whose she was. No one would dare meet her eyes, never mind grab her wrist.

Saliva welled from the corners of her lips, stretched wide open as they were. I leaned in and licked it up, a deep rumble escaping my chest. Charlotte's breath stuttered. She was shocked by the act, but I knew if I reached into her panties right now, they'd be a mess.

Charlotte Burke, in charge of two people's lives, responsible for everything in her world, tired, overwhelmed, and alone. *No more.*

Her tongue brushed past my fingertips, caressing. Her body welcoming my depraved control.

Oh, sweet little Charlie, I'm going to teach you how to lose control. I'm going to teach you how to sin like only a good girl touched by the dark can, in a way that will make the angels weep.

"Delicious. How sweet your submission tastes, Miss Burke. I look forward to more of it. And if you're wondering when that will be, how, where . . . don't bother. It's not something you can control, try as you might. You gave me your word, and you'll stand by it. Do you understand?"

She murmured low in her throat, her mouth too wide to form

words. Gently, I withdrew my hand. I wanted to hear her sweet surrender in her own voice.

Her bottom lip was puffy when I let go, and she snapped her lips closed. She seemed shocked at what had happened, her eyes shining with accusation at me.

"Are you going to pretend that didn't turn you on? Go ahead, and I'll prove you wrong." I put my hand on her belly, pointing downward. "How about this, *bambina*. Call me a liar, and I'll slide my hand down your panties and check. If you're not dripping wet, then I will never, ever touch you again. In fact, I'll call our whole deal off . . . you'll be free to go, both you and Lucy. You'll never see me again."

She blinked rapidly. She was trying to think her way around my offer and twist it to her advantage. "You mean you'll trust me not to talk to the cops?"

"Not even close."

"Then why even offer?"

"Because I know I'll win. I know your pussy will be slick and wanting, making a needy mess in your panties. I bet you prefer cotton, right? Sensible, breathable, and now . . . soaked with your desire for me."

"You're wrong. I don't want you."

"Then let's test it and see. If you're right, then you'll walk away free and clear. But if I'm right, you'll never lie to me again."

She licked her lips, considering her options. My hand itched to slide lower. I needed to feel her wet folds. I was in real danger of becoming addicted to tangling with this woman, only twenty-four hours after we'd first met. I had no idea what I'd be like in a week. She'd be lucky if she wasn't chained to my bed in Casa Nera by then.

I couldn't rule out the possibility.

I didn't give her another moment to stall. I knew I was right.

She'd shown me deep down inside her soul the other day, and now I could read her. My fingers slipped under the waistband of her pants and slowly crept downward. Flames leapt higher in her cheeks when I got to her damp panties. No, not just damp.

Soaked.

I hooked them to the side and swiped a finger through her creamy arousal, then lightly brushed over her slit and hooded clit. She gasped, her mouth falling open.

"If you don't want me, then care to explain?" My bored tone hid my raging desire.

Fuck, her pussy was hot and slick. Soft curls on her mound brushed against my fingers. It had been so long since I'd fucked a woman with hair. Hell, it had been a long time since I'd fucked in general. Even fucking could get boring, it turned out, when faces all blended into one bland mass, and shiny, waxed, and primped body parts were so interchangeable, I couldn't have picked a woman I'd fucked out of a group of her friends if my life depended on it.

The women who went after me—for money, or power, or just to make Daddy happy by creating an alliance with my family—waxed like they hated themselves. It was all so very monotonous. Diet to be slim as a board, wax until hairless, pluck, paint, nip and tuck.

Charlotte's body wasn't like that. She worked too many hours to spend a lot of time at the salon, and she didn't have enough money for surgery. I'd bet her list for getting date-ready had exactly two items: taking a shower and shaving her legs.

My fingers played in the curls covering her pussy. I wanted to see it. I wanted to see it studded with white pearls of my cum.

"It doesn't mean anything. It's just biology," Charlotte interrupted me from my reverie, her voice full of helpless anger.

I lapped up her emotion. She burned so fucking brightly. A

light in the dark, and, like all nocturnal creatures, I couldn't resist its pull.

"So you get wet like this whenever a man speaks to you? It's nothing personal?" I persisted, enjoying the fury in her eyes.

She didn't want to be proved a liar. She was ashamed of her body's reaction. She thought something must be wrong with her to enjoy being manhandled and ordered around. She thought she was sick. She had no idea that the fever had consumed us both. I was just better at managing it.

"No! I—it's just pheromones and chemicals," she trailed off as I tugged on that delicious thatch of hair on her mound, just hard enough to make her gasp.

"If I didn't know better, I'd think you're trying very hard to use scientific jargon to explain one very simple thing." I pulled my hand carefully from her pants, missing the warmth of her body immediately.

I brought my fingers to her lips. Her eyes widened, horrified, turned on, scared. Who even knew anymore? It didn't matter. When she tried to twist her head away, I gripped her chin with one hand and slid my wet fingers into her mouth with the other.

"You're attracted to me. Every time you lie about that, I'll make you taste yourself."

My lips hovered over hers. I could smell her musk on her breath. I needed a taste. Taking my fingers from her mouth, I swiped my tongue across her lips, and she let slip the softest moan. I immediately wanted more. Me, the man who had gotten bored of everything. It was a revelation.

Just then, before I could kiss her properly, the way she was silently begging to be kissed, the door opened beside us. From the corner of my eye, I saw a group of four women stroll in, and stop in their tracks when they saw us. I had Charlotte trapped against the wall with my hips, my cock a pin of desire holding her in place. My hands cupped her face, my lips brushing against hers.

"Mr. De Sanctis!" I recognized the voice of one of the organizers, aghast at having walked in on such an intimate moment.

I straightened up, releasing my grip on Charlotte. She bolted, hurrying away like her ass was on fire as I turned a professionally aloof smile on the women.

By the time I left the restroom, Charlotte was halfway across the dance floor. She glanced back at me, her face flushed.

Giada passed her, raising an eyebrow at me as she approached. "Playing with your food, Ren? Watching you with her, I can't decide if you're going to kill her or marry her. That's not like you."

"What can I say? She's different."

Giada smiled. She pulled her phone from her clutch and nodded as she swiped it open. "She sure is different."

She handed me her phone, and I took a moment to process the image. Detectives Whitely and Vane, the two motherfuckers who'd been on my tail for months, sitting at a small table in a cramped kitchen. The photo had been taken with a long lens, clearly from a neighboring apartment window. Despite that, the cops were easy to make out, as was the woman standing opposite them, dressed in only a towel.

Charlotte Burke.

"Bitch has a death wish," Giada laughed.

I handed back the cellphone. *What a little minx.* That she could seem so innocent and beguiling, standing there with her sweet, lying lips wrapped around my fingers, and also be going to the cops behind my back? My blood surged through me, excitement pouring through my veins. A worthy partner to clash with, after so long. If this were chess, one of my favorite games, Charlotte had just put herself, and her queen, her sister, in check. I wouldn't hesitate to take advantage of that fact.

"Shall we go and get her? I've got a new crossbow I've been looking forward to playing with." Giada's catlike smirk was red like blood. "Maybe she just needs a reminder of the consequences of being a dumb bitch."

I nodded. "A reminder she'll get. Keep your crossbow for hunting down the Castillos. You know, your job."

I watched Charlotte moving around tables, casting nervous glances our way. My reminder wouldn't be tonight, while my fingerprints were still imprinted on her tongue. Tomorrow, I'd show her I couldn't just get to her in the dark, or in my territory. She needed to know that I could get to her wherever, and whenever I wanted. This was my city, and no one here would protect her from me. Her wrathful and vengeful god.

Something to look forward to, after so long.

Charlotte worked at Camden Community Hospital in downtown A.C. At this time of day, early afternoon, the place was already packed. There was a chaotic buzz in the air akin to the atmosphere after a fight. Maybe that's what doctors and nurses did all day; fight off death, prolong the inevitable for another day. It was a shitty, underfunded hospital and it showed, with its stained walls, blurry windows, and general air of postapocalyptic chaos.

My men entered the building before me and asked for Charlotte at the front desk. The wide-eyed receptionist watched us warily as she checked her system.

"Student nurse Burke is working in the ER right now," she said, chewing her lip nervously, maybe rethinking the wisdom of telling men like us where to find Charlotte, but also not wanting to challenge us.

I turned toward the ER and started along the hall, my men flanking me. There was so much white in the damn place it was blinding. I was a creature of darkness, and my dark home in Casa

Nera didn't hurt my eyes like this hallway did. Blaring fluorescent lights and white tiles. Even the staff who passed were in white. It was like some parody of heaven, and me and my men were black-clad demons.

In the ER, I spied Charlotte immediately. She walked between curtained cubicles efficiently, her face beautiful and serene despite the chaos around her.

"Bring her to me," I said to Elio, my shadow. He nodded and moved away.

Ten minutes later, I sat behind a curtain, my mind going over the idea of the Burkes talking to the cops, playing with a knife as I waited. I guessed it was the younger, more idealistic one, Lucy, and not practical Charlotte. Not that the cops could do anything to me. I had enough leverage on the chief of police to get away with anything I wanted in this city. Still, it was a transgression that couldn't go unpunished.

The curtain drew back with a sharp snap, and Charlotte stepped into the area. She gripped a clipboard with a paper sheet attached like it was a shield that could protect her from me. As soon as our eyes connected, she flinched so hard, she dropped it.

"What are you doing here—" she started and nearly leapt forward as Elio's silent shadow crowded in on her, forcing her farther behind the curtain.

He pushed her firmly into the curtained room, so close that if I reached out, I could have gripped her thigh. The thought wasn't unappealing. Then Elio backed up and ducked out of the space, pulling the curtain closed behind us.

"Why are you here?" Charlotte repeated, her voice just above a whisper.

Her words were strong, but her eyes glittered in fear. They

dropped to the knife in my hands. It was a little trick I'd mastered young, twirling a slim blade easily between my fingers. I liked knives; I'd been comfortable with them since I'd learned *paranza corta*, the Sicilian art of knife fighting, when I'd been only a boy.

Charlotte's gaze fixed on the knife, and she paled, seeming to swallow her words of protest at my presence.

"We need to talk, Miss Burke."

She stared at me, wordless.

"Sit, please." I pointed my blade at the exam bed beside my chair.

"I can't stay here if you're not hurt. I'll get in trouble for—fraternizing during work hours," she said quietly.

"Fraternizing?" I cocked an eyebrow at her words, faintly touched with amusement. Christ, this woman was intriguingly unpredictable. I liked that about her.

I put the knife against my palm, flipping it and catching it by the blade. "Meaning?"

"Meaning you need to be a patient for me to stay here with you," she said, gaining confidence in her ridiculous ploy.

The mistake law-abiding citizens like Charlotte always made was that they thought that there were rules that could keep them safe. They thought that some higher power, an authority over all, would enforce order.

She hadn't understood that *I* was now the authority over everything in her life.

"Here, how about now?" I asked carelessly, catching my knife and then dragging it across my palm. The cut burned slightly as blood welled and dripped on the floor.

Charlotte gave me a horrified look. She needed to understand that I didn't fear her superiors or the police. I didn't fear pain or even torture.

"What have you done?" she muttered, the compassionate part of her that was such a fucking liability kicking in. She reached my side and took my hand in hers. Her skin was sinfully soft.

I shrugged nonchalantly, the cut forgotten now that she'd moved closer. I'd never really had a chance to study her in adequate lighting. She was even more lovely than in firelight. Her nut-brown hair was gathered into a low ponytail, as sleek as an otter's hide. She had two beauty marks on her neck and one on the delicate shell of her ear. Someone should commission a portrait of this woman. Oil on canvas, maybe sitting in the orangery at Casa Nera, or the library.

She tutted over my hand, reaching for gauze in the small cabinet next to the exam table.

"You know why I'm here, don't you?" I prompted.

A faint blush tinted her cheek. *Yes, she knew.*

She gathered herself, ignorant to the fact that her stunning face was as easy to read as my favorite book.

"You just really wanted to see what an ER was like on a random Saturday afternoon?"

Her brave attempt at dispelling the tension had me smiling. I shook my head. "Try again."

She took a breath and pulled a small rolling table toward us, resting my hand on it. Truthfully, I didn't give a fuck about getting my hand bandaged, but her willing touch felt good.

"Confess your sins, Charlotte. You're the kind of person who will feel better once you do," I advised her.

She swallowed hard, and her eyes flickered up to mine for a second before glancing away. "I don't know what you mean."

My injured hand tightened around hers in a flash. "Don't lie to me. Don't. Ever. Lie. To. Me." My tone was lethal.

She paled. My fingers pressed against her pulse in her wrist, and it fluttered wildly beneath her fragile skin. "Was it you or Lucy?"

Her flush told me all I needed to know.

"Confess and repent," I ordered her. "Promise me that you'll make sure it never happens again, that you'll lock her up if she tries to go there again, shackle her to the door to stop her. Make me believe it," I urged.

Charlotte stared at our joined hands. "And?" she wondered.

"And I'll give you one last chance . . . to save your own life."

She was silent for a long moment. I loved the battle on her fine features. Her pride battling with her practicality. The good girl in her soul arguing with the one who'd do anything to survive. I saw the moment she lost against the devil on her shoulder.

When she opened her mouth, I interrupted. "On your knees, isn't that how sinners ask for forgiveness?"

Her eyes flashed fire at me, far too furious to be the meek little lamb she was pretending to be, and yet, she followed my instructions. Her face ended up level with my knee. I stroked my hand through the fall of her ponytail, pushing it back from her neck, my eyes daring her to stop me.

She didn't. She had excellent control over her fear. I'd enjoy breaking that control to pieces and seeing what it revealed beneath. My hand framed her neck like a tattooed necklace, pressing in at the sides just enough to force her eyes wide. She flushed, and her lips parted and reddened, like I'd touched her clit instead of her throat. So responsive and lovely. So wicked and depraved.

"I can't figure out if you're afraid or excited," I confessed.

The room around us had faded away, and there was just Charlotte and the feeling of her lifeblood rushing desperately under my palm.

She wet her lips, and my heart lurched. "Do you really care?" she asked.

I considered the question for a moment before shaking my head. "No. In my experience, they're very much alike. You told me that you understand men like me . . . What is it you understand?"

Her lips parted to answer, but no words came. She was willful and loyal. Good in her bones in a way I'd never been, not even as a child; my blood didn't allow for that. She also had no idea of her true appeal. I'd bet my life that Miss Charlotte Burke didn't have a lot of experience with men. I liked that thought. I liked it a lot.

"Have you ever been properly fucked?"

She clearly wasn't expecting that question as her eyes widened comically.

She recovered quickly and scoffed. "Are you asking me if I'm a virgin? I'm twenty-six."

"I'm not talking about a little piece of inconvenient skin. I didn't ask if you'd ever been pawed by some sucker who was punching above his weight. I meant have you ever been fucked *properly* . . . Have you ever seen stars behind your eyes while some lucky bastard pumped his cum into you? Have you ever come so hard, you forgot how to talk . . . how to breathe?"

My hand still ringed her throat, and her pulse hitched another notch upward. "You can't expect me to answer that," she muttered.

"I don't need you to, *bambina;* it's obvious. But don't worry." I leaned in and rested my forehead against hers. Just being skin to skin felt soothing. Right, in a way I'd never experienced. "We'll remedy that soon enough."

A throat clearing sent Charlie jumping back, her face twisting guiltily. She leaned back and nearly fell in her desire to turn around. I steadied her from my seated position and took my time making sure she was fine before swinging my head toward the intruder.

"Boss." Elio pushed the curtain open and shouldered in. "There's some business that needs your attention."

"*Arrivo.*" I looked back at Charlotte. "But first, a little reminder that you can't escape my eyes in my city." I gripped the back of her neck, like a newborn kitten, and pushed her face forward.

Behind me, Elio produced a syringe and handed it to me. I wouldn't let him put the tracker inside her. No one but me would break her creamy skin. That was my privilege.

I slipped the needle under her skin as her hands shot up to rest on my thighs, her nails digging into my legs as she gasped. I injected the tiny tracker in the back of her neck where it wouldn't move. She also wouldn't be able to cut it out too easily, with her neat and capable skills.

"What have you given me?" she asked, her voice calm. There was that impeccable control.

"A new leash. Don't test its bounds; they're shorter than you can imagine. We'll continue this conversation later, Miss Burke."

I handed the syringe back to Elio and released her neck. She looked up at me immediately. I cupped her angelic face with both hands. Leaning in, I placed a chaste kiss on her forehead. A pardon for her sins, for now.

"Answer your phone when I call, *bambina,* and be on your best behavior. Lucy, too, or I'll get upset. You wouldn't like me when I'm upset."

8

RENATO

My business waited for me in the warehouse on Clements Drive.

Elio filled me in on the drive over. "A representative of the Castillo Cartel. I don't know who the fuck he is, but he has enough men to make a mess."

This confrontation had been a long time coming. I was starting to think that the head of the cartel had no interest whatsoever in how many of his men I killed, as we'd been cutting them down for nearly a year and there'd been no sign of repercussions.

It was almost a relief that something had finally rattled their cage enough to draw them out. There would be no eradicating them as long as those in power stayed hidden.

The man was wearing a suit, unlike those lower than him in the organization, and he clearly wasn't a man who walked into a rival family's territory lightly. His security detail, a force of nearly fifty men, communicated his awareness of that fact.

"What an unexpected pleasure," I said, entering the warehouse. My own entourage was only Elio, but my men who were stationed at the warehouse surrounded the Castillo thugs, and tensions were high.

"Renato De Sanctis, we finally meet in the flesh. I've heard a lot about you." The Castillo spokesperson smiled broadly. He was a confident fucker, but he had to be to just show up here like this. "I'm Juan Ruiz Eduardo Castillo."

"Well, Juan, I'm afraid I haven't heard a thing about you."

"Not all of us like the infamy that comes with running a large operation."

"So, you're here why?"

The air was full of unspoken violence, with men on both sides eyeing each other, sizing up the opposition's defenses. The only kind of conversation that could take place between men like me and Juan was in this sort of circumstance. One where an aggressive action from one side was sure to be answered in kind. Our mutually assured destruction formed a fragile, temporary truce.

"Are you someone of importance to the Castillo family?" I asked.

Juan laughed. "Forgive me if I don't choose to pin a target on my forehead. I'm merely an objective party. An ambassador. You're an intelligent man, De Sanctis, and you have a code. I come to you for information, and only that. I will make no aggressive move toward you at this moment, at this meeting."

"Ask your question, then, Castillo." I folded my arms across my chest and waited. I could predict what he had come for, but why exactly the cartel cared so much about a random initiate trying to be accepted into the family, I had no idea. I intended to find out.

Castillo nodded. "A little bird told me that a new recruit disappeared in your territory the other night . . . a young guy, just getting his feet wet in the business."

I shrugged nonchalantly. "People who wander into the wrong territory, young or not, need to look after themselves."

Castillo chuckled darkly. "Maybe so, but this guy was responsible for twenty-five grand of product that's now missing."

"Sounds like the cost of recruitment to me. The kid probably cut and ran with the stuff. Surely this isn't an issue worthy of your attention."

Castillo inclined his regal head, seeming to agree with me. "I'd think that, too, if he wasn't family to the boss. A cousin on his mother's side. It's a small connection, but family is family, after all."

Fucker. My face was unmoved by the revelation. A poker face was the biggest asset you could have in tense negotiations, and mine was one of the best in the biz.

Juan studied me for a long moment, looking for a weakness. When he didn't find one, he chuckled again. "Family can be a pain, and I barely know the kid, but that doesn't mean his life is worthless. Blood is blood, as you know."

I nodded. The Mexicans and Italians were united in that belief. *La famiglia prima di tutto.* Family above all else.

"Well, I wish I could help you, but I don't know anything about the kid."

Juan's expression was unreadable for a beat, until he sighed. "Well, keep an eye out for me, will you, as a professional courtesy. He had a girlfriend, some little gutter rat. She might know something. She has a sister, too, a pretty thing." Juan's eyes fell meaningfully to the bandage wrapped around my hand.

His threat was clear. He knew about Lucy and Charlotte.

He knew that the idiot kid was dead, and he was going to do something about it, probably to the Burke sisters first, and then use their confessions to start something with me. Maybe he'd even force them to go to the police before they disappeared.

"I wish you luck in your search, but I warn you in future, think carefully about wasting my time with your personal business."

"But of course, what else for the *capo dei capi* of New Jersey?" His dry mocking scraped along my nerves, but I hadn't gotten where I was by starting petty fights. I simply stood and nodded to him as he headed toward the doors, his men surrounding him in a shield of bristling weapons.

Elio stood beside me, and we watched the Mexicans leave. My men shifted restlessly, the lingering tension stinking up the air.

"You think he's the boss?"

"Could be."

Maybe, maybe not. It was impossible to tell, and moving too soon would spook them. I needed to root the Castillos out of the state completely, and that meant being patient. His less-than-subtle threat toward the Burkes was clear.

"That's going to be a problem," I muttered to Elio. Charlotte and the earlier feeling of her throat in my grip pulsed through me.

He shrugged. "Only if you care about what happens to the nurse and her sister."

Right.

Elio could always read me better than anyone else. "It's for the best, really. They can clean up the girls. We don't have to do a thing about it. Win-win."

His meaning was clear: Let the cartel take their pound of flesh from the Burkes.

I didn't care if the Castillos knew my men had killed their little thief. We were at war already; they just refused to face it. I already planned on wiping out every single one. Maybe a flat-out battle with them would achieve the objective sooner and flush out the leaders. Besides, Charlotte had spoken to the cops and broken our deal, as soon as she'd had the chance. She couldn't be trusted. It really was a win-win. And yet, even as I nodded, I knew I wouldn't let it happen.

I'd been bored for years. The last few days were in color, after a decade of monochrome. What was the point of all the wealth and power I'd amassed if life had become bland and boring?

Giada's words came back to me as I stared off into space. *Watching you with her, I can't decide if you're going to kill her or marry her.*

Marry her.

Of course.

"What are you going to do?" Elio asked, his voice carefully devoid of emotion.

He never gave his opinion unless I asked for it. He was unreadable and stoic, just as strong mentally as he was physically, but I wondered if I might finally be able to shock him.

"I'm going to marry her," I told him. As soon as I said the words, they fit inside me like the missing puzzle piece I'd been seeking.

To his credit, my *sottocapo* was only mildly surprised by the announcement.

I started toward the car, Elio at my shoulder. "I need a wife and an heir. She wants to live. It's a simple solution."

Elio nodded. "I'll get the eyes on her to pick her up."

"No." The word left me before I could question it. "I'll go myself, and you get the sister." *I don't want anyone else touching her.*

"Yes, boss," Elio said.

"When you want something done right, do it yourself. This has turned into a delicate situation, and I don't trust anyone else with it." It was pure lies, but Elio wasn't going to call me on it, if he knew what was good for him. "Let's go."

There was something dark and twisted in my belly as I got into the armored SUV and slammed the door. Something simmering and hot. Something new.

It felt a lot like excitement.

9

CHARLIE

I moved through work in a haze after Renato left. It felt like I'd just survived another near-death experience. I didn't know how much more of it I could take. The cops came to our apartment, and hours later, Renato knew. I couldn't get anything past him, and going to the cops about the murder wasn't going to guarantee our safety.

My neck throbbed where he'd injected me with the tracker. I couldn't stop imagining it, lurking just under my skin, letting him know where I was at all times.

Kneeling before him to "confess my sins" had also shaken me. The man was deviant. Dangerous in a way I'd never known. He was the living embodiment of everything the nuns at Mercy House had warned us about. A dark and powerful temptation to sin. And my idiot body didn't hate that. Shame coated me, thick and sticky. Maybe I should give myself a cold shower, now that I was old enough to police my own impure thoughts.

I dragged myself home at the end of my shift and collapsed at the kitchen table. I'd never been so exhausted.

Lucy shuffled out of her room. The run-in with Renato had

shoved everything else out of my head. The guarded look on my sister's face reminded me of our fight.

She leaned against the kitchen counter and folded her arms. I looked at her, wondering which way she was going to go. She opened her mouth, like she wanted to say something, and then closed it. Eventually, she took a deep breath and spoke.

"I think that guy came here today . . . Miguel's buddy."

Suddenly, making up after our fight didn't seem so important anymore. My heart stopped for a beat. "Tell me."

"Someone knocked at the door. I was in bed, so I didn't get there quickly. Before I could open it, they started pounding. It was scary. They waited around for an hour, maybe more, before leaving. I think he's going to come back."

"He is definitely going to come back," I muttered, chewing on my lip.

"So, what should we do? Go to the police?"

"And tell them what? Some guy keeps knocking on our door? There's no way to tell them what kind of threat that really is without admitting all of it and putting us in the De Sanctis crosshairs."

Lucy rolled her eyes. "So, what do we do, then?"

I studied her. I'd worked so hard to build this life for us. I was almost done with school, and I had connections at a real hospital. There was a good chance I could get a job and start to earn more soon. All of Lucy's friends were here; her entire life was here. But Renato De Sanctis wasn't a man to cross, and Miguel's boss was looking for his money. The police were watching us, and it was a tightrope that I was tired of walking.

Our lives here had become too dangerous, and nothing else mattered in the end.

"We each pack a small bag, and we go. Tonight. As soon as it's quiet. We leave here, and we don't look back and we don't stop until a thousand miles are between us and them."

"We're running away?" Lucy's eyes narrowed.

I had no idea what she thought of me suggesting the idea, and I was past caring. I wanted to live. I could worry about everything else later.

I nodded. The panic in my chest had slightly eased as the plan took shape in my head.

"We're running away, and we're going tonight." I reached for the silverware drawer and pulled it out, finding the smallest, sharpest blade I could. It needed to be sanitized, and then it was good to go. It wasn't ideal, but it was the best we had. The tracker itched under my skin, but not for long.

"First, I need you to do something for me."

In the end, it only took an hour to pack up our entire lives and abandon the apartment we'd called home for the last five years.

We bundled up in layers. Soon, it would be truly cold, and while I didn't know how far we'd end up running, it seemed a good idea to take as many clothes as we could easily carry.

We left the house and took a long, twisting route around the neighborhood before heading to the jitney stop.

It was only a few stops to reach the bus station. I stood at the counter, cap on and a mask hiding the lower half of my face. I was grateful that wearing a surgical mask had become more normalized. It certainly made hiding our identities easier.

Small town or big city? A direct route or something with a lot of stops? My mind conjured pros and cons for every alternative.

In the end, I went for lots of stops and a random small-town destination that was a stopover for other larger destinations. I could only hope that if anyone did follow us, they wouldn't be able to follow the trail. I paid in cash for the tickets and sat with Lucy as we anxiously waited to board the bus.

Inside, we settled into the cramped seats for a long journey. Neither of us had phones anymore. We'd left them on the city jitney, going around and around town.

I stared out at the bus station as we pulled out, looking at every new face, peering into every dark opening.

Every time the bus paused, I worried it would stop and someone who was hunting us would get on. But it didn't happen. Slowly, we worked our way out of the city.

I dozed, haunted by dreams of opening my eyes to find a dark shadow walking up the aisle toward us. Renato De Sanctis, knowing every move I made before I'd done it.

This is pointless. He's always watching. Even before he'd injected a tiny microchip under my skin, he'd known everything about us. The chip wasn't the only eyes that Renato De Sanctis had on us.

Even though I knew as much, I had no other bright ideas about what to do. I was truly trapped.

With nothing else to do but stare out the window, Lucy grew tired quickly and fell asleep on my shoulder. I stroked her hair like I used to when she was just a kid. I had nothing but the night passing outside the window to distract me from how horrible my reality had truly become in less than a week. Everything I'd worked for was gone, just embers in a fire that had ripped through my carefully laid plans. All the nights I'd worked extra shifts, all the classes I'd forced myself through, so tired I could die, had all amounted to nothing. I'd worked my entire life to provide something real for Lucy, and now I had nothing. Not that she appreciated all the sacrifices I'd made. Ugly resentments and hopeless disappointment threatened to overwhelm me.

The road looked familiar as we worked our way deeper into New Jersey, away from the shore. It was the same road we'd taken the other morning. We were going to pass close to Casa Nera. A chill went over me at the very thought.

I snuggled deeper into Lucy, trying not to picture those blood-red halls with the imposing paintings staring down at me, or the dark and terrible basement level with a corridor of cell-like rooms.

We pulled in at a rest stop an hour in. "Lucy." I tapped her arm gently. I hated to wake her, but the chance to use the bathroom was too important to pass up.

She woke slowly and groggily took in her surroundings. For a second, she looked serene and carefree, just like the old Lucy. But then she seemed to remember the situation we were in, and her features became tight with worry. "Are we there already?"

"God, no. We just need to go to the bathroom. The next break might not be for a long time."

"Okay," she mumbled and slid out of the seat after me.

The night air was cold, and I was glad for our layers as we crossed the parking lot and made for the restrooms. Waiting in line, I couldn't help watching the other people around us. Were they running from something, too? Or were they just taking a trip at a discount rate?

"I'm hungry," Lucy muttered as we inched along in the line.

"Want me to get you something from the store?"

She thought for a moment. "Chips?"

"Okay, sure. Save my space," I said to her, peering around.

The store was right there, and Lucy was waiting in line with about twenty other people. In plain sight seemed like the safest place to be right now.

I headed into the shop, the harsh overhead fluorescent lights reminding me of the hospital at night.

The hospital. My heart clenched thinking about it. I had been so close to finishing my degree. Within touching distance of my dreams. Now, they were ashes in the wind. If someone was looking for us, calling the hospital and trying to get my credits transferred would be a very stupid thing to do.

I grabbed a couple of bags of chips and some water bottles, paid cash, and headed outside. The line had moved up a little, and Lucy was nowhere to be seen. I stood outside and waited for her. After what seemed like ages, the door to the ladies' room opened and someone came out. Someone who wasn't my sister.

She wasn't here. She wasn't in line or in the restroom.

I stepped out of the line and spun around, searching for her.

"Lucy?" I called, worry threatening to steal my breath away. "Excuse me, did you see where my sister went? She was just in front of you in line?" I asked the older lady standing behind me.

"I'm sorry, I was checking my messages," she said and waved her phone.

Okay, great. I stepped farther from the line and spun around again. Maybe she'd gone back to the bus? I started toward it, a sinking feeling in my gut. Of course she hadn't. Why would she? She knew I'd panic when I couldn't find her. Ignoring logic screaming at me that something was happening, I checked the bus. A few people had made it back to their seats now, but Lucy wasn't one of them.

I got back off and jogged around the parking lot. At the far end, trucks were parked, and in the other direction was the highway, cars whizzing by.

There was the rest stop building, with its bright lights and people, the gas station, also full of bystanders, and then there was the area with the overnight trucks. The shadows between the hulking vehicles called to me. There was nowhere else to look.

A fine drizzle fell as I crossed the lot. The light from the gas station didn't quite penetrate the darkness at the far corner of the lot, and I steeled myself to step into the shadows. I had to find Lucy. I strode in. It was quiet. The cab light glowed in a distant truck parked on the periphery and the driver fiddled with something on his steering wheel. The rest were dark, their drivers asleep for the night.

I moved up a long corridor formed by two trucks. It was quiet this far from everything else. So quiet, I made out the sound of footsteps first. They weren't even trying to be stealthy. Someone walked parallel to me, their steps nearly in sync with mine. When I stopped, they didn't.

I was frozen with fear in the middle of that dark walkway when he appeared at the top. Rounding the bend, he faced me and stopped. He was wearing a long black wool overcoat with the collar turned up. Tall and broad and utterly inescapable.

Renato De Sanctis. Of course it would be him. The demon from my nightmares and the man I had promised to obey.

You knew he'd find you, didn't you?

Yes.

"Run from me right now, and you'll regret it, *bambina*." Renato's voice reached me clear as crystal, without his even raising it.

I shook my head, fear mixing with adrenaline. "I think I'll regret going with you more."

"You have no choice. Accept that now," he said, advancing slowly toward me. He sauntered as though he had all the time in the world.

I shook my head again. A puppet on a last broken, desperate string. "I think I'll regret not putting up a fight more," I whispered.

Renato's mouth quirked in a devastatingly handsome half-smile. "You can't fight destiny, Charlotte. It'll find you, every single time. *I'll* find you, every single time."

You can't fight destiny. His words were so similar to the ones I'd said to myself a thousand times before, it threw me for a second.

"I took the tracker out."

"Of course, you did. But did you take out the men watching you?"

I backed away as he approached. "I'll scream. The people from the bus will hear and come looking for me—the truck drivers, everyone."

He shrugged. "Scream away. Scream to your heart's content. Just know that I could kill every single person who dares to check on the sound . . . and no one could stop me from walking right out of here." His dark eyes flickered back to mine. "I could have my men gun down every single person on the bus, and my lawyer would have me free by sunrise."

I couldn't speak. His words had punctured my lungs.

"Do you want their blood on your hands?" He took a step toward me.

"You're bluffing. You wouldn't want that kind of attention."

"Well, we can't always get what we want. That's a lesson you're about to learn the hard way. The attention isn't ideal, but I can afford it. They can't save you."

"Where's my sister?" I veered off topic before his words could freak me out too much.

He smiled, and it had a wicked edge. "I'm sure she's around here somewhere. Don't worry. Elio's on it."

Just the thought of the mercenary enforcer getting his brutal hands on my sister was enough to send me spinning around and running.

10

CHARLIE

We never should have run. We should have gone to the cops.

No. It wouldn't have mattered. There was never any other outcome to this. From the moment Miguel had died, it was always going to come down to this.

There was no going back.

I ran in the direction of the bus; despite his warning, I was sure he was bluffing. Renato De Sanctis, *capo dei capi* of New Jersey, hadn't gotten to his position by gunning down groups of innocent bystanders. The fact that he'd even given me and Lucy the chance to keep quiet proved that he had a code of some kind, even if it wasn't anything I could understand.

I ran as hard as I could between the parked trucks. After the last one, the bus was only a short sprint away.

I was *so* close.

I almost made it.

A split second before I escaped the looming truck shadows, his hand snagged my arm. My momentum sent me spinning around and right into his arms. Renato's hand clamped over my mouth, sealing my scream inside. I bit at his fingers as he carried me deeper into the darkness, and the sounds of activity and potential witnesses faded. My teeth met something too smooth and thick to be normal skin.

Gloves. The man was wearing the gloves.

I was so fucked right now.

New panic beat at my chest as he dragged me effortlessly into the shadows, deeper into the truck stop. No amount of kicking seemed to dislodge his steely arm around my waist. I was utterly powerless. Beaten.

"I told you not to run, Charlotte. You're only making this harder on yourself," he murmured in my ear.

I fought to calm my raging fear. *Think, Charlie.* He expected me to keep fighting, clearly. Maybe I could use that. At my hip, a hard object. Something fastened to Renato's belt. A gun.

He carried me behind the last truck. There was a freeway on-ramp there, and a car was parked with the headlights on, illuminating us. It looked just like the black, painfully expensive car that had taken me and Lucy to Renato's house. He wasn't alone. Big surprise.

I was so screwed. I had one chance, and knowing my luck, it wouldn't work, but I wasn't going down without trying.

I let my body go limp, a dead weight that Renato wasn't expecting. He cursed in Italian when I fell to the ground, leaning down to keep his arms around me. While he did, I wiggled my hand behind me and grabbed his gun. By the time he straightened up, I had it in my hand. I squirmed away from him, and he let me, clearly realizing what I'd done.

I took a few steps back and leveled the pistol at him.

He stood a few feet away, looking completely unruffled. The bastard smirked. "Clever girl. You're quite the survivor, aren't you, Miss Burke?"

"Shut up! I'm the one with the gun, and I get to talk now."

He lazily raised an eyebrow and then nodded, gesturing for me to continue. His curved lip made me feel like he was only going along with this because he was amused, not because he was afraid I'd kill him.

"You are going to leave Lucy and me alone. We'll leave town, and you'll never see us again . . . You won't come after us, the cops won't know where we've gone—we'll disappear."

Renato pursed his lips as if he was contemplating my plan. "And with what resources would you achieve this disappearing act? So far, it's not convincing."

"I'll find the money. I have friends who can help me," I said quickly. Truthfully, I had one good friend who might try, a friend from nursing school who lived in Michigan. She was the only person who really knew me, after Lucy.

Renato shook his head. "I'm afraid I can't allow another person to enter this equation. In fact, I need the opposite of that to happen."

A tear squeezed out of my eye. "She's only nineteen," I muttered. "Don't you have any siblings?"

Renato nodded. "Yes, in fact, I do. A younger sister."

"So then you know how it feels to need to protect them."

Renato sighed. "Charlotte, this ends tonight."

He took a step toward me, and I leapt back, the stolen gun still pointed at him. "Don't come closer! I'll shoot you, I swear I will," I warned him.

"Do you think you could manage it? Your hands are shaking."

"I can manage it," I snarled. "For Lucy—I can manage anything."

Renato stopped his slow approach and tilted his head to the side, watching me carefully. "Anything? I've heard that before. Could you really manage anything, or would you fight and scream and refuse what you'd already promised to do?" Renato's smile was infuriatingly unbothered. The sick bastard was enjoying himself.

"Is this fun for you? Toying with your victims before you kill them? Are you getting off on it?"

He chuckled. "I admit I preferred when you kneeled and prayed to me to spare your life . . . but this has its own appeal." He checked his watch. "But we don't have all night."

"Stop! I'll shoot, I swear to God," I babbled wildly as he started toward me. I slipped the safety off, my fingers smearing sweat on the metal.

"Go ahead, *bambina*. Take a man's life in cold blood and sink into the darkness . . . let it grow in your heart. Give up on your chances of heaven and fall," he mocked, now striding my way fearlessly.

He was nearly close enough to swipe the gun from me. I was out of time. Instinct took over, and my finger jerked. His eyes locked on mine, and something passed between us in that second. Something real and honest. A terrible moment of truth. I might be a good person and one who had dedicated her life to helping people, and yet I would kill for the right reason. I would cross that line and take that sin onto my own soul.

The gun clicked. I pulled the trigger again, the muzzle now pressed point-blank against Renato's chest. Another click. Renato waited as my gaze fell to the empty gun and then back up to his face.

"You knew it was empty?" I blurted as he smoothly took it from me. I was done. I couldn't run. He wouldn't let me get away again. "You walk around with an unloaded gun?" The arrogance of this man was infuriating. Even now, at the end, it pissed me off.

He held the gun with the ease of someone used to handling firearms. He aimed it at the ground behind me and pulled the trigger two times in succession. One empty click, and then a bang.

The shot was the most terrifying thing I'd ever heard. I flinched and bent over at the waist, my fight-or-flight response screaming at me to run again.

"Of course not," he replied calmly, like I hadn't just held a loaded gun on him and pulled the trigger. "But I wanted to see how far you'd go."

I swallowed hard. He switched the safety on and tucked the weapon away. I didn't think I'd be getting my hands back on it. His black gloves shone in the moonlight overhead.

"And now?" I asked, suddenly weary. I had been fighting for so long—days, weeks, decades—and now, I was done. I was finally done.

"And now, I know," Renato said.

He stared at me, a new look in his eyes that I couldn't read. Who knew what a man like him thought about? He was impossible to predict, and I gave up trying. I was out of my league here.

"You're not going to shoot me? What're the gloves for? Strangling?" I rambled. A shrill laugh left me, and then another one. I sounded insane, but I couldn't do anything about it right now.

Renato watched me giggle, even as fresh tears slid down my cheeks. He glanced down at his hands. "The gloves? It's cold out tonight."

I blinked at him and giggled again, then dissolved into a fit of laughter. An edge of hysteria threatened to consume my mind, and I'd given up the fight.

"So, what now? Will I be bludgeoned to death? Am I going to fall off a bridge, or maybe the hotel roof? Maybe I'll just overdose, that would be nice and clean, wouldn't it? Too bad I don't have a history of drug use . . ." I was definitely rambling now, and when I finally shut my mouth, Renato sighed.

"You have quite the dark imagination."

"You were giving me another chance, remember? You gave

me the tracker, and you were waiting to see if I could keep my promise."

"And you were *clearly* intending on doing so. It's what, a few hours later, and you've already gotten rid of it and are trying to flee the state." He tutted disapprovingly. "I'd say I was disappointed, but honestly, it doesn't matter. I've finally decided what I'm going to do with you, little nurse."

Just then, the passenger door of the waiting car opened, and light flooded the dim interior. Elio stood in the open doorway and watched us. I looked past him into the interior of the car, and my heart squeezed hard.

Lucy lay sleeping—or drugged, I had no idea—in the back seat. Her white cat pajamas looked so out of place in this dark, terrifying scene.

"You're coming with me, Miss Burke, for better or worse, until death do us part."

I jerked my head toward Ren, unable to comprehend his words.

"I need a wife and a mother to my children."

He stepped toward me, and I was too frozen in shock to move. His leather-gloved hands gripped my shoulders and tugged me toward him.

"And?" I breathed.

A shadow of a smile passed over his lips. "And—you're going to be both."

11

RENATO

Charlotte stood mute with shock. She got into the car like a good little girl. I'd expect nothing less since I had her sister sleeping peacefully on the back seat. Charlotte had already proved she'd do anything to keep that girl alive, and soon, anything would mean becoming my wife.

I was really warming to the idea now. Once it had taken root inside me, I couldn't imagine a better solution to my heir problem.

"Where are you taking us?" Charlotte asked, huddled in the back seat as far away from me as she could get. She gripped her St. Anthony medal like it was a sacred object capable of keeping me away; like I was a vampire from a teen movie.

"Home. Where else?"

She stared at me. "You don't really want to do this. There has to be another option."

"Even if there was, I chose this one. I'm the man who gets what he wants, or takes it—remember, *bambina?*"

She chewed her lip with sharp teeth, her mind furiously roving over possible objections and discarding them. She finally seized on one, a light of futile hope burning in her eyes. "But you're mafia royalty. You should be marrying some woman who will bring you connections or more power—something like that, right?"

"I don't need a wife to bring me connections or power. I make my own money and forge my own alliances," I replied smoothly.

Charlotte's hands were bunched into fists on her lap, her impulsive temper simmering under her calm facade. "I don't understand . . ." she started, her tone a stitch away from a demand.

"You don't have to understand. You don't have to agree. It changes nothing," I told her, waiting for that lid to blow.

"You want me to marry you?" she asked in a disbelieving tone.

"And carry my heirs. Yes."

She snorted. "Like I'd ever have kids with you."

"I'm afraid marriage and kids is a package deal. You can't have one without the other."

She glared at me. "Right, and I'm choosing between what? Living long enough to pop out your tiny dictators or dying right now?"

I inclined my head, letting her draw her own conclusions. Her frustration turned to fury, and I knew she was about to attack me, just like she'd attacked Elio the night we met.

The moment her self-control snapped and she lunged for me, I was ready for her. The veil of compliance and politeness fell, and just as she opened her mouth to unleash her impotent rage, I reached out and tugged her into my lap.

She gave a grunt of surprise as she landed on my knee, her plump ass fitting perfectly against my thighs. One arm banded around her waist, keeping her put, and I pressed my other hand against her smart, obstinate mouth, sealing her accusations inside.

She attempted to struggle for a moment, but there was barely an inch of give in my hold. Her fingers scrabbled at my hand, attempting to dislodge it from her mouth, but her short, trimmed nails were useless against my gloves.

"Shh, *anima mia*, there's no point in struggling," I told her.

Her ass was pushing against my dick, and I'd been hard since the moment I'd decided this woman would be my wife. The very idea of it sent blood surging to my cock. And the thought of getting her pregnant? It was the biggest turn-on of my life. It was unusual to discover a new kink at my age, especially when I'd seen and done so much. And yet, the idea of this woman, and her alone, swollen with my heir—it was already my new favorite fantasy.

"It's not going to do anything but get me off," I added.

She stilled, her heaving chest pressing my arm, her short nails digging into my sleeve. Her breath blew in hot pants as I flexed my hips against her, rubbing my stiff cock on the curve of her ass. She stiffened with shock at the visceral proof of my need.

"That's right, Miss Burke. I like it when you struggle. I like it when you argue with me and challenge me. I like you fighting me with all that glorious, fiery righteousness, and then sinking into my hands like butter when you surrender." I pressed my middle finger, still encased in the glove, between her lips, until she had no choice but to open.

My leather-wrapped finger sank inside her mouth, and her teeth tested the thickness of the leather. I chuckled. "If you think biting me will prevent me putting anything else in your mouth, you're wrong," I muttered.

She froze for a moment and then wiggled again, trying to squirm away from me. I held her tightly, my finger resting on her tongue, until she calmed again.

"You should know, since I don't plan on keeping secrets

from my wife, that this is barely about Lucy anymore or what you saw."

Gently, I slid my finger out of her mouth and then plunged it back in, slowly fucking her mouth with my digit.

"Now, it's about us. Something about me you'll come to learn: I always keep my word. Always. I don't like to repeat myself, and once I decide on something I want, I don't stop until I get it. What this means for you is that from this moment on, you're mine . . . permanently. You'll be my wife and the mother of my children. Nothing, and no one, can save you from that fate. The sooner you accept that, the sooner you can get used to your new life. Be grateful that you get to live one."

She was growing tired of fighting me, her weight sinking deeper onto my thighs, my cock aching to a painful degree. I wanted to thrust up against her innocent ass until I came like a teen dry humping his girlfriend over the back of a pew after Sunday school. But I wasn't a kid anymore. I was a man. I had control over my urges. For now, at least.

Instead, I wrapped my arms tighter around my wife-to-be and rocked her. She was so tense, taut as an overstretched violin string. I was calm. Peaceful, almost, having charted a course for the future that solved my ongoing heir problem—and for once, I was on a course that actually excited me. I was also holding the object of my obsession in my arms. Was I already obsessed with this woman? Yes, undoubtedly so. I'd been obsessed since the moment I saw her.

"So, what will it be, *bambina*? Death, or me and my demon spawn?"

She was quiet for so long that I suspected she was actually considering both options equally. Then she turned her head toward me, and I released her mouth from my grip.

"I choose you," she whispered. "I want us to live, so I choose you."

"Good girl," I muttered, and before she could ruin the sweet moment of her surrender, I slipped my finger back between her lips and held her firmly.

It was barely noticeable at first, but the fight ebbed from Charlotte. She liked being constrained so tightly; I could tell by the way she grew increasingly boneless. She liked being rocked. She had to be exhausted. Burned out from fear and lack of sleep. If I counted up the hours I knew she'd worked in the past three days, she was already approaching superhuman status to be awake at all. Anyone else would have been passed out by now, but Charlotte was willfully holding on to consciousness through sheer tenacity. My soon-to-be wife had grit. And it was hot as hell.

I rocked her a little more as she leaned into me. Her tongue brushed over my finger, and I slipped another between her parted lips. This time, she barely fought me. I was developing quite the fascination with putting things in this woman's mouth. She was getting calmer, sleep crowding in on her now that she'd been caught and restrained. The inevitability of it all washed over both of us.

Her mouth fastened more tightly around my fingers. Tentatively, her tongue moved over the leather, and she sucked. She probably wasn't aware that she was sucking my gloved fingers like a pacifier. A shrink would have a field day with that unconscious movement. But Charlotte no longer had to worry what anyone else would think. Fear of judgment was a thing of the past for her. The only opinion she'd need to worry about was mine.

I gathered her against me, keeping my fingers in her mouth to comfort her, and let her sleep. The smell of her cheap shampoo filled my senses. She was pushed to a brittle point, underfed, overworked, living in a tiny shoebox, and subsisting on shitty processed foods. Not anymore. I would change all of that for her. As my wife, she would live in the kind of luxury most people could only dream of.

If she was a good girl who learned to thrive within the limits of her freedom as my wife, then we'd get along just fine. If not? Then I'd teach her. And I'd enjoy every sinful moment.

12

CHARLIE

I woke suddenly, jumping at the sensation of cool night air rushing across my face. I was lying down in the back seat of a car, and Elio stood beside the open door. "You're awake. Let's go."

The previous hours came rushing back. The rest stop and Lucy disappearing. Renato walking out of the shadows like a reaper arriving to take my soul. Sitting in the car with him holding me so tight I used up the last of my strength trying to move him. He hadn't moved an inch.

I'd fallen asleep? Well, the human body did have limits; I supposed I should have known that. There was a strange kind of adrenaline dump now that we'd been caught. The worst had happened. No need to stay awake anymore.

Casa Nera was even more creepy in the moonlight. Elio picked up the sleeping Lucy and escorted us inside. Armed men strolled the grounds. They watched us from the driveway, their eyes curious as we went inside. I looked around, wondering if this was the last time I'd see the outside of this house. Renato was nowhere to be seen.

If this was just a nightmare, I'd really like to wake up now.

Inside, Elio wordlessly guided us through a maze of corridors, all darkly decorated and reminiscent of a stately house from the 1700s. We followed him up an impressive staircase flanked by stained glass windows that bathed us in ruby-red light as we walked. The stairs continued upward, but Elio stepped onto the first-floor landing and headed along the corridor. He stopped at a massive door near the end.

"You can sleep here tonight. The housekeeper, Carmella, will help you settle in." *Settle in?* Well, at least we weren't sleeping in the dungeon in the basement.

He opened the huge door, effortlessly maneuvering my sister through without so much as brushing a lock of her hair against the imposing wooden doorframe.

"Do you live here, too?" I wondered as I followed them inside.

Elio nodded shortly. "This compound has housed the De Sanctis family for decades."

Family. My brain hitched at that word.

Elio saw my reaction. "Soon, that'll be you and your sister, too. Family."

"Yeah, right. You need more than a piece of paper and a gun to the head to be family," I muttered, going to a lead-paned window and looking out at the dark woods beyond the property.

"*La famiglia prima di tutto*. The family before all else. Those are words that Renato lives by."

"Didn't he kill his own father? That's the rumor, anyway." I wrapped my arms around my chest.

Elio shrugged. "There's more to family than a name. I suggest not getting on his bad side."

"He has a good side?"

Elio paused on his way to the door and glanced back at me. "The fact that you're standing here is evidence of that."

"Meaning?" I crossed my arms, squaring up for a fight with

someone I was pretty sure wasn't allowed to harm me, as opposed to his boss. My emotions were a whirling maelstrom in my chest, and they needed out.

Elio paused for a moment. "Do you want to die?"

His question threw me, and I scoffed. "Does anyone answer yes to that?"

"You'd be surprised. You've been given a pardon by the most merciless man I've ever known. You should be grateful for it."

"A pardon? Becoming a broodmare for a monster is a pardon? You've got some really fucked-up principles."

He nodded. "Maybe I do, but guess what? You're living in our world now. You need to adjust your ideas of right and wrong. Good and evil. I've known Ren since I was a boy, and he's always been precise, ruthless, cunning, and cold. This is—" Elio broke off, his deep voice hinting at his own confusion.

"This is what?" I pressed. I couldn't stand not knowing what he was about to say.

"It's different. You're an exception." Elio seemed as puzzled as I was, as if he couldn't really believe his own words. His ruthless, infamously merciless boss was breaking his own rules, *for me*. Elio's gaze ran over me, looking for what it was exactly that drove his boss to spare me. He was clearly drawing a blank, as he shrugged and turned to the door.

"But why? Why me?" I stepped forward, the words bursting from me. Suddenly, I needed to know the answer to that more than I needed to breathe.

Elio pulled the heavy door open and glanced at me over his shoulder. "Ask him yourself."

In the morning, I woke at six, as I usually did. Lucy still snored softly beside me. I stared at the elaborately corniced ceiling, taking a second to remember where I was.

Right.

The devil's castle, in the middle of Bumfuck, New Jersey.

I need a wife and a mother to my children. You're going to be both.

I resisted the urge to turn over and try to sleep again, hiding in dreams. I needed to figure out exactly what the deal was before Lucy woke up and freaked out. My sister usually slept late, and given how she'd missed her usual routine night after night—thanks to Miguel's murder and her being drugged with something—I'd bet she'd be out for even longer today.

I got out of bed, dressed quickly, and crept from the room. The door wasn't locked. Renato was confident in his security. As soon as I stepped outside, I saw why. Two men in black suits stood in the hallway. Their gazes fell on me as soon as I appeared.

"Good morning, Miss Burke. Do you need something?"

I thought for a second. "Coffee."

"I'll take you to the kitchen. I'm Sonny, by the way."

"Charlie," I mumbled in response, eyeing the other guard who seemed like he'd be staying outside the door to watch over Lucy.

"Don't worry about Vinny. His job is to make sure your sister is safe. Nice to meet you. Welcome to Casa Nera."

Make sure my sister was safe. *Safe?* Did Sonny really not know that we were here against our will? He didn't seem to, as he walked cheerfully through the hall, leading me around corners that all looked the same. He was downright chipper, which felt rude considering I was still half expecting Renato to change his mind about us and kill us anyway.

When we got to the first floor, Sonny explained the layout of the house and then took me to the kitchen. It immediately became my favorite room. It was cozy and had a lived-in feel. Warm ochre walls flowed into terra-cotta tiles, and white Carrara marble with delicate veins adorned the long wraparound counters and island. Potted plants with herbs and bottles with different oils were scattered around the space, and the air smelled faintly of lemons. Pans hung over the island, lovingly shined and well taken care of. Someone spent a lot of time in this room and was proud of it. That someone stood by the sink when I walked in.

"Carmella, this is Charlie. The boss's woman."

So, Sonny was under the impression that I *wanted* to marry his tyrannical boss?

"You do know that it's not by choice, right? I mean, we're going to all stand here and pretend that this is a cause to celebrate and not the start of a lifelong prison sentence?"

Silence met my blunt statement. Sonny shifted his eyes from me to the older lady by the sink—the housekeeper, Carmella. The silence stretched for a long moment before he spoke again.

"The boss is going to have his hands full with you. But don't worry, he's used to handling difficult women." With that, Sonny pulled out a chair and sat, just in time for Carmella to hand him a plate with a fat, buttery pastry on it.

I grabbed her hand as she passed me. "Me and my sister are here against our will. Will you help us?"

She turned to me, eyeing me critically. "I will make sure you are fed well."

"That is not the kind of help I'm talking about."

"But that is the only kind of help you'll get from me, *ragazza*. I don't go against Renato, and I don't support anyone who does," she said and stepped away, her face showing how pained she was from having to interact with me.

So, it seemed if I was banking on help from this corner, it would be a long time coming. Renato clearly knew how to surround himself with people who were just as insane as he was.

Carmella set a plate in front of me with the same type of pastry she'd given Sonny. As soon as the smell of chocolate and butter hit me, my stomach growled loudly. I debated the wisdom of refusing to eat out of protest. My thoughts were clearly easy to read.

Carmella tossed her head. "Why do women these days never want to eat?" she mumbled.

My tummy rumbled emptily.

Figuring I might as well eat the damn thing—seeing as I hadn't eaten much since before the gala, and I was going to need my strength to survive all this—I pulled out a chair and sat, taking a bite of the pastry. It was still warm and melted against my tongue.

Sonny chuckled. "Thin is in, Carm, didn't you hear?"

"In the magazines, maybe, but not in real life, and not with men," she replied confidently.

I wished I'd ever been that confident about men. The other sex remained a mystery to me most of the time.

"Maybe not all women care that much about what men want," Sonny continued, surprising me as he shot a look my way. "Charlotte is a nurse, right? From what I hear, she's dedicated to her work."

I blinked at them, suddenly included in the conversation with a mouthful of pastry.

I nodded, not able to elaborate with food in my mouth, but he was close enough. I was an aspiring nurse, and I worked more hours than anyone else I knew. If that wasn't dedication, it was at least desperation, but there was no need to go into that with two strangers.

Carmella's eyes narrowed, and something changed in her expression. Her tight lips loosened a touch, and her forehead smoothed. She nodded to herself a little.

"Va bene."

Carmella's quiet words and softer expression made me feel like

I'd just passed a test of some kind. The expression on the housekeeper's face had changed from wary contempt to something closer to respect. I didn't know how to feel about that.

"It's good, isn't it?" Sonny prompted, grinning down at my rapidly disappearing pastry. He'd finished his in three big bites and now sipped coffee.

I nodded reluctantly.

Carmella placed a cup of coffee before me. "Let me guess, you like black coffee?"

I raised an eyebrow at her. "Don't tell me you're some kind of coffee psychic who can tell what a person likes just by looking at them."

She flicked her gaze over me, and I suddenly wished I hadn't invited her scrutiny. I hadn't washed my face, and it had to be a mess of the makeup I'd worn last night. My hair was tangled and fuzzy. My eyes felt gritty. I was in absolute shambles.

"You look like someone who doesn't have time to take care of herself. Someone who works too hard and survives on scraps here and there, and a whole lot of caffeine to power through." Carmella's voice told me she knew she was right.

Bullseye.

Sonny snorted. "Just like the boss when he got back from Napoli, no?" he addressed to Carmella.

She nodded.

Renato had once been as tired and pressed to a sharp point as I was on a regular basis? I couldn't imagine it. The man seemed too collected. Too in control of everything and everyone around him.

"You look after your sister, don't you?" Sonny continued, again making me wonder how much he knew about me. "Kids are tough."

"She's not a kid. Well, nearly not. She's nineteen."

"Nineteen is a kid in some ways, and not in others. You don't seem that much older yourself, if you don't mind me saying."

"I'm twenty-six," I muttered and took a sip of coffee.

This conversation wasn't making me feel good about myself. I usually worried that I was getting haggard and old before my time, thanks to my stressful life and taking care of Lucy. Now, it seemed my lifestyle wasn't as aging as I'd worried it was. It was an odd relief. But why did I even care? The day I cared about whether Renato De Sanctis, self-appointed dictator over my life, thought I was pretty would be the day I jumped off the roof. It would be a clear sign I'd been body-snatched.

"*Buongiorno, tutti,*" a deep voice spoke from the door, sending nerves flaring through me.

Renato walked into the kitchen, passing behind the counter to kiss Carmella on the cheek. It was like a tiger had strolled into the room with no sign of a handler or collar. It was too much. *He* was too much.

The older woman smiled at him, patting his hand, and they conversed in Italian. I took the chance to study the man holding me captive. Casa Nera clearly had a gym, because he'd been working out, judging by his gym wear and the sheen of sweat on his bare arms.

Those arms were something else. I couldn't stop looking at them. His body was a monument to strength and beauty, hidden until now beneath his designer suits. His arms bulged with muscle when he moved them. No wonder he could toss me around like I was a kid. Compared to his size and strength, I practically was one.

"Good morning, Charlotte."

Renato's words jerked me out of my inspection, and I met his warm, dark eyes. "Why are you calling me that? I thought I was Miss Burke to you?"

He nearly grinned as he leaned his elbows on the counter, bringing his face closer to mine. "Now that you're going to be family, I'd say it's time to drop the formalities."

I wet my lips, the conversation turning my mouth dry. "Maybe I like the formalities."

Renato shrugged his well-developed shoulders. "Too bad. I don't. What you'll come to learn about this house, and this family, *bambina,* is that I make the rules. My word is law, and I'm the judge, jury, and executioner here. Don't forget that, and behave accordingly."

I nodded. "Right, note to self: Don't piss off the dictator, or he might change his mind about killing you in cold blood, like he nearly did last night." The words flew out of me before I could stop them.

The kitchen fell silent for a long moment. Sonny broke the tension by slapping the counter and letting out a hearty laugh. "Boss, we've got a live one here! I'm sure you'll enjoy teaching your new little wife how to behave."

Renato sent a dark look at Sonny, who spluttered into his coffee. "No disrespect, of course," he added hastily.

The teasing sent blood to my face. I stood, my chair scraping loudly over the tile. I turned around and got one step before Renato's voice lashed out and held me in place. "I didn't give you permission to leave, Charlotte, nor did you ask for it."

The painful silence drew out. If I left now, like I wanted to, I was going against Renato's explicit command. He wanted me to ask him for permission, and I just couldn't bring myself to. But I also didn't want to make a scene and then lose. He could do anything he damn well pleased to me here, and there was nothing I could do about it. He could probably do anything he wanted to me *anywhere* and get away with it. The idea made me feel powerless and weak, and I hated it.

"Lucy will wake up soon and be scared. I don't want her to be alone when she comes to." My voice was full of pride, and I couldn't bring myself to turn around and meet the tyrant's eyes. My skin was hot between my shoulders, right where I imagined Renato's eyes were staring.

"Very thoughtful of you. Sonny, stay and finish your coffee. I'll escort Charlotte back to her room."

I nearly changed my mind and sat down again. After last night, I really didn't want to be alone with Renato. The whole thing was seared in my mind, and yet it was hazy in a way, too. Maybe all trauma ended up feeling like that—and thinking you're about to die in a parking lot or shooting someone point-blank definitely qualified as trauma.

I left the kitchen, walking quickly to try to keep ahead of Renato.

He chuckled at my first wrong turn. "It's this way," he pointed out.

I stopped and spun back. He waited for me at the bend I'd just hurried around. When I reached him, he gestured to a different hall, and I started forward. This time, Renato's hand circled my wrist and jerked me in to him, forcing me to slow my pace.

"Not so fast. There's no need to go racing around. I'm sure your sister will sleep a little more."

"What did you and your henchmen give her last night?" I demanded. I'd been worrying about what they'd drugged Lucy with all night, though her vitals had seemed steady.

"Nothing more than a responsible doctor would for someone in her condition."

"Her condition?" I arched a brow at him.

"Overwrought . . . not thinking straight. You know exactly what I mean."

"Of course, because it's so unreasonable to freak out when

your boyfriend is shot dead in front of you and your life is threatened."

We stood nose to nose. Well, not really, seeing as his nose was so much higher than mine. He stared down at me with an indecipherable emotion in his eyes. This wasn't like me. I didn't challenge authority figures or rock the boat. I didn't get up in people's faces, ever, but something about this man made me forget the woman I'd worked so hard to be. Sensible, hardworking, and an expert at avoiding attention.

Nobody had ever paid such close attention to me. Not until Renato.

This dangerous killer.

A ghost of amusement passed over Renato's striking face. "Be careful, little nurse. You're in my house now, and like I just told you—I make the rules. I won't tolerate temper tantrums or accusations. You gave me your word, and I expect you to honor it."

"Or?" It was like someone with a death wish had possessed my mouth and was now running the show. My brain couldn't seem to overpower my anger and frustration.

"Or there will be consequences."

"So, every time I do something, or Lucy says something that you don't like, we have to be scared of being taken out to the garage and put down like dogs?" There it was. A core fear that couldn't be ignored. How long would the axe of death hang over our heads? I didn't know if I could take it much longer.

Renato studied me for a long moment, his gaze tracking across my face, from my splotchy old makeup to my lips, lingering there, and then returning to my eyes. "You're really not afraid of anything, are you, Charlotte?"

I wet my lips, my mouth dry as hell again. How did this man use up all the space in every single room he was in? "Not true. I'm scared of you. I just want to know what to expect. I *need* to know."

"You need to know so you can try to control it. You need to exert some kind of power over the situation so you can feel safer, because you need to be in charge, isn't that right?"

Renato's words slid over me, prickling my nerves. I didn't like that he was psychoanalyzing me. I didn't like that he was seeing all my soft, unprotected parts.

"What you need to understand, and soon you will, is that you're never going to be in charge of your life in the same way again. You're never going to go somewhere or do something without rules. You're never going to be the one keeping you and your sister off the street. You're never going to be the one paying down huge student loans and struggling to put food on the table. You're never going to be the one whose shoulders bear all the burdens . . . even the ones you never asked for. Soon, that'll be your husband's job. *My* job."

His words sank through me like stones, hitting the bottom of my heart with odd thumps. They both infuriated me and perplexed me. I didn't know what to make of those promises. I was a modern woman. I didn't need a husband to take care of me and make decisions for me.

Fuck him.

Renato reached out and tucked a loose strand of hair behind my ear. "You're not alone anymore, Charlotte. You're no longer the only adult in the room. The grown-ups are here now, and you will never be alone again. It's time to let go now, *bambina*. It's okay to just stop worrying about everything. You have no choices here. You've surrendered . . . it's over."

His hand abruptly left my hair and cupped my chin, and my pulse rate shot up, thundering through my veins. Why did I keep antagonizing this dangerous man? What the hell was wrong with me? *He could have killed you already; there's a reason why he hasn't.*

Stress had burned out my survival instincts, and now I was just a crazy person who didn't mind swimming with sharks, or something else as dangerous as talking back to the *capo dei capi* of New Jersey.

"I'll never stop worrying about Lucy, and I'll never let you make every single decision for our lives without a fight." I snorted softly.

His thumb brushed over my lips, and my face was caught in his firm grip. I couldn't look away. I couldn't move an inch. Last night and the oddly comforting feeling of falling asleep with his fingers in my mouth returned to me.

"You know, *anima mia,* Sonny was right. If you prove to be too much of a handful, we'll have to remedy that."

His finger brushed over my lips again. It felt good, sinfully so. I hadn't been touched by a man who actually knew what he was doing for longer than I could remember. Not until this man first touched me at La Leonora.

My love life had been one of the dullest, most disappointing parts of my life. I'd started to think it was me. I was the common factor on all the dates I'd been on with perfectly nice guys. There was something broken inside me that couldn't be fixed, or maybe it just wasn't in my genes. I didn't get the shivers when someone messaged me or feel growing excitement to see a boyfriend after time apart. I had never fallen apart in a man's hands and then wanted to repeat the experience with him. In twenty-six years, I'd had sex with a grand total of three men, and each one was less memorable than the last. I'd never come close to an orgasm with any of them, and lately I barely bothered masturbating.

Maybe it was the nurse in me, but understanding the mechanics of stimulating certain areas with high nerve density and why it was pleasurable really took the fun out of things. Either that, or the patina of shame that coated my skin at a stranger's touch—shame instilled in me at Mercy House—was simply too thick to wash off.

And yet, as Renato ran his thumb over my lips, he might as well have been touching my clit for how good it felt. I remembered the heat inside me when half his fist had invaded my mouth. I'd never been as wet as I'd been with his fingers in my mouth, controlling my ability to speak. Shame flooded me at the memory.

"You tell me to let it go, and I don't have to worry about paying the bills. Do you think seriously that'll comfort me? A woman who has worked her entire life to be independent and free? You think I've just been waiting for a man like you to come along and save me?"

"I told you already that I'm no white knight, Charlotte. I'm the villain in your story, and no one is coming to cut you free from the belly of this beast. No one."

His finger still touched my lips, and impulsively I opened my mouth and rested my teeth on it, debating the wisdom of biting him. There was no glove there to stop me now.

"I wouldn't, if you value being able to sit this week."

His warning sent heat curling through me. What was he warning me about, *really*?

"I'm a heavy-handed disciplinarian," he added, a slight smirk curving his lips as he took in my flustered expression. Just the thought had me squirming, and from the satisfied look on his arrogant face, he knew it.

"Fight it all you want, but we both know it's true. I own you, and your sister, and I can do whatever I want with you. I didn't have to let you live. If you understood how unlike me that was, you would be getting down on your knees and opening this smart mouth for something else entirely."

He kept his thumb between my teeth, confident that I wouldn't draw blood.

"Next time I hear an outburst like today's, that's what I'll expect. Soon, by your own agreement, you will be my wife, and this won't be a sham marriage. I want more than that from you."

I released his finger, silently acknowledging that I was bluffing.

"How much more?" I asked in a whisper, panic building as he leaned in and pressed his forehead against mine. I could smell him. Leather, amber, and vetiver, with a hint of clean male sweat. My body hummed at the scent.

He ran his nose down my cheek. He wasn't even holding me in place now; my own body was doing it for him. I couldn't have run away if I tried. I was spellbound. My brain wasn't in the driver's seat anymore, my body was, and it wanted to be touched by this man. That was the sobering truth I couldn't deny. The call was coming from inside the house. Who needed enemies when your own body was hot for your captor? The shame of my reaction was crippling.

Renato's gaze tracked across my face, seeming to recognize the conflict there. He saw my resistance, and he also saw my want. I couldn't hide anything from him. I'd never felt so vulnerable. His lips ticked upward, making him blindingly handsome for a moment, and his lips brushed over mine.

"Everything."

His whisper sent a gale of heat billowing through me, and when he captured my mouth in a hot kiss, sliding his tongue between my lips, I lost all ability to think.

For me, kisses after a date were dry cheek pecks. Real kissing was to be done in bed behind a locked door, with the lights off, followed by a shower. *Wash away your sins.* It wasn't in full view of anyone who might walk past, in the hall, right after breakfast. The same heat that had fogged up my brain in the bathroom at La Leonora hit me, and I couldn't help but melt. After all, what was the point in fighting it? I'd given him my word, and now, he could take what he wanted from me. I shouldn't have felt so excited by that.

His lips moved against mine, his tongue hot and wet and obscene in its languid thrusts. He kissed me like he was fucking my mouth with his tongue. The pleasure was intense; it was ungodly. The indoctrination of my youth played on an endless loop in my head. I'd tried time and again to push it out, living my life like other young women my age, but I'd never quite managed it. Even the ones who went to church regularly had happy, functioning premarital relationships, without the shame and guilt that dogged me. I envied them. Another sin to add to the list of my transgressions.

Renato tugged my bottom lip between his teeth and bit down. I moaned, heat radiating through me in waves. I rocked my body against his. I couldn't help it; an instinct I had no control over was tugging at my strings. I was lost. Powerless. Out of control. *Free.*

An involuntary moan left me when he pulled back and cool air danced across my overheated skin. I could feel his smug satisfaction at how I'd lost myself to his touch. I was depraved. I was shameless. I was wet as hell.

"You have one thing wrong," I panted, attempting to claw back a shred of dignity to hold before me like a shield. "When all this started, I never agreed to marry you," I bit out.

"No, you didn't. You agreed to worship me. To pray to me. To follow my every command." He brushed my stray hairs away from my flushed forehead.

I still had on yesterday's makeup, and I hadn't washed my hair this morning. I had to be a shiny mess, so why was he watching me with such hunger?

"Think of yourself as a sacrificial bride for the devil, if it makes you feel better . . . Trussed up in white silk, captive in my kingdom, mine for the rest of time."

I had no response for that. I only stared at him, aghast.

He brushed another kiss onto my lips, sending heat curling through me.

"You promised me your soul. Don't forget that. I'll settle for your hand and a couple of heirs. Now, go upstairs and see your sister, before I decide to drag you to my room and start making our firstborn."

When I got back to the hallway outside our room, heat throbbing in my face, my body traitorously warm and needy, a loud smash met my ears, just as Vinny, the guard outside the door, spoke into a discreet radio clipped to his shoulder. A piercing scream filled the air, muffled by the heavy wall and thick door, but unmistakable. Both me and Vinny turned and stared at the wooden surface.

"I think your sister is awake," Vinny quipped.

"You think?" I muttered as I approached the door. "Let me calm her down." I tried the handle, and it refused to budge.

"It wasn't locked before."

"That's only if you're together. If she's on her own, the boss is worried she'll . . . have trouble coping with her new situation." Vinny's voice was carefully devoid of emotion.

I met his eyes. He wasn't a bad-looking guy, and I'd put him around my age. He had sandy-blond hair and faded blue eyes. He met my gaze unflinchingly. This was a man who had locked a nineteen-year-old girl in a room and then stood guard outside it. A man who knew we were both here unwillingly. How did someone become like this? A person capable of such cruelty? I really had stepped into another world, one where up was down and right was wrong.

"Wow, it seems like the boss has a lot of experience holding innocent women hostage. Thank God he has good guys like you to do his dirty work for him and keep them in line," I snapped at Vinny and headed to the door.

"Lucy? It's me," I said, knocking at the same time.

"Charlie?" Lucy's voice sounded ragged.

Shit. I should never have gone exploring and left Lucy to wake up on her own.

"Let me in," I instructed Vinny, and to my surprise, he complied without arguing.

It seemed the De Sanctis men really didn't know what to do with Lucy. Overwrought women weren't their area of expertise, after all. Maybe they usually just killed them. The thought wasn't comforting in the least.

Inside the room, my sister had worked her magic and completely trashed the place. She was uniquely qualified to make a mess, so she was in her element. She'd cleared off every surface and broken the mirror. She'd stomped the feathers out of the pillows. She'd even torn down the curtains. Carmella and Lucy really weren't going to get off on the right foot.

As soon as she saw me, her eyes filled with tears. Our fight roared back into my mind, breaking my heart all over again. Was she still upset over what I'd said to her? Was I still upset at her cruel words? Maybe a little, but it didn't matter now. That was how it was with sisters. Every word could cut a new scar on your heart, but when you needed each other, no one else compared.

"Charlie!" Lucy cried, stepping over the wreckage on the floor and flying into my arms. "I thought they'd done something to you. I thought you were dead."

I was surprised by her emotion, and my battered heart warmed at the display. Despite our differences, we were sisters. We could get over anything.

"So you thought you'd piss them off some more by being the most annoying houseguest?" I was going for teasing to lighten the mood. Maybe I'd lost my mind, too. I certainly deserved to at this point.

"It's not funny. Where are we?" Lucy demanded. Her eyes suddenly widened. "Wait, did we go to the cops? Is this a safe house?"

"I hate to break it to you, but safe houses don't rival five-star hotels."

We both looked around the ruined room.

"This is the De Sanctis family compound."

Lucy turned pale, her angry flush fading as reality hit. "Why?"

Blowing out a sigh, I turned to the bedding on the floor and began to pick it up. I couldn't face her while I told her about our predicament.

"Because we're going to be staying here, for a while, until the heat with the cops blows over and—"

"You said they'd kill us. Why did they bring us here?" Lucy cut me off.

"Why? Are you so eager to die?" I challenged instead, only delaying the inevitable.

There was something shameful about the truth, and I couldn't wrap my head around why I was embarrassed to tell my sister about Renato's terms. He hadn't really explained why he was doing this, only that he had decided on me. He didn't seem like the romantic type, so maybe it had something to do with the cops. I couldn't make sense of it, even in my own head.

"Of course I'm not. But tell me why we're here?"

"Well, there weren't a lot of options, so I went with the least painful one. The cops can't compel family to give evidence, so we're becoming family. By this time next week, I'll be married to one of the De Sanctis men, and then this will all just be a distant, unpleasant memory." That explanation made more sense, so I decided to run with it. It felt better to imagine that there was a concrete reason for why the master strategist mobster had chosen me to be his bride. It made me feel safer, somehow, for reasons I couldn't consider too closely.

Silence fell in the wake of my bright, chipper tone, so brittle and fake one wrong move would shatter it to pieces.

"You'll be married to a De Sanctis man? *Married?*"

"Yes, married."

"Which one?" Lucy's voice was careful. I could hear in her tone that she feared my answer.

I simply held her gaze, and she started to shake her head.

"No. Are you kidding?"

My face was pretty easy to read.

"I'll be married, and we'll both be alive. That's all there is to say about that, unless you have a time machine. Help me clean up."

13

CHARLIE

Lucy calmed down as we tidied the room and fell into a restless, sullen silence. I was worried about her, but there wasn't much I could do but be by her side. We hung out in the room for most of the day, watching TV and reading. I chewed on my nails, a bad habit, and worried about everything my desperate mind could get its mitts on.

When would I have to see Renato again? What the hell would the hospital think about my sudden absence? What about Detectives Whitely and Vane? They would suspect that something weird was going on. Maybe they'd just think me and Lucy were dead. That would certainly be more in keeping with the De Sanctis code of business. How was I going to keep my head on straight when Renato touched me?

I took a shower and was just drying off when a knock sounded at the door.

Elio stood outside. "Come with me, Renato needs you." He turned away.

"Wait!" I gestured to my towel. "I have to get dressed."

"Be quick," Elio said.

I closed the door and grabbed my clothes, changing quickly.

Despite my taking only a few minutes, Elio looked impatiently at his watch when I emerged again.

We set off at a brisk pace. I had to nearly jog to stay at his side. He took me down to the lowest level. I balked at the top of the stairs.

"I don't want to move down here," I called to Elio's departing back. *Crap*. Here I was, pushing Renato and talking back to him like I had any power in our relationship, blithely forgetting what he could do to me if I pissed him off too much.

"Just come," Elio called back.

I had no choice, really. He'd just come back and get me. I ventured down into the darkness.

Below, the air was dank and muggy. I followed the De Sanctis enforcer through the gloom toward the room at the end, where lights blazed. It was the same one I'd been in before. The makeshift medical room. I should have been relieved to step into the bright lights after the gloom of the corridor, but the sight that met my eyes didn't allow for that. Men filled the room. Dangerous, tattooed men sporting suits and grim expressions. I'd never seen so many De Sanctis men in one place. It was overwhelming.

Even more attention-grabbing was the sight of blood. Crimson all over the floor, like an overenthusiastic art student had gone to town on a concrete canvas. A man sat in the middle, partially covered with a blanket. Every single pair of eyes landed on me as I entered after Elio, but they all fell away when Renato's eyes met mine.

He was right there, a king amongst his merry band of hardened criminals, and he stared right at me.

The touch of his dark, magnetic eyes was like a caress. His gaze gripped me and locked me in place as effectively as a large hand wrapped around my throat.

"Charlotte, we've been waiting for you," Renato said, his deep voice doing something to loosen my sudden paralysis.

It was like becoming absorbed in watching a savagely beautiful panther sitting behind safety glass. His voice, low and intimate, made you feel like that glass had suddenly shattered all around you, or worse, you were in the cage with the predator. There was an edge to him now. He shot a look at Elio, and I read it easily. We'd taken too long to come. He was tense, worried about his wounded soldier, maybe. Odd that there would be a side to Renato, the merciless kingpin, who cared about the health of a random henchman. Maybe I didn't know him as well as I thought.

I stepped forward, moving like a windup doll, jerking back to life.

"What happened here?"

"My man is hurt," Renato replied smoothly, rising to his intimidating height and stalking toward me. "I need you to help him."

"How did he get hurt?" I asked.

"He was in a car accident. Help him."

There was no room to argue with his commanding tone, and besides, since my first sight of the bleeding man, the caregiver in me had been distracted, itching to get close and triage the situation.

"Why didn't you call an ambulance?"

"You were closer, little nurse."

"Right, like I'm the same as a hospital," I muttered, pulling the metal supply cart toward me and surveying the contents. I reached for the disinfectant and doused my hands liberally before snapping on gloves. It was hot in the room with all the brooding and intimidating bodies packed in.

"When did this happen?"

"Not long ago. It was only a few minutes' drive from here, and he was brought here immediately."

I nodded and focused on the job at hand.

"Do you need something?" Renato asked, standing just behind my shoulder, watching me closely.

"Some space would be good," I snapped, and shifted into nurse mode. It was easier to pretend that this was just another patient with well-meaning family hovering nearby.

Renato didn't say a word, and apparently a look was enough to communicate his desires to his men, as they filed out, talking in low tones. Elio remained, lounging on the edge of a crate pushed against the wall and lighting a cigarette.

"Seriously?" I asked him over my shoulder.

He shrugged and spoke to Renato in what I guessed was Italian. I couldn't make out much, but my high school Spanish gave me the gist of the situation. A turf fight with a rival family.

The bleeding man groaned, and I focused on him, shuffling forward on the dirty floor and spreading my jacket out beneath me, keeping my hands as clean as possible.

"What's your name?" I asked him.

"P-Paolo . . . I'm Paolo," the man muttered.

Up close, I could tell he was around my age, late twenties. He had blue eyes, clouded with pain, and as I got closer, they latched on to me.

"I-I don't want to die. Please," he muttered quietly.

"I know. It's okay . . . I'm going to look and see what we have here," I soothed, falling back on tried-and-tested phrases to calm and yet not make promises. Promises always bit you in the ass.

His head bled copiously. I was shocked that he could speak at all. I checked around the back of his head, hiding my grimace. The man had suffered head trauma, of that there was no doubt, and it always presented differently. I couldn't know the outcome of that right at this second, so I moved on to his middle.

Shifting the blanket, I fought a gasp at the sight of his battered torso. I had no idea how this man was still conscious.

"This man needs to go to the hospital—now!" I called over my shoulder. "He's minutes away from losing too much blood. He has blunt-force trauma to the chest and internal bleeding. It's incredible that it hasn't killed him already. He needs surgery and blood, and honestly, a miracle."

Paolo panted and gripped my arm. "I don't want to die there . . . I can't."

"But I can't save you here," I protested, panic pressing down on me. Truthfully, no one could save him. His body was wrecked. I had no idea how many organs were bleeding and ripped beyond repair. He was already dead. It was a sobering realization.

"Please, no . . ." Paolo shook his head, his eyes losing focus.

I twisted around and stared at Renato, who watched the scene without emotion.

"Can he be saved?" Renato murmured.

No. It's too late. Dread slid through me. Honestly, even if an ambulance had arrived immediately at the scene of the accident and taken him straight to the hospital, it wouldn't have changed anything. There were too many broken parts, and not enough time to fix them. It was a cruel twist of fate that he was awake and coherent enough to understand what was happening to him.

This man was going to die, and I was the only person here who could have done a damn thing about it, and I was powerless. People died all the time in the hospital, but it didn't feel like this. I was never alone with them. I was never the only one whose shoulders it rested on. There, it was clinical and professional. Here, in the stuffy dark, with Paolo's fear filling up the room, there was an intimacy to his demise that hit me hard in the gut.

Renato must have seen the truth in my expression because he merely nodded and then took off his suit jacket. He rolled his sleeves up. He had ink on his arms, but I couldn't make out what it was.

He nodded to Elio and approached. I knelt in the pool of the dying man's blood, knowing there was nothing I could do about it.

"Breathe, Charlotte," Renato said, crouching next to me.

A warm feeling surrounded me. It was Renato's jacket, thrown around my shoulders.

"Breathe now," he ordered and took my chin in a firm grip, breaking me from my reverie.

I hadn't realized I'd been shivering until the heat of Renato's coat surrounded me. I dragged a rough breath into my lungs and then another, my eyes snapping to his.

"Good girl." He leaned down and forced my hazy gaze to meet his. "It's not your fault."

Renato's deep voice warmed my chilled skin. Hands closed on my shoulders, and then I was standing. I stared at the man who planned to marry me. He stood in a pool of blood, his dark eyes fixed on me.

"You tried your best, *bambina*. It's not your fault," he repeated.

Elio turned me away from Paolo and Renato and led me to the crate he'd been sitting on. He smelled like tobacco, and the scent mixed with the harsh metallic tang of Paolo's lifeblood coating the floor.

I sat on the crate, and Elio stood against my side, a wordless wall of support to keep me upright.

Renato now sat beside his dying man. Red smeared his white shirt and his skin. He sat in the puddle of blood unflinchingly and laid a hand on Paolo's shoulder, leaning down to make sure he could see him. Paolo seemed to wake up from his delirium a little as he realized who held his hand.

"Elisia and the baby . . ." he muttered. His face was paling more and more by the second. It wouldn't be long now.

"Are family. They will have everything they need and want, as long as they both shall live. They will want for nothing, *fratello mio*."

Paolo nodded, a touch of a smile brushing his bloodless lips, then he shuddered. "It's so cold here—I miss the sun. The sun on our skin, like when we used to swim in Capri." He broke off and shuddered again.

Renato patted his shoulder and put his forehead to Paolo's. "That's where we are now, isn't it? I can feel it on my skin; I can smell the oranges from the grove by Torre Saracena."

Paolo's eyes closed, and that slight smile settled on his lips. It was the last expression he would ever make.

After he was gone, Renato sat for a long moment, his head still pressed to the dead man's. I couldn't tear my eyes from the scene. The bloodstained kingpin mourning the loss of one of his men.

When Renato rose, he carefully laid Paolo down, and Elio went to help, closing the eyes of the deceased.

I stood forlornly, clutching the edges of Renato's jacket in my bloody hands. I went to slip it off. He crossed to me, his shirt a Pollockian nightmare of bloodstains.

"Keep it." He glanced meaningfully at my dripping-wet hair. "Don't get sick."

"So, I'm supposed to think you're worried about my health now?" The words burst from me before I could stop them. I was shaken by what had just happened and blurting out desperate things. I couldn't reconcile the man I'd just seen comforting a dying soldier with the one who would take two women hostage and force one of them to marry him.

His gaze ran over my face, his dark eyes seeming to drink me in. I couldn't take his intense inspection. He used up all the air in the room.

"You promised to look after his family. Will you really?" I heard myself ask, my brain searching for some way to break the tension between us.

"Something you will come to learn about me, little nurse, is I always keep my word. Always."

He leaned in, bringing his lips only inches from mine, so close his breath gently caressed my top lip. He held that pose as I wondered wildly if he was going to kiss me again. Was this one of those kisses that gangsters gave you before killing you? I had to binge some mob movies. I had no fucking clue what to expect from this man, and I feared my heart might give out worrying about it.

"My word is my bond, and yours will be, too . . . Don't forget your promise to me, Charlotte. I never said you had to be a happy bride, just that you had to keep your word."

Then he pulled away, and I sagged, unsure whether I was relieved or disappointed. Just the fact that disappointment even flashed through my mind was evidence that I was losing my grip on my sanity.

"Elio will take you upstairs."

I followed Elio wordlessly from the room, leaving Renato in the shadows behind us. The men outside crossed themselves morbidly as I passed, making me feel like an angel of death in my bloodstained T-shirt. Then they headed back into the room with Paolo.

"What are they doing?"

"Giving Paolo a proper send-off, and then the boss will go and let the widow know the news. She just had a baby a few months ago," Elio continued quietly.

I swallowed a sudden, intense urge to cry. "That's horrible."

Elio simply nodded as we reached the stairs and started upward. "That's life."

14

RENATO

Hours later, I stepped into the walk-in shower in my room at Casa Nera and let Paolo's blood wash down the drain. Visiting a widow with her dead husband's blood drying on my clothes might be macabre, but in my world, it was a mark of respect and admission of responsibility. His blood was on my hands as the boss, and I'd support his family from now on. His widow, Elisia, had been inconsolable. I'd brought Carmella with me to speak to her. She had enveloped her in the kind of comforting hug that she excelled at, and I'd stuck to the facts. Her husband was dead, killed in the line of duty, with honor. Because of that, she would live on the compound, provided for, as long as she wanted.

I sluiced water through my hair and reached for the body wash. The smell of blood and the stink of the lowest level of Casa Nera was trapped in my nose.

As I lathered the gel between my hands, the faint scent of jasmine floated to me. It reminded me of Charlotte.

Charlotte Burke. The sight of her standing in my overly large jacket, her face pale, her usual sass and defiance dimmed by the sight of the dying man, filled my head. She'd been wearing unremarkable, shapeless clothes, her long brown hair screwed up in a topknot, her face devoid of makeup, and yet she was the most compelling sight I'd ever seen.

Her kind of simple, unspoiled beauty wasn't common. It was rare as hell, and I wanted to see more of it. It was an indulgence; I shouldn't be getting distracted. There was work to be done. Commissioner Reynolds and his slimy friend, Judge Ellens, had been causing problems for me at La Leonora, and the Castillos were still trying to undercut me and steal my clients. There was a lot to think about, and yet, as a man who had always appreciated the classics, letting my mind linger on Charlotte was a temptation too strong to resist. I allowed myself to image her soft curves as I ran the suds down my body, palming my cock.

After death, men wanted to fuck to remind themselves they were alive, or so history would tell us. In my case, there was no way I'd rather celebrate still being alive than to sink inside Charlotte and fuck her until she screamed my name.

Memories of the first night we'd met took over my mind. The thought of her kneeling at my feet again, begging, promising to do whatever I asked had precum leaking from my tip. I spread it around the head and pumped myself, long strokes up and down, picturing her sweet, upturned face. I imagined pushing between her lips as her first task to keep her and her sister out of trouble.

I'd made my darkest fantasies a reality, and soon, I'd have her roaming the halls of Casa Nera in easily pushed-aside dresses of thin silk, ready to sit on my lap, spread her legs on my dining table, or crawl beneath my desk and open her plump lips wide whenever I was home and hungry for her. I was a careful, meticulous man. I was calculating and measured. That was how I'd built my *famiglia* up to the kind of power it enjoyed today, and to become that man, I'd never let emotions cloud my judgment. I rarely allowed myself to want.

But I wanted her, and I'd have her, every single way I desired, any time, any place, for as long as we both lived. She'd fight me on it at first, of course; the woman didn't know how to be meek. Soon, she'd understand that the tension between us was nothing ordinary, and she'd give in and become mine, mind, body, and soul. A couple of fat, happy babies would keep her from hating me too much.

The thought of sinking into Charlotte and ordering her to bounce on my lap while I worked had my cum boiling in my balls. But it was the thought of my soon-to-be wife round with my baby, her nipples large and her breasts heavy with milk, that had me finishing against the wall in ribbon after ribbon of white, coming so hard my balls ached a little in the aftermath.

I rinsed off, my breath as heavy as my conscience after Paolo's death, and made my way out of the shower.

I wanted a bedroom for us renovated, a nursery created, and of course, checkups for her health to be conducted, to make sure she was ready to be pregnant. Making sure she was off any kind of birth control was a top priority.

For the first time in years, I was making plans that involved my private life with something other than jaded nihilism. She had blazed into my life, and now I couldn't remember it without her. I'd been waiting to meet her all along, and now, with my captive bride locked up safely inside, with no possibility of escape, I was as close to happy as I'd ever been. Content with her company or obsessed with possessing her?

They both meant the same to a man like me.

15

CHARLIE

"Lucy? You haven't eaten anything." I nudged my sister where she lay in a lump under the covers. She was sleeping so much, she had to be falling into a deep depression, but I had no idea how to fix it.

She ignored me, though I could tell she was awake. She was disappointed in me, I suspected. All her life, I'd taken care of her, provided for her, and been larger than life in her eyes, like a parental figure. Now, she'd seen that I was just a person, like her, and I had no magical powers to fix things. In fact, my fix was awful: marrying into a Mafia family to keep us alive. Lucy's delusions about the safety of the world and our place in it were being spoiled, and there was nothing I could do about it.

"I have to go downstairs. I'll be back in a little while," I told her.

She didn't answer. She was grieving the loss of the life she'd imagined for herself, and I got it. We'd both lost a lot in recent days.

I headed down to the first floor of Casa Nera, for once taking every correct bend in the corridor and ending up in the second drawing room, where my presence had been requested by Elio's batshit-crazy sister, Giada. The woman from the charity benefit, it turned out, had been a member of Renato's inner circle and not a girlfriend. I didn't know how to feel about that. She was a lot to handle.

I knocked and stepped inside, and then froze. The beautiful dark-blue-and-gold room looked different. The velvet couches and side tables had been pushed to the side, and a huge set of mirrors had been set up, with a raised dais in the middle.

"Finally, you're here. I nearly finished the bubbly while I waited," Giada huffed. She was leaning back on a couch, her heavy boots perched on top of a gleaming, polished mahogany table. She hefted the heavy bottle toward me. "Here, have some."

I approached her warily. "What's the occasion? Is this a wedding dress fitting?"

Giada snorted. "What gave it away?"

"I really don't need a fancy wedding dress for this fiasco. Just bundle me up in a burlap sack and write 'hostage' across it. I'm sure that's all anyone will see when they look at me, anyway," I muttered and took the bottle. I needed the liquid courage to face my rapidly approaching reality.

Giada laughed and slapped me hard on the thigh, making me jump. "Girl, you crack me up. I, for one, can't wait for the fireworks show that your marriage is going to be." She glanced toward the doorway. "Shh, here's the designer. Better lose the attitude and be good, or I'll tell Daddy."

I raised an eyebrow at her. "Daddy?"

"Renato," she clarified.

A hot flush worked through me. Was that jealousy? *Hell no.*

"You call him Daddy? What kind of relationship do you two have?"

"Sibling rivalry . . . He's not *my* daddy." She grinned at me, the edge of sharp wickedness sending more heat flooding to my face. "He's yours."

"Yeah, right," I muttered, standing and turning my face away so she couldn't see my reaction. My body was a fucking traitor, and I hated it. I swigged more booze and jumped guiltily when a throat cleared behind me.

"Good afternoon. I take it you're the bride? Please disrobe, and we'll begin."

The designer was a small, steel-haired man who seemed to be in his seventies. He had a strong Italian accent, and the air of someone who expected to be revered.

The people pleaser in me hurried to comply.

Ten minutes later, I stood on the dais, a half-finished gown of raw silk, chiffon, and sinfully smooth satin hanging off my body.

"Fuck! Vito, that dress is hot," Giada proclaimed, looking away from her phone long enough to whistle loudly. "You're channeling virgin sacrifice right now and it's working."

A virgin sacrifice for an angry god.

"Very *Phantom of the Opera* vibes. I love it. It'll even be hot when it's ripped off and on the floor on your wedding night."

I stared at myself. I could hardly recognize my reflection. I'd never been so glamorous. The dress was hauntingly exquisite. Giada was right. There was a magical quality to it that enchanted me.

I wasn't a pretty-dress kind of person. I was a scrubs-and-Crocs person. Someone who valued clothes for their practical usefulness, not for the aesthetic. *Ripped off and on the floor.* Giada's goading words were no doubt designed to scare me. She needn't have bothered. I was scared enough already. It wasn't just the thought of Renato De Sanctis claiming his conjugal rights that scared me, but what I'd become in his hands. My body wasn't to be trusted around him.

Vito moved around me, pinning the waist and highlighting my curves. I'd never looked so beautiful. The back was completely open, as was the still-unpinned cleavage. I couldn't wait to see what it would be like when it was done. As soon as I thought that, shame filled me.

Well done, Charlie. You're like the lamb who can't wait to see what the butcher's knife feels like. This isn't a wedding gown, it's a pearl-and-lace jumpsuit for a lifer. It's just white instead of orange. Get a fucking grip.

Then Giada spoke, and all fluffy, romantic thoughts vanished from my mind. "Hey, when you send an email, do you go by Charlie or Charlotte?"

"Charlotte. Why?"

Giada nodded and tapped at her laptop, and soon the sound of an email zooming off into hyperspace chimed.

"What did you just send?" I demanded and pushed Vito's hand away, twisting to look at her.

"Your resignation from the hospital and your degree program."

"What?" It was a sudden punch in the gut. "Why?"

Giada shrugged like it didn't interest her in the slightest. "Boss's orders."

"Boss's orders?" I repeated, my voice shrill. *"Boss's orders?"* I nearly shouted.

Giada nodded. "If you don't like it, take it up with Ren."

Something inside me snapped. It was my sense of caution and self-preservation. Turned out, you could only push someone so far until you found their breaking point. I'd just found mine.

"Fine. I will," I ground out, clenching my teeth so hard I tasted metal.

Then I spun on my heel, anger and frustration building inside me like a volcano about to blow, and stormed out of the room.

Sonny struggled to keep up with me as I strode through the house.

"The boss is in a meeting," he warned me as I closed in on Renato's study, the only off-limits room in the house.

"I don't care," I fumed.

He stepped in front of the door.

"What? Are you under instructions to carry me off if I try and disturb His Majesty?"

Sonny snorted. "Fuck, no. I'm not to touch you under any circumstances."

"Oh, really? That's good to know." I advanced on him, and he jumped back to avoid touching me. Triumphantly, I reached for the doors and pushed them open.

"Good luck," Sonny murmured and ducked out from behind me.

Seven men sat around a long rectangular table, with Renato at its head.

A few flinched at the sound of the doors crashing open, and one reached for his piece and then stopped himself. Of course, no one drew a weapon in Renato's presence without his permission. The man really got off on controlling others.

"Charlotte. To what do we owe the pleasure?" Renato purred. He didn't look annoyed by my sudden entrance.

I folded my arms, and his gaze dropped to my chest. Anger sparked suddenly, and his faint bemusement morphed instantly to fury.

"Leave us."

The word had hardly left his lips before the men assembled were scrambling to leave the room. I met his fiery gaze throughout the scraping of chairs and general air of fluster while the room emptied.

The door closed behind the last man, and we were alone. Nerves prickled along my spine at Renato's dark look. My courage, born of righteous anger, was deserting me now, when I needed it the most.

He stood slowly, smoothing a hand through his dark waves, the veins rippling in his strong forearm. Why did he have his sleeves rolled up? Didn't he know what that did to innocent bystanders? He probably did and enjoyed it. He was a sadist, clearly.

"Before you start your tirade on your latest issue with your situation, let me be clear." He strolled to me and then reached out a hand to my half-sewn bodice.

I jerked with surprise when his finger landed on the curve of my breast. Not on the material of the dress, on my skin.

Gasping, I glanced downward. My reckless movements had unpinned the edges of the gown, and my breasts threatened to spill free. My nipples were barely covered, the inside curves of both tits on display, with the rest pressing dangerously close to escaping.

Renato's tanned hand was huge and shocking against the pale curve of my tit. It was just so male, and held such an aura of restrained violence, I couldn't look away. His finger traveled over the plump swell, slipping under the curve, somehow kneading me with one finger. Better than anything I'd ever felt before.

Then his hand drew the material closed over my exposed skin, his fingers brushing over my straining nipples. *Fuck,* my nipples were hard little stones beneath his accidental touch. Needy, wanton, and blithely oblivious to the fact that I shouldn't be turned on by this man. *This monster,* my mind reminded me. But it was too late for my body. It was desperate for more.

"You will not walk around this house in such a state of undress. You will not let any man here, except me, your husband, see what lies beneath your clothes, or you'll suffer the consequences."

My mouth had gone dry as hell. "What consequences?"

"You'll find out if you don't listen to my warning, *bambina*. I don't allow threats in my presence, and that includes all this." He slid a hand from the neckline of my gown down to my waist.

"My body? It's hardly a lethal weapon," I muttered, squirming on the spot. I needed to cross my legs or find some way to relieve the pooling heat gathering between them. He was making me wet, and he was barely even touching me. What dark sorcery was this?

"That's for me to decide. Remember, my house, my rules. Now, what brings you here, half-dressed and ready to kill?"

He released his grip on my gown, and I hurriedly pulled the gaping bodice together, straightening my back and trying to locate a lucid thought.

"My job. The psycho you have working for you just told me that, apparently, I'm quitting my job and nursing program?"

Renato moved to the window beside his desk and looked out, hiding his face from me. "Yes, of course you are. What's the problem?"

I swallowed the hurt from his callous tone. "I've worked for years to become a nurse. It's all I've ever wanted."

"I think your life has taken you far from what you wanted by now, hasn't it? Surely you can't think I'd let you travel to the shore every single day to be out of the house from dawn till dusk. I might have extended you mercy, Charlotte, but don't push it."

"So what? I'm just supposed to stay in this house all the time, lounging around . . . waiting to die one day?"

"You can treat the De Sanctis men who are hurt. Let me assure you, they're in constant supply."

"You can't possibly think that's the same? Working at a hospital helping people, or patching up mobsters in a dungeon?"

"Are their lives worth less than other people's?" Renato challenged, turning to watch my reaction. "Is their pain and suffering less valid? Do their families care less if they die?"

"You're twisting my words," I ground out.

"Maybe you're using the wrong words," Renato responded quietly.

I took a deep breath. "Okay, fine. Being a nurse and working in a big hospital has always been my dream. You're killing my dream. Does that make more sense to you?"

Renato thought for a second, his eyebrows drawing together. *Christ,* the man was handsome.

After an excruciating pause, he spoke. "You once asked me if I believed in God. Do you?"

The crucifix on the wall stared down at us, judging my thoughts. "It's not a case of whether or not I believe in God. God has never believed in me," I finally said when his inspection became too much.

"Poetically put." He nodded appreciatively at me before continuing. "But I think you have more faith than you realize. You have faith that challenging me like this won't get you killed. You have faith that telling me your dreams, and begging me not to kill them, will move me . . ."

"I'm not begging."

"Aren't you?" He stalked toward me.

I fought the urge to back up.

"You are a burning ball of contradictions, *anima mia.* You keep me guessing what you'll do next. You have a whole lot of faith, even if you don't realize it."

"I don't—" I attempted.

He reached out and touched my cheek, robbing me of words. The back of his finger smoothed over the apple of my cheek. "You have faith that I can be a better man than I've ever proved myself to be, and I don't know which one of us is the greater fool . . . you for believing, or me . . . for even considering it."

He stared into my eyes, so intense, one wrong move would blow us both apart. We were a powder keg and a match, desperate to meet.

His fingers slid up my cheek and pushed my hair behind my ear. "If you believe in God, which I'm sure you do, somewhere deep down inside, then know this . . ." He leaned in as he spoke, putting his lips to my ear. His warm breath sent shivers across my skin. "He gave you to me. We were destined to meet. Fate has woven us together, and those threads can never be untangled. God wanted me to have you . . . and now that I do, I'll never give you back."

I swayed, suddenly weak in the knees. Was it fear sending a gale of heat through me, followed by an icy shiver? Everything in my body tingled, heightened by his deep murmur and the utter blasphemy of his words. He was crazy, and yet his voice murmuring in my ear was the hottest thing that had ever happened to me.

Maybe I was more broken than I'd ever realized.

He stayed there for a long moment, his lips resting on my skin. If I turned my head, my mouth would meet his.

I waited.

He waited.

I didn't move.

Gradually, he drew back. "I'll think about your points, and you think of why I should allow it." A smirk passed over his insufferably handsome lips. "Maybe you can convince me."

His dry tone was laced with amusement, like my pain and suffering were fun for him. And what response did his mocking give me? Wet panties and a pounding heart. Hard nipples that I wished he'd take between his teeth.

"I hate you, you know that?"

"No, little nurse, I don't think you do, and that bothers you more than anything."

I pushed back from him, and he let me.

"I do hate you, and one day, you'll get everything you deserve. I might have a complicated relationship with God, but I believe in karma. In the end, you'll burn for your sins," I said quietly but full of conviction.

He stared at me for a few beats before nodding. "Amen. Now, get out of here before I change my mind about letting you leave."

My courage all spent, I took his advice and left, feeling his eyes on my naked back the whole way.

16

CHARLIE

"I can't believe the prisoner is getting out for the day. How exciting," I grumbled, staring out the window of the bulletproof SUV currently driving along the A.C. strip, heading to Vito's dress shop in La Leonora. I was being sarcastic, but honestly, being out in the fresh air and off Casa Nera grounds was pretty exciting.

Giada laughed. She sat next to me on the back seat. Her brother drove, and Sonny sat in the passenger seat.

"Well, if you make a break for it, I'll be sure to tell your sister you abandoned her myself," Giada murmured.

Like I needed the reminder that Lucy was locked up in Casa Nera while I was here. Even if I could escape, there was no way I could get Lucy out, so that was a no-go.

Rain hit the windows, and the wiper scraped the glass. Fall was sliding into winter, and normally, I'd be enjoying the decorations that were starting to go up and the air of excitement that filled the air. Christmas cheer was free, after all, and I loved it.

"This is stupid. I don't need a designer dress. Who's even attending this farce? What a waste of time."

"While I share your sentiments about weddings, I'm tired of hearing you complain, so shut the fuck up," Giada snapped. "You don't have to remind everyone that this is against your will with every breath. I'm starting to wonder who you're trying to convince."

I rolled my eyes at her but dropped it. I was tired of complaining, too. It wasn't going to help me, clearly.

We got out at the back of the casino and went inside. Giada looped her arm through mine, and Sonny and Elio followed closely behind.

Vito's shop was lavish and stuffed full of extremely ornate, over-the-top dresses. His style seemed to be based on the "more is more" principle of design.

His assistant led me down a long corridor toward the dressing room while my disreputable-looking entourage sat in the waiting room. Vito wouldn't allow them to get too close to the dresses.

I stepped into the room and the assistant drew back a curtain, revealing the half-finished dress and a set of underwear that had my eyes popping out of my head.

The underwear in question consisted of a white bodysuit that reminded me of a corset, with elegant boning to nip my waist in, a garter belt hanging from the bottom edge, and transparent lace that left absolutely nothing to the imagination. It was all cobwebs of handsewn lace, satin straps, and embroidery. It probably cost more than my old apartment's monthly rent.

The assistant left, and I sank down on the pink velvet chaise longue. I stared at my reflection for a long time. My St. Anthony medal shone in the changing room lights.

Are you a lost thing, bambina?

I've always been lost.

Did I still feel lost? Everything I'd built for myself had come crashing down, and I was just trying to survive through it and come out the other side somehow. *I'm starting to wonder who you're trying to convince.*

A soft tapping sound stole my attention from my spiraling thoughts.

I glanced around. It didn't seem to be coming from the doorway. The sound continued. I got to my feet slowly, nerves jumping to high alert.

One wall had a gauzy curtain over it, and others were painted eggshell white, without even a window to tap on. I went to the curtain and drew it back.

Shock froze me to the spot.

There was not only a window there, but a glass wall with a set of French doors leading out to a tiny courtyard, with a chair and table. The courtyard butted up against a parking lot and a row of garbage bins. More shocking was the two people who stood in the courtyard, watching me.

Detectives Vane and Whitely. My heart all but leapt into my mouth, and my mind went completely blank.

Whitely pointed down at the door handle. There was a key inside the lock on my side. I turned it with a trembling hand. Cold air hit my face when I pushed it open.

"Miss Burke. Are you okay?" Whitely asked.

"I-I don't know what you mean," I started slowly.

Detective Vane tutted and clapped a hand on my wrist, tugging me out into the drizzle. "We don't have time for you to gape like a goldfish. We can help you, but you need to listen, now."

"Help me?" I repeated. Part of me was screaming to tell them every single thing and fall into their protective arms. Maybe they could save us. Maybe they could send Renato and all his men to prison so Lucy and I could go back home.

Maybe . . . Maybe not.

More likely, the dark malicious king of Casa Nera would rip

me from their hands and punish me even more for breaking my promises again.

"Yes, help you. Well, you help us first, and then we'll help you."

"I don't get it. What's going on?" I tried to make my brain catch up with everything that was happening.

"We know that De Sanctis got to you. We know what he's forcing you to do."

"Are you offering to take me and Lucy away from him?"

Detective Vane scoffed. "I'm flattered that you think we could. No, in fact, this whole situation is an opportunity, and one we can't afford to let pass us by."

Whitely jumped in. "You're going to be up close and personal with the boss. In his home, around his most trusted men. You can be our eyes and ears. You can bring him down."

"What? Are you asking me to spy on him?"

"Exactly. Be our inside person, the one with access to the big boss, and in return, when he goes down, we'll make sure nothing bad happens to you or your sister." Whitely looked earnest as he spoke.

"How will you make sure of that?"

"Don't worry about that. Just know that we'll keep you and Lucy safe." Whitely sounded like he believed it, but when it came down to the might of the De Sanctis family, or the cops, I knew who *I* believed in.

"I don't trust you," I told them after a moment. "I don't want anything to do with this."

Detective Vane gave me a chilling smile. "You don't really have a choice, Charlie. If you want your sister to stay out of jail, you'll do this."

"Excuse me?" I demanded.

"Did you know her little boyfriend, Miguel, showed up? Well, his body, anyway. He was executed, and the last person he was seen with was your sister."

"You think my nineteen-year-old sister executed someone?"

"It doesn't matter what I think. It matters what a jury thinks. We've got the body, we've got a witness putting them together, and I heard that his family is searching for him, or at least, for whoever hurt him . . . It doesn't matter who gets to her, cops or Castillos. She's in big trouble."

"You're unbelievable! You're not here to help me at all, are you? You're just vampires looking to suck the blood out of an unfortunate victim."

"We hold the line between good and evil in this city, Miss Burke. Or maybe your allegiance has already shifted. Fell in love with the bad guy, did you? How predictable," Detective Vane sneered.

"Dolores, please!" Whitely snapped at his partner. He turned back to me. "We're telling you this about your sister not as a threat, but a warning. Things are in motion that you don't know about. You need to do this while you can. Get the evidence, get us our own eyes and ears inside Casa Nera, and then we'll guarantee your safety."

I shook my head wildly. "No. I'm not doing it. I'm not endangering myself and my sister more for your case. If you could easily take down Renato, you would have already done it."

"We *will* do it, with your help. We're not asking, Charlie. Unless you want your sister arrested within the next few hours . . . you'll do this." Detective Vane pressed an envelope into my hand. "Plant this in Renato's office before lunchtime tomorrow, or we'll take it to mean that you're not going to help, and that means you're our enemy."

"Tomorrow?" I protested, trying to shove the envelope back to her.

She refused to take it. "Tomorrow, and just remember that we could drop by Casa Nera anytime to arrest Lucy and tell Renato you're cooperating with us. Let's see who he believes."

She waited a moment for her points to sink in and then shoved me back through the door, jerking her head in the direction of the waiting room.

"Now get your ass into that dress before the psychopaths outside realize you're taking too long."

When I got back to Casa Nera, I was numb. I'd reached my limit on being threatened from all directions. Lucy watched TV with Carmella in the den. Her evenings with Carmella were the only times she voluntarily left her room. She seemed to have a soft spot for the gruff housekeeper.

I went to the kitchen, foraging for something to stress-eat. Sonny watched me silently as I grabbed a box of fancy chocolates and a tub of leftover pasta. I took my haul upstairs, waving to Carmella and Lucy as I headed toward our room to eat my sorrows away.

Once alone, I fished out the envelope Detective Vane had given me from my bra and opened it. A tiny electronic device the size of my pinkie nail stared up at me. A bug, just like in the movies.

I could have laughed if I wasn't so close to tears. They wanted me to plant this somewhere near Renato, to spy on him. A hysterical laugh escaped me at the thought of mercurial Renato finding out about a betrayal like this. Mr. Don't Lie to Me Ever. Mr. Don't Break My Rules or You'll Regret It. The cops wanted me to commit suicide by angry mob boss, and I had no idea what to do about it.

I changed into the silky cami and tiny pajama shorts Carmella had found me. I still didn't have much to wear, seeing as we'd left our bags on the bus the night of our ill-fated escape attempt.

The Casa Nera housekeeper's taste tended to run a little too romantic and skimpy for my liking, but beggars couldn't be choosers.

Before I knew it, the chocolate was gone and the pasta, too. My belly was full, and I needed to move. I needed out of this room. I tried the door handle, and it turned easily again. Lucy hadn't come back. Sometimes she fell asleep in the den downstairs, and Vinny simply kept an eye on her there. Renato's prisoner security was flexible, I'd give him that.

Outside the bedroom, my own guard, Sonny, sat on a folding chair, his head back against the wall, sound asleep. It was late now, and the house was sleeping. So, there were some cracks in Renato's security systems after all.

I closed the door and tiptoed away from Sonny.

The mansion was warm inside. Rain pelted against the windowpanes on the landing, the shutters rattling forcefully in the wind. Inside Casa Nera, the air was cozy. In our apartment in Atlantic City, the weather outside equaled the climate inside. We had leaks and drafts in the winter and humid, hellish heat in the summer. That was just the reality of living in a five-floor walk-up with no A/C and busted heating.

My bare feet sank into the thick dark carpet as I quietly crept down the hall.

I headed downstairs. A grandfather clock ticked loudly in the main hallway. I decided to go in the other direction from the kitchen. I hadn't explored much of the rest of the house, but I knew there was a gym and a pool. At the very thought, my entire body hungered to be submerged in clean, cool water. I couldn't actually swim very well at all, but I wasn't scared of water, as long as I could touch the bottom.

Was it weird to go poking around at night and skinny-dip in someone's pool? Maybe. But this whole thing was weird. Normal had lost its meaning. It didn't matter anymore. There was only what was real, and Casa Nera was painfully real.

I followed a set of stairs down to the next level. At the bottom,

I was greeted by a well-lit hallway and the faint smell of chlorine. The low-level lighting lit my path as I continued forward.

A gym sat on one side behind a glass wall. It was an impressive sight. I guessed if you had all the money in the world, what else did you spend it on? Might as well have a full gym in your mansion. There was also a full-size boxing ring sitting in the middle. The place was deserted, giving me confidence that no one would venture down here at this hour.

I veered to the right, toward the faint perfume of chemicals. I'd always wanted to learn how to swim, but it was time-consuming and expensive. Lucy had been spot-on in her harsh accusations the other night. All I did was work, and I was a joyless person. Someone who had learned how to survive and didn't have space for anything else.

I turned a corner, pushed through double doors, and found it. A swimming pool. It was as beautifully styled as the rest of the house, though I didn't know why I expected anything less of Renato De Sanctis. The man had shown himself to have impeccable taste. He had the air of a well-traveled, experienced man who was effortlessly in control, always. He was measured, cool and calm, and instinctively dominant in every situation I'd seen him in.

He was a lot, and so was his house. It was such an extension of the confident older man, that just by me wandering around, the thought of him lingered in my head. Really, my haywire brain was taking any opportunity to shove him to the forefront of my thoughts.

The room was pale sandstone with citrus plants spaced around the walls. It was more of an orangery than simply a pool. Beneath the blue water, an artistic mosaic was embedded in the floor, and at the far end of the room, a fountain trickled.

I walked toward the steps before I could question it. I just needed to feel the water on my feet for a second, I promised myself.

The steps descended gently into the aqua-blue water. The first touch revealed it was warmed to exactly the right temperature.

I stepped down another stair and enjoyed the way the water swirled around my ankles. I ventured farther in. I wanted nothing more than to strip down to my underwear and submerge myself completely, but that would be a bad idea, considering I had no idea who might visit this pool. Was this house off-limits to lower-level made men in the family and only open to those closest to the boss? Elio said he and his sister lived here, but were there others? I had no idea, and frankly, at this point, I might prefer a random stranger stumbling across me than Renato himself. That man was a danger to my sanity.

The lemon-and-orange-scented air was humid, making the fine hairs that had escaped my ponytail stick to my neck and forehead.

A blurred shape moved out of the corner of my eye, calling my attention. The frosted glass wall that separated the hallway from the pool was translucent enough for me to make out a tall figure moving rapidly alongside it, right toward the pool doorway. My moment of peace burst like a bubble.

Crap! Someone was coming after all. Who was it? Please be Sonny, looking for me. Please be Elio coming for a midnight dip. Please be anyone but *him*.

I turned quickly and took a step upward. Maybe I could get out and hide behind a potted lemon tree until whoever it was left? It was a ridiculous plan, but in the heat of the moment, and feeling like I was doing something forbidden, it made sense.

I looked up when the door started to open, with only one more submerged step left to go.

And that was my downfall. Literally.

My foot slipped off the smoothly curved marble step, and I fell backward. I registered a dark shape coming through the doors just as I flew back and hit the water with a hard smack. The cool water rushed over my head, flooding my nose and open mouth.

The water hit my lungs, and I convulsed. *Goddamn it.* In my panic, I sucked down liquid like someone with a death wish.

Arms wrapped around me as I thrashed and flailed in the water, my limbs flapping wildly beneath the surface.

"Stop fighting me, Charlotte! I'm trying to help you, for fuck's sake." Renato's voice was a deep growl. Of course it would be him. The devil himself. *Of course.*

He held me against his body, his arms tight around my middle. I coughed relentlessly, hacking up all the water I'd swallowed. The one silver lining was that I didn't need mouth to mouth.

He carried me to the edge of the pool, and I rested my hands on the curved lip, my breath coming in pants as my lungs worked to expel every last drop of water.

Renato kept one arm wrapped around me and moved the other to my hair, stroking my wet strands. It was soothing as hell. "You're okay, *bambina.* I've got you," he murmured quietly.

I swallowed hard and stared straight ahead. His body drifted against mine in the water.

"I'm fine from here, thanks." My voice was a rasp.

"Are you?" he asked, and after a moment, his arm fell away.

I wasn't ready for it and immediately went under. My flailing had forced us into the deep end of the pool. I couldn't touch the bottom, and my hands lost their grip on the edge.

I sank like a stone, my body sliding down Renato's, just as his hands landed under my arms and he yanked me up.

"*Cristo,* can't you swim?" he demanded when I resurfaced and grasped desperately on to the ledge, harder this time.

Renato turned me to face him, pressing his body into mine to keep me above water. The man was in a white shirt, and it was completely see-through. I could see tattoos through the translucent material. His dark waves were slicked back with water, and clear beads dotted his olive skin and caught in his dark lashes. It was criminal how good he looked, which was fitting, I supposed.

I shook my head slowly, trying desperately to calm my racing heart.

"If you can't swim, then why were you down here, alone at night? If I hadn't come along . . ." he started.

"If you hadn't come along, I wouldn't have fallen," I protested hotly.

He stared at me for a long moment and then shook his head. "*Ora sai come ci si sente.*"

"And what does that mean?"

He simply shrugged. "Better learn Italian if you want to understand your husband."

Something moved inside me at the way he'd said the last word. *Husband*. It was nearly a growl, and my insides squirmed.

"And I'm supposed to believe you want me to understand you?"

"Everyone wants to be understood by someone. Everyone wants to be seen by someone, don't they, Charlotte? Even you."

His face was so beautiful wet, it was distracting as hell.

I shook my head stubbornly. "I don't want to be seen by you."

"Then why are you wandering around here at night? Who were you hoping to run into?"

"No one!" My voice was nearly a squeak. If it was weird to be having this conversation, with his body pinning mine to the pool wall, I forgot. There was something calming about his presence. Like nothing bad could happen to me when he was there. *Well, duh, that's because it already happened,* my subconscious reminded me.

His mouth stretched into an arrogant grin. "No one. Of course not. You barge into my meeting half-dressed, looking like the forbidden ingenue, and trust me not to bend you over my desk and have my wicked way with you. You swallow my fingers like a good girl and get offended if I point out how wet you are. You talk back to me, disagree with me, tell me you hate me, and then you cling to me when I kiss you."

I opened my mouth to clarify, but there were no words there. He seemed to sense my confusion, a triumphant smile flickering across his lips.

"You want to be seen by me. You like how it feels when I cross all the lines you've been taught to fear. You like the way it makes you feel when I touch you. How long are you going to fight me, little nurse?"

Then he leaned in and kissed me. There was nothing soft or gentle about his kiss. Nothing hesitant or unsure. He was a man who took whatever the hell he wanted, and right now, he wanted to kiss me breathless—and he did just that.

His lips slammed against mine, his tongue stroking along the seam of my mouth before ruthlessly plunging inside. I briefly tried to push him back out of pure instinct, like if a tiger suddenly licked your hand and you weren't sure if it was going to eat you or not.

My struggle went exactly nowhere, and I soon realized he wasn't going to eat me. But I secretly wished he would.

I stopped fighting against him and pulled him closer. He wrapped my floating legs around his waist and pushed me into the tile behind me, grinding his hips against mine. A long, thick hardness pushed up at my center, pressing against my pussy. I could feel every roll of his hips and nudge of his cock through my flimsy pajama shorts.

His tongue moved along mine, making me shake. He was so hot, burning me up everywhere he touched. His mouth was warm and wet, and his skin blazed against mine through his soaked shirt. He ground his hard-on in circles between my open legs, right against my clit, and pleasure flooded me. One hand held me up under my ass, while the other rose to my throat. He gripped me by the neck, tilting my head back so he could devour me more thoroughly, his tongue plunging in and out of my mouth in long, drugging kisses that made my head spin.

Every rock of his hips sent pleasure skyrocketing through me. A peak grew inside me. Holy hell, I was gonna come just from being dry humped by this man.

"Stop—I can't. I'm going to . . ." I panted out in a whisper. My words were at odds with how tightly I held on to him.

"You're going to come, and there's nothing you can do about it, *anima mia*," he growled in my ear before taking the lobe in his mouth and sucking on it, a feeling that shot a straight, liquid pulse of pleasure right between my legs.

"There's nothing wrong about coming for your husband. There's nothing wrong with what you're feeling. You're going to come for me, and it's only going to keep happening, so get used to the idea."

His hand moved from my neck as my head tipped forward to rest on his shoulder. He was right; I was definitely going to come, and there was nothing that could stop it. I was so sensitive, shuddering on a precipice, and there was no escape.

He took my wet ponytail in his hand and pulled my head back so my glazed eyes met his.

"You're going to come and let me see it. I want to see every single part of you unraveling, *bambina*," he demanded, staring right in my face, his dark eyes drinking up the pleasure etched across my features. "Don't try to hide . . . I'll only find you. You already know that."

I stiffened, a harsher drag of his engorged cock hitting my swollen clit just right. *It's just nerve endings, remember, Charlotte?*

It seemed laughable to think of sex that way as Renato drove me toward a knee-shaking climax. It wasn't just nerve endings and hormones; it was so much more.

I came hard, my whole body collapsing forward and spasming so firmly I bit my goddamn tongue. Renato stared at me as my lips parted and his name left me on an uncontrollable gasp. The moan that escaped me sounded nothing like me at all. It was completely foreign. I had the sudden idea that there was a whole side of myself that I had ignored and denied, a part just dying to be set free.

This man freed it, whether I wanted him to or not.

Renato watched me as I came, not missing a single detail. He never stopped moving against me, the water furiously lapping against our chests, until the pressure of his unrelenting hardness became too much to take and I flopped into his arms, all pretense at holding myself up gone.

"*Brava,* Charlotte. You did so well. You're perfect, just perfect," he muttered, pressing kisses along my jaw.

I was floating, not just physically, but mentally, too, until he kissed my neck and bit at the chain of my St. Anthony medal. "You're not lost anymore, *bambina*. I've found you, and I'm keeping you," he murmured against my skin.

I stiffened, reality crashing in. *What the hell was I doing?*

I pushed away from him and nearly went underwater again. Grabbing on to the ledge, I pulled my way along the side of the pool, feeling like a bedraggled cat desperate to reach dry land.

Renato simply watched me until I was struggling up the steps. My satin pj's clung to me like a second skin, the shorts rucked up, revealing my ass cheeks. I could feel his eyes on me as I sloshed up the steps.

"I never gave you permission to leave, little nurse, nor did you ask for it."

"I have to get back to Lucy," I stammered—a lie, and we both knew it. I froze on the warm tile. I really didn't know if this man would drag me back if I attempted to leave without his permission. Worse still was the part of me that wondered what he would do next. I was sick in the head. There was something wrong with me.

He didn't let me leave but changed the subject. "How is your sister?"

His sudden question threw me and I turned around to face him. "She's okay. Quiet. Upset, no, devastated at the wedding news. So, a pretty normal reaction." I put my wet hands on my burning cheeks.

"Yet your reaction is far from normal by that definition," Renato pointed out. He was so damn close, I could see flecks of gold in his rich, brown eyes.

My laugh sounded bitter. "You only think that because you don't really know me," I started.

"Don't I? Charlotte Elizabeth Burke, daughter of Mary and John Burke, both deceased, grew up between the ages of thirteen and eighteen at Mercy House Children's Home. Only sibling is Lucy Elizabeth Burke."

"Stop! Don't." I was breathless as he recited the tragedies of my past.

"Don't what?"

"Don't make me even more afraid of you."

Renato's eyes sharpened on me, like he was pouncing on a weakness. "Are you really afraid of me, Charlotte? The things you say to me, the way you act . . . it doesn't match that sentiment."

"And what makes you think that? You won't be my husband, you'll only ever be my jailer—"

"If I was your jailer, I'd have you tied to the wall in the basement. I'm not a merciful man. Nothing about what's between us is normal—not for me, and I'll bet not for you, either. You can't pretend that you don't feel it forever, little nurse. I won't let you."

I crossed my arms over my wet top. "I would have to be crazy not to be scared, wouldn't I?" My tone was so uncertain.

"Are you asking me or telling me?" Renato asked, smoothing a hand through his wet hair, watching me from the water.

"I-I have to get to bed. I should never have come down here. I didn't mean to run into you," I said, wringing out my hair and nervously looking around, panic beating at me from within.

"I checked for you in your room before I came here, so you had no choice but to run into me," Renato said quietly.

"Why?" I asked, cotton-mouthed.

"Because I can't seem to stay away."

Those words only sent my leaping pulse higher. Why was his soft confession making my heart pound so hard? He was staring at me like I was someone important to him.

Someone special.

No one had ever looked at me that way.

Then I remembered the bug in the envelope upstairs. He wouldn't look at me that way if he knew what I was planning on doing.

"You should let us go. Just let us go. It's the best outcome for everyone," I muttered, my energy deserting me all at once. I was so tired I could barely keep my eyes open.

My rising emotions fizzled out flatly, the excitement in my veins from my first orgasm at someone else's hand dying abruptly.

I didn't stay to listen to another word. I turned on my heel and hurried back to my room, not daring to look back even once.

17

RENATO

"The details on the car accident with Paolo," Elio said, bright and early the next morning.

I'd spent the night reliving the moment in the pool. Specifically, the exact moment Charlotte had come in my arms, her pussy rubbing relentlessly over my cock, while I stood and did my best to hold on to my flagging self-control. In that moment, I'd wanted to sit her on the edge of the pool and eat her sweet pussy for hours. Teach her all about proper fucking before getting out and ravaging her right there on the wet tile. An animal tearing at an angel, marking her as his.

Instead, I'd let the desire simmer and sink into my soul. I didn't even jerk off, even though I was desperately hard and my balls were so full they ached.

When Charlotte gazed up at me with her beguiling eyes and moaned my name, I'd decided right then that I'd wait for my wife's touch. The next time I came, it would be wrapped up in a body part of hers, whether it be her hand, mouth, cunt, or ass. I would accept nothing less.

I studied the black-and-white CCTV shots that Elio had

pulled. He then placed a tablet in front of me and hit play. Paolo's car came into sight. He headed in the direction of Casa Nera.

Out of nowhere, a car appeared from the left and slammed into him.

Both cars spun with the impact. After a moment, Paolo's car door opened, and he fell out. He hauled himself to his feet and fired a shot at a couple of dark shadows I couldn't make out, lingering beside the other busted wreck. One shadow fell, and the one left standing dragged it off the screen. Then came the sound of screeching wheels. Another vehicle.

"They took their man," Elio said emotionlessly.

"And left mine to die, alone on the street like roadkill," I muttered darkly. The sooner I stamped out the Castillos, the better. I'd allowed them too much grace, hoping they'd understand how stupid it was to continue their business under my nose, in my town, but it looked like they were too dumb for that.

"They're searching for the Burke sisters. They want to settle the score of the boy."

"Is that really all they want? I can't help but think they want more than that. They want to provoke us, and the question is, why now? We've been killing them off for months. Why are they escalating now?"

"Maybe they smell an opportunity. There's a dead body and a witness who can point the finger at the family."

I nodded. "Exactly. It seems like someone smarter has taken over Castillo operations. They might be emerging as a real threat, and we don't take real threats lightly."

"I'll step up surveillance on their areas. Maybe we can get a face for this new mastermind."

"Once we do, we stop holding back. How are the other plans coming?"

Elio sighed. "If you're asking how your fiancée handled her

dress fitting, badly would be the answer. I don't think you're going to have a smiling, blushing bride tomorrow. It probably wasn't a good idea to invite so many prominent people."

"When the head of the family gets married, everyone should know. Take plenty of pictures for Salvatore to frame back in Napoli."

Elio chuckled. "If you're planning on long wedding toasts, I'd dial it down. She might actually stab you."

I nodded. "She might, but then she'd be the one responsible for patching me up, so I'm sure she wouldn't do anything too terrible. She values human life too much."

"Even yours?"

"I'm willing to bet my life on it."

Elio grinned. "Literally, in this case."

"How are the renovations coming?"

He grimaced. "The nursery is proving tough. It could use a woman's touch. This house doesn't exactly lend itself to baby colors."

"Get Carmella's help. And the master suite?"

"The walk-in closet is done, and the bathroom."

"Very good. You know, if this gangster thing doesn't work out, you can always take up a side gig as a contractor."

"With all due respect, fuck you."

"Apologies. You know I'll never let you work a side hustle. We're too old for that. What about the other thing? The college thing?"

Elio blew out a long breath. "Giada inquired. Apparently, she can change her program into a full-time one, even at this late stage, and finish it up quickly. After that, she'll be placed in a hospital. Giada can make sure she ends up at St. Roberta's, not far from here. Twenty minutes max."

"Okay. You can go." I turned to my laptop and opened the lid.

Elio headed for the door. He paused on the threshold. "You're in a good mood today," he observed.

"Am I?"

He was quiet for a moment, and his tone was curious when he broke the silence. "Are you really going to let her finish school?"

I shrugged. "Why not? She's a capable, intelligent woman. Why deny the world that? As long as she's coming home to me, I don't care. And as long as she works with a protection detail in the hospital, then what's the harm?"

My mother's face ran through my mind. She'd had so much to give, and instead she'd wasted away. The world had been darker without her light. My life had been darker. My sister, too, an artist who had nearly faded away in the jail-like environment my father had fostered in Casa Nera. A little bird with clipped wings, flapping in her cage but never breaking free, not until she'd met a man who would have died to set her free. A man who had broken every single rule there was to save her. My brother-in-law was a lot of things, but no one in their right mind could deny his devotion. I understood him better than I'd ever understood my father.

When something was precious, you took care of it, and people were the most precious, irreplaceable things of all.

Elio frowned at me. "If I didn't know any better, I'd think you were actually falling for this woman and not just solving a problem."

"Psychoanalyze me on your own time. Get back to work."

18

CHARLIE

I woke with a pounding headache and fear churning in my gut.

The bug.

I had to plant it today. I lay in bed for a long moment. At some point, Lucy had made it back to our room. She was snuggled under the covers, facing me. I studied her sleeping face. What was I going to do? It was bad enough being forced to marry into this family, but now, the police were pushing me into betraying them, too.

Soon enough, I'd have a target on my back so big it would be visible from space. Just like the rat in the maze I'd always been, I could see that the walls were finally closing in, and the exits were barred.

Detective Vane had been clear. Plant the bug before lunchtime today, or they'd come and arrest Lucy. She wasn't stable enough to stay quiet during an interrogation. She'd break; she was already bursting at the seams, barely holding it all in. She'd crack and tell the truth, and Renato would take her out.

My father's rosary beads were wrapped around her fist. I stared at the round beads and touched one with the tip of my finger. Lucy shifted, and the entire chain fell into my hand.

I got up quietly, washed my face, and pulled on a borrowed oversize sweater and leggings. I wrapped the rosary around my wrist for good luck. Then I took the tiny bug from the envelope, clutched it carefully in my palm, and made for the doorway.

I'd gotten Sonny off my tail by sending him to the kitchen for a needle and thread. I couldn't think of anything else on the fly. Since I was sure Carmella would be hot on it, I had to move fast.

I stood outside Renato's office where it connected with the library, my heart pounding loudly in my ears. Since I had free access to the library, being caught there would be far less damning than being caught in the office. I knocked quietly, hoping against hope there wasn't anyone inside browsing for a book.

No one answered. For once, luck was on my side. I pushed open the door and peeked around the side. The long room was empty. I stepped inside and shut the door.

The double doors that led to Renato's study stood open. Just the sight of the room transported me back to the first night I'd met the boss of the De Sanctis family. There was a different rug in there now, and no sign of the men who had died there. I felt no sadness for them, and maybe that made me just as much of a monster as Renato, but it was their rash actions that had put us here, in part. I'd never mourn them.

I headed through the connecting doors to the study. Where should a bug go? Near a phone, maybe, or somewhere people would be talking. Did I even care about finding the best place? No. I didn't. All Detective Vane said was I had to plant it. She didn't say where.

I headed toward Renato's desk. It didn't have a lot on it, and there were no easy places to put the bug where it wouldn't stand out. A plant sat on the corner of the desk, and before I could overthink it, I dropped the bug into its soil. It seemed to disappear in the dirt.

There. I did it.

"Charlotte?" Renato's voice spoke from just behind me.

I whirled around, my ass coming to rest on his desk.

Crap. In my haste, I hadn't noticed that the floor-to-ceiling door leading from the library to an outside patio area was ajar. He must have been out there the whole time. Had he seen anything?

"I-I was looking for you," I said. My mind was drawing a blank about what to say. How could I explain being here?

"Were you?" Renato asked, approaching. He had a cashmere sweater on, and the V-neck revealed the golden skin of his collarbones. With his dark waves pushed off his forehead, and his sweater sleeves rolled back to his elbows, he was the picture of effortless elegance with a lethal edge. It was a lot to handle so early in the morning.

"Yes, I—"

My words died as he reached the desk and peered down at the place he'd caught me leaning over. The goddamn plant. He was going to see the bug.

"I was thinking about the other night," I blurted.

He looked curious, but it wasn't enough to distract him from his mission. He headed toward the other side of the table, getting closer to the bug.

I panicked and reached up to touch his face. He immediately stilled. His cheek was chiseled under my palm and I allowed myself the indulgence of sliding my fingers over his stubble. The raspy feel sent a liquid heat pooling deep in my belly.

His eyes snapped to mine, and his expression was burning. "Is that right?" He made no effort to move my hand from its intimate position, cradling his cheek. He moved his arms to either side of me on the desk, caging me in.

It dawned on me, dimly, that I might have jumped from the frying pan into the fire, but there wasn't anything I could do about it now.

"And what exactly were you thinking about?"

"My nursing program. You said to convince you to let me finish, but I don't know how."

"With your rich imagination, I'm sure you'll come up with something," he said, his gaze bouncing between my eyes and my lips.

My body grew hot at the memory of last night.

"Think, little nurse. What do I want from you?" His deep voice twisted up my insides.

"Sex?" I muttered.

Renato smirked. "I suppose no one can accuse you of being a romantic, can they?"

He leaned in, bringing his face so close to mine I started to feel dizzy. He was pulling me deeper into his orbit, and it was disorienting. "Sex, we will have. What else do I want from you?"

I wet my lips, my mouth suddenly dry as hell. "I don't know. Kids?"

"Kids we will have, too. Try again . . ." He studied me for a moment and then sighed. He started to pull back, his focus shifting from me to the desk.

Fuck. The bug. *Do something, Charlie. Anything!*

My hand tightened on his jaw before I could question it, and then I was pushing myself forward. He jerked to a stop when I pressed a chaste kiss to his lips, seeming just as startled as I was. I moved my lips over his, desperately trying to distract him from discovering what I'd been up to.

My panicked attempt to distract him worked better than I ever could have hoped.

Despite the clumsiness of my touch and the chasteness of my unsure kiss, he groaned against my lips and yanked me closer. He kissed me like he wanted to consume me, and I burned in his arms. I had no choice, I reassured myself. I needed to distract him. That was the only reason I'd climbed on the pyre and lit a match.

Liar. I ignored the voice in my head and lost myself in his touch, burning up all over like he'd started a fever in me.

"This, *anima mia*, is what I want from you," he said, his lips falling to my neck. "Your unequivocal surrender."

I melted in his arms, a heat that scared me building inside my core. I felt empty and needy and just wanted more of his touch. I wanted reassurance and proof that I was alive. I wanted to feel safe, just for a second, and I was pretty sure there was no safer place in the world for me than in this man's arms.

"Lose the pants," Renato ordered, his hands roaming over my ass.

I froze, staring up at him.

"I said lose the pants. I want to see your pretty pussy, right here, on my desk."

I was still frozen with shock when he sighed and tugged down my leggings, taking my panties with them. The cool air snaking around the open patio doors hit my skin, and I shivered.

He guided me onto the desk. What the hell was happening? I should do something. I should stop this. Logical thoughts filed through my head and barely stopped. But then I was bare-assed on the desk, and the man who had consumed my entire life stood between my legs.

"Now, let me see," he said firmly, pushing my knees apart.

I blanched. It was broad daylight, and I'd never been so exposed. My fumbling sexual experiences had happened in the dark, under covers and a thick cloak of self-consciousness and shame.

It's okay. You're just distracting him from finding the bug. This is what you have to do, a soothing voice spoke inside my head. Yup, okay, and that must be why I was so excited about it, too. Sure.

Renato pushed my legs farther apart and made a noise that was half my name and half a growl. "Do you have any idea how wet you are?" he asked, his voice oddly reverent. "It's glorious."

Fuck. Couldn't he leave me a shred of deniability to help soothe my broken pride?

I lay back and stared at the ceiling, humiliation washing over me. I was supposed to be distracting him so he wouldn't find the bug. I wasn't supposed to be getting so turned on by that distraction that I was making a wet mess on his desk.

He ran a hand down my inner thigh, making me jump. "How beautiful you are, Charlotte. I knew you would be, but I'm still unprepared."

I squeezed an eye open at his words. Beautiful? I risked a glance at him. He wasn't looking at me, he was staring between my spread legs, his fingers petting my wet curls. "Let's see if we can make you even wetter," he murmured, his eyes never leaving my pussy as he leaned in and licked me.

I nearly shot off the table. The list of men who'd gone down on me was so short I could count it on one hand. But while I'd been eaten out before, I'd still never come from it. It seemed an impossible feat. It was too awkward and imbalanced. Too much of an imposition to be doing something so one-sided. Selfish.

His elbows pushed my knees apart, splaying me helplessly before him. Liquid heat moved through me, dripping down my spine. He ran his tongue up and down my slit, from my clit to my asshole and back, while I stared at him, aghast and turned on.

His tongue was long and hot, dipping inside me and then back up to circle my clit. After a few minutes of that, while I got wetter and wetter and my leg muscles turned to jelly, he straightened up, his eyes never leaving my pussy. He rolled up his sleeves where they'd fallen, as if he was preparing to get his hands dirty, and brought his pointer and middle fingers to his mouth. He pushed them inside, wetting them, and then leaned in, putting his blunt fingertips against my entrance.

"What are you doing?" I asked breathlessly.

"Showing you what this beautiful body was made for," Renato replied, his eyes fixing on mine as he pushed his fingers inside me. They were long and thick. Renato swallowed a curse. "If you're this tight on my fingers, then you're going to grip my cock so perfectly."

He pumped his fingers in and out of me, pressing firmly against the spongy spot on my inner front wall. The elusive and, at times, seemingly mythical G-spot. My wetness coated his fingers, and the sound that filled the air was embarrassing as hell. A wet, sucking squelch. I fell backward and screwed my eyes shut.

"Don't do that, little nurse."

"I can't help it. It's just biology, remember?" A nip to my inner thigh made me yelp. I leaned back up and glared at him.

"No, *bambina*. Don't close your eyes and squirm with embarrassment. Don't spend a second feeling ashamed of how your body reacts to my touch. It's a fucking turn-on," he growled, then leaned in and licked my slit as he continued to finger-fuck me.

His tongue found my clit, and he circled it relentlessly, his fingers driving me toward the edge.

My fingers sank into his hair and tugged at him, trying to move him away. It was too much. Suddenly, the fire that he was stoking felt scary. I was out of control. I didn't know how I was going to react. I was rushing toward the hardest orgasm of my life, and I didn't think Renato was the type to give me mercy and stop. I wanted it but I feared it.

I pulled at his hair, and he only went harder. With his tongue moving at such an incredible pace, and his fingers massaging that secret spot inside me, I saw stars. My body tensed, and pleasure washed over me in a wave that never seemed to crash.

Wetness gushed out of me, spraying my legs and the leather inlay on the desk. My pussy clamped down on his fingers, pulling his hand deeper into me. My knees clenched around his head, squeezing involuntarily.

Renato didn't stop through all of it. Not even for a second. He pushed me through and spun out the pleasure in never-ending spirals that pulsed through my every nerve.

"That's right, Charlotte. Look how beautiful you are, my perfect, perfect *bambina*."

I twitched around him, my body full of sparkles. His words sank into my heart and lodged somewhere deep. So deep, they became a part of me.

My muscles went slack, and my knees fell open. Renato lapped at my pussy, and I writhed at the feel. He licked my center and then moved on to my thighs, licking my skin gently, cleaning me up with his tongue. He followed those gentle ministrations with kisses.

"From now on, Charlotte Burke, you'll put aside your shame and guilt, let me take care of you and your sister, and stop pretending that this thing between us isn't electric. I will always keep you safe, from everyone but myself."

He pulled me up so I was perched on the edge of the desk, his arms supporting me. He put his lips to mine, and I tasted myself there.

"Brava, bambina. Brava."

19

RENATO

I was in a good mood. In my line of work, it was rare that I felt much in the way of happiness. I could feel content with our bottom line, relieved that my men and their families were provided for. I could be satisfied that I lived another day or survived a bloody scrabble for power. I could experience dark delight in ending those who threatened me.

But happiness was rare.

For me, happiness had become the taste of Charlotte's sweet cunt in my mouth. It had become the way she melted into my arms when I kissed her, the fight leaving her when we touched.

I left her to recover from our little interaction in my office, though I already knew I'd be hunting her down again later. Now that I'd had a taste, I was addicted. Just once was enough to make me insane for her. Regardless, there was work to do, and I was sure my little nurse was struggling with the morality of falling to pieces in her captor's arms.

I'd let her come to terms with that before I wrecked her all over again.

Now, I was in the basement of Casa Nera, taking care of business. I flicked my lighter on and off, and the man who was tied up in the chair in front of me groaned around his gag. His eyes glowed in the reflection of the flame. I yanked the gag down enough for him to speak.

"You were near my property, deep in the woods. Far too close for comfort and not exactly a popular walking trail. What were you doing there? And don't bother lying. I'll know."

"I swear, I was just lost. I didn't know it was your place. I don't even know who you are!" The fear in his eyes betrayed him immediately.

"Ouch, that's quite a blow to my ego, isn't it? I suppose I should introduce myself." I stood and stripped off my jacket.

A knock at the door revealed Elio, carrying a nifty treasure in a bucket. Glowing hot coals. The smell filled the room.

The guy in the chair turned gray when he saw them. I knew he was lying. He was Castillo Cartel, and the stupid fuckers thought it was a wise idea to try to scope out Casa Nera.

Maybe displaying dismembered body parts on castle walls should become the standard again. A healthy reminder that being hanged, drawn, and quartered wasn't fun.

I took one of the coals from the bucket, holding it with tongs, and hovered it over the bound man's neck. He wriggled, like that could save him.

"Who sent you here? I want names."

"No one, I swear," the guy whispered.

Idiot. "Very well. You've made your choice," I said dispassionately and yanked the gag back up. Then I pulled his T-shirt open at the neck and dropped the hot coal inside.

He screamed, writhing in pain as the scorching coal slid down his body, melting flesh as it went, and stopped somewhere near his gut. His eyes bulged with pain. The coal burned through his shirt quickly enough, and I flicked it out with the tongs.

"Again, I'll ask you—who sent you? Tell me his name."

"I said I don't know! I didn't get told to do it directly. Juan Castillo, maybe, I don't know."

"Okay, now we're getting somewhere. Since that motivated you so well, we'll repeat the exercise, but this time, I'll drop it down your pants," I warned.

"No! No, I seriously don't know anything, man. I was just told to get close and see your setup, see if the women were here."

"The women?"

"The bitches that got Miguel killed."

Bitches? Oh, kid, this is really going to hurt.

"Why does Juan want them so badly?"

"I mean, he'd like to even the score, and he wants to take you out. There's someone else helping him, though, some old white guy who lets us bring our product in along the shore and gets the cops to look the other way."

Now that was interesting. "Elaborate."

"I don't know anything else, I swear. I've told you everything, I promise." The guy was crying and shaking now. The smell of burned flesh was enough to make me queasy, and I had a strong stomach for that kind of thing.

"Okay, relax. You did good. Well done," I reassured the blubbering mess of a man. Really quite pitiful, here at the end of his life. I could have made it quick to reward him for the information he'd given me; a final gift for a dying man. But he'd fucked that up.

He'd lost that chance when he'd called Charlotte a bitch.

I flicked a glance at Elio, who moved behind the guy and held his head in a punishing grip. Taking another hot coal in the tongs, I shoved it into his screaming mouth. Elio forced his jaw closed and held it shut against the fiery coal on his tongue. The man screamed wordlessly, unable to shift his face from my *sottocapo*'s grip.

For calling Charlotte a bitch, he'd have his tongue burned out of his worthless mouth. For attempting to spy on Casa Nera and my family, his body would fertilize the roses that Charlotte would carry in her bouquet.

The circle of life was a beautiful thing.

I patted his shoulder and gave him a smile as I made my way out of the basement.

"Are you whistling?" Giada accused as I strode into her office later. It was as chaotic as her personality, and I hated to spend a minute longer there than I absolutely had to.

"I don't know. Was I?"

Giada narrowed her eyes at me. "Got it bad, I see, for our resident medic. How interesting. Good job you decided to marry her instead of kill her."

"I was never going to kill her," I revealed. While I'd initially planned to give Charlie a week to prove her worth, the blazing fire between us quickly burned that plan to dust. And even if I'd gone through with it, I knew now that no matter what the outcome of that trial period, I never would've been able to kill her.

Giada raised an eyebrow at me. "Then what was your grand plan?"

"I'd simply keep her here until she didn't want to leave," I supplied.

She snorted. "Ah, the Stockholm syndrome backup plan? Nice. Anyway, to what do I owe this honor?"

"Any luck finding the Castillo stronghold? I refuse to believe they aren't hunkering down somewhere to make their shitty plans."

"These guys are paranoid. It doesn't help that you've been cutting holes in the ranks left, right, and center."

I shrugged in response to that accusation.

"Anyway, I'm coming up empty right now."

"I need to find them," I reminded her. I'd been wanting to wipe out the Castillos from Atlantic City for months. There hadn't been a time limit to flush them out before. Now there was. They'd threatened my property—my future wife. I wouldn't allow them to live.

"I'm on it. In other news, I came across something interesting earlier."

"What is it?"

"When I was monitoring the usual traffic from the property, I found something. Actually, I found three little somethings. Now, the signature on these is minuscule. If you weren't searching for it, it wouldn't present as anything to worry about. But . . . I still remember what it looked like the last time someone tried to get a bug in here."

"Someone brought a bug in here?"

"Yes, indeed. Probably yesterday. I need to scan to find its exact location."

Charlotte and her sudden, out-of-character kiss filled my head. The little minx had been jumpy and nervous. She'd also been poking around my office for no reason.

"There's one in my study, maybe in the potted plant," I said, immediately knowing I was correct. I'd completely underestimated my reluctant bride if she was capable of sneaking into my office, distracting me by letting me eat her cunt, and walking out without a hint of guilt. I wasn't sure whether to be worried or impressed.

One thing I was, however, was furious.

Detectives Vane and Whitely had been a thorn in my side for

months, and now they thought they could use Charlotte against me? They dared try to manipulate my wife?

It was time for this particular game to end and another to begin.

This time, it would be *my* game, and I didn't plan on losing.

20

CHARLIE

"The Boy I'm Gonna Marry" played over the speakers as I stepped into La Leonora. It was loud as hell and echoed around the beautiful building. The happy song contrasted sharply with the air of tension that hung over our small group. The music was the icing on the cake. Was Renato fucking with me?

Today, the casino was dressed up in the most opulent fashion. Apparently a De Sanctis wedding was not a discreet affair, and from the tank-like cars lined up on the strip and the groups of lethal-looking bodyguards swarming around, it seemed like the guest list boasted some of the most notorious kingpins on the East Coast.

Despite the general air of violence in the atmosphere, it was odd to realize that I felt safe. Surrounded by Renato De Sanctis's guards, on his property, I was untouchable. It was a sharp contrast to the days before he'd taken us to Casa Nera when I'd been jumping at shadows and running from the Castillo Cartel.

I entered the building with an entourage of guards, gripping Lucy's hand in mine. Giada stood on her other side and every now and then reached out and squeezed her shoulder. A friendly reminder that a crossbow-wielding psychopath was her designated babysitter.

La Leonora had a chapel on site. I was appalled at the very thought of getting married in a church, considering what kind of wedding it was, but no one cared about my protests.

"Now, you have a couple of hours to transform into a beautiful *sposa* and turn that frown upside down. I don't want wedding pics of a long-faced bride on the mantel," Giada quipped, directing me and Lucy toward the bank of elevators.

We were flanked on all sides by Sonny, Vinny, and a few other men.

There was no escape.

We got ready in a penthouse suite. Vito had a whole army of assistants running to follow his every barked instruction. Lucy sat in the window and stared down at the city. Sonny and Vinny laughed and joked, seeming jovial. Giada watched us all with hawklike cunning and alternated between slicing razor-thin slices of peach and sharpening her blood-red talons with a paring knife.

"Can someone turn the music off?" I asked, nearly lunging for a passing champagne flute.

I grabbed it and downed the contents. The fizz was pleasant, but there was no softening of my anxiety. I went searching for another one, being stealthy in case Giada was under instructions to make sure I didn't get wasted before the ceremony.

She smirked at me. "Knock yourself out. It's nonalcoholic. The groom doesn't go for passive drunk compliance. That's no fun."

"You're a monster, and so is your boss. Fucking lunatics, all of you," I muttered, setting down the glass and turning to the mirror. Somehow, I'd been transformed. The dress had taken three people to put on me, and I had no idea how I'd go to the bathroom in it. Only the veil remained, hanging on a special stand. It was so long that even if I ran from the ceremony, the groom would have a long leash to catch me by.

I looked more beautiful than I'd ever known I could. My cheekbones stood out, and my eyes were huge. Even my lips were overlined and bigger than usual. I didn't look like myself. Maybe after today, I'd never go back to the person I was before. Maybe the old me would die for good once I took the last name of a certified killer. I'd be reborn as someone else, someone I couldn't recognize.

Lucy watched me in the mirror while the stylists cooed over the frothy confection I was wearing. Her look of disdain morphed into flat-out disgust when her eyes reached my face. I flinched like she'd bitten me. She got up and kicked at the table next to her, sending glasses flying everywhere. She whirled around and headed toward the bedroom, slamming the door behind her so hard a picture fell off the wall and smashed on the floor. Sonny crossed himself like Lucy was possessed.

"I know she's your little sis, but . . . do you want me to kill her for you?" Giada mused, inspecting her nails. "I'd make it quick, as a courtesy to you."

I swallowed down the jagged shards of pain at seeing Lucy so upset and made my way toward the bedroom.

"She's just upset. I'll speak to her."

"She needs more than speaking to, Charlie. She's an ungrateful little brat, and she's barely affected by all of this. She got you into this mess, and now you're the one getting her out of it, and she can't even be nice to you. That kid needs a kick in the head," Giada muttered. "Volunteers for kicker position?"

She raised her hand, as did Sonny.

I took a deep breath and pushed open the bedroom door. Lucy was lying on the bed, staring up at the ceiling.

"What's up?" I asked her, unsure how to tackle her stormy mood.

"What's up? Just look in the mirror and answer your own

question." Lucy's voice was hard, full of vitriol. "You actually seem happy, you know that? It's pathetic."

"Happy? I'm not happy," I disagreed.

"Are you sure? You looked it earlier. Don't you understand that none of this is real? Renato is probably laughing at you behind your back."

"What the hell have I done to you to deserve this attack?" I demanded, my patience snapping.

"What have you done? You've changed sides, by the looks of things."

"Changed sides? I'm marrying Renato to keep you safe."

"Maybe it started that way, but now, I think you just want to." Lucy swung herself up from the bed and glared at me. "Admit it. You like living in his luxurious prison and not having to go to work, just sitting around, eating food that a chef cooks for you." She folded her arms and raised her chin at me. "I bet you even like the big bad mafia boss backing you into corners and kissing you. You like him, don't you?" Lucy's lip curled even more. "Don't lie to me, I already saw you two."

"You saw us?" I repeated, shame flushing down my body in a great, hot wave.

"Yeah, I saw you. Some captive you make. It took you, what? Less than a week to become a desperate housewife for your captor?"

"A desperate housewife?" A laugh left me before I could stop it. And then another. Drowning out my urge to cry, bitter laughter surged out. It came so hard it bent me over.

"What's wrong with you? Did you finally just lose it?" Lucy watched me warily.

"Maybe I did," I gasped. This dress didn't offer much room for laughing your ass off. "Maybe I really did." I sobered, the shame inside me morphing into something else.

Anger.

No, not just anger.

White-hot fury.

"Maybe it really is crazy to be relieved that there's a solution to all of this, one that lets us both live. Maybe it's crazy to feel relieved at not having to worry about money for once, or having a hot meal that you didn't have to make yourself."

Lucy narrowed her eyes at me. "So much for your high-and-mighty morals and being a good person, right? Do you realize you're feeling grateful to the man who put us in this position?"

I scoffed and walked closer. "Let's be clear. *You* are the one who put us in this position. You and your boyfriend. Renato De Sanctis didn't ask you to break into his warehouse and try to steal his drugs. He also never asked his two goons to shoot Miguel, in fact, he punished them immediately for going against his wishes, right in front of me. You put us in this situation. *You.*" I stopped in front of her. "How dare you judge me?" I took in Lucy's ugly sneer and red-rimmed eyes. I couldn't understand her. My emotional bandwidth had shrunk in the last few days. I had used it all up with my own worries.

"Guilt."

Renato stood in the doorway of the bedroom. I hadn't heard him enter.

He stole my breath away. He was in a tux. Midnight couture hugged his built body, perfectly designed to fit his proportions. He wore it flawlessly, a man used to luxury. He stepped into the room, and his eyes fixed on me.

"She feels guilty for getting you into this situation and is lashing out, trying to push you away while at the same time seeking a sliver of hope that maybe this forced marriage isn't as bad as it seems for you. Isn't that right, Lucy?"

One glance at Lucy's face confirmed Renato's words. Her sullen expression shifted guiltily.

"What your sister doesn't understand yet, is that all she did was introduce us. The rest of what we are and what we will be, is between us."

Renato had crossed the room and now put his hand on the small of my back. It warmed me in a way I didn't want to examine too closely. My anger ebbed in the face of his calm. His effortless dominance relaxed me somehow, and I let go of my aggression toward my sister. He was right, wasn't he?

I turned and stared up at the man who had stormed into my life and tipped everything on its head. I never felt judged by this man. Was it so wrong to like that?

It's all fun and games until he finds out you've betrayed him and decides to cancel the deal.

My sister obviously felt guilty and was lashing out, but wasn't there truth to her words, too? Maybe that's what hurt the most.

"I'm going to speak to your sister now," Renato said to Lucy, leading us out into the living room of the suite.

The room still teemed with Vito and his assistants. "Leave us," Renato instructed quietly, but his words held power.

Suddenly, the suite was emptying, with Giada escorting Lucy out. I stood in front of the wall of windows, the bright sun of the early winter day shining its pure-white brilliance on me. Renato looked down at me in the morning light and frowned.

"Who did the makeup?" His words were like a whip.

Vito stopped just short of disappearing out the door. "My daughter, Elena."

"Send her back in ten minutes," Renato instructed, and with a regal jerk of his head, dismissed Vito.

The door clicked shut, and we were alone. I hadn't seen Renato since the other day, when I'd come in his arms, mercilessly pushed over the edge by his wicked tongue. My entire being flushed hot when I thought of it.

"What are you going to do that's going to ruin my makeup?" I wondered curiously. I never could tell with him. My mind went immediately to the gutter.

He raised an eyebrow. "While I like where your mind is headed, you don't seem like yourself with all that makeup on." He approached me, grabbing a plastic packet of wet wipes as he passed the vanity table. He pulled one free and offered it to me. "I want to see your face. The real one."

I huffed. "Why do you care? Surely, I should feel beautiful on my wedding day, sham or not."

"You're more beautiful without it. I want you to look like you."

I took the wet wipe, denying the feeling in my chest his words had evoked. My skin was already starting to itch, and the makeup felt like a heavy mask. I couldn't imagine wearing it all day long, under bright lights.

I rubbed at my cheek with the wet wipe, and about three pounds of makeup lifted off. I suddenly grew self-conscious about how I'd look with a partially made-up face and set to wiping off the rest. Renato waited patiently, even handing me fresh wipes and getting rid of the used ones.

Finally, he set down the packet and nodded. "Much better."

"So, you came here just to make me wash my face?"

"I came here to give you this," he corrected and produced a black velvet box from his tux pocket.

He handed it to me, and I opened it carefully, my jaw dropping. Inside was a dazzling ruby necklace, the huge red stones surrounded by diamonds. Matching earrings sat above it.

"They were my *nonna*'s and have been in the family for generations."

"Wow," I touched the stones, marveling at the twinkle. "You've always been rich, then?"

Renato's mouth pulled to the side in a half-grin, and then he was lifting the jewels out of the box. "Think of them as a wedding gift."

I'd never seen such beautiful jewelry, even at the fancy galas I'd served at La Leonora.

"My *nonno* was a powerful man. He wasn't born into it. He made the first steps toward De Sanctis power in Napoli. Back then, the man who ruled the city was called Stromboli. The story goes that my *nonno* saw Stromboli's daughter one day while she was walking in the garden of their home. He was the driver. He was twenty-five, and she was eighteen. He fell in love at first glance.

"Ten years later, when her father died, he named my *nonno* his successor, despite the fact that he had three sons. No one knows what passed between the dying man and the man who was his chauffeur, but within a week, my *nonno* had married Stromboli's daughter and seized power. As he grew in power, they say he became more and more paranoid about his bride's safety. He lavished her with gifts and built her a house that only a queen could dream of, but he didn't let her outside."

"Sounds like your kind of relationship."

Renato smiled, but it was sad somehow. "My father was of the same mentality as my *nonno*. A gilded cage for flightless birds. Turn around."

I complied slowly, hyperaware of his hot breath on the back of my neck. His hands circled around me, fitting the necklace into place.

"Why would you give these to me? Am I doomed to repeat your *nonna*'s fate?" He fastened the clasp, and the platinum felt cold against my skin.

"She never wore them. She had nowhere to go. It was her silent protest at how her life turned out. She accepted the gifts but never wore a single one."

I didn't know what to say in this unexpectedly intimate moment. I had nothing to reciprocate his family secrets with. My mother died giving birth to Lucy, and with every day that passed, I remembered her less and less.

"I'm giving these to you because I've never met anyone else I'd rather give them to," he murmured. "And I want you to *wear* them, little nurse, and not just today."

His touch made my skin burn. How could my body behave like this? Soaking up even the slightest brush of this man's fingers like they were water in a desert? Did he mean he wouldn't keep me locked up in a luxurious cage, like his grandfather had done to his grandmother?

"They suit you. Priceless jewels for a one-of-a-kind woman."

His thumb stroked up the nape of my neck, sending tingles out in waves across my shoulders. We could both feel it. The tension between us was like nothing I'd ever felt before. My body was attuned to his. I could tell where he was with my eyes shut. It was like my body lit up when he was near and faded into darkness when he was gone.

And I was spying on him.

"Are you sure we have to do this?" The question left me before I could stop it. The thought of the bug, sitting right now in the potted plant in Renato's office, kept playing on my mind. Not because betraying him was undeserved, but because I was sure it wouldn't turn out well for me or Lucy. We were just collateral damage in a game being played between giants.

"I'm sure. Today, you will be my wife. And if someone should try to take you from me?" he added. "No one could stop me from taking you back. Not the cops, not a guardian angel with a flaming sword, not even the pearly gates themselves could stop me. Remember that."

Not the cops? Fear doused me at his words. Was he talking generally, or did he already know? I didn't dare meet his eyes for fear of what I'd see.

"I'll let you handle the earrings," he suggested, stepping away.

I swallowed past the dry hunk of awkwardness lodged in my throat and simply nodded.

A knock sounded at the door, and Elena, the makeup artist, entered.

"Keep her natural. I want her to look like herself," Renato snapped to the girl before striding toward the doorway.

"But the photographs . . ." Elena started.

"Will be perfect."

I turned around just in time to see him disappear without a backward glance.

I peered down at the ring on my finger, marveling at the weight of it.

The ceremony had passed in a blur, and now the reception was speeding by, bringing us closer and closer to the wedding night. I felt so nervous I could throw up.

Was it nerves or excitement?

Ignoring the traitorous voice in my head, I glanced around the huge ballroom where the reception was being held. It was so full of flowers and glittering lights, it hurt to look at. Stares followed my every move. Questions were whispered in my wake.

Who is she?

Why her?

Renato was off half the time, speaking to dangerous-looking men with armed guards. Giada and Lucy sat with me.

"How did all these people come at such short notice?"

"When Renato De Sanctis invites you to a wedding, you come. It doesn't matter if you have to fly back to the country to come. The only people who are off the hook for being out of the country are his sister and her family. They get the blood pass. Everyone else? It would be the ultimate disrespect not to show."

I pulled a face, and Giada laughed. "Let me guess, you're the kind of person who never throws a party in case people don't come?"

Ding, ding, ding.

I glared at her, and she laughed again.

"Look on the bright side—from now on, they'd better come, or they'll have to deal with your husband."

Lucy had fallen into a sulky silence. She was dressed in black, as were half the guests, but my sister had decided to dress hers up with Doc Martens and ripped fishnets. If there was a poster child for teen rebellion, it was Lucy right now. She was tracing patterns in spilled sugar on the tablecloth when she sat upright and waved at someone.

"You know someone here?" I exclaimed. That was more than I could say. I'd been passing the time by sitting and staring out at the crowd, and my hands, and the flashy-as-hell ring on my finger. It matched the necklace and earrings perfectly. *His grandmother's jewels.* It felt odd to wear them, and I had no idea why he trusted me with them. Considering our dynamic, I was more likely to head to the bathroom and toss them down the toilet than cherish them. Even as I thought it, I knew I would never do it.

Maybe he knew me better than I liked to think he did.

"It's Quinn," Lucy said and waved again. "From this summer. Lifeguarding."

Ah, yes, the first and only job that Lucy had ever held down was this summer at the beach.

A slight red-haired girl about the same age as Lucy came rushing over. "Oh my God, I can't believe you're here!" The girl smiled at my younger sister and held her arms open for a hug. To my shock, my prickly sister hugged her back.

"I kind of had to come . . . it's my sister's wedding." Lucy laughed and introduced us. "Quinn, this is my sister, Charlie."

A low whistle filled the air, setting my nerves on high alert. Someone appeared behind Quinn and draped an arm over her shoulders. Someone tall, broad, tattooed to hell, and with trouble written all over him. He wore a black jacket and white shirt, and his tie was hanging loosely around his open collar. His green eyes flashed at me as he held out a hand.

"I never thought I'd see the day Ren took a wife, and I definitely never expected it to be someone so young and lovely. I'm Brandon O'Connor, but you can call me Bran." He leaned in, a charming smile stretched across his handsome face. "Just blink twice if you need rescuing, beautiful."

"Yes, Charlie, blink twice if you want to be whisked away to Hell's Kitchen to live with the Irish Mafia instead of Italian." Giada's sweet tone was venomous.

Bran leaned away from me and turned to look at the curvy Italian spitfire sitting just behind me. Giada tossed her hair and waved her red-tipped talons. "If you want to rescue someone, Irish, try taking someone who won't bring a war down on your house."

Bran's eyes fixed on Giada, and he grinned wickedly. "Like you, sweet cheeks?"

Giada laughed. "You'd never survive me."

"Sounds like a fun way to go, though, I have to say," Bran said. The look he was giving Giada made me feel like I was an intruder.

"I don't think we've been introduced, beautiful. I'm Bran." He held out a tatted hand to her. "And you are?"

She smirked in his direction, flipping her knife between her fingers. "Out of your league," she finished for him.

His grin said that he was hardly deterred by her put-downs.

I cleared my throat to break the tension. "I'm just going to visit the ladies' room."

"You want me to hold your dress up for you again?" Giada asked lazily, focused once more on her little knife that she liked to carry.

"No!" I flushed and stood, turning and nearly falling when my body collided with Renato's. His eyes were fixed on Bran and Quinn.

"Congratulations, Ren. I have to say, when Niko said you were getting married, I just couldn't picture it, but here she is, and she's lovely. Far too lovely for you," Bran's voice purred over the compliment.

Renato took my hand in his, failing to rise to the bait. "Isn't she? If you'll excuse me, I'm going to dance with my wife," he simply said and swept me out to the dance floor.

The band paused whatever they'd been playing and struck up a waltz as soon as we reached the middle of the floor.

"I don't know how to dance like this," I worried as Renato pulled me toward him.

"It doesn't matter. I'll lead, and you follow, just like in life," he said and smirked when I glared at him. "Ah, there she is. I've missed this angry look all day."

"Meaning?"

He turned me with ease, and I found he was right. I didn't need to do much but go the way he guided me.

"Meaning, you show me a part of yourself you don't show many others." He spun me under his arm, and I nearly tripped on my long gown. His hands were there, falling to my waist and keeping me from tripping. "I like it."

"What can I say? I guess you just bring out the worst in me," I muttered through clenched teeth.

"It's a talent," he agreed, making me smile with his easy acceptance of my accusation.

We danced on, and the feeling of hundreds of eyes watching me lingered. Everyone watching, judging, wondering what the hell had happened between us that had brought us here.

"What's the matter?" Renato asked, reading my change in mood.

"I hate being the center of attention. Today is my nightmare, everyone watching us."

"I thought it was a nightmare because you're marrying me?"

I blinked up at him and his self-satisfied smirk. "You're still at the top of the list, don't worry."

We danced in silence for a while, and I gradually became aware of how the heat of his hands on my back made me shiver. The smell of him, and the way I missed it as soon as he pulled back, haunted me. It was all too much. It was just enough. It was more than I'd ever expected from life. It was everything I'd hoped would never happen to me. Thoughts of the cops and Lucy fell away for just a moment, and I was just a woman who'd married a man who turned her heart inside out. I had no idea what that meant. I feared him and I wanted him in equal measure.

Most of all, standing there under the intimate lights, dancing in this man's arms, it felt like fate had finally caught up with me. It was all inevitable, really.

That shouldn't have been as comforting as it was.

21

CHARLIE

It had been the longest day of my life, and yet as we drove up the long, winding driveway to Casa Nera, I saw that it wasn't over. The house was lit up like a Christmas tree in the darkness.

"What's going on?" I wondered. A huge number of men had gathered outside in the front courtyard.

"The family are here to pay their respects," Renato answered. He didn't look tired at all. If anything, he had a restless energy, like the day hadn't been enough for him. Apparently, he needed more than a mere wedding to tire him out.

Elio pulled to a stop beside the house, and over a hundred heads turned our way as we left the car. Renato held my hand to help me out, steadying me in my wobbly heels and restrictive dress.

As we stood there together, the moon shining down on us, a clap started and spread across the entire group of collected men. I looked over the crowd. They smiled, cheered, and shouted congratulations.

Overhead, a loud bang sounded. The gangsters had clearly

been expecting it, as no one pulled a gun. I jumped out of my skin, and Renato's arm came around me. He was so solid and warm. I looked up and smiled as fireworks burst across the sky, dazzled by the display.

"What do you think, *bambina?*" Renato asked me. His eyes were reflecting the jewel-colored lights, and it was hard to look away.

"It's beautiful," I murmured.

"Yes, it is, isn't it?" Renato agreed, his gaze never leaving me.

We watched the fireworks until a bell sounded. "Time to go inside." Renato wrapped my arm around his and turned me toward the house.

"Where now? Doesn't this day ever end?" I asked. "I don't know if my feet can take much more."

"Not a problem," he said, and without another word, scooped me into his arms to cross the threshold.

My heart all but jumped into my mouth. Too many feelings swirled inside me. Shock, confusion, fear, and something else. It felt an awful lot like relief. *Great, they've made me just as crazy as them.*

"You can put me down now," I muttered to him as he carried me through the house.

"Maybe, but I won't." His voice was calm and deep.

His confident hold comforted me somehow. I was supposed to be scared of this man, but his grip on me made me feel like I'd never fall.

"Because?" I wondered, studying the place where his starched collar met his tanned neck. It looked positively edible. He was too tempting; it really wasn't fair.

"I don't want to," he answered.

Then we headed into the largest room in Casa Nera. I'd always wondered if it had been a ballroom at some point. Tonight, it was lavishly decorated with fresh flowers and stylish but elegant banquet tables. A fire roared in a hearth big enough to climb inside.

Another round of applause started when we entered. Casa Nera staff stood against the walls, clapping vigorously.

Bottles of champagne popped all around the room as Renato took me to the table in the center and sat me on a plush velvet chair.

Men from outside filed into the room, talking loudly. A lot of slapping shoulders and smiles. It wasn't the vibe of a deadly mafia family at all.

Then the line formed. My chair was in the middle, and starting there, the line snaked back out of the room, it was so long.

Renato stood behind my chair and placed a hand on my shoulder.

Elio was first. The *sottocapo* approached. He gave me a slight grin and bowed his head, holding out his hand.

"It's okay, Charlotte, that's why they're here," Renato said, unruffled.

I put my hand in Elio's, and the deadly mercenary brought it to his lips and lightly kissed the back. "*Non ti deluderò, sangue del mio sangue.*" The Italian rolled effortlessly off his tongue, and he smiled at me and moved away.

"What does it mean?" I asked Renato over my shoulder.

"I will not fail you, blood of my blood," Renato translated, covering my shoulder with one of his huge hands and sending a warm jolt through me.

I didn't have time to ask more than that, since another made man approached, reaching reverently for my hand.

They kept coming. Strangers who bowed their heads and promised me their allegiance. I didn't know what the hell to think. There was something ancient about the ritual, and the formality of it suited Renato. Everything about him had the edge of history and tradition, though he clearly bent the rules whenever he wanted to.

The ceremony, because that's what it felt like, went on for nearly an hour.

"What was that?" I asked Renato later, when the men drank champagne to toast their fearless leader's nuptials and I finally had a moment alone with my new husband. *Husband?*

Just the idea was ludicrous, and yet it had happened.

Renato messed around with something on the table. He'd doused his hands in sanitizer, the harsh chemical smell seeming out of place in the ballroom that looked straight out of another era.

He took my hands in his, and the shock of his powerful fingers sliding over mine went all the way down to my toes. He smoothed the sanitizer over my hands meticulously.

"Don't tell me you're secretly a germophobe?" I wondered.

He simply smirked. "We're not done yet, *anima mia*. And that was a pledging ceremony . . . like knights of old, getting down on one knee and promising their lives to their rulers."

"Rulers?" I repeated.

Renato hummed in agreement and tugged me to my feet. A hush fell over the assembled men.

"My family is now your family, Charlotte De Sanctis, and every single one will protect you and your sister until their last breath. You'll never hunger or want for anything again. You'll never be alone again. You're a very powerful woman now, Charlotte. You command an army of men who would die for you. They came tonight to pay homage."

My head spun; I couldn't take in his words. But the sight of a knife in his hand soon cleared the brain fog. "What is that?" I asked nervously.

He took my hand, freshly sanitized, and held it up for all to see. The ruby-and-diamond ring sat on my fourth finger. Renato nudged it up a few inches and set the tip of the knife on the skin underneath.

"Flesh of my flesh, blood of my blood," Renato intoned.

The fucker was going to cut me, right here in front of everyone, like some kind of barbarian. "Only this band—our union—holds the blood inside. Only this ring keeps you safe. A shackle you can never break," he said quietly, and then pushed the blade against my skin.

He twisted it with the expertise of a man well versed in leaving scars. I bit my tongue so as not to cry out. The slice burned, and blood dripped down my hand as Renato pushed my ring over the weeping wound, stopping the bleeding. It would leave a scar. A ring I could never take off. Marked, forever, as his.

He turned the knife around, holding the hilt in my direction. I took it from him slowly. The point was poised over his chest as he fiddled with his ring. I could kill him right here and now, before anyone could stop me.

No. You couldn't. His men would cut me down immediately, and anyway, I was pretty sure he could disarm me in a second. He was so confident, though. He knew I wouldn't try it. He knew the spell he had woven over me and the power he held.

You're a very powerful woman now, Charlotte.

He offered me his bare ring finger, and I cut him just like he'd cut me. He pushed his wedding band back on, just like he'd done with mine, and pressed our bleeding hands together. Ruby droplets scattered across the skirt of my white gown, matching the ring. It seemed fitting somehow. Of course, a deal with the devil and a marriage born in hell would be sealed with blood.

I was the demon's bride, and I looked it, standing there with blood spattered across my dress, my hand clasped in a red grip. The applause was deafening, and then the shouts began.

"Bacci!"

"Kiss her, boss!"

"Bacci! Bacci!"

I barely had time to warn Renato before he was leaning forward.

"Don't." Suddenly the thought of kissing him in front of everyone and the thunderous cheers became too much. Too much attention, too much anticipation, too much guilt that I'd enjoy it, too much fear of what that meant.

"Stop me," he murmured against my lips, sliding his hand around the nape of my neck and then kissing me hard.

His tongue pushed between my lips, sending a gale of fire roaring through me. He kissed me mercilessly, like he wanted to devour me, and I sagged into his chest and let him.

No, I didn't just let him. I kissed him back. My mouth moved over his, and the feel of his hot skin burned like liquid fire. I stroked my tongue along his, and he gave a deep rumble of appreciation. When he pulled back, I nearly stumbled, but he was right there, holding me up.

What the hell had I just done? I shouldn't be kissing him or swooning against him. Lucy and I were his prisoners. I was losing my head here and forgetting who was good and who was bad.

Renato was the villain, the blackhearted mob boss who had just forced me to marry him, and I was going weak at the knees from his unwanted kisses. *Are they unwanted, though?* I shoved that thought violently from my head.

In the rest of the room, oblivious to the roller coaster of guilt and shame I was riding, the music started up and the party began.

The De Sanctis men who hadn't been invited to the wedding—the sheer number of them made that impossible—were here to celebrate their capo's new bride.

Renato leaned in to speak to me. "You have ten minutes to show your face here."

"And then?" I wondered, though the heat creeping through me warned me of what he was going to say.

"Then we're going upstairs, *bambina*, and you're all mine."

22

RENATO

Charlotte's hand was cold in mine as I led her from the ballroom. The music and noise of celebration fell away as we made our way through the twisting labyrinth of Casa Nera.

There was no tiredness to my step. I'd been waiting for this moment all week.

Tonight, I'd fuck the woman I'd chosen to be my bride, the one strong enough to stand up to me and carry the De Sanctis legacy and heirs with grace. Charlotte wouldn't crumble in the face of adversity. It just wasn't in her character. She didn't know when to quit. It was one of the many things I admired about her.

I took her hand when we got to the stairs, and we started upward. I reached down and grabbed a handful of her heavy skirts and lifted them for her, catching a glimpse of her thigh-high suspenders. My cock had already been hard the entire day, since the moment I'd walked into the penthouse suite where the bridal party was getting ready.

She'd been standing in the window, the winter sun blazing down on her, looking like something holy. I might never recover from the sight. She'd already worked under my skin like a splinter, and nothing would take her out. Not even discovering that she was spying on me.

I wanted her to tell me about the cops herself.

I wanted her to trust me.

If this woman could trust me, the sinner to her saint, then she would fully belong to me.

We got to the master suite. I hadn't been sleeping there. It was a set of rooms that hadn't been used for decades. They'd been my mother's rooms. Elio had had them completely overhauled. I didn't want to live with ghosts anymore.

Charlotte was nervous; I could see it in the slight hunch of her slim shoulders and the way she kept glancing at me through her lashes.

We walked into the room. I was pleased to see that Carmella had gotten it ready. Candles were lit, red rose petals scattered on the bed. I'd asked for four lengths of silk to be left at the bottom of the huge, four-poster bed, and I already spied them there.

Waiting for their captive.

Charlotte looked around with awe. She walked around the perimeter while I took off my tux jacket and hung it on the valet stand. At the sound of my cuff links hitting their mother-of-pearl tray, Charlotte paused her inspection of the room and looked at me. I tugged my silk bow tie off and tucked it into my jacket pocket. Her eyes scanned me, and her cheeks went pink.

What a delightful contradiction she was. At times as brave and ballsy as any of my men, and at others, a blushing ingenue. I never felt our age difference more than when her cheeks were rosy and her eyes were avoiding me. It made me want to corner her, take her on my knee, tilt her chin up, and pry her secrets out of her.

Secrets like hiding a bug in my office.

I took a long breath, pushing the fury I felt at Detectives Vane and Whitely from my mind. Charlotte was *mine*. Claimed, wed, and soon to be bred. How dare they interfere with my woman? I knew what they were thinking. Their small minds were pitifully easy to read. Charlotte was powerless, without influence or connections—exactly the kind of person they could lean on and suffer no consequences should she crack under the strain.

Well, now she had power, connections, and billions to her name. Let's see them break her now, with me at her back.

"This room is so beautiful. I've never seen it before," Charlotte babbled.

I knew this tactic. She was stalling. I reached for the buttons of my dress shirt. I undid them quickly, and my shirt joined the rest of my clothes.

"You talk a lot when you're nervous, *anima mia*. Did you know that? It's your tell."

"I'm not much of a poker player."

"Tells are useful in all sorts of games." Like the game of chicken we played now, without her knowledge. She would continue to spy on me, and I would wait and see when she would stop, her guilt getting the better of her. The day she confessed to me would be the day I'd know she'd accepted her new reality. It would show that she trusted me more than the cops. That I'd worked under her skin just as much as she'd gotten under mine, and the playing field would be level again.

"Undress."

She stopped in her tracks at my order and spun around. Her blush had spread across her décolletage, too. A heavenly rose color.

"I mean, I know we just got married, but you can't think—"

"We're not about to fuck because we just got married," I interrupted her, approaching her slowly in case she bolted for the bathroom and locked me out. I'd just had this room renovated. Kicking in a door would be annoying.

"We're about to fuck because I haven't been able to stop

thinking about the taste of your cunt since yesterday. It's mine now, and I won't waste one more second without indulging in it."

I reached for her dress, and she put her hands over mine. "Wait. This is all a lot," she whispered. Her eyes rose to mine. "I think I'm freaking out."

"You look completely calm to me."

"Maybe I do have a poker face after all, then." Her gaze landed on my chest.

It was the first time I'd been shirtless before her. She frowned at the tally marks tattooed in even rows across my heart.

She had to swallow twice before she could speak. "Are those the people you've—" she broke off, struggling. "I mean, is it your kill count?"

Her hand floated in the air over my skin, and suddenly I wanted nothing more than to feel her flesh against mine. I took her fingers and guided them to the marks, encouraging her to touch them.

"Not a kill count. A loss count," I corrected her. "Every good De Sanctis man lost under my leadership is here."

"The night we met you killed two of them yourself," she reminded me.

"I said *good* De Sanctis men. Men with honor, who deserve the name. I carry them with me, so I never forget that my men's lives are in my hands, and their families', too."

She swallowed hard. "And I thought it was hard being responsible for Lucy," she joked.

"Being responsible for one, or one hundred, is the same. A burden and a gift."

Her eyes lifted to mine. She shook her head, an incredulous smile playing on her beautiful lips. "You have no idea how often I've thought those words. I've never said them out loud, though.

They go in the 'secrets we take to our grave' pile . . . for me, anyway."

"You can tell me anything, Charlotte. Confess your secrets, and I'll carry them. You're my wife now."

"On paper, right? I mean, how else?" she asked, her breathing coming harder as she spoke.

"I'll show you how else." I reached for her dress again, my hands going to the column of tiny buttons down the side. They were tedious as hell, but I was a patient man, and I had waited my entire life to find a woman I wanted to marry. *This* woman. Nothing would make me rush now.

The tension was thick as I slowly undid the dress, giving Charlotte plenty of time to consider what was coming. My wife seemed to feel some sense of shame every time her body responded to my touch. She was embarrassed about how wet she got. Ashamed about the way her nipples begged to be sucked, and how she liked to be held down, helpless and out of control.

I planned to teach her to take pride in her pleasure. To demand it.

The dress sagged as soon as the last button was undone, and I pushed it off her shoulders. It pooled at her feet in a waterfall of chiffon, silk, lace, and pearls.

She was wearing a corset-style undergarment, with garters that held up sheer stockings. It was all a creamy, virginal white.

I helped her step out of the dress and pulled her away from it to the huge mirror that sat opposite the bed.

Standing behind her, I wrapped her long hair around my fist, trapping her head in place and waiting until her eyes found mine in the reflection.

"What do you see?" I wondered, one hand in her hair, the other roaming over the front of her body.

My tanned, tattooed hand was a stark contrast against her white undergarments. Her attention fastened onto the back of my hand. I moved first to her neck, circling it with my palm. Her pulse beat steadily. She might be nervous, but she wasn't afraid.

Charlotte knew no fear, unless it was asking for something for herself.

I pressed lightly, and her chin tilted up, instinctively giving me better access. Yes, my little nurse was perfect.

"What do you see, Charlotte?" I repeated.

I moved my hand downward now, heading for her breasts. The corset had a half-cup design, with an overlay of delicate, cobweb-fine lace. I could see her nipples through it. I closed my fingers around one and pinched it lightly.

Her lips parted, responsive as hell.

"Answer me," I ordered her.

"Me and you," she shot out. "I see me and you."

"Hmm, is that right?" *I only see her. Nothing can distract me from her.*

"But who are you?"

"I'm your wife," Charlotte muttered, arching her back subtly to move her nipples closer to my fingers.

Fuck, yes. I loved how that sounded.

"Hmm, yes, you are. My wife. All mine."

I ran my hand down her abdomen. "You are also a very beautiful woman. Loyal, smart, and brave . . ." I trailed off as I reached the hem of the corset. There were a couple of inches of flesh and then her panties. They were the same lace as the corset and completely transparent. I could see her thatch through the white swirling pattern.

I slipped my hand between her legs, and she jerked. She was all pent up; I could feel the tightness in her muscles. I tutted in her ear when she tried to keep her thighs together and deny me access. Her eyes, usually hazel, had turned dark and full of want. She had no idea the things she was capable of. None at all. I was going to show her.

I slid my fingers across her pussy, fingering her through the lace. Her juices coated me despite the barrier of fabric. "Shall I tell you what else you are, *mia moglie?*"

Her gaze fixed on my hand working between her thighs, and her hips flexed against me in subtle movements I doubted she was even aware of. I leaned my face on her shoulder and spoke to her reflection.

"You are perfect, Charlie. Perfect. You light up the room."

Her breath hitched, and she trembled.

"You fascinate me." I kissed her neck.

She melted into my touch, her resistance ebbing.

I spun her in my arms and kissed her. Her lips parted immediately, and my tongue slid inside. I kissed her with long, languid strokes of my tongue that hinted at what I would soon do to her cunt. I lifted her by the waist and pulled her to the bed with me. Blood pounded in my veins, demanding that I finally take this woman, fill her up, mark her as mine, keep her forever. I was tired of denying myself. I couldn't hold back one more second.

I searched for the ties to the damn corset as she wriggled like a live wire in my arms, not taking my lips from hers for even a moment. She pulled at me, her fingers sinking into my skin and clawing me closer.

"That's right, *bambina,* show everyone who I belong to," I growled in her ear.

She shivered and kissed me harder, pressing her tits into my chest until I thought I'd go crazy if I didn't taste them. She wriggled her hips against me, her hot pussy greedy for more friction, and if I didn't get her underwear off in the next ten seconds, I was going to rip the entire thing to shreds.

"Is this lingerie or a chastity belt?" I muttered as my hands continued to find nothing but lace and mesh.

Charlotte snorted with sudden, unexpected laughter and then froze. It was loud and inelegant. It was real. I found myself smiling, and it felt damn good.

I stroked her hair back from her hot forehead and reached for one of the blades I kept hidden near the bed. "I'm sorry if you love this. I'll buy you a new one."

Leaning back, I did the only thing I could think of and carefully positioned the blade at the lace of the cup. "Hold still, little nurse."

She held her breath as I cut the lace apart on both sides and then sliced the sides of her panties. Tossing the knife, I pulled a hard nipple in my mouth and moaned. Fuck, that was perfection right there. The cut-open cups of the corset propped her tits up, and the cuts left just enough space for her nipples to pop through. I took my time licking and sucking the puffy buds while I worked her with my fingers, sinking three digits inside her. Tonight, she needed to take my cock, and she was so tight, it might even hurt. She needed to be stretched.

I fucked her with my fingers, rubbing my thumb on her clit until she came. Her muscles tightened on me and then slackened more than ever as she crested on waves of pleasure. I took the opportunity to push her legs apart and move between them.

Her hands gripped my shoulders, and she shuddered in my arms as I rocked my cock up her soaking entrance.

"I just came," she muttered in a daze.

She was adorable. She was so used to coming being a rare occurrence, she had no idea that one time was nowhere near enough for a proper fucking.

"And you'll come again, and again, until my name is all you can say." I pressed inside, and her slick muscles parted beautifully for me. "I'm going to fuck you until you're as addicted to my cock as I am to the taste of your cunt." *As addicted as I am to your smile.* I withheld that particular thought. It felt more intimate somehow.

We both paused when I reached the end of her, my hips pressed flush against hers. It felt unbearably good to be inside her. She moved first, wriggling on my cock, urging me deeper.

I chuckled as I moved. My little nurse had no idea what she'd been repressing. She was going to be a wildcat in bed, I could tell. Once she stopped shaming herself for enjoying the things we did together, she'd be unstoppable. I was a lucky bastard.

No, not lucky.

I fucked her a little harder, and she gasped, a breathy sound that turned me on even more.

I made my own luck. Charlotte was the perfect example. I'd seen her and I'd kept her. Put my fucking ring on her finger, and now, as soon as I could manage it, I'd have her round with my child. Mine, forever.

She clung to me as I fucked her harder. Leaning up on one arm, and keeping my cock sunk deep, I reached between us with my other hand, circling her clit. She cried out.

"You have nothing to feel ashamed of, little nurse. You're my wife, before God and witnesses. Nothing we do together is wrong."

I fucked her slowly at first, building to a punishing pace. She clutched onto me, panting my name. I had a new favorite music, and it was my name rolling from this woman's lips. When she contracted around me with a scream, I followed right behind. She held me so willingly and clenched my dick so hard, there was no holding back. I pulsed inside her, burying my cock in the warmth of her wet pussy.

Pushed in to the hilt, I cupped her sweating face and captured her mouth in a searing kiss. Her glazed eyes looked into mine. I'd never known it was possible to be so intimate with another person. To really see inside a soul. Not until I'd met this woman.

My murmur sounded raw. "Every time we touch, it's holy, and nothing you think or feel can change that. My perfect, perfect wife."

I was born a sinner, and I'd die one. I'd long since given up hope of salvation, and yet coming inside my wife felt like a glimpse of Heaven. It was the closest I'd ever come, and it was enough for me.

23

CHARLIE

I woke from a dead sleep to the slightest pinch on my arm. The last few hours rushed back to me. The wedding, the reception, Renato cutting my finger and then bringing me upstairs. Coming so hard I'd seen stars. My body was warm and limp, wrung out by pleasure.

"You're a heavy sleeper, *bambina,*" Renato murmured from my side.

I turned to look at him. The sight was absolutely terrifying. He was wearing a sterile glove and had a case of medical instruments set out on the bedside table.

"What are you doing?" I panicked.

"Nothing you didn't already expect," he said and dropped something into a metal dish. It landed with a clink.

I thought of that sharp prick that had woken me up, the pain just above my elbow. There was only one thing there.

"My birth control implant," I guessed. "You removed it."

"Of course I removed it." He snapped off the glove and balled it up. He then wrapped a stretchy bandage around my upper arm, securing it just tight enough to seal the small incision he'd have made to remove the implant.

I'd removed enough of them to know the procedure well.

"You don't need it anymore," he continued.

That calmly delivered sentence was terrifying. He really planned on having children with me. *With me.* Nobody in my life had ever shown me that level of commitment.

Commitment? He just married you, just made his men bow to you. What kind of commitment are you looking for? I had no answer for that.

"You didn't think a medical professional should remove it? Or maybe you were too worried what they'd say about removing an implant from an unconscious woman?" Going on the defensive seemed the safest bet right now, when my body was still warm from his touch and my mind had softened toward the man who held my future in the palm of his hand.

Renato stood and leaned over me, smoothing the bandage and inspecting his handiwork. He was precise in all things, whether that was shooting someone perfectly between the eyes or carrying out minor medical procedures.

"Firstly, I didn't ask a medical professional because no one but me will ever hurt you. I promise you that."

"That is not as reassuring as you seem to think it is!" I interjected, prompting Renato to press a silencing finger against my lips.

"Secondly, you are no longer just some unconscious woman. You're my wife."

I twisted my head from his hand, electricity starting in the pit of my belly. "Stop saying it like that."

"Like what? Wife? You're my wife, *bambina*. I think it has a nice ring to it."

I swallowed my nerves and confusion. My arm didn't hurt. He'd clearly injected me with a local anesthetic. He moved around the bed toward the bathroom. I should hit him, or fight somehow, but my body was too languid to make the effort. He hadn't even drugged me, just worn me out with sex and the longest, most emotional day of my life.

I stared at the bandage on my arm. I'd known this would happen, hadn't I? He'd been clear that he needed an heir. It was literally his goal, and he made no secret of it. But I *did* have a secret.

My implant had been about to expire, and one of the doctors on rotation encouraged me to sign up for a clinical trial testing a new birth control shot. The shot was good for three months, and I'd just gotten it a few weeks ago. So, while I hadn't gotten around to taking out my old implant, I knew I should be protected for another couple of months.

Still, my new husband was clearly serious about getting me pregnant as quickly as he could. It should have scared me more than it did. Maybe my fear sensors were just burned out. Too much adrenaline had made me immune. I was numb. But I didn't feel numb as I watched Renato head to the shower, pausing in the doorway to look back at me.

"You're very calm about this," he observed.

Crap.

I shrugged. "You warned me. Death, or marriage and kids with you. I chose you."

"Yes, you did."

He watched me for a moment longer, and I considered trying to look worried but dismissed the idea. I was a terrible actress. Instead, I pushed my hair back over my shoulder, where it slid right back like a waterfall.

Renato still watched me. "Are you sore? A shower could help," he suggested, his gaze lingering over me.

"I'll take one later."

"Or you could take one now, with me," he said quietly. He

chuckled at my expression. "Are you really blushing after everything we did last night? I'd think a shower was on the tame end of the spectrum."

I hated that he could read me so damn well. Was I really so transparent? Or had no one ever cared enough to try before?

"I can't get the hole you made in my arm wet," I snapped, sliding down in the bed and hiding my face in the pillow.

"Sure, you can't, *bambina*," Renato smirked.

Thankfully, the shower came on a little later and the door closed. I blew out a long breath and rolled onto my back, staring at the beautifully corniced ceiling.

I brought my left hand up over my head and peered at my ring. It sparkled in the light that flooded through the wall of windows lining one side of the room.

My arm wasn't the only place that bore Renato's handiwork. Blood had crusted around my wedding ring, reminding me of the ceremony the night before. I'd have to clean it. It didn't hurt that much, but I wasn't someone who fussed over small cuts and scrapes, anyway.

I was more worried about the bug sitting in the planter in his study. I hadn't heard from the cops again, but I knew they'd be in touch.

Maybe I should just tell Renato the truth? As soon as I thought it, I knew I couldn't. This was a man who'd just cut my birth control implant out of my arm. He had no boundaries. His idea of right and wrong was completely different from mine. I had no clue how he'd react. I couldn't risk it. I just had to play along with Detectives Vane and Whitely until I could figure out what to do. I needed a little damn time to think.

The shower shut off, and I jumped out of bed. My leg muscles protested wildly as I staggered out of the bedroom and down the hall toward the room I'd shared with Lucy. I noticed Sonny wasn't around. I guessed that meant Renato would take the night shift. Who needed a prison guard when your own husband was on the job?

Vinny sat outside Lucy's room. He jumped up when I came into sight and then whirled away from me, averting his eyes.

"Good morning, Mrs. De Sanctis," he said gruffly.

"Good morning. It's just Charlie," I reminded him, wondering at his odd posture. "What's wrong?"

"Nothing, nothing at all, I just don't think I should be . . . um . . . seeing you in that outfit, not that I was looking," he mumbled.

I was wearing a silky-soft nightgown with a lace back, part of the bridalwear given to me by Vito and his team. *Right.* Renato and his high-handed orders about what I could wear in front of his men.

"Sorry. It's my fault. I won't tell him if you don't. Just let me in to see Lucy." I waited impatiently as he unlocked the door.

Lucy was reading, and she raised an eyebrow at me when I went inside and shut the door behind me.

"Good morning," I muttered, knowing that Lucy had a whole lot to say, judging by her expression, but too distracted to give it much thought. I set about searching for the envelope in one of the drawers.

Lucy watched me with an unreadable expression. I found the envelope and folded it into my palm.

"Are you okay?" I asked.

"Sure, as much as a prisoner in the world's most boring prison can be."

"What do you want to do?"

"I want a phone. I miss talking to my friends." She turned to look out the window at the woods. The fall leaves had painted a blaze of oranges and reds in the trees beyond.

"I'm not sure you'll get a phone, yet." I chewed my lip. "Maybe it's a good time to think about what you want to do next."

"Meaning?"

I sat opposite her. I'd been thinking about the topic since the end of summer, when most of Lucy's classmates had gone on to study or work while she'd remained behind, stuck.

"Well, do you want to go to college, or maybe get a job? What do you want to do with your life?"

Lucy rolled her eyes. "You're so naïve. You seriously think that either of us is going to be allowed to do anything we wanted to do? I'm sure my new brother-in-law is just looking for the right candidate to marry me off to next, and that will take care of the younger sister problem."

A chill went through me at her confident words. "No. He wouldn't. That was never on the table. He gave me his word he'd take care of you if I married him."

"And Renato De Sanctis is the kind of man who keeps his word? Yeah, right."

Renato's confident voice spoke in my head. *I always keep my word. Always. My word is my bond.*

"That's not going to happen, so just put it out of your head and think about what I asked. Do you want to study? Work? What do you want to do with your life?"

"What life?" Lucy exploded, whirling away from me.

She was so agitated, I wondered how she'd managed to keep it under control until now.

"We have no life. We died, and this is hell."

I shook my head. "Don't be ridiculous. I did all of this so we could live."

"Maybe I don't want to live like this. Under the microscope of killers, waiting to see what they'll do with us. No freedom. No space. No escape. That's no life."

"Life is what you make of it. Stop crying about the past; it's gone. Focus on the future."

"We have no future!" Lucy snapped, glaring daggers at me. "I can't live like this."

"You have no choice." My tone sounded harsh, run ragged by the continued stress of the past week. "This is our reality, and we aren't quitters, so get on with it."

"That's your advice? Just get on with it?"

"That's what I've always done, isn't it? *Look after your sister*, so I got on with it. *Provide a roof and school and food for her*, so I got on with it. *Marry a mobster to keep us safe*, so I got on with it."

Slow, ironic clapping interrupted me. "Congratulations on being able to make yourself do horrible things." Lucy's eyes blazed with unshed tears. She was a ball of emotions, and I didn't know how to help her.

I reached out for her arm, and she jerked away. I backed away and sighed. "I don't have time for this right now. I'm taking a shower and getting on with my day."

My sister stared at me for a long moment, as if she was disappointed at my response to her outburst, then shrugged. "Yes, wouldn't want to keep the warden waiting."

I couldn't afford to get dragged into Lucy's pity party. I was starving and needed a shower desperately. I could smell Renato all over me. I was sticky with his cum, and it made me feel debauched in a way I never had before. I left her there, stewing in anger and resentment. As time passed, it was becoming harder and harder to communicate with her without fighting.

I hopped into the shower in my old room and washed as quickly as I could.

I shivered, running my hands over my body. Everything was so sensitive after his touch last night.

You have nothing to feel ashamed of, little nurse. You're my wife, before God and witnesses. Nothing we do together is wrong. Every time we touch, it's holy, and nothing you think or feel can change that. My perfect, perfect wife.

Just remembering the words—spoken as I'd come for the second time, my body stuck to his with sweat and both our cum—was enough to make me shudder. Those words perfectly fit the jigsaw of broken pieces inside me that had shattered during my childhood. That fact alone told me that my new husband did indeed see me, in all my repressed, tightly controlled glory. *My perfect, perfect wife.*

I headed downstairs, dressed in one of the borrowed leggings-and-sweater combos that Carmella had given me. At some point, I was going to have to get some new clothes.

The kitchen was crowded when I got there. Elio sat at the counter, and Sonny and Giada argued over the last bowl of some imported Italian cereal in the pantry.

Carmella turned a smile on me as I walked in. "*Auguri.*" This was the warmest she'd ever been with me. She pulled me into a hug. She was soft, like a cushion, and smelled of sugar cookies. I stayed longer in that embrace than was normal, but she didn't say anything. She simply patted my hand when I finally leaned back.

"Thank you," I murmured to her.

"*Grazie*. Thank you is *grazie*," she encouraged.

"Don't tell me you're going to start giving Charlie language lessons against her will now?" Sonny teased the elderly housekeeper.

"She should speak the language of her husband. The language of her family." Carmella tossed her head with the kind of energy that wasn't going to be deterred.

"She's right. When you go to Italy, it'll be nice to be able to speak to the family." Elio's voice surprised me. He wasn't exactly the chatty type.

I sat next to him, just as Carmella placed a cup of coffee in front of me. *Will Renato really take me to Italy?* I'd never even left New Jersey.

"*Zio* Salvatore is going to love you," Giada called from the counter where she looked for a bowl.

"Salvatore?"

"Renato's uncle on his mother's side. He runs Napoli like Ren runs Atlantic City. He's been waiting for happy news from this side of the world for years."

"Happy news?" I took a sip of my coffee.

"Baby news," Giada snorted, cradling her bowl of cereal victoriously.

Her words and the unexpected taste in my mouth sent the liquid up my nose. I snorted and coughed, choking on my mouthful. "What is this?" I asked.

"It's decaf. Expectant mothers shouldn't overindulge in caffeine. It's not good for the baby," Carmella tutted from the pantry.

"But I'm not pregnant!"

"Yet," Giada added.

I ignored her and addressed Carmella. "I'm not pregnant yet, so there's no need to drink decaf. I need the caffeine. Please, give it to me, or I'm scaling a wall and heading for the nearest coffee shop."

"Scaling a wall? No need for that here. Casa Nera is full of secrets . . . like hidden passages where you come out way down the road," Giada smirked at me.

"Really?" I asked.

"Really," she confirmed.

"Giada, basta." Elio's snap made me jump.

"Don't worry. I agreed to this farce. I'll see it through," I muttered and tried another sip of decaf. It wasn't actually that bad.

Elio focused on a point over my shoulder. "You're not the one I'm worried about."

I twisted in my seat and spied Lucy lingering by the doorway. Carmella immediately went toward my younger sister and put her arm around her, ushering her into the kitchen with the energy of a mother hen.

"Lucy! I've been waiting for you. Today, we learn how to make bread."

"You're learning how to cook?" I asked.

"Why? Is it not allowed?" Lucy snapped back at me right away.

Our painful conversation upstairs circled my head.

Carmella patted Lucy's hand. "Easy, *cara*." The housekeeper caught my eye. "Lucy will be with me for a while."

I nodded, gripping my coffee cup like my life depended on it, and made my way out of the kitchen. I needed some space.

I was watching TV later when someone knocked at the den door. I'd never had so much free time. I wanted to finish my program and work in a hospital, just like I'd told Renato, but I couldn't deny it was nice to have a break. I hadn't had proper time off in years.

Sonny poked his head into the room. "Just thought you should know some stuff arrived for you. You might want to be upstairs to direct where it goes," he said cheerfully and disappeared.

I left the room and went to see what the hell he was talking about.

Casa Nera staff rushed up and down the stairs, hauling up boxes and returning empty-handed. Their destination was the new room I was to share with Renato. I hurried after them, pausing on the threshold as I took in the scene before me. Boxes of all shapes and sizes had been put on the bed, the floor, basically any surface they could fit on. It was quite the sight to see hulking men in dark suits, with earpieces, trying to balance five shoeboxes at once.

"What is all this?" I asked.

"Deliveries from the boutiques in La Leonora," Sonny said and grinned. "Boss knows how to go all out." He looked proud, like buying more than a year's worth of clothes for someone was normal.

I sent everyone away as soon as all the packages were in the room. I felt bad enough they'd had to go out of their way to carry them all upstairs. I could have done it alone, but it would have taken me the better part of a day.

I lingered in the doorway for a long moment, feeling like an intruder. An imposter. The pretend wife.

"Nice haul." Giada peered over my shoulder. "Ren has good taste, though a little conservative, but maybe you like that. To be real, he's not letting you out of the house in anything too short or revealing. You just have to accept that."

"I don't like showy stuff," I murmured, my gaze tracing over the well-known designer brands emblazoned across the shiny bags.

"Of course you don't. He gets you. It's almost kind of sweet."

"It is not," I argued back faintly. I couldn't even fathom the cost of everything in the room. It was the kind of extravagance I had no experience with. Never mind buying designer clothes; I usually struggled to justify buying *new* clothes and not getting something from Goodwill.

"Something Renato De Sanctis will never be is sweet," I continued, edging into the room. I peered inside one of the bags and looked up at Giada. "It's shoes."

"Why are you whispering? Are you scared they'll hear you?" she replied in a loud mock whisper.

She reached into the box and opened it. A pair of flat, chestnut-brown leather riding boots emerged. Perfect for the weather, and so classic and beautiful, I had to touch the smooth surface.

Giada handed them to me and then turned and glanced at the

rest of the room, packed with boxes and dress bags. "Okay, I suggest this. I'll open, and you sort. Deal?"

"Is this really all for me? Maybe we should check before we open it all?"

Giada frowned at me for a moment and then laughed. "Oh, Charlie, I seriously never know what you're going to say. No shit, it's for you. You are the wife of the boss now; you can't keep walking around in Carmella's old leggings. Relax and let your husband spend his money on you. You deserve it, and you need to internalize that thought."

"Great, the criminal is giving me self-help advice now?" I muttered.

Giada cackled. "I sure am. Now, help me, or I'm taking those boots as payment."

I gripped the boots to my chest, and she laughed again.

"That's the spirit. Learn to be selfish for once in your life. There aren't any prizes in heaven for being the most self-sacrificing. That's just a myth."

I rolled my eyes, but a sense of excitement ran through me that I couldn't deny. Just the idea of having my own clothes again was more than appealing, but beautiful, soft, unworn clothes? As ashamed as I might be to admit it, I was excited.

We dug into the boxes.

I found a note inside a soft bag full of lingerie. The folded piece of paper was like a grenade, exploding my tentative happiness. Giada had gone for snacks, and I was tackling the more personal items alone. The underwear sets I'd already unpacked were beautiful in a way I'd never known underwear could be. The voice in my head that I recognized as one of the sisters' at Mercy Home was immediately critical. *What a waste of money.* But the woman inside me, the one who never bought herself anything new, loved it.

My hand closed around the piece of paper at the bottom of the satin bag. I pulled it out.

Who would put a note in here? My fingers shook as I unfolded it.

> *We have his phone last pinged in your apartment block, and we have her guilty, tearful testimony about his disappearance in the books. Don't test us. Choose a side. V*

"Okay, I know I went for food, but I brought margaritas," Giada sang loudly as she sailed into the room holding a tray with a huge jug of pink liquid and two glasses.

"What's wrong?" She stopped immediately, taking in my stricken expression.

"Nothing," I lied, feeling sick.

"It's clearly not nothing." Giada sighed and set down the tray, pouring two glasses of pink margaritas. She handed me one. "I'm just going to assume you found the bag of toys."

I was gulping down my drink and nearly choked. "Toys?"

She grinned wickedly and clinked her glass against mine. "Cheers to men who want to fill every hole on their wives at once but would shoot any other man who dared to touch her."

Fill every hole? Embarrassment flooded through me, and I clapped a hand over my face. Then I remembered the note in my pocket, and I jumped on the chance to distract my mind. "Show me."

24

CHARLIE

That night, I was trying to read in my new bed when Renato appeared in the doorway. Trying, because the words kept moving. An entire pitcher of margaritas was a little past my tolerance level, it turned out.

Despite feeling like I was on a merry-go-round, I was glad to be done sharing a room with my sister. Her sullen mood was contagious, and I couldn't live like that. I had to carry on with things. After all, I'd agreed to all of this. And with the police breathing down my neck, it was hard enough to keep my *own* mood stable.

"What are you reading?" Renato's sudden voice from the doorway made me jump.

I dropped the book on the bed and glared at him. He lounged in the doorway, staring at me.

"How long have you been there?" I asked accusingly, unsettled by his warm expression.

"A while," he murmured and came into the room, taking off his suit jacket and revealing a black dress shirt. It was unbuttoned at the throat, and a hint of his tattoos peeked through.

My gaze lingered on the long, muscled curves of his torso. The man was insanely hot. I couldn't deny it. My gaze found his face, and his knowing smirk had me picking up my book again, embarrassed.

"It's okay, *bambina*. I like when you watch me. I like watching you, too," he pointed out. He undid more buttons on his shirt, leaving it open, and I studiously avoided looking at his inked torso.

He wandered toward the bed in the open shirt and his black dress pants, perched low on his hips. He stopped beside me and slid a finger under the satin strap of one of the new pajama sets that he'd bought me.

"This suits you," he mused.

I fought the urge to squirm under his touch. "If you want to waste your money, I'm not going to stop you," I quipped.

The bed dipped when Renato sat on the edge beside me and closed my book. I gave a pained sigh, looking everywhere but at him.

"Spending money on my wife isn't a waste. You deserve to have nice things. Tell me whoever made you feel differently, and I'll teach them that fact, slowly."

I shrugged. "Life taught me that, so just calm down. There's no one to shoot for it, thanks for asking."

Renato's mouth pulled up in a half-grin that was sexy as hell. He glanced at my lap. "What are you reading?" He turned the book and raised an eyebrow. "*The Prince*. Machiavelli. Light bedtime reading, then?"

"Your library isn't exactly stuffed with rom-coms, or books in English for that matter," I blustered. Truthfully, I'd been drawn to the book because it was one of the most dog-eared. Like a book could help me understand the man sitting beside me. *Yeah, right.* Still, something was better than nothing.

Renato lifted the book and set it on the bedside table, then spoke quietly.

". . . since love and fear can hardly exist together, if we must choose between them, it is far safer to be feared than loved."

He shifted his eyes to mine. "I've studied the thoughts in that book for years, but I've only just come to understand the meaning of that particular quote."

His tone was cryptic, and with him so close, it was hard to concentrate on anything. The margaritas from earlier still swam through my veins, making me relaxed and fearless in front of this man who owned me. *Does that mean I own him, too?*

"Are we really going to be sleeping here together every night?" I asked, my mind latching onto the next stray thought that came along.

"Yes. We're married, this is our room."

"You just don't seem like the kind of man who . . . sleeps with one person." Crap, I had no idea who was controlling my mouth, but they were doing a terrible job.

Renato raised an eyebrow. "What gave you that impression? I believe the only woman you've seen me with besides yourself is Giada."

I waved a hand over him. "It's all of this. This whole thing," I elaborated, like that would help.

A faint grin touched Renato's mouth. "Are you complimenting me, *mia moglie?*"

I snorted. "Why would I? Like you need anything else to make you cockier?" The last word seemed to stick on my lips, making me laugh. "Cocky, get it?" I laughed a little more. I probably shouldn't have drunk so much when unpacking. I hadn't realized I was so wasted until this moment.

Renato raised an eyebrow at me.

I swayed into him. "Cocky, because you have a big *you know*," I explained in a loud whisper.

He caught me when I nearly toppled over. "Who is responsible for this?"

"Giada helped me unpack."

"Enough said. Did you eat dinner?"

"I forgot." I sighed. "I was trying to read your book, but the words kept moving around."

I closed my eyes for a second, and the world lurched. Yikes. Okay, that was definitely too much tequila for a lightweight like me.

"Come on, little nurse. Let's get you something to eat."

I opened my eyes. Renato stood beside me, holding his hand out. My stomach growled at the prospect of food, and he chuckled.

"I don't need help. I'm not drunk," I protested as I stood and immediately fell against him.

"Sure, you aren't." He ran his gaze down my outfit, and his eyes darkened. "I knew you'd look good in the clothes I bought you."

"I *only* have clothes to wear that you bought me."

"Good." He pulled me closer, running his hands from my shoulders to my waist.

His touch felt good. I melted against him. "Except for Carmella's old leggings," I pointed out.

"I'm having them burned. Come on, let's find something for you to eat," he said gruffly, brushing my hair back from my face.

My new husband could cook. In my semi-drunk state, all I could do was watch him with my mouth hanging slightly open. Hopefully, there was no drool.

He rolled his shirtsleeves up to the elbows and just took charge in the kitchen. We were alone, the clock ticking toward midnight. I sat at the island, leaning my head on my hand and trying to stay upright, observing the man who had stolen my life and replaced it with another. He was cooking me an omelet, and it was disturbingly attractive.

The air filled with the smell of ripe cherry tomatoes, chopped basil, and pressed garlic, sizzling gently in olive oil.

"I feel like I should offer to help," I muttered.

"And that's your problem right there, *anima mia*. You don't always have to help. Sometimes, you can let people do things for you," Renato said, cracking eggs with one hand and whisking with the other.

His strong, tattooed wrist rotating the whisk with ease did something to me. God, I really needed to sober up. I played with the chess pieces from a board lying on the counter. I'd seen Giada and Sonny playing there in the morning sometimes.

"Spare me the armchair psychology BS, or I'll do you, too," I warned him.

He laughed. "I'd love for you to do me, *bambina*."

Ignoring the innuendo, I wrapped my arms around my knees and pushed against my stomach, hoping the position would muffle the growling. Now that I could smell food, my stomach had woken up and demanded to be fed.

"Fine. You're the king of the castle," I proclaimed. "And everyone else is locked outside. You have to control everything around you, every player on the board is yours to move . . . You can't look away or relax, because then if you make a mistake, you might lose someone and have to add another tally mark." I pointed toward his chest.

He'd left the omelet to cook and leaned over the counter toward me. I turned to the chessboard, desperate for anything at all to distract me from the beauty of this man in the low lighting. I chose black for Renato, because of course. I pushed back all the other figures, isolating the king.

"Very astute. Maybe drunk therapy should be a thing—" he started.

I brought my finger to his lips and shushed him, braver in my drunkenness than I normally was.

"I wasn't finished. You do all that, and you have all this, and everyone thinks you're this god, untouchable, all-knowing, holding power over life and death . . . and it's true, but you're up there in your tower and you're all alone."

As soon as the words left me, a warning sounded through the thick fog in my head. *Wait, what did I say?* I tried to recall as Renato stared at me.

"Well, heavy is the head that wears the crown, after all."

"Machiavelli?" I wondered.

He was so close to me, and the air had grown thick as we'd spoken. He hadn't pulled back when I'd leveled my drunken psychoanalysis at him. In fact, he seemed closer than ever.

"Shakespeare," Renato corrected gently. "*Henry IV.*"

Right. A timely reminder that this man was way out of my league in terms of experience and worldliness.

"You know a lot. I bet you've read all the books in your library, haven't you? You're much smarter than me. I've never been out of the state, did you know that? Never been on an airplane. I can't really speak any other languages fluently, but I bet you know that. You know everything about me," I murmured.

Renato watched me with a kind of fascination I couldn't deal with in my hazy state. It was too intense. This man was intense about everything, and yet I hadn't seen him stare at anyone the way he stared at me.

"No one looks at me the way you do," I heard myself say. My already flimsy filter was MIA at the moment.

"No one talks to me the way *you* do," he responded, reaching out and cupping my cheek. It felt affectionate and intimate. My heart beat strangely.

"Because you'd kill them?"

Renato smirked and reached toward the omelet pan to turn off the heat. Then he straightened up and rounded the island toward me.

The chessboard sat beside me in the funny configuration I'd set up, with the king encircled by a few squares of space on all sides.

I spun around on the stool to keep him in sight. He wasn't the kind of man you turned your back on. It would be like putting your back to a panther and trusting it not to pounce.

He stopped before me, stepping so close I had to open my legs for him to fit. He reached past me toward the chessboard. He picked up the biggest piece from the opponent's side of the board and set her down beside the lonely king.

The queen.

The *white* queen.

The black-and-white couple sat at the top of the board, isolated, but not alone. Not anymore.

Renato turned to me and cupped my face, stroking both thumbs over my cheeks, looking at me like I was something precious.

Something holy.

I opened my mouth to speak, desperate to fill a silence too intimate to bear, but there were no words waiting for me. I had no way to distract myself from the expression in his eyes and the undeniable knowledge that something was happening between us. Something huge and real.

His lips met mine, and it was a kiss unlike any he'd given me so far. It was as gentle as a man like him was capable of being. He brushed his lips against mine, and it was a request. I parted my lips in a gasp. The heat of his hands on my face, the closeness of his body . . . it was intoxicating. His tongue slid into my mouth and tangled languidly with mine.

He kissed me like he was tasting every inch of me. Savoring.

I dug my hands into his shirt, tugging him closer, holding him in place.

He smiled against my lips. "Don't worry, *mia moglie*. I'm not going anywhere," he murmured.

"What does *mia moglie* mean?"

"My wife," he supplied, pressing kisses along my jaw toward my ear.

"What about *bambina*?"

"Baby girl."

He reached my ear, and heat flooded me. *God*, I liked that.

"*Anima mia*?" I'd memorized all the things he called me, desperate to know their meaning, but scared, too.

He paused and pulled back, pinning me in place with his dark gaze. I wondered if he was going to leave me hanging with that one, but then he spoke.

"It means 'my soul.'"

I wet my lips, only dimly aware of the rest of the room. This moment felt important somehow, or maybe it was just the alcohol in my veins, making this powerful man seem less scary for a second.

"I thought men like you didn't have one," I said quietly, without reproach.

"We don't, but don't worry about me, little nurse." Renato smiled wickedly as he leaned in and spoke right in my ear. "You promised me yours, remember?"

Then, with the most embarrassing timing in the world, my stomach let out a protest so loud, the intimacy of the moment was shattered.

Renato chuckled, leaning back and heading toward the delicious-smelling omelet.

"Enough philosophizing for tonight. Let me feed you."

"And then?" I wondered, my gaze feasting on the omelet as he put it on a plate and cut it into neat, bite-size rows.

"And then . . ." He threw a dishcloth over his shoulder and speared the first bite of eggs, holding it to my lips. "Bedtime."

25

RENATO

"Ren? Did you hear me?"

Elio's voice pierced through my reverie. Charlotte had been circling my head all morning, probably because she'd promptly passed out as soon as we'd gone upstairs last night and left me with a raging hard-on. She'd reached into my barren chest in the kitchen and taken my withered heart in her perfect small hand . . . and then blithely went on to eat eggs and forget about it.

But I hadn't forgotten it. Not by a long shot.

"Yes, I heard you. Commissioner Reynolds wants to meet. Why?"

"He didn't say."

"I'm not extending his credit again. He's already in the hole for nearly a hundred grand." I pinched the point that ached between my eyes.

Rich, powerful men like the police commissioner were the bane of my existence. They were too influential to waste by killing off, but they were fucking leeches.

"Do you want me to tell him that? Or just bar him from playing until he pays some off?"

"Bar him. I don't have time for this. He thinks he can make demands? When he knows full well that I have more than enough evidence on his police department skimming? Bar him and keep him out of my sight. Let him sweat."

Elio raised an eyebrow but otherwise didn't comment. I needed Commissioner Reynolds more than ever lately, with Detectives Vane and Whitely sticking their noses where they didn't belong, but I'd had enough of the guy. Plus, every word that was said in my office was going straight to the nosy detectives' ears, thanks to the bug they'd had Charlie plant. Let them take that piece of info to their boss and see how it went.

"Giada also found this," Elio continued and placed a photo in front of me.

It was Commissioner Reynolds, and the slimy, suited Castillo who'd walked into my warehouse a week ago. The one the dead guy from the woods had named. *Juan Castillo*. The posture of the man, and the amount of security that surrounded him, confirmed my suspicions. This was the head of the Castillos, and he'd been right under my nose the entire time. I should've cared more about that than I did right then. But I was distracted, and the reason was asleep in my bed.

Work was tedious beyond belief today, and every second I devoted to work felt like time that I could've spent fantasizing about my wife.

My wife.

Was she awake yet? I checked my watch and stood.

She'd slept enough, and it was time she did something about the ache in my balls.

She was still asleep. Burrowed under the covers, only the trailing length of her brown hair visible when I entered the room. The curtains were still drawn, and I closed and locked the door behind me, anticipation roaring in my veins. After just one taste, I was already hopelessly addicted to being inside this woman. It was a compulsion. I wasn't even going to try to fight it.

I watched her sleep for a moment, sinking into the armchair on her side of the bed. She shifted toward me, as if her body naturally gravitated in my direction, even in sleep.

She was wearing the silky camisole I'd picked out for her. It gaped at the cleavage, and I could see a hint of one dusky nipple. I'd never shopped for or with a woman before. I had no interest in it. But my wife was a different story. After a lifetime of cheap secondhand clothes, she deserved spoiling, and I was just the man to do it.

Besides, I liked the thought of her wearing clothes I'd bought for her. I liked that there was a small part of me she'd carry with her all day. Soon, I hoped there would be a much larger part.

The De Sanctis family doctor had reassured me that conception could occur pretty much as soon as the implant was removed. I planned on being very diligent about keeping Charlotte's tight cunt stuffed full of cum so whenever her body was ready, she could easily get pregnant. The compulsion to breed my wife had little to do with producing an heir or pleasing *Zio* Salvatore, if I was brutally honest with myself. I just wanted a part of me to live inside this woman, tying us together forever.

I undressed, making no attempt to be quiet, and she stirred slightly. My bambina had really tired herself out yesterday unpacking all her new clothes and getting wasted with Giada. I had to talk to Elio's sister. Drinking wasn't good for an expectant mother, though technically, Charlotte wasn't pregnant yet, and it had been good to get behind her defenses and see inside her head.

She didn't hate me nearly as much as she pretended to.

I could work with that.

I stripped everything off and searched for the box I'd had

delivered along with everything else. Charlotte had hidden it right at the back of her walk-in closet. I took what I wanted from it and headed back out to the bedroom. Next, I tied her wrists and ankles to the bedposts. She was so pliable and trusting in her sleep.

I will always keep you safe, anima mia, *from everyone but myself.*

She woke just as I fit the ball gag in her mouth. Her eyes widened as she tested the bonds and attempted to speak. Her gaze roamed around the darkened room, wild and panicked for a moment, before they met mine. The panic and fear in her eyes melted away when she saw me. It was a moment I knew I'd never forget.

She trusted me. Despite lying to me and hiding bugs for the police, my little nurse trusted me.

"Shh, don't worry, *bambina,* we're just catching up on what I planned to do to you last night, before you passed out."

Her eyes widened again. She was remembering last night. She swallowed, and the sight of her neck moving was beautiful.

"Are you hungover?" I asked.

She nodded a little.

"Do you want me to make you feel better?"

Her pupils were blown with want, her body already responding to the very idea. I'd suspected she would like being tied up since that night in the bathroom at the benefit. I tapped the ball gag.

"This is because I know how much you like having something in your mouth," I murmured.

She flushed bright red, but nothing in her expression disagreed with me.

I headed to the end of the bed and picked up one of the toys I'd brought with me, then positioned myself between her legs.

She strained to look down at me, curious, panicked, embarrassed. I couldn't keep up with the emotions chasing across her beautiful face.

I turned on the toy, and the low hum filled the room. Lowering it to her pussy, I moved along her side so I could suck her pretty tits while she got wet for me.

She jerked as the vibrator touched her. She still had on her nightgown, but it was thin and didn't seem to diminish her sensation. I lowered my mouth to her nipple, hard and poking through the lace covering, and bit down lightly on it, working her clit with the toy.

She moaned past the gag, her gaze glued to me as I used my teeth to pull the silky straps of the camisole off her shoulders and expose one tit at a time. Her nipples were darkened hard points when I rolled them between my lips, sucking, biting, and licking circles around them. Her hips bucked against the vibrator, seeking more friction. I worshipped her tits until her skin turned pink and her nipples were puffy. She rose toward a climax, just from the tit play and the toy alone. I kissed her hard when she came, moaning around the gag and convulsing in the silk ties.

I turned off the toy and tossed it aside, moving down her body. Her slip was going to be tricky to take off, so I reached for one of the slender knives I kept in my drawer. There were similar knives all around the house. You never knew when someone might get past all the security measures in place at Casa Nera, and in that case, a knife could be the difference between life and death.

She watched me carefully as I cut the top of her nightgown, the material parting easily beneath the blade, and then ripped it down the center and spread it open. She was bare before me, tied and vulnerable, and breathtaking.

Setting the knife aside, I couldn't wait one more second to taste her. I leaned down and lapped at her wet pussy. She was soaked from coming already, and as I slipped three fingers inside her, her cunt gripped my hand like it wanted to suck the whole thing inside. Reaching for the toy again, I flipped it in my hand and wet it liberally in her juices, sliding it inside her.

She groaned, thrashing as much as she could against me. I leaned in and sucked on her clit. She wasn't going to last long; her chest flushed pink, her hips already stuttering, but I wasn't stopping. I dove into her pussy with my tongue, circling her clit like a man possessed, fucking her with the toy. As she rose and rose, I flicked the vibration back on, and she exploded on my face. A jet of liquid hit me, and she screamed around the ball gag.

"Fuck, yes, *bambina*, soak me through with your cum," I rasped, my lips pressed to her pussy before tonguing her clit more, making her convulse against me and squirt more of her pleasure on herself. I looked up at her face and drank in her expression.

Tears had run tracks down her cheeks, her eyes bright and hazy at the same time. She panted and stared at me like I really was her chosen god. I stowed away that look of reverence inside the cold, dark recesses of my heart to treasure.

"Good girl, Charlotte. See how well you come for me, *bambina*. But we aren't finished yet," I told her.

Her breath hitched as I settled myself between her legs. Her thighs, and the bed around us, were wet with her cum, and it was fucking glorious.

I wanted to bathe in it, fuck in it, live covered in it. Proof that my quest—to make this woman as obsessed with me as I was with her—was working.

I pushed inside her, my aching dick not able to take one more second of torture. She was slick and hot and so tight it was hard to push in. Once I was in all the way, I reached for the strap around her lips and tugged it off. Her mouth was red and swollen. She whimpered as I licked the tears from her cheeks and then kissed her.

I lost myself in that moment, kissing this woman who had stolen my heart when I'd thought it had forgotten how to beat. I kissed her and fucked her until she came again, tightening around me like a vise, and then I followed, pumping cum into her, marking her insides with my best intentions, hoping that my seed would stick and root deep.

When I slid free on a rush of white, my fingers were there, pushing it back inside her hole. My thumb circled her clit, and she cried out. "I can't come again, I just can't," she panted desperately.

The way her beautiful, tearstained eyes pleaded with me was a fucking turn-on.

"You beg so prettily, *anima mia,*" I told her, pressing my white, slick fingers inside her while thumbing her clit. "But I promised to show you what proper fucking was, and I'm a relentless teacher."

I leaned in and kissed her when she came again, muffling her scream. My breath was in her mouth, my fingers in her cunt, and my name in her heart, right where I wanted it to be.

26

RENATO

The North Shore Club was the place to see and be seen by Atlantic City's elite. Mostly, it was rich old men playing golf, feeling up the staff, and pissing in the bushes. A real circle jerk of privilege and corruption. I owned every single one of the members there, in one way or another. I wasn't like my father, who'd watched one too many movies and relied on a "horse's head in the bed" approach to managing the business. Fear and threats could only take you so far. I preferred leverage and mutually assured destruction. We were not the same.

People who'd crossed my father, they'd gotten their asses beaten, or a member of their family might have been taken hostage. People who crossed me? I buried them socially, professionally, and then, once they'd suffered through that, physically.

It wasn't enough to kill a man like those who frequented the North Shore Club. You had to embarrass him first. You had to destroy his reputation. *Then* you killed him. Everything at its right time.

I waited with Elio until Commissioner Reynolds and Judge

Ellens were at the hole farthest from the club before heading toward them.

"Good morning, gentlemen, what a coincidence. I didn't know you played here." A lie, of course, obvious to everyone present. I knew every goddamn thing about these slimy excuses for men.

Commissioner Reynolds recovered first. "Renato! I didn't know you played. I've never seen you on the links before."

"What can I say, my work keeps me busy, and I neglect my hobbies. Something I suppose you aren't familiar with, Commissioner. You never neglect your hobbies, do you?"

The commissioner's face turned red as he gave a strangled cough.

Reynolds's hobbies were pretty standard. Drinking, snorting whatever illicit substances he could shove up his nose, gambling away his life savings, and chasing down some poor escort for the night, disappointing her with a poor performance. I knew exactly how poor because I'd seen the footage. With Giada's skills at my disposal, it was easy to get exactly the kind of evidence that could ruin a man.

"Meaning?"

"You've been going hard lately. We talked about credit before, if you remember?"

Reynolds licked his lips. "I remember."

"*Bene*. So, that particular part of the conversation doesn't need repeating. How do you know Juan Castillo?"

Reynolds blanched, and Judge Ellens got fidgety, suddenly very interested in the grass at his feet.

"Who?" Reynolds asked weakly.

I smirked at him. "You're going with that?" Playing dumb wasn't going to work for me, but Reynolds had never been the brightest bulb.

"What?"

I sighed heavily, irritated by the fact that I might get blood on my suit. I hefted the club in my hand, giving it a short spin before I smashed the heavy head against Reynolds's cheek. A couple of teeth flew out onto the grass, and the man fell to his knees.

"Did that jog your memory? Shake something loose?"

Reynolds gripped his jaw like it was broken or dislocated. Maybe it was. I didn't care. Elio handed me a stack of photos, and I tossed them on top of Reynolds.

"I want to know where this man hides out, and don't try and tell me you don't know." The CCTV showed Reynolds meeting Juan, the same smooth ambassador who'd recently strolled into my warehouse on Clements Drive.

The *patrón* of the cartel.

"What does he want?" I asked, dropping to a crouch beside Reynolds.

"Just those two nobodies, the nurse and her sister—and to get rid of you. Obviously, I told him to take a hike."

"Sure, you did. Let's get something straight. You can't fight me, Reynolds. You can't take me, not even with the Castillo kids behind you. You can't change my grip on this city, and you can't erase the leverage I have over you."

I stood. Judge Ellens cowered by their golf cart. This was the same judge who signed off on all the questionable paperwork Commissioner Reynolds sent his way, and yet he was dumb enough to look surprised that he'd pissed someone off.

"Detectives Vane and Whitely. Do they work for you?"

Reynolds rolled around on the ground, clutching his mouth and spitting blood down his chest.

"Call them off, if they do. If they don't, find a way to make them back off. I'm tired of them, and the next time I have to come and talk to you about it will be the last." I held out a hand for the sand-and-seed bottle used for maintaining the course, and I frowned at it as Elio passed it over.

I'd been planning on pouring some sand down Reynolds's throat to get the message across, but the disgusting pigs had pissed in the bottle.

I sloshed the bottle threateningly over Reynolds's body. "I see you with another Castillo, and this conversation goes very differently. You can't take me on in my city, Reynolds. Don't even try it." I poured the piss-ridden mixture over him before tossing the bottle at Judge Ellens, who fumbled as he tried to catch it.

"See you soon, gentlemen."

27

CHARLIE

The grounds of Casa Nera were pristine in the late December afternoon. The woods beyond the walls were still wearing their fall foliage, and the sky was a clear, pale blue. The faint scent of woodsmoke hung in the air, like someone was burning leaves nearby.

Gravel crunched underfoot as I walked away from the biggest house on the compound and headed around the back. Sonny dogged my steps, staying at least a few yards behind. Here and there, I glimpsed armed guards on patrol. I recognized one of them as Angelo, the guy whose face I'd patched up my first night in Casa Nera. The night I'd promised Renato to worship him. Angelo waved at me, smiling broadly. I returned his warm gesture.

Around the back of the sprawling mansion house was a small wooded area, a vegetable patch with a greenhouse, and a tiny stone building. Today, for the first time I'd seen, lights blazed inside the small windows of the cute building.

"What is that?" I asked Sonny, waiting for him to catch up.

"It's the late Mrs. De Sanctis's chapel. Renato's mother's. He keeps it well maintained. She loved it in there."

"Can I see?" I was already walking toward the doors.

Sonny hustled after me, hanging back in the doorway, like he was scared to step across the threshold onto holy ground.

Renato's mother had her own chapel? It was small and quaint, like it had been transported brick by brick from Italy. The kind you might come across in some pretty mountaintop town, with its red bricks, ivy-covered facade, and lead-paned stained glass windows.

Inside, a cross hung on the wall over the simple altar, and to the right, a marble Madonna looked benevolently across the humble pews. This wasn't a church to show off in. It was the church of a true believer. It wasn't ornate or impressive. It was simple and beautiful. Candles were lit on nearly every surface, the air heavy with incense.

I drifted down the aisle and slid into a pew. I hadn't been inside a church since before my Da died (except for my wedding, of course, which hardly counted). Because of the pain I'd felt as a young kid, feeling abandoned and unloved by the adults in my life, I'd turned my back on my father's beliefs. I couldn't see my faith returning anytime soon, but that didn't mean I didn't feel comforted by the peace and stillness of the place.

I closed my eyes and let that peace sink through me. *Please. Someone show me the way.* I wished someone would answer, because I was in real danger of falling in love with a devil and had no idea how to stop it. The thought of the bug circled my head and tormented me. Should I just destroy it?

"This was my mother's chapel." Renato's voice made me jump. I opened my eyes and glanced at him. He lounged in the doorway, staring at the marble Madonna.

This morning had been the filthiest and greatest sexual moment of my life. I'd had no idea I was capable of four consecutive orgasms. Hell, until I'd met Renato, I hadn't known I was capable of an orgasm that involved another person, period. I'd always been too tense, distracted, or hurrying toward the finish line. I'd always been too worried what the guy was thinking about me. Always too in my head and cut off from my body.

Not anymore, however. My husband didn't allow me space to run away or hide from him. He didn't even let me hold on to my precious sense of control that helped me keep my head clear. He was a whirlwind that I had no choice but to surrender to.

And I was dangerously close to becoming addicted.

Renato sauntered into the chapel and sat next to me on the creaking pew. "My father never came here. Not enough people around to demonstrate his faith to. He had another place in the city. There was a fire there. We don't use it anymore. For him, faith, like love and loyalty, was a performative act. If no one was watching, did it even matter? Not to him."

Inspired by his openness, I reciprocated. "My Da loved to go to the local Catholic church in our neighborhood. We had so many friends then. Everyone loved him. He was a character, you know? Larger than life. We were so poor, but we never really knew it, not until he was gone. He could make being hungry a game somehow. He always knew what to do, and I never have," I trailed off, feeling suddenly awkward about how much I'd shared.

"You do just fine. Your sister isn't an easy person."

I bristled. "You don't know her. She's not looking for trouble. She's a good girl, the best one, she just fell in love with the wrong guy. Love can do that . . . not that I'd expect you to know that."

I felt Renato's eyes swing to me. "Meaning?"

"Meaning . . . I haven't seen anyone else get close to you, and you married me, a perfect stranger—"

"Have you?" he interrupted.

"Have I what?"

"Ever been in love?"

No. Never even close.

"I love my sister." It was a pure statement of fact.

Renato nodded and then raised an eyebrow. "Sure you do, but that's not what I asked."

"If you're talking about romantic love, then sure, maybe, here or there."

"Maybe, here or there?" Renato repeated, sounding amused. "It seems like you don't know any more about it than I do."

I shrugged, and his expression tugged a reluctant grin to my face.

"Why do you seem happy about that?" I demanded. I didn't want to argue with him, because, after all, he was right. I'd never been in love with any of the men I'd dated. It felt too pathetic to confirm his words, so instead, I played with a rosary. "You know, when we were really little, my Da used to tell us to grab a rosary bead and make a wish."

"That's not how rosary beads work," Renato said.

I rolled my eyes. "I know. I'm just saying. He wanted to make all of our wildest dreams come true, and he didn't achieve any of it. Instead, we were alone . . ." I broke off.

"What was your wish?" Renato asked, relaxing back and sliding his arm along the pew behind me.

"I can't tell you that, obviously. Then it won't come true," I pointed out.

He grinned at me. "My sister—you'll meet her one day—she always wanted to be an artist. I never wanted anything like that. My dreams weren't a profession or possession. I wished I could make her feel safe. I wished I could have saved my mother. I wished I could be the person that the people I loved trusted."

I turned a shocked face to Renato. That had been raw, startling honesty, and I wasn't sure why he'd decided to share with me.

He pushed a hand through his thick waves. "Force of habit. Confessing in church."

"I wished I'd never be alone again," I blurted, inspired by his honesty. It felt too imbalanced not to reciprocate. "I wished that someone in the world would choose me, not because they had to, like Lucy, but because they wanted to. I wished I'd be enough for someone."

Renato's eyes, fine like aged whiskey, met mine. He raised a rakish eyebrow at me. "I find it very hard to believe that no one has tried to choose you over the years. I find it hard to believe you felt like you needed anyone to. You're a very capable woman."

My cheeks warmed at the compliment, and I gave a half-hearted shrug to hide my embarrassment. "Well, the scars from being picked last in gym are deep and everlasting, every shrink knows that."

Renato chuckled and gave me an appraising look. "You don't know how to take a compliment, do you, *bambina*?"

I took a deep breath and tried to steady my pounding heart. My depressing conversation with Lucy the morning before returned to me. I should stick to safer ground around Renato, or I'd risk losing my head completely. "Lucy is worried that she's going to be a prisoner forever. That you'll marry her off to some made man and get rid of her. She's worried that her life is over before it's even really begun."

"I promised you I'd take care of her. I can assure you marrying her off isn't what I consider taking care of her. Of course, since you're my wife, Lucy is now my younger sibling as well. I'll treat her like she's Sofia, my sister."

I stared at him distrustfully, though I couldn't stop the hope flourishing in my chest. Like always, he read my feelings as if they were written on my forehead.

"My word is my bond, remember?"

I nodded, trying to stay cool. I knew it. I knew he wouldn't go back on his word. I had no idea why I was so certain. It didn't make any sense. It was illogical, and yet it was true. My heart pounded like I'd been sprinting.

Then, Renato went and made my pulse thump even harder. "Once all the dust settles, your sister will need to make a real life here. She needs a clear head for that. You do, too, if you're going to finish your nursing program."

I spun around to look at the enigmatic boss. He was cloaked in the half-light of the chapel. I couldn't read his expression, which was nothing new. "You mean I get to finish my degree?"

He inclined his head. "But enough of this part-time nonsense. You'll go full-time and be done with it. These things shouldn't drag on."

I reached out and embraced him before I could stop myself, hugging him around his shoulders. Given how broad they were and how I was sitting beside him, it didn't make for a firm hold. He grabbed me when I nearly toppled off the pew.

"What? Are you happy?" he asked, looking down at me.

I nodded vigorously, and Renato smiled. I had the feeling that not many people saw him smile. I tucked it away inside my heart.

"If you're so happy, come sit on my knee," he said quietly, and the mood veered suddenly into hot, dangerous territory.

I hesitated a moment, thrown by the request.

"Don't overthink it. Just do it," he said.

"Renato," I started with a sigh. The man was determined to corrupt me, and here in a church, no less. He really was a devil.

"Ren."

"Ren," I corrected myself. I pulled back, his command hanging in the air, unanswered. I cleared my throat. "Why did you come in here?"

"To see you."

"Don't you have work to do?"

"I always have work to do," he said wearily. Pinching between his eyes, he suddenly looked exhausted. "Believe it or not, I'd rather make my family money by cleaning it in my casinos than shooting people in seedy warehouses by the shore. My father's legacy has taken a long time to clean up and make profitable."

He seemed so tired for a moment, and so burdened, something in my chest moved. I knew that look. I'd worn that look. When you just felt done with everything, but people depended on you, so you forced yourself to keep going.

I stood before I could question myself, moving along the pew and perching on his lap. He was frozen with surprise for a second and then wrapped an arm around my middle, helping me balance. I tried to sit up, but it was uncomfortable as hell, so I sank back and rested against him. His arms came up to hold me in place. My mind skipped happily to the thought of studying full-time.

"I know I don't have to thank you for something I had a right to do anyway," I started.

Renato tutted. "You're as bad at giving compliments as receiving them."

"But . . . thank you. I know it's a headache for you and you didn't need to let me, so, thank you."

I twisted back around, exhilarated by the conversation. It felt like I was finally moving forward after being stuck in limbo for a week.

"I never convinced you, though," I added, remembering that infuriating conversation where he'd goaded me to find a way to convince him to let me study.

"Didn't you?" he murmured.

We were both quiet, the peacefulness of the setting washing over us. He was warm and steady beneath me. I couldn't figure him out. Was he a lighthouse in a storm or the waves that would crash me against the rocks? He seemed like both and neither at the same time.

What would become of Renato's mercy once he found the bug? There would be no hiding from his wrath then.

Worry about that later, kid. Tomorrow, you could be dead.

Right, Da. The way I'm going, it's certainly a possibility.

One thing I knew for sure. I had to get rid of the bug.

We had dinner in the dining room. Lucy and I ate in silence. Renato was out, working in his office at La Leonora. The vibrance of the A.C. strip felt a million miles away from the quiet peace of Casa Nera.

After a mostly silent dinner, I headed toward the library. Now that I'd decided to destroy the damn bug, I couldn't wait to do it. It didn't take back the fact that I'd planted it in the first place, but it would help my case once he found out. I knew in my heart that he would, sooner or later.

The library was still as I let myself in. The last time I'd ventured in here was the night before, when I'd been looking for a book to read, somehow figuring in my drunken state that it would help me sleep. I'd considered taking the bug then, but Giada had crashed in like a drunk baby elephant and I'd lost my moment. I hadn't been sure, then. Now, after the chapel this afternoon, my mind was made up.

I stepped into the room and closed the door. A fire burned in the corner, illuminating the armchair and side table that sat across from it. That was where I'd found *The Prince*.

At the other end of the long room, the door to his office was ajar. Just like last time, I sneaked through the space into his study. Rounding the desk, I shoved my fingers into the potted plant and sorted through the lumps of soil. I had a moment of pure panic when I couldn't find it, but then my fingers brushed the tiny, hard shape. I pulled it out and stared at it. Was I really doing this? Had I really decided to trust Renato?

Yes. Between him and the cops, he was the devil I knew.

I headed back to the library and crossed to the fire. At the fireplace, I held my hand over the flames and opened my fist. The bug fell into the fire, a slight popping sound signaling its demise.

It was gone.

It felt like one weight had lifted off my shoulders, only to quickly be replaced by another.

I left the fireplace, adrenaline surging through me. Could I really trust him with my and Lucy's safety? He'd killed two men who had disappointed him right in front of me. He valued loyalty above all else.

The time to come clean would have been when the police had first made contact and given me the bug. But I'd been angry and impulsive and made a mistake. *Which I have now corrected,* I tried to reassure myself as I grabbed a book from a shelf of English novels. I liked the library. It had such a cozy feel, I decided to stay there a little longer. Besides, my brain threatened to melt from too much trash TV. I was more than ready to get back to studying for my degree.

I sank down in the library chair. A sweater hung over the back that smelled like Renato. I pressed my face into the material and took a long inhale. Mm, that was the good stuff.

I must have dozed off there in the chair. When I woke, a big, tattooed hand lifted *Tess of the d'Urbervilles* from my lap.

"Hardy doesn't make for light reading," Renato said quietly.

It was the third time today he'd surprised me with a sudden appearance, and the third time my heart had jumped to see him. I turned my face up to him. He was in black again, his face tight and unreadable. Whatever his business had been tonight, it had taken a toll on him. I thought of the chapel, when he'd admitted to how tired he was. He'd felt like a kindred spirit at that moment.

"Here, sit. I should go to bed," I mumbled, half asleep. I stood and stepped past him.

He snagged my wrist before I could take two steps. "Stay."

He sat and spread his legs slightly, pulling my attention to the hard-on pushing through his trousers. I blinked at it, wondering what the hell had caused that.

"You, *bambina*. Just you. The thought of you waiting for me at home."

I hadn't realized that I'd spoken out loud. He flexed his hips, and it seemed for a second like he might burst through the zipper.

I swallowed hard, desire kicking me in the stomach, hot and wet. I didn't know what to do with myself. Then I noticed a strange shine on Renato's chest. I reached out hesitantly, and when he made no move to stop me, tugged his shirt to the side and took in the new inked tallies, covered by a clear wrap. Two lines had been added to his loss count.

A visceral flashback of the other night hit me, and the new dad, Paolo, dying on the ground. Renato had become human to me in that moment as he'd comforted his dying man. He had stopped being just a monster, a creature of darkness without feelings. He had feelings. He had honor. He had a code. He was just a man, and men could do terrible things to each other, but I would bet my life that this man would never do terrible things to me. I didn't know where that conviction had come from, only that it was suddenly there inside me.

"Will you stay with me, *anima mia*?" My soul.

I nodded and took the book from him. He watched me closely, perhaps wondering where I was going to sit and what I was going to do. A sudden desire stole my breath, and I wanted to do it so badly, I couldn't stop myself.

This morning had been all about me, all about my pleasure, and it had been a gift I'd never thought I deserved to receive. I wanted to affect him like he affected me. I wanted to hold him by the balls and feel powerful for once. Not only that, but after the bug fiasco, I wanted to apologize, and there was no way I was confessing to it. I could apologize like this, without ever revealing why.

I handed him my book, opening it to a random page. "Read to me."

He watched me over the book, his strong eyebrows pulled forward in a slight frown as I lingered at his knee, and then understanding dawning as I sank to my own.

I reached up for his fly and tugged it down, then needed his help for the belt buckle. His cock pressed against the material so hard it was unyielding and difficult to maneuver.

Finally, I freed him, my confidence wavering when I took in the thickness of him. Even his length was beautiful, marbled with veins and flushed pink, the tip wet. His desire for me.

"You can take me, *bambina*. I could come from just your eyes on me," Renato said quietly.

I drew a deep breath and circled him with my fist. He was so big. Why had I thought this was a good idea? *Right*. I wanted to even the playing field between us. I wanted to pay penance. That was it.

I moved my mouth to his cock and let spit drip onto the mushroom tip. His fingers tightened on the book.

"Keep reading, or I'll stop," I murmured, moving my lips over the sensitive head as I spoke.

He gave me a look of approval, cleared his throat, and started to read.

"'I was born bad, and I have lived bad, and I shall die bad in all probability. But, upon my lost soul, I won't be bad towards you again, Tess.'"

I bobbed on him, pushing my mouth down around his girth as

far as I could, which wasn't that far, admittedly. His voice grew tight nonetheless, and one hand came to rest in my hair. I lost myself in that moment, trying my best to turn him inside out, like he did me, and him reading on and on, his voice wavering now and then as I swirled my tongue around his head or dipped in into the tip. When my mouth got sore, I leaned my face against his thigh and simply rested there, his dick lodged in my throat, and started again when I had the energy. His calm, measured reading while I sucked him turned me on.

When my jaw was aching and my panties wet as hell, he reached down and took my jaw in his grip. "Enough, wife. I'm only human, and I don't plan on coming anywhere that isn't your sweet cunt. On my lap, now."

He tugged my shorts down, then he urged me to face away from him and sink down. As I lowered, he entered me.

I gasped, sitting on his knee, impaled on his cock; I was so full. Renato hummed his approval in my ear and picked up *Tess of the d'Urbervilles* again and started to read.

I squirmed on his dick. With his free hand, he played with me, circling my clit as his hips made shallow nudges upward.

I leaned back against him and let him spread my knees as wide as they could go, his fingers flicking my clit and moving down to the place where he was buried inside me, and then back. Even the slight thrusts were getting to me. I wanted it to last all night, and I wanted him to fuck me hard and come inside me.

After a few minutes, he snapped the book shut.

"Fuck, I can't even pretend to concentrate while you're rocking on my cock like this." He dropped the book on the table, and his hands went to my hips. My feet were planted on the floor, and now he encouraged me to rise a little and then sink back down on him.

"That's right. Ride me, *bambina*," he grunted.

He dragged my T-shirt up over my ass, so my panties, pushed to the side, were on full display. He lifted me and lowered me, setting a pace that made me bounce like crazy on his lap.

His hands spread my ass cheeks and further pushed my panties aside so both my holes were bared to his eyes.

"Touch yourself while you fuck me, *bambina*. Touch your pussy and come on me," he instructed, his voice strained.

I rubbed my clit as I rode him, his cock dragging along places inside me I hadn't known existed, the new angle opening up another world. I flushed with heat and that lingering shame that always hit me whenever Renato was inside me and it felt so good. I tensed, the veil of shame I'd learned young descending over me and tugging my pleasure away.

Renato tutted, seeing the change in my posture. "You are perfect, Charlie. Perfect and good and pure as the driven snow. Nothing you do or feel is wrong, *anima mia*. Nothing. Now, *come*, milk my cock with that tight little pussy and soak me with your cum."

As I came, my vision turned white for a long moment, and all I could say was his name over and over like a chant. He followed, spilling inside me, lighting me up with his warmth. When the pulsing stopped, he pulled me back against him, tucking my legs up so his cock could stay right where it was, sealing his cum inside me, and rocked me faintly. It was so warm by the fire, and the feeling of being in his arms, safe and satisfied, pushed all other thoughts from my head, except one.

I was passing the point of no return with this man, and I had to stop my descent.

28

CHARLIE

Two mornings later, Sonny drove me to the Trenton campus of my college for class. I'd never been so excited. Getting out of the car and crunching over the fall leaves, with a new backpack and clothes carefully selected from my new designer wardrobe, I felt like a student starting her first day of high school.

Just over a week had passed since the benefit where I'd had to serve Doctor Dan and his friends, but I felt like a different person. So much had happened to me, not the least of which was the big-ass ruby-and-diamond ring on my finger. I had suggested taking it off, but that idea had been met with a wry, final shake of my bodyguard's head.

Renato wanted the damn ring on my finger, and I was pretty sure Sonny was under instruction to put it back on if I tried to take it off, or worse, call my husband.

I decided I'd rather not test that theory, so I wore it.

Considering that yesterday, I'd finally had the health checkup that Renato had been threatening, I didn't want to rock the boat. I was pretty sure my birth control shot was about to be discovered with the blood test. There was no way to make the hormones wear off faster, so I still had a good seven weeks of protection, and I had no idea how my baby-obsessed husband was going to react. His addiction to filling me up and holding me in place, full of his cum, was pretty transparent. He wanted me pregnant, and soon he'd find out that wasn't going to be possible for another seven weeks. That moment was coming, and I had no idea exactly when.

However, since that moment wasn't this one, and I was at school and Renato wasn't here, I wasn't going to let my anxiety ruin my day. In the grand scheme of things I was keeping from him, a temporarily higher hormone level barely made the cut.

Today was special and just for me. Making the decision to run from Atlantic City had already meant giving up everything I'd accomplished here, including my degree. Now, I had another chance. An unexpected opportunity to follow my dreams when I'd thought they were gone for good.

I entered the building where my lecture was, soaking up everything about the place. The flyers on the wall, the smell of burnt popcorn emanating from the common room. I grabbed a coffee from the takeout cart and waved to some people I knew in my program. The only dark spot on an otherwise happy day was my lurking shadow.

When it was time to pay, Sonny handed money over and took his Americano from the barista.

"You know, you don't have to watch me in here. You can wait outside in the car."

"The lot is way in the back. I need to be close at hand, just in case," Sonny muttered, looking suspiciously at every student who passed us.

"Just in case what?"

"Those Castillo fuckers try and get some revenge. An eye for an eye, you know. That's not just in the movies. It's painfully real."

We walked along in silence for a moment. People passing us sent smiles my way, only to blanch when they clocked the hulking man in a suit glowering at them. There was no hiding Sonny. He was large and in charge, or so he liked to think, clearly. He seemed to have been trained in the same merc school as Elio, because he scanned corners and moved with the same tactical grace as the *sottocapo*.

"Did you serve with Elio?" I wondered as we reached my classroom.

"How did you know that?"

"Just a guess. You know you can't come into the lecture hall, right?"

Sonny nodded and pointed to a spot by the door. "I'll be here. If you need anything, Mrs. De Sanctis, just scream, and I'll be there before you run out of breath."

"Call me Charlie, please. Don't make this weirder than it already is," I begged him.

He avoided my eyes, moving to his position beside the doors. "Mrs. D. Final offer," he finally agreed.

With a resigned sigh, I turned to the doorway.

"Before you go, how long is this?" Sonny shot out before I left.

"Three hours."

His look of disgust made me laugh. He crossed himself quickly, swearing under his breath in Italian.

"You'll survive, and if you get tired, I can come look for you at the coffee shop?" I suggested.

But he was having none of it. "I'll be here," he said firmly, planting his feet.

"See you later, then," I teased and went into the classroom.

Students were settling into their seats, and I selected one on the end and sat. I had my notes and books. Somehow, Renato had managed to get a minion to track down all our things from the bus. He'd also had everything moved from our old apartment to Casa Nera. I had all my notes and secondhand textbooks back.

And now that I had my old clothes back, I could see how shabby they looked next to my new designer threads. I was considering donating them, but that felt wasteful and spoiled. I actually felt guilty toward my own clothes for wanting to toss them when something better came along. I was clearly losing my sanity a little bit more with each passing day.

The lights dimmed as I checked the class schedule. A guest lecturer? Who could it be?

As if my thoughts had summoned him, he suddenly appeared. "Well, Nurse Burke, I'm relieved to see you're still alive."

Oh, no.

Doctor Dan stood at my side, peering down at me with a self-important smile.

"Are you the guest lecturer?"

"I sure am. I hope you don't mind being taught by a co-worker. Or is it former co-worker? I heard you transferred to St. Roberta's. A nice small place with less violent crime. Nice location if you can land it," Doctor Dan went on.

I'd forgotten how much the man liked the sound of his own voice. I used to mistake that drone for confidence, but meeting Renato had changed my opinion. There was power in silence. Not being compelled to fill every gap in the conversation was confidence.

"I'm going to be studying full-time, and then, yeah, I'll probably be finishing my rotations at St. Roberta's." I wasn't surprised to hear that Renato had already arranged for me to work at the hospital closest to Casa Nera. Weirdly, I didn't mind it. St. Roberta's was a lovely little hospital, and it was generally considered a dream come true to land it for rotations. I wasn't about to look a gift horse in the mouth. My pride wasn't that fragile.

"Well, we miss you around Camden Community Hospital."

The lights dimmed in the hall, and the projector came on. I pointed toward the front. "I think it's time to start."

Dan nodded, though he seemed like he had more to say. Luckily, he was out of time.

He headed to the front, preening as he waved to the audience. Great, three hours of hearing Dan talk about how awesome he was. Just what I needed. He wasn't a bad doctor at all, but he couldn't go five minutes without bragging.

I took a sip of my hazelnut mocha, picked up a pen, and braced myself.

In the end, the time went by quickly. He'd talked about shifts in the ER, which was interesting, and I'd missed studying so much, when I checked the clock, I was shocked to find out how time had flown. As soon as we were finished, people surged from their seats. I packed my bag and made my way out of my row.

"Charlotte? Can I have a word?" Dan called from the front.

I seriously considered pretending I didn't hear him, but in the end, my good manners were too deeply ingrained.

"What is it?"

"Did you enjoy the class?" Dan perched a hip on his desk and smiled benevolently at me.

I nodded. "Sure, it was really interesting. You're a good teacher," I said, hoping he was just looking for a little ego boost.

"I know, that's why they always ask me back. One day, when I get too tired or burned out at work, I'll go into teaching. There's something about eager young students that just makes me excited about the topics again." He smirked.

Eager young students? There was something slimy about the way he'd said it, and I imagined him as an older man, graying at the temples, like Renato, but with none of his style or dark charisma, hitting on students more than half his age.

"We're going to miss you around Camden Community, but to be honest, it was always a bit of a ball ache that we were co-workers. It's such a cliché, the nurse and the doctor." He chuckled. "I try and avoid that sort of thing, but now, it's easier."

"I don't follow." I glanced nervously at the door. It was only a matter of time before Sonny came looking for me.

"Us. I apologize for being drunk at the gala," he began.

"No need. It's water under the bridge. But I should stop you there. I can't date you."

Dan frowned, seeming annoyed at being cut off just as he was getting ready to hit on me. "Why not?"

"Because she's married, and I'm not the type to share," Renato's deep voice filled the room.

A frisson of alarm zipped through me.

He stood in the doorway, leaning against the threshold with indolent grace.

"Excuse me?" Dan asked, his reedy voice fading as he took in the man staring at him with murder in his eyes.

Renato straightened up and sauntered into the room. He took his time walking down the stairs that led to the lectern. When he reached us, he pulled me to his side and kissed my cheek.

"Why are you here?" I wondered.

"I wanted to pick my wife up after her first day." His gaze roved over my face like he'd missed me terribly in the few hours we'd been apart.

"Your wife?" Dan repeated skeptically.

Renato turned to him, his warm expression melting into something terrifying. "Yes, my wife. Charlotte and I are recently married. You may congratulate us." He raised his chin and waited, with all the imperiousness of a king. He'd definitely been royalty in a past life.

"Congratulations, I guess," Dan stammered. He looked closely at Renato, probably trying to place where he knew him from. The head of the De Sanctis family was notorious, but Princeton boys like Dan—pampered and coddled and brought up far away from the real world—might have missed the memo. Maybe he recognized him from the gala.

Dan's gaze fell to my hand, scanning for a ring. Renato laced his fingers through mine and lifted it to his lips, kissing the back. The ring was obvious.

Dan's mouth fell open. "I-I didn't know," he started.

"And now you do. From now on, you don't ask my wife to stay late to be alone with you. You don't attempt to flirt with her, or even speak to her about anything unrelated to the subject you're teaching, and above all . . ." Renato's tone dropped, holding a deadly hint that sent fear skittering down my spine. "You never, ever talk down to her. No one disrespects my wife. No one."

The tension was high as hell, and I looked at my husband. He was mad. Renato didn't get mad like other people did. He didn't rant and rave. He didn't even shout. I'd never heard him shout. The quieter and more controlled he was, the more deadly.

"Let's go. There's a cute coffee place on campus. Buy me a hot chocolate," I said to Renato.

He stared at Doctor Dan in a way that was making the other man sweat. He turned pale under that withering stare.

"Ren, come on." I tugged at my husband's hand, and to my surprise, it worked.

He broke his death stare and looked down at me.

"I want a hot chocolate, and someone I know likes to buy me everything I want, so here's your chance," I told him and attempted a smile.

A beat passed, and then Renato's lips lifted into a grin, Doctor Dan forgotten.

"If my wife wants a hot chocolate, then that's what she gets."

He tucked my hand into the crook of his arm and turned us, without another glance at Dan. "You know, Carmella can make a far better hot chocolate for you. None of that instant powdered crap they use in coffee shops."

"I like the powdered crap," I protested, relieved the storm had passed.

We left the room, and Sonny detached himself from the wall. Renato tossed a glance at him as we passed.

"You're not going to do anything to Doctor Dan, are you? He's just an idiot."

Renato patted my hand. "That's indisputable. Now, where is this coffee place?"

I twisted before we turned the corner and looked back at the door to the lecture hall. The door was closed, and Sonny was nowhere to be seen.

Renato watched me over his espresso cup as I excitedly went over the lecture. He didn't interrupt and he didn't seem bored, either. When I was done, I sagged back against the seat.

"Okay, your turn to talk," I said and picked up my hot chocolate, taking a sip and grimacing at the temperature. I'd talked for so long it had gone cold.

Renato caught someone's eye, and before I knew it, he'd ordered a new drink for me.

"Do you always get what you want? You are aware that they don't do table service here?" I asked as he settled back and smirked at me.

"Sometimes they do, I suppose."

Rolling my eyes, I stood and stepped past him to head to the bathroom. "You're just that guy who gets everything he wants, every single time, aren't you?"

He caught my wrist as I passed and stopped me. "Not everything. I'd like you to straddle me while you tell me about your classes and let me fuck you right here in this chair, but I can't."

Heat flushed through me. His words made me feel wanted and wicked. I wanted him just as much. It was a frightening realization.

"Well, there's always the car home," I pointed out.

Renato smiled, and it was so breathtakingly hot I fought the urge to fan myself. He pressed a kiss to the inside of my wrist and then released my hand.

"You have five minutes, in that case."

I spun on my heel and headed for the restroom. I had no doubt that he meant it. He was going to fuck me in his fancy SUV while Sonny drove us home. Thank God there was a privacy partition.

I stepped into the bathroom, fizzling excitement in my belly. It was quiet, and it only got more so as I flushed and zipped up my jeans. Heading out to the sinks, I stopped in my tracks. There was a reason it was so quiet. A person stood barring the door, and another leaned against the sinks.

Detective Vane and Detective Whitely.

"Miss Burke, or should I call you Mrs. De Sanctis? You're a difficult lady to get alone."

I seriously considered backing into the cubicle and locking it, but Renato would come looking for me soon, and finding me here with the detectives? I was terrified to see his reaction.

"I have nothing to say to you." I jerked my head toward the door. "Let me out, my husband is waiting for me."

"Waiting for you or watching to make sure you don't run away?"

"What do you want?" I demanded, but I knew, of course. They were never going to just let me go without a fight. They saw a hole in Renato De Sanctis's inner circle, and they wouldn't be giving that up so easily.

"What happened to the listening device? It was transmitting perfectly fine and then, nothing."

"I don't know," I blustered.

Detective Vane stared at me closely, her face calculating. "You got rid of it, didn't you? You've switched sides, haven't you, Charlie?"

"Sides? I was never on your side, or his. I'm on my side."

Whitely made a frustrated sound. "And you want to throw in your lot with a kingpin. This man is dangerous, Charlie. He's a killer."

I waited for a long moment, taking slow breaths, my brain working furiously over the predicament. "Are we done here? I'm assuming you don't have a warrant?"

Detective Vane stood and folded her arms. "No, no warrant. But we do have evidence leaked from inside Casa Nera. I bet your husband would just *love* to know he has a mole, and that it's his wife."

A pang of regret went through me. Great, now that I'd made the mistake of planting the bug in the first place, Detective Vane would try to use it against me.

I shrugged. "Tell him, I can't stop you."

She laughed. "You think he cares enough about you to overlook it? Don't you know how families like his work? Loyalty is the most important thing. Omertà, look it up."

"Are we done?" I repeated, injecting a bored note I didn't feel at all into my voice.

Detective Vane's face grew red. She was getting pissed off, so I had to be doing something right.

"Okay, say you actually trust the killer you married. Let's imagine you really do have shit for brains, or he has a magic cock. What about your sister?"

"What about her?" I demanded. This woman was absolutely

coming unhinged to speak to me like this. Her erratic behavior felt dangerous.

"We have a warrant for Lucy, all ready to go. She was at the scene of the crime, she knew the deceased, and his friends say he was cheating on her. That's what we call opportunity and motive."

"Circumstantial at best."

Detective Vane shrugged. "Sure, maybe, but if she confesses to what happened, whatever it was, then we have a witness. Do you really think Lucy can take hours of interrogation? She looked pretty fragile the last we saw her. I wonder if seeing crime scene photos will jog her memory. Maybe if we tug the right thread, it'll all come tumbling down."

My thoughts raced around my head. My old motto of surviving another day screamed at me, and my responsibility for Lucy counterbalanced the new feeling of trust that had developed between me and the dangerous man I'd married. I was pulled in all directions and had no idea how to fight my way out of the spiderweb.

I swallowed hard and gripped my St. Anthony medal. It was my go-to move. It always comforted me.

You're not alone anymore. A pair of white and black chess pieces, united against the horde, a perfect balance. Renato's ring on my finger and the cut beneath. *Only this ring keeps you safe, only our union protects you.* I was so tired of being alone. I was so weary of being the only one making all decisions and sacrifices. I was done.

I needed someone to lean on, and I chose him.

"Do what you want. I won't speak to you again without a lawyer present, and if you want to speak to our attorney, contact the De Sanctis offices. Now, fuck off and leave me alone."

I pushed past Detective Vane. Whitely stepped aside when I got to the doorway and wrenched it open, spilling out into the hall and coming to an abrupt stop.

Renato leaned against the wall outside. He was the picture of ease, his knee bent, foot planted on the exposed brick, his expression soft when he met my eyes. I knew that expression. It was just for me. He didn't look at anyone else that way.

Did he know what'd just happened inside the restroom? Did he know the police were in there, trying to get to me? I had no idea. Nothing in his pose gave him away, if he did know.

"That was more than five minutes," he pointed out, straightening up.

"I'm sorry, I got caught up," I muttered and went to his side. I needed to get him away from the restroom area. I waited for a painfully long moment to see if he was going to say something about the cops.

"It's okay, wife. I don't mind waiting for you," he said and took my hand in his, interlacing our fingers.

I nearly collapsed with relief.

His lips curved into a smile. We walked away from the bathroom.

"Now, though, we have a car ride to get to."

29

RENATO

"I saw the pictures," Sal told me over the phone later. My uncle liked to practice his English whenever he could, even if it wasn't the easiest to understand. "She looks like a handful."

The description of Charlotte made me smile. "You have no idea."

Sal chuckled. "*Bene*. Sometimes, you need the fire, other times, you just need a steady hand to hold. *Lealtà. Fede*." Loyalty. Faith.

"*Sì, Zio*."

He'd bust a gut if he knew that Charlie had just been cornered by two detectives in her college restroom, or worse, that my wife had planted a bug in my office.

But she'd also destroyed the device and stood up to the cops. I'd never been so proud, or more certain.

Charlotte had fallen for me, despite her better judgment.

She was mine, even inside her own head.

She was mine to save, mine to protect, and mine to keep. The power was heady. She really did make me feel like a god.

Outside, the late-afternoon December sky was heavy with

snow and white flakes flurried past. The first snow of winter. A blur of red passed the window, and I stood and looked out.

"Well, good. Now, by the time I arrive, maybe there will be *buone notizie* about a baby?"

"I'm married now. Let that satisfy you for the time being. The heirs will be here soon enough." I didn't tell *Zio* Sal that Charlotte's medical report, lying on my desk, had revealed another secret my little nurse had been hiding from me.

Her hormone levels were currently too high for her to conceive. She'd had a birth control shot, probably right around the time we'd met, and she hadn't told me about it. She kept me on my toes, and she certainly made life interesting. After feeling jaded and bored with my existence for so long, suddenly there were things to enjoy all around me. It was her doing. My little ball of goodness and light. My angel to taint and twist. Mine, forever.

In the small rose garden that sat outside my office windows, Charlotte and Giada threw snow at each other. Charlotte was wearing a red parka, and twin blooms of color burned in her round cheeks. She laughed, and it was the most fucking beautiful thing I'd ever seen.

Sonny stood to the side, looking cold and put upon. Giada was busy rolling stones into the snowballs, until I knocked on the glass and she sent a glare my way. I wagged my finger at her and pointed to Sonny. No one was throwing stones at my wife.

"Are you listening?" Sal demanded in my ear.

Giada and Charlotte turned their attack on the bodyguard.

"Sorry, I am now."

Sal chuckled. "Don't tell me the mighty Renato has finally fallen. So, you love this woman?"

"She's my wife." It wasn't a yes, but it wasn't a no, either. I had next to no experience with love, so recognizing it wasn't a skill of mine. I'd never met a woman I was tempted to love before my little nurse. That fact alone made her rare.

I watched Sonny try to evade Charlotte and Giada and then slip to the ground.

Sal's laugh faded, and I could just picture his resigned expression. "Well, I wish you good luck, my boy."

Good luck?

"Save your wishes for someone else, *Zio*. I make my own luck." I caught sight of my reflection in the glass. I looked like a stranger for a moment. It was the smile. It was new, and Charlotte was responsible for it. I didn't need luck ever again. I had her, and she was all I wanted.

I left the medical report on my bedside table. Tempting bait for a curious little nurse. While I might understand why my hesitant new bride had hidden the birth control shot from me, that didn't mean I wouldn't punish her for her deception.

I took a shower before bed, and when I came out, Charlotte had taken my bait. She just couldn't help herself. She jumped guiltily as I appeared in the bathroom doorway, clutching the folder.

"Those are your medical results. I thought you'd like to see them."

She nodded. "Have you seen them?" she asked faintly.

I shook my head, playing with her. "Maybe you can talk me through them?"

She swallowed. "It's okay, there's nothing really important."

"Isn't there? Still, I like to hear you talk medical jargon, it's a fucking turn-on. Tell me your results, *bambina*," I pushed, sitting on the bed and patting the spot next to me.

She hovered uncertainly and then sat. She opened the file and stared at the charts. "Well, I'm not anemic, that's good for a start."

I gave her a few minutes to talk through everything she could before pointing at her hormone level results. "And what about this? What does this mean?"

Her cheeks turned pink as she thought furiously. "Well, hormone levels can fluctuate," she began but didn't get any further.

I reached out and took the folder from her carefully, setting it on the bedside table, then circled her wrist and pressed a kiss to her palm before tugging her. The sudden motion sent her face down across my lap, her ass landing just where I wanted it.

"What the hell?" she started, pushing herself up on her elbows and twisting to look at me.

"I believe I've told you to never lie to me, haven't I?"

She was quiet, her mouth open, but couldn't summon the words to defend herself.

"Don't make it worse, *bambina*. Just repent and do your penance."

"Penance?" she asked, her voice breathy.

She had on the silk shorts that drove me mad, and I traced the lines of the soft material, pulling it up to her cleft so the globes of her ass were exposed. Perfectly round and full, they fit my hands like they'd been designed just for me.

"Yes, penance," I growled at her, enjoying the way she wiggled on my lap. My wife was far too excited about getting caught in a lie. I brought my hand down on one ass cheek, enjoying the satisfying sound of her inhale and the meeting of my flesh against hers.

"Hey," she murmured and looked at me over her shoulder. "Are you seriously going to spank me for keeping it from you?"

"I am, and you're going to take it like a good girl, aren't you?"

I smacked the other side, and she jerked against me. I ran my finger down the bunched material in her cleft, tugging it just right so it rubbed her clit.

"Aren't you?" I leaned in and whispered in her ear.

She shivered, her thighs rippling with goose bumps.

I smoothed my palm in a circle over her ass. "Aren't you, Charlotte?"

"Yes," she muttered. She seemed torn between maintaining her pride and begging me for more.

I brought my hand down on the first side, and she groaned. Really, it was no wonder that my little nurse hadn't had anything resembling good sex before me. She didn't have vanilla tastes in bed, and I'd be surprised if any men she'd met could handle her. They clearly hadn't been able to, because my wife was coming properly for the first time in her life, and I planned on making her as addicted to my touch as I was to hers. I needed the shorts off. Slipping a knife from my pocket, I cut through the satin of her shorts and ripped them off.

"How many of these do you think you deserve for lying to me?" I asked with a growl.

She wet her lips. "Twenty?"

She tore a real laugh from me with her suggestion. "Most people would try and lowball, but not you. You take it on the chin, you're fair as hell, and most of all . . . you love this, don't you?"

I slid my finger between her legs, pulling her cheeks apart so I could see her weeping hole.

"You really fucking love it, my perfect girl," I murmured in her ear and then reached in my pocket and took something out. "But this is a punishment, and we shouldn't forget that."

She tried to see what it was, and I showed her. A shining gold plug shape with a diamond top.

"My ace in the hole, literally." I smirked as I stroked her asshole, encouraging the wetness dripping from her slit to coat the soft pucker.

"You are not putting that in my ass," Charlotte said unsteadily.

"Am I not?" I goaded her, teasing her rim with the smooth end of the plug. "Not only am I putting it in and spanking you with it, but I'm also going to fuck you with it in so you can feel me in both holes. Got it?"

Her eyes were round, and dark fascination burned in them. She was curious. My beautiful ingenue of a wife was curious about being fucked in both holes. She really was perfect.

I smiled at her tentative eagerness. "Let's begin, shall we? Use your words, little nurse. Do you want me to spank you again? Plug you up and fuck you?"

She swallowed hard, excitement sparking from her intrigued gaze. Then she nodded and sent all other thoughts flying from my head.

30

CHARLIE

Tell him.

Confess and repent.

I woke to those words circling my brain. Last night had been . . . I didn't have words to explain what it had been. My body was warm and relaxed, and Renato's arms held me tightly to him. My ear pressed against his chest, right over his heart.

I had to tell him the truth about the bug and the cops. It was a secret I couldn't hide anymore.

Because? I didn't *want* to have a secret from him. In the last few days, everything had changed between us. This could be something real if I let it, and I wanted that suddenly, with an intensity that made it hard to breathe. Because I was falling for him. I couldn't stop the fall. He was working into my heart like a splinter. He saw me. He got me. I'd been denying an entire part of myself my whole life. I'd beat myself down and cut off my needs and wants, like they were selfish to even consider. He had lifted that veil from my eyes. It wasn't selfish to want one goddamn thing for yourself.

And I wanted him. I wanted to be his. I wanted to belong in this family.

And to do that, I had to tell him and let the chips fall where they may. He would be furious, probably. He'd punish me, undoubtedly, though after last night, it wasn't exactly a deterrent anymore. *What if he goes back on the deal? What if he decides he can't have a wife he can't trust?* Regardless, I still trusted him more than the cops.

Renato shifted under me, stroking my hair. "I know you're awake."

I cleared my throat.

"Don't tell me you're shy this morning, after last night?"

"Aren't you mad that you've been having all this sex to make me pregnant and it's been a wasted effort?" I leaned up on my elbow and looked down at him.

"You really think any time I'm inside you is wasted? Fucking you, my wife, is the highlight of my bleak life. I'd have fucked you no less if I'd known earlier, and I'll fuck you no less when you're pregnant. I'm not fucking you just to get you pregnant," he said. "I'm fucking you because I can't stay away. Coming inside you is my new hobby, and making you come on me is my new obsession. You're just going to have to deal with that, *anima mia*."

My soul. *Tell him.*

"I have to tell you something," I blurted quickly.

I opened my mouth, my confession on my tongue, but I never got the chance. A loud banging at the bedroom door made me jump. Renato frowned. No one disturbed him when he was in bed. They wouldn't dare unless it was something important.

He slid out of the bed and went to the door. He was wearing loose black pants that hung on his hips. His broad, tattooed chest flexed as he wrenched the door open. "What is it?"

Elio stood right outside, looking worried, which was scary as hell given how little emotion the *sottocapo* usually showed.

"The cops. They're outside. They say they have an arrest warrant for Lucy."

I jerked like I'd been shot. They'd actually done it. They were really going to arrest Lucy, as if she could have executed her own boyfriend with a bullet to the head. What the fuck?

I jumped out of bed and reached for a sweater to put over my silk camisole.

"What are you doing?" Renato asked, sounding unflustered.

"Getting dressed. I'm not going to the station in my pj's," I muttered. I felt sick. This was awful, and yet there was a part of me that had just been waiting for it to happen. It was an odd and terrible relief.

"You're not going anywhere," he said to me, then turned to Elio. "Get Lucy."

"Ren—" I started.

But he had already pulled me into his arm and hugged me. "It's okay. I'll take care of everything."

"I have to tell you something." I pushed out of his grip just as Elio appeared with Lucy.

She rubbed sleep from her eyes. "What's going on?"

Renato stared down at me. "You're going to see some of the original Casa Nera. You're going to wait there with your sister for a little while, and then come back out, just like hide-and-seek."

"Ren," I started a third time, but a banging at the front door echoed through the entire building.

"Casa Nera will hide you both, until it's safe," Renato said decisively, pulling on a shirt and buttoning it with ease. "Come with me."

I yanked on jeans and shoved my feet into sneakers, then took

Lucy's hand. We hurried downstairs after Elio and Renato. We went all the way down to the basement level. Lucy blanched when she saw the cells.

We walked along the hall, and Elio seemed to disappear at one point. A hidden doorway, made of the same stone as the rest of the walls. It was so dark down there, it was impossible to see.

"Go along there for about five minutes. You'll come to a room. Sit and wait there. No one will find you. I'll come for you when the coast is clear."

"The cops are going to tell you something," I cried desperately, stepping into the hidden passage.

But there was no time.

"Don't worry about the cops, I'll handle them," Renato insisted.

I grabbed his arm before he could close the section of wall that would hide the opening.

"I have to tell you—"

"I know," Renato finished. "Charlotte, I know." He reached up and cupped my cheek.

"You know?" Tears filled my eyes. I'd been worried about him finding out for days, and he'd already known? What the hell was he going to do about it? Was he furious with me?

"I know. Trust me, *bambina*. Now, you just need to trust me," he reassured me, and his eyes met mine, just before the wall closed and darkness fell over us.

Lucy held on to my sleeve and crowded close to me. "What's happening?"

"They're here to arrest you for involvement in Miguel's murder."

"What?"

"Don't worry. Renato won't let them get to you."

Lucy snorted softly. "Sure, he's so self-sacrificing. He just doesn't want me to tell the truth."

"Do you realize we're talking about the only person who is on our side right now?"

"On our side?" Lucy sniffed. "No one is on my side."

I ground my teeth with frustration and pointed along the dimly lit passageway. "Let's get away from the door. After you."

Lucy trudged along, and I followed, imagining strangling her the entire way.

We reached the room, and Lucy paused outside.

"You know, Sonny told me about these tunnels. Renato and his sister used to use them to sneak out when they were young. People have been kept prisoner in this place for decades."

"You're not a prisoner," I muttered.

Lucy stilled and tilted her head. "Do you really think that?"

If we are, then I'm falling in love with the jailer. It didn't sound great.

Lucy sighed. "Maybe you don't feel like that anymore, but I do. I'm still a prisoner and I don't want to be anymore."

"Meaning?"

"Meaning, I'm going to see what's at the end of this tunnel, and if it's freedom, I'm never looking back."

"Lucy!"

She took off before I could grab her. I set off after her, running up the uneven corridor.

"Lucy, don't be stupid. It's dangerous outside, the cops are looking for you."

She was getting away from me. She'd always been fast.

I ran faster, my sneakers getting a better grip on the damp floor than Lucy's flip-flops.

"Lucy!" My cry echoed around the walls.

It was growing lighter. We neared the end of the tunnel. I wanted to laugh for a second, and then I wanted to cry. This moment here perfectly encapsulated my life. Running after my sister, leaving my heart and best interests behind me.

I tripped over a raised stone and fell to my knees. Pain radiated up my legs. I watched her getting farther and farther away.

"Stop. Please, just stop," I cried.

She didn't hear me or turn around. A stray thought blew across my mind, freezing me to the spot. *Just let her go.*

I tensed. Let her go? She'd gotten us into all this, but then again, wasn't she the reason I was falling in love with a man for the first time in my life? Wasn't she the reason my path had crossed Renato's?

You can't fight fate, it'll find you. Your God gave you to me. This was all destined to happen.

Renato's words circled my mind as I fought with myself to get up. My fate and Lucy's were linked forever, and I could never not care. It wasn't who I was. Loyal to a fault. A sister to the end. The bitch who never quit.

I started after her, my knees burning. She'd reached the end of the tunnel and was trying to figure out how to open it. I pushed myself faster, but I didn't make it in time. The door slid open, and she disappeared out into the winter morning.

I reached the door just as it closed and fumbled with the catch. It was tricky, and it took me a few moments to manage it. I stumbled out into the light and looked around for Lucy.

She stood in the middle of the road. Where were we? Was this around the back of Casa Nera?

Lucy stared at something farther up the road than I could see. She was still as a statue. A white van roared toward her.

"Get out of the road!" I screamed, running for her.

I grabbed her just as the van stopped. The back slid open, and four men jumped out. I recognized one of them immediately.

The thug from the hospital. The one who had been asking about Lucy. The Castillo guy.

They snatched Lucy first, clamping a hand over her mouth to muffle her screams. Two of them carried her into the van, while the other two advanced toward me.

I was still close to the tunnel. I could have made it back and locked the door from the inside.

My gaze fixed on my sister.

I couldn't leave her alone. I didn't fight when they seized me. I wanted in that van beside Lucy. They pushed me in carelessly, and my scraped knees burned painfully against the floor. They bound our hands roughly with duct tape, shoved a bag over my head, and then the sound of the doors shutting rattled my teeth.

After another moment, the van started.

"Lucy, are you okay?" I worked my wrists behind my back, sawing them back and forth, trying to free them.

She moaned. They must have taped her mouth after her hands, probably because she'd been screaming so much.

"It's okay. Don't worry. It'll be okay," I muttered like a chant. I needed to hear it myself, because things felt pretty far from okay right now.

Renato knew about the bug. He'd already known. Did he hate me? Was he playing with me? The part of me that was used to being alone crowed its triumph. *See*, it snarled, *you are supposed to be alone. Who could ever love you? He was just playing with you, and you believed it. Pathetic.*

Renato's deep, confident voice from my memories spoke in my head.

You are perfect, Charlie. Perfect and good and pure as the driven snow.

You light up the room.

You fascinate me.

I got hold of the writhing insecurity in my head, the voice that warned me never to trust anyone else. The one that had been born to protect me and my sister. The one I didn't need anymore.

"Don't worry, Lucy. Renato will come for us. He'll find us, and he'll take us home," I reassured her.

Lucy made a quizzical sound through the tape. *Are you sure?*

"I'm sure."

31

CHARLIE

I didn't know how long we drove. I wrestled with the tape on my wrists. A sawing motion loosened it. I was sweating, and my wrists burned with the friction by the time I managed to slip it off, but bringing my arms around my front was worth it.

I pushed the bag off my head. Lucy was lying on her side, her eyes wild and desperate. I crawled to her over the van floor, being as quiet as I could. I reached Lucy and gently pulled the tape off her mouth, holding a finger to my lips to signal for her to be quiet.

Loud Spanish conversation crowded the air from the cab. The dialogue was rapid, but I could make out the gist of what they were saying. They were taking us somewhere to switch vehicles, and from there, they'd split us up to make it harder for Renato to keep up.

Terror beat through me at the thought of being separated from Lucy and having no way of finding her. My *husband* would have no way of finding her. I couldn't just let that happen.

Renato hadn't put another tracker in me, as far as I knew. But he was always three steps ahead, always strategizing. Had he really let me wander around without a backup plan? It didn't seem like him at all.

"Shh, don't scream. We need time to think," I whispered to my little sister.

She held on to me and nodded. I stared down at my bleeding wrists, racking my brain for a plan of some kind, and my ring caught a strand of light through a crack in the newspaper taped over the window.

Renato's ring. The family heirloom. The one his paranoid *nonno* had given his *nonna*. The one Renato had warned me to never take off.

"Shh, just listen," I whispered to her harshly, dragging my ring off. I peered at the intricate pattern of interlocking diamonds and rubies.

This ring is the only thing keeping you safe and alive.

"Don't take this off, no matter what," I breathed and took her hand and then paused, rethinking it. The ring would be obvious on Lucy's finger. The Castillos knew that she hadn't married Renato.

"Open up," I demanded.

She frowned at me but opened her mouth and let me put the ring on her tongue.

"Try not to swallow it, but keep it in there. There must be some waterproofing to a degree," I muttered furiously. Not stomach acid–proof, though. "Don't swallow it unless it's a last resort. They might not even take the tape off again, and it'll be fine. If they do, hide it like you used to hide gum in your mouth from the teacher. You were so good at it." I smoothed Lucy's hair back from her sweating, tearstained cheeks.

She obediently tucked the ring into her cheek, her hands gripping me like she never wanted to let me go.

"Okay, we don't have time," I muttered and lifted the edge of the tape over her lip.

"Wait," she whispered urgently. Her dark-eyed gaze scanned my face. "I love you. I know you probably hate me now, I ruined everything, I'm sorry. You're everything to me. All I have. The only one who never left."

I enveloped her in a fierce hug.

Lucy's hand grabbed me when I tried to shuffle back to my seat. Awkwardly, with her bound hands, she pressed Da's rosary into my palm. She'd taken to carrying it around lately. I took it and wrapped it around my wrist, a little strengthened by the treasured object.

"I'm pretty sure the ring has a tracker in it. Renato will be using it to look for us. He'll come wherever it is and he'll find you."

Lucy's eyes questioned me.

"In case we're split up. I need him to find you," I explained.

Lucy's eyes filled with tears, which streamed down her cheeks. Full apple cheeks of youth.

"What about you?"

"I'll be fine. He'll find me next," I told her.

"How?" she wondered.

I didn't have an answer for that, so I just pressed a kiss to her forehead. "This isn't goodbye forever. It's goodbye for now."

"How do you know he'll come?"

I didn't know how to explain to my sister what had passed between me and the man who'd stolen our lives and given us new ones. I didn't know how to sum up in words the complicated and foreign things we'd shared, and how those weren't feelings that were easily set aside. How could you explain taking the measure of another person's soul?

"He'll come. He's a man of his word." *A man of his own twisted kind of honor. A man I respect, now, at the end of it all.*

"Promise?" Lucy's voice wobbled.

Yes, I just hope it's in time. Instead of sharing that morbid thought, I nodded and attempted a smile, taping her mouth shut so they wouldn't suspect we'd done anything.

The van came to an abrupt stop a few minutes later. I was calm. Lucy was still crying, her face twisted in torment. I could only hope her distress would make the men less likely to free her mouth, in case she screamed a lot. I'd found a crowbar beneath the mess in the back. They really didn't think much of our ability to defend ourselves, seeing as they'd left an actual weapon with us.

I waited by the side of the door, poised to do any kind of damage I could. I had no illusions about being able to take more than one man, and I already knew there were several. But one, I could handle, and maybe with the weapon and the element of surprise on my side, I could even knock him out. It was against my nature not to go down swinging—literally, in this case.

The back of the van opened. I swung as soon as a head came into view. The crowbar hit the back of the man's head with a meaty thwack. There was a shout, and he slumped down. Men jumped into the back, grabbing at me and getting too close for me to swing again. I fought as hard as I could. I was a wild animal protecting her young. I scratched and bit, screamed my throat raw.

They pulled me out of the back of the van. The man I'd hit was lying on the ground, bleeding from the head. He was still. My eyes caught on the sight, and my brain stalled. A fist connected with my face, and the last thing I saw was Lucy being dragged from the van.

Then it was lights out.

32

RENATO

"So, Detectives, I really don't see any need to arrest Lucy Burke." Ronan Black, my attorney, relaxed back in his chair and smirked.

The laptop sat on the table, and carefully cut CCTV played over and over again.

Detective Vane looked like she wanted to shoot him in cold blood right there. "And you had this footage and didn't think to share it."

"What can I say, we just discovered it the moment you showed up at the house," I said with a grin that made her face redden dramatically.

"Sounds like serendipitous timing to me," Ronan said with a shit-eating grin.

"And where are the two men who were involved in the killing?"

I shrugged. "I have no idea. I've never heard from them again. We weren't exactly friends. I had no idea what they'd done."

"Where's the audio on the file?" Whitely interrupted.

"I'll ask my IT guy, she's outside. Maybe it can be recovered, who knows?" I smiled at the detectives.

We all knew it would never be recovered, just like the rest of the video would never be found. There was the moment of the Castillo kid's shooting, and that was it.

Detective Vane held my stare, waiting for me to twitch. I met her probing look and smiled. She pushed back from the table abruptly and cursed loudly, her elbow hitting her coffee mug. It fell to the floor and shattered into pieces.

"Oops, butterfingers," Ronan remarked lazily, tapping idly on his briefcase. "I take it we're done here, Detectives? Seeing as you're completely wrong in your accusations and have absolutely no evidence to charge either my client or his sister-in-law with anything."

Whitely straightened as both Ronan and I stood. A muscle worked in his jaw as he watched us.

"For now," he finally spit out.

"In that case, have a great afternoon."

We swept out into the hallway as a cop hurried to open the interrogation room door.

Outside, in the waiting room, Giada and Elio were watching for us. Instead of Giada's usual wisecracks, she looked serious. I stopped as soon as I stepped into the room. Elio's hands clenched into fists by his sides.

Something was wrong.

"What's happened?" I crossed to them in three long strides.

"It's Lucy. It seems like she found the secret passage, the one that comes out on Multree Street."

"And?"

"I had to check the footage to see what happened. The Castillos picked her up. They've been watching, waiting for a chance to get to her. The timing is suspicious as hell."

"*Bastardi.*" I shoved a hand through my hair, tension pulsing through me.

Charlie would be distraught about her sister. I had to get her back as quickly as possible. If something happened to her . . . No. I couldn't afford to think like that. They needed a bargaining chip. They wanted a shot at me. Killing their hostage wouldn't get them anywhere. I could be reasonable and rational about this. It was the only way to make sure I didn't make any mistakes. Charlotte would never forgive me.

"There's something else," Elio said heavily, stopping me in my tracks. "Charlie went with her, trying to stop her from leaving, I guess. Sonny was watching the entrance to the passage inside the house, and he missed it all."

I whirled around and grabbed my best friend. An explosion of violence. I yanked him close, unable to bear the words he was about to say but knowing they were coming.

His pale eyes met mine, and I knew.

"They took Charlie, too. They've got your wife."

33

CHARLIE

I woke in a cramped position, my legs screaming at me to straighten them. The smell of gasoline filled my nose, making me dizzy. I had a terrible headache, red tinting my vision as I looked around. I was bound and gagged again, and this time, in a tiny trunk. My face hurt, and my ribs weren't much better. Clearly, they'd kept on kicking me, even after I'd passed out.

We were still moving, the vehicle rocking over rough terrain.

Lucy wasn't here. Fear threatened to paralyze me as I lay there. I couldn't afford to hyperventilate in the trunk. I'd run out of air too fast.

I had to repeat a simple chant to catch my breath.

Ren will find Lucy. He'll bring the might of the De Sanctis family down on these fuckers and not one will walk away. He'll save her, and then he'll save me. He'll save her.

My hands were bound behind my back, and my shoulders ached. Somehow, in my sleep, my fingers had found the rosary beads. I ran my fingertips over the smooth spheres.

"*Make a wish, kid.*" I heard my da's voice in my head.

But rosary beads didn't work like that. I knew that better than anyone. Instead, I held each bead and prayed to the vengeful god I had promised my soul to.

My husband.

We stopped somewhere for a long time before we started moving again. I had to pee. I couldn't hold it, so I didn't. What did I care about messing up my kidnapper's trunk? Sure, it was embarrassing, but it was just biology. I wouldn't let them make me feel ashamed.

When we finally stopped, I'd begun to think I was going to run out of air. My head pounded from the blow and then the hours of exhaust poisoning.

When the trunk opened, I wasn't in a state to fight or do anything but be roughly manhandled out of the space. Laughter and taunts reached me. Maybe passing out would be preferable after all?

My knees, hurt earlier from falling in the tunnel, scraped painfully along the gravel road while they dragged me into a building.

I glanced around as I managed to get my feet under me. I wanted to walk into whatever was coming, not be dragged. It was a house, a big fancy one. Windows along one wall revealed the shore and boats docked at a private marina.

"Hurry up," someone grunted behind me and pushed me forward.

A picture of a family hung on the wall. White, middle class, and perfectly ordinary in every way. I didn't recognize any of them.

We went through double doors into a huge lounge. The middle-class suburban luxury theme continued with velvet couches, a fireplace, and fake flowers on every surface. A chessboard sat in the window and a huge TV loomed above the mantel. It was an utterly ordinary scene and didn't fit with the general aura of violence coming from the man waiting for us there. He wasn't the man in the picture outside. This man spoke in rapid-fire Spanish to his men, then turned a charming smile on me.

"Mrs. De Sanctis, what an honor." A Castillo. Maybe *the* Castillo. The one Renato had been searching for. He pointed to the couch. "Sit."

One of the men said something about my having wet myself, sniggering.

The boss shrugged. "It's not my couch. Sit."

I sank down on the soft surface, dizzy. My head was really sore. I might have a concussion. I tried to breathe deeply to calm my nerves.

"Let me introduce myself, I'm Juan Ruiz Eduardo Castillo."

"I guessed," I managed to get out around my swollen lips. "My husband's been looking for you. He'll be so pleased to finally find you."

Juan laughed. "Except he hasn't found me, you have. Well, technically, we found you and your sister, finally."

I swallowed hard. "He will, though. As long as you have either of us, Renato will find us, and he won't be forgiving."

"What great confidence you have in the man who kidnapped you in the first place," Juan mused.

I held my tongue and glared at him. He approached me, laid a hand on the back of the couch, and brought his hand to my bruised cheek. "I wonder what this dirt is hiding? Whatever it is, it was enough to enthrall a discerning man like De Sanctis. Maybe I should find out for myself."

I refused to respond to that, channeling Renato's deadly silence. I simply stared at him.

He tilted his head to the side, considering me. "Rumor has it that the untouchable king of A.C. has fallen in love. A weakness, at last, after so long. And then there's your sister."

"What does she have to do with anything?"

"She was there when Miguel died. He was a Castillo, you know, and we have a tradition in our family." He took a switch-blade from his suit pocket and flicked it open. "An eye for an eye," he said, watching my eyes widen in fear. Savoring it.

"How original. Did you come up with that yourself?" I bit out. I couldn't help myself. Whatever was going to happen here was going to happen regardless of what I said or did. So, fuck them.

A flash of anger rippled through Juan. He brought the knife to my eyebrow and trailed it down my face, circling my eye. "Shall I take it literally? Would Renato still want you if I blinded you?"

I met his stare unflinchingly.

He broke off after a moment of tense silence and chuckled. He withdrew his knife, and I took a quick breath, the dizziness still clouding my thoughts.

"I see what interested him about you, Mrs. De Sanctis. Your job isn't to bleed. It's to be bait. Your sister, though . . . she'll bleed for Miguel. She's the eye I'll take in exchange for the loss."

I felt sick. "The police are looking for her, did you know that? Searching for her might lead them to your men."

It was a weak argument to make, but I had nothing else.

Juan smirked. "Who do you think told us where to look for her?"

His words hit me like a bucket of ice water. *What the hell?*

"Whose house do you think this is? It isn't mine," he said, crouching in front of me and waving his hand around. "People in high places are sick of the stranglehold Renato De Sanctis has over this state, and they're finally going to do something about it. The King of A.C.'s kingdom is about to come crashing down. You and your sister are just the beginning of it."

"You think you and your little ragtag operation of thugs can take on the De Sanctis family? You're delusional."

"You'll see. Maybe I'll keep you around long enough to see your husband kneel to me, and then I'll kill you and make him watch before I end him. That has a nice symmetry to it, doesn't it?"

"Sounds like a loser's wet dream," I spit at him, trying to hide my fear at his words. "You're no match for him on his worst day."

A muscle twitched in Juan's jaw. He glared at me and then shrugged. "Maybe. Maybe he won't even come for you, his forced, unimportant little wife. Maybe we're both delusional to think that he'd care at all about you or your sister."

No. You're wrong. He'll come for me, as surely as the sun will rise in the east. I didn't voice that conviction, it was too damning, but I knew it in my bones. All my life, I'd struggled to trust that someone would come through for me, but now, it seemed impossible that Renato *wouldn't* come for me. He'd rip the world apart to find me. There was no question.

"Take her upstairs and out of my sight. She stinks," Juan said with a cruel smile.

Choke on it, fucker, I thought mutinously as I was manhandled out of the room.

"Wait!" Juan called before his goons could drag me away. He rose smoothly, making a show of fastidiously picking lint off his shiny pin-striped suit as he approached.

Another layer of fear washed over me, deeper and more terrifying than before. What was he going to do? It was easier to talk back when he was safely across the room. This man was nothing like my husband. He had no soft spot for me. He could do whatever he wanted.

Juan stopped in front of me and whistled, circling a finger in the air, indicating for his men to turn me around. Then I was facing away from the boss and waiting to see what the hell he wanted.

Juan whistled. "A religious woman, are you, Mrs. De Sanctis?" His hand brushed over the rosary wrapped around my wrist.

"If I said yes, would you let me go?" I attempted.

He snorted. "Cute." He fumbled at my wrist and sharp pain sliced my skin. I was hauled back around and Juan stood before me, smirking. The rosary was in his fist, cut open. He folded his knife and tucked it away. The place where he'd cut me burned. I felt naked without the rosary, for some reason.

Juan lifted the beaded necklace and turned it around, studying it. Had my husband tracked Lucy with it? Juan smirked.

"Here," he tossed the rosary to one of his men. "Take this out and ride around with it. Let's not make it too easy on the King of A.C. Making him sweat a little will make him more open to negotiating, and if not, maybe worrying about this bitch will disturb that damn infamous calm and he'll fuck up."

Juan leaned in, sending me reeling back. "If that's the case, then I'll be moving into Casa Nera by the weekend."

The thought of the Castillo Cartel moving into Casa Nera was abhorrent. I didn't know when exactly I'd started to consider that place home, but somehow, it had happened. It wasn't dark and disturbing, not really. It was cozy and classic, an ode to history, which my husband was determined to preserve. Most of all, the thought of the De Sanctis men being killed by these thugs hurt my heart. Surely, it was impossible. The De Sanctis family was too powerful.

"That'll never happen. He outclasses you in every way," I said, when Juan was clearly waiting for an answer. Juan's hand connected with my face before I even saw it move. Pain blossomed along my jaw as my teeth clicked hard, cutting the edge of my tongue. Blood filled my mouth as I fell to the floor. Nice timing Juan and his thugs had, given that they'd let go of me just in time for their boss to slap me around. I landed hard on my side, my hands tied behind me with no chance of breaking my fall. My shoulder hit the small table in the window, sending the chessboard crashing to the floor. The pieces scattered, but one remained.

The King. Standing alone.

"Get her up," Juan drawled lazily. Clearly hitting a woman in the face helped him calm down. "Your husband should have taught you how to speak to a man."

I lifted my head, blood dripping from the corner of my mouth. The pain clashed with fear and anxiety inside me, but I couldn't let this man see it. I wouldn't give him the satisfaction.

"He's going to make you regret that," I said, my tongue thickening in my mouth.

"Let's see, shall we?" Juan mused and then flicked his fingers toward the doors. "Take her."

"To a bedroom?"

"No. The basement. We wouldn't want the King of A.C. to think we didn't know how to treat his wife."

34

RENATO

I lost time. It jumped in huge leaps, and I couldn't keep track. I was at the station, and Elio was telling me about Charlotte, then I was back at Casa Nera, in the weapons room.

My men geared up beside me. There was no small talk or grim humor today. It was silent. I strapped on my knives, guns, and ammo over my tactical gear.

"Ren. We should go without you. You're the one they're waiting for," Elio dared to say beside me.

I didn't bother responding.

"We need backup."

I ignored him. Waiting for someone else meant leaving Charlotte in Castillo hands for longer, and that wasn't happening. We'd taken too long to find Juan and his hideout, and now my wife was paying the price. It was my fault, and I had to fix it.

Bristling with weapons, I strode through the house. Giada fell into step beside me, her tablet in her hand.

"The GPS in the ring has stopped moving. It's at an abandoned motel on the edge of Atlantic City."

"Send the coordinates to Elio."

"Done." She stayed with me as we made our way through the main hall.

Behind me, more than fifty armed men followed. Carmella watched me walk past, her mouth pressed into a worried line. She crossed herself as I passed by.

"Monitor the police channels. I don't trust this timing. Something is going on," I told Giada, reaching the outside steps.

"Agreed, but I can do that with you," she said, dogging my steps. "I want to come."

"No. I need you here, my eyes in the sky."

"Please, Ren, they're my family, too."

I stopped. Her heartfelt words reached into the coldness that had filled my chest since the police station.

"I know, but I need you here. You're our eyes, Giada, and we need you. *They* need you."

She swallowed hard, fighting an internal argument but losing. She nodded reluctantly. The rest of the men filed out of the house and into the waiting cars.

Gravel sprayed out as the cars pulled out of the courtyard and down the winding Casa Nera driveway.

"We don't know what we're walking into," Elio said quietly, still not dropping the topic. He handed me a phone. "Call your sister and Nikolai, at least."

"She's in Russia, on fucking vacation, if you'd care to remember."

"Call."

Time skipped again, my mind unable to focus on anything clearly.

We'd stopped a block away from the abandoned motel.

I'd barely been able to focus on the phone call with my sister and her husband, the *Palach*.

While they lived in Maine, too fucking far away to be any help to me, as a member of the *vor v zakone*, Nikolai had access to Russians all over the country. Not only that, but his brother led the bloodthirsty Chernov *Bratva* out of New York. New York was a lot closer than Maine. I'd only met Kirill Chernov a couple of times, most recently at the wedding, where he'd come to pay his respects. In return, I respected his power and the efficiency of his men. I wasn't too proud to ask for help, but I also wasn't waiting around for the Russians to arrive.

"Let's move." I was first out of the vehicle.

My men hurried to spread out. The run-down neighborhood was quiet at this time in the afternoon. Giada was live in our ears as we headed toward the building where the ring was located.

"I don't see anyone in the buildings around you. This is amateur hour, clearly," she said over the headset. She used satellites and thermal imaging to look for threats like snipers.

"And in the motel?"

The clacking of her keyboard filled my ear. "Room eleven, right in the middle. Five heat signatures. One is alone in a room, the rest outside in the other room."

One alone? Would they split up Lucy and Charlie? A sense of foreboding filled me.

We advanced on the motel. Loud music played in room eleven.

"Okay, two people in the back room now, and three in the front," Giada updated as we got closer.

"Copy," Elio said into his headset.

He was ex-military, and the scariest motherfucker I'd ever met. I trusted his tactical skills. He sent men around the back, and we waited a couple of beats before advancing on the front door.

A quick shot made short work of the doorknob, and a kick sent it crashing to the floor. My men entered, and shots rang out. Music boomed, and blood spattered the walls. It was over quick. Too quick. I was a man possessed; I couldn't focus on anything but the door to the bedroom. Kicking it in, I raised my gun toward the guy who bent over a bound, trembling figure on the bed. My gaze took in the scene dispassionately. She still had her clothes on, and she was tied up, with tape over her mouth.

Lucy. The disappointment crashed against me.

I aimed my gun at the man who had whirled around, clearly shocked to find an entire team of men busting in on his attempted assault. My bullet caught him between the eyes, and he fell.

I strode to Lucy and helped her upright. I ripped the tape off her mouth before I could calm my silent panic.

"Where is Charlie?" I demanded immediately. "She has to be in this room."

Lucy was crying, huge glassy tears dripping down her cheeks. Slowly, through the sobs racking her, she opened her mouth, and I saw it. The wedding ring with the tracker, my *wife's* tracker, sitting pretty on her little sister's tongue. I plucked it out of Lucy's mouth before she choked on it.

"She's not here. She gave me this, and then . . . they took her. I don't know where," Lucy cried and then grimaced with pain.

"Boss," Elio urged.

I realized I had gripped the girl's arm hard with one hand, enough to bruise the bones. I released her, and Elio crouched beside her.

"Did you hear that?" I asked Giada, who was listening silently in my ear.

"I heard," she said, her keys already clacking. "I didn't think to track both of the devices because they were together, which was so fucking dumb. I'm sorry."

Both of them?

Right.

I snapped my head to Lucy. "Where are your father's rosary beads?"

35

CHARLIE

I think I passed out for a while in the cellar. The dank, clearly unused lower level of the house was cold and dark. I'd been hog-tied at the wrists and ankles and left on the dirt floor. When I woke up, I peered at the light coming from underneath the heavy metal door that had been locked from the outside.

The sliver of light was darkening, and I guessed the time to be around dinner, if the growling of my stomach was any indication. I hadn't eaten all day, and my stomach was a cavern. My head was still sore. I should really have it checked . . . if I survived, of course.

I wondered if Renato had found Lucy yet. I could only hope that he had.

He'd find me, too. I was sure of it. The only questions were, how long it would take, and what would happen to me in the meantime?

Helpless tears pressed against my eyelids. My life had been destroyed just to be built back up, and now, I teetered on the edge of losing it all again. The pain I felt at losing the tiny glimpse of life I'd had with Renato put into perspective how unhappy my life had been before meeting him. He was the storm that had blown my existence apart, and only then had I realized I'd been hanging on by a thread. Working too much, worrying too much, scrimping and saving and trying to survive.

But there was more to life than just surviving, and I'd forgotten that. Maybe, thanks to my childhood, I'd never really understood that. Happiness was a privilege reserved for others. That belief had been lodged in my bedrock, and Renato had pried it free.

I didn't care that he was a man destined for hell for the things he'd done for his family. I didn't care that he'd forced me to choose between him and death. Now, at the end, my morals didn't amount to much at all in the face of love.

Love. Maybe it was the impending death talking, but the word kept circling my head. Was it even possible to fall in love with someone so fast? I guessed it was just as possible as getting to my age and never loving anyone but my family. I hadn't been aware of it happening, and I might not even have realized it if I weren't tied up, on a cellar floor, facing nearly certain death. A circumstance like this forced you to think about what you'd miss, and who you were losing.

So, faced with that, I couldn't deny that I loved him. He was the first and last man I'd ever love, and if I died today, I knew in my heart he'd take care of Lucy. I trusted him.

And like that, the habit of a lifetime gave way for an exception. He was my exception.

Tears tracked slowly down my cheeks. I should have told him about the bug right away. I should have told him I loved him, even if it was too soon. I lived in his world now, and in his world, where you experienced life-and-death scenarios on the regular, was a declaration of love so crazy?

My regretful musings were distracted by a sound from outside.

A key turned in the lock with a rusty groan and then the door banged open. The two guys who'd taken me barged in. One was carrying a tray. My stomach growled at the smell of soup.

"Look who's decided to wake up," one of them sneered, kicking me in the side when he got close enough.

"Yeah, this bitch gets to wake up, when she put Julio in a coma? It's not right," the other one muttered. Julio? Must have been the guy whose head I'd smacked with the crowbar. I really didn't like to make things easy for myself.

I watched them warily as they moved around. The light from the doorway illuminated the cold basement. Cities of cobwebs wreathed the unused wine racks, and the rustle of paper shavings and old newspapers in the corners told me I wasn't alone down here in the dark. It looked like the basement was in use after all, but the inhabitants were of the four-footed, scurrying variety.

Stooge Number One pulled my gag from my mouth and got close to me. "What do you have to say for yourself, bitch?"

I didn't bother responding. I had nothing to say, and I was pretty sure there was nothing I *could* say to stop whatever these guys were about to do. I was powerless, and it burned.

My stomach chose that moment to growl again, and both my tormentors laughed.

"She's hungry. She's still got an appetite after nearly killing someone. Don't worry, we've got you covered."

One of them held the tray.

"The *patrón* said to make sure you didn't die, that you had some water . . . He wants you around so that Renato can watch when he kills you."

The other guy was stroking my hair back with malicious gentleness.

"I said we'd take care of it." The one holding the tray laughed.

His friend moved back, just in time to avoid getting splashed with soup as the tray was tipped over my head.

The soup was hot and splashed down my chest and middle, burning through my sweater. The guy who had dumped the soup on me tossed the entire tray over my head once they'd laughed their fill at the sight of me writhing in pain under the hot liquid.

"What a mess you are, girl. I'd clean up if I were you, before your husband comes. You don't want his last memory of you to be all dirty like this." Chuckles filled the air, as well as the sound of the heavy old door opening. "We'll be back later, bitch. Enjoy your meal."

The door slammed and the sound of the key turning in the lock confirmed that I was once again completely imprisoned inside this cellar; nothing more than human bait for Renato.

Tears streamed down my cheeks, now that I was alone and free to fall apart. I'd be damned if I let them see me cry, but now, alone? I couldn't stop it.

The soup quickly turned cold and the cool draft blowing beneath the door made me shiver. The smell of carrot and ginger filled my nose. Mixed with the earthy mold smell of the cellar, it turned my stomach.

I lay there, crying in the dark, my whole body shaking, shoulders screaming in their hunched position. I didn't know how much time passed, but it was clearly enough for the rats who had made the basement their home to get curious. The rustling of their feet drawing closer only made me cry more. They smelled the food, and it was all over me. I didn't dare shut my eyes; I was paranoid that if I did, I'd wake up crawling in rodents trying to suck soup from my clothes. Even as it got later, I fought to keep my eyes open, and twitch just enough to scare any animal from venturing too close.

Renato will come for you. He will come. Trust him.

I repeated the chant through my mind, rubbing each comforting thought like a precious wooden bead. My own mental rosary.

He would come.

He would.

36

RENATO

"Scan all around the area again, search every building and shed, and fucking overturn every leaf again until you find her!" My shout echoed around the study, and the men standing before me flinched—well, all but Elio.

He waited until my voice had faded from the air. "You heard the boss. Search again. Do it now."

The men filed out. Between them, they made up the next level of management in the family. They would make sure it was done. I'd never had a reason to doubt them before. They were good men. Yet, as soon as they filed out, I doubted my orders. I needed to be the one to search everywhere.

I didn't realize I'd voiced that particular doubt aloud until Elio spoke again. "They're your loyal men. You can trust them."

"Don't tell me what I already know," I snapped.

Elio merely nodded. *Fuck*. I was losing control. This wasn't me. This mess of violence and impulse. But since the moment Giada had zeroed in on the rosary beads, and I'd ripped open an abandoned car's door and found them sitting on the seat, I couldn't think straight.

Red colored my vision. Fury that was so hot it boiled in my

veins tormented me. Yet despite all of that, it wasn't the anger that was making me abrasive.

It was fear.

I'd never been so afraid.

Elio left the room, and the door had barely closed before my arm lashed out and struck the laptop on my desk, sending it clattering to the floor. It wasn't enough. My anger surged through me, turning into violence.

The books on the bookcase were next, and then the entire case. It crashed to the floor with a thunderous bang. Next the desk itself became a punching bag. The lamp sitting on the end became a good weight to bludgeon the art on the walls, and the plant where Charlotte had hidden the bug became confetti, crushed under my feet on the carpet.

Time skipped forward again. I couldn't keep it in place. My hands ached, the knuckles torn and busted. My breath rasped in and out, and the barren hole in my chest where a heart had beat for a few precious weeks ached.

When time came back to me, I was spent. My arms throbbed, my shirt was dotted with blood, and the room was a wreck.

Nothing remained but the portrait of my mother, serenely smiling down at me, and the wooden cross on the wall above. Wrecking the room had brought me to my knees right below the portrait and the cross. The polished wood of the cross gleamed, and the strict lines of the shape judged me.

I was a man who had feared nothing. A man who'd had nothing to lose for a long time.

That had all changed. I was pushed to a point; a brittle, broken, jagged shard. My infamous control was hanging in tatters, and a stranger stared back at me from the pieces of glass littering the floor.

"Forgive me," my voice rasped in the sudden silence. "Forgive me, damn me, drag me to hell . . . just bring her back."

For the first time since I was a boy, following his mother's coffin to the burial site, I began to pray.

Before another hour had passed, I was back out, searching the areas around where the abandoned car with the rosary had been found. Night had fallen, and with it, snow swirled in the air. It was bitterly cold and all I could think of was that my little nurse was out there somewhere right now, cold and alone.

Lost.

A vivid memory of the first night we'd met filled my mind. When she'd pleaded for mercy, and that St. Anthony medal she wore had caught the light, staying my hand.

Are you lost, bambina?

I've always been a lost thing.

We moved in teams around the neighboring countryside, spreading farther and farther out in circles. My phone rang when dawn was creeping over the horizon.

"I got my brother's message." Kirill Chernov's voice spoke in my ear. "Sounds like you need a little help in the Garden State."

"What kind of help can you offer?"

"It depends on the situation," Kirill mused. He sounded far too cool for comfort, compared to the hot and burning storm of emotion inside me.

"The situation is that my wife has been taken—" I cut off, reining in my pure, undiluted fear. "Something I've heard you have experience with."

Kirill chuckled. "Any chance you have a half-brother waiting in the wings to cause havoc?"

"Unfortunately not," I snapped. He was talking about the time his brother, Nikolai, had kidnapped the captive little bride Kirill had been keeping in his penthouse. His childhood sweetheart and lifelong obsession. Kirill had stopped at nothing to get her back. Now, I knew how he felt.

"Then go to your enemy list. I'm confident you have those. No one becomes the *capo dei capi* of New Jersey without stepping on a few toes."

"I know who took her. I just don't know where."

"Well, my enemy's enemy is my friend, isn't that the saying? I'm sure you've done your research on the men who took her, so the question is—who has something to gain from helping them?"

Fuck. I was distracted and unbalanced. Making mistakes I couldn't afford. This wasn't like me. Now, when control and precision mattered the most, I was a fucking mess for the first time in my life.

I finished talking to Kirill and dialed Giada. I was immediately surprised to hear Lucy's voice in my ear.

"Lucy? Are you okay? What's wrong?"

"Nothing. I just can't stay in my room anymore. I want to help," she said quietly.

I nodded, my urgency pushing everything else aside. "Giada already checked out Commissioner Reynolds's and Judge Ellens's residences in the state. I need her to check out more distant connections, exes, siblings, fathers-in-law . . . everyone."

"Okay, I'll tell her."

It only took Giada five minutes to call me back. She didn't waste any time.

"700 Riverside Drive, Crestwood—Commissioner Reynolds's ex-wife's brother-in-law's place," she said quickly. "It's twenty miles from where the rosary was found."

"Send coordinates to the rest of the men."

"Done. Ren!" Giada shot out before I could hang up. "Go and bring her home."

"Just try and stop me."

37

CHARLIE

I woke to a wiggling feeling on my chest. Several wiggling feelings. Screaming, I twisted as much as my cold and stiff body could manage, dislodging several of the rats that had been roaming over my neck and chest, nibbling at the food remains. Panic climbed up my throat and threatened to throttle me. I was powerless. I couldn't move, I couldn't run, all I could do was lie there and take it.

Dry tears pressed against my eyelids. I had no liquid left to spare for them. I was so thirsty, the thought of water had started to take over my mind. It had to have been nearly twenty-four hours by now. Light flooded under the door. Dawn lighting up the world. I was so cold, I was shivering uncontrollably now, my arms and my feet numb. My cheek that was pressed against the dirt was also without feeling.

Was I going to die here?

No. I couldn't allow the thought to sink through me. Losing hope was dangerous. I saw it all the time at the hospital. People needed hope to keep fighting.

It sounded noisy outside in the property beyond the basement.

Men were shouting in the distance, and there were a lot of scuffling steps, like people running back and forth.

Slowly, a noise echoed through my paralyzed thoughts, and sank in. What was that sound? A loud repeated banging tore through the air. It was like a banging drum, beating quickly. No, not a drum.

Now that I focused on it, it was too distinctive to be anything other than gunshots. Machine guns in the distance. I didn't have to be an expert to know that sound. My heart all but jumped into my throat.

Renato was here.

The door to the basement busted open, and two of the thugs from earlier came in.

"What's happening?" I asked.

They yanked me to my feet, and one shoved a gun into my side. "It's showtime. Hurry up," he grunted.

Renato was here. He'd found me. But I was bait, and I didn't want my husband getting hurt.

I struggled against the men, but the gun dug harder into my side.

"Listen, *chica*, you were bait, and now that the fish has nibbled, we don't need you. Don't be difficult."

"That's an impossible request," I muttered, looking wildly around for something I could use to defend myself or slow down our progress. "Ask my husband. Sounds like he's outside. I can introduce you, if you want."

"Shut it, bitch, or I'll gag you."

The threat was enough to shut me up. Even the thought of this man putting anything in my mouth made me feel sick. It was ironic how Renato had played with gagging me, finger-fucking my mouth with his black gloves, and it had only turned me on, even when I'd been trying to run away from him, yet the threat of it from these guys had me nauseated. Proof that my husband was my exception in every way.

A voice spoke from somewhere in front of us. The light streaming in was so bright after hours of darkness, it blinded me, and I couldn't make out the features of the dark silhouette that filled the doorway. But his voice? I'd know that voice anywhere. That voice was home.

"No one gags my wife but me."

My heart squeezed hard. Hope flashed through me like a forest fire. How had he gotten here so quickly? The gunfire still sounded far off. Had he snuck in by himself? Questions shot through me like lightning, but all of that fell away as I searched for a glimpse of him.

My captors had just turned toward the voice when one cried out and dropped my arm. Renato stood in the doorway of the basement, a gun in his hand. He had it pointed toward us and shot in quick succession, and the other guy holding me fell, dragging me to the floor beside him.

Both men were writhing on the floor when Renato reached me. He pulled me toward him, his face intense and stormy. All in black, he seemed like a mercenary for the Devil himself. I couldn't stop staring. It was hard to believe that he was real.

He looked me over, anger hardening his features. "You're hurt." His voice was utterly lethal.

"I'll live, now that you're here," I rasped. "You came."

"Of course I came. I told you, *bambina,* not even an angel with a flaming sword could keep you from me."

He surveyed me, taking stock of my cuts and bruises, and my bloodied, soup- and pee-stained clothes. A look so dark crossed his face I nearly flinched away from him. It was like the light went out in his eyes.

He stroked his fingers down my cheek and turned to the first fallen Castillo, who'd tried and failed to reach his gun. Renato rose and stepped over his flailing body, picked up the weapon, and pressed it to the man's hand, pinning it to the floor.

"Need a hand with that?" he asked, his dispassionate mask back in place as he pulled the trigger.

The man's hand exploded in a burst of blood and bone. The sound was deafening. I crab-walked back to stay out of the spray zone. The other man tried to get up and run, but he'd been shot in the legs, and he only managed to hobble a few steps before falling. Renato took a knife from a hidden pocket in his sleeve.

"It's nothing personal for us, man. It's just the boss's orders."

Renato stalked him down, his black gloves flexing in the overhead lighting. He crouched over the man and pointed the knife at me.

"Nothing personal? Who marked her face up? Who pressed their worthless fingertips into her skin? Who touched her at all?"

The man on the floor shook, and the smell of pee filled the air. There was a poetic justice in seeing him reduced to the same state he'd put me in.

"Who scared her?" He dragged the knife down the guy's face and leaned in to speak to him in a low tone. "When I take your worthless life, I'm going to cut off your head and have it delivered to your family. It doesn't matter where they live. I'll find them. I'll make it my life's work. They'll get the head, and then, that night, while they cry and mourn your loss, I'll slip into their homes, nice and quiet, and do the same to them. Then I'll send their heads to their families . . . and in time, I'll have wiped out everyone who held even a drop of your blood from the world."

I swallowed a jagged protest at those truly horrifying words.

Renato wasn't home right now, and I couldn't stop this monster on a mission.

The man whimpered, and Renato smiled. "Don't worry, I'll be

sure to tell them exactly why they are dying before they go." With that, he ripped his knife across the man's neck, and blood sprayed against his shoulder and cheek. He didn't even flinch. He looked like a real live demon at that moment.

He stood, surveying his handiwork, and took a gun from his waistband. He pumped two shots into the guy whose hand had been blown off.

I couldn't look away, even though I wanted to. It felt like if I did, he'd disappear and I'd wake up, delirious from dehydration on the basement floor, still handcuffed.

Renato crouched beside me, cleaning the knife on his pants before carefully cutting my bonds. Then he pulled a small pack from his back. He'd barely opened the water before I was reaching for it and gulping it down.

"Go slow, you might bring it up again," he muttered, watching me with that same dark murderous look that warned that his revenge killing spree was far from over. He went back to the pack and pulled out a dark sweater, threading my injured wrists through the sleeves like I was made of glass. The sudden warmth made me shiver even more for a second. My arms were coming back to life and they hurt like hell.

"We have to move," he said after a moment of watching me, taking stock of every shake and sigh. He stood and then pulled me up carefully into his arms.

"Where are we going?" I asked quietly, unsure if I was talking to my husband right now or the demon who wore his face.

"To finish this," he said, gently tucking a hanging lock of filthy hair behind my ear, so softly, it was like I was something precious.

It was such a contrast to the way he'd just acted, I was transfixed by the sight. My husband was measured and calm. Controlled in all ways. Not anymore. He was as close to savage as I'd ever seen a man. The contrast was only more dramatic in a man like Renato, who was a master of his emotions. I clung to his neck and pressed my face into the bloodstained skin there.

He took me out into the freezing dawn. Sonny stood outside, gun in hand, his face bloodied and battered. The smile of relief that passed across his familiar face tugged at my heart. The back of the property was quiet, and I could see a jagged hole in the wire fence that bordered the snowy woods. Had my husband cut his way in here, sneaking past numerous armed guards, with only one man as his backup? We passed by the side of the house, heading around to the front. Clearly, sneaking in the back while attacking the front had been part of the plan, if the chaos that we walked into was anything to go by. I wasn't prepared for the sight that greeted me around the corner.

The grounds were strewn with fallen men. The sound of gunshots echoed all around. The snow that had fallen was bloodied.

De Sanctis men had filled the yard, crouched behind different things for cover. Their cars had busted open the gates, and the sides of the black SUVs had taken fire.

The cartel members hid behind the walls of the porch and, I could only assume, other places around the property. Shots were exchanged in both directions. We stepped into the shadows beside the house, and stopped where there was a vehicle parked, providing excellent cover.

"Well, Giada?"

Renato's voice surprised me, until I spied the discreet earpiece in his ear.

"I've got her. Where are they?"

I couldn't hear her answer.

"Where's Elio?" I wondered, peering around at the shadows and the men crouching, staying out of the line of fire. It looked like an impasse. Renato's *sottocapo* was never far from his side.

"He's on his way," Renato said.

"De Sanctis!" A loud shout echoed around the grounds. It sounded like it came from above us.

There, surrounded by his men, on a balcony overlooking the scene, was Juan. His men were arranged in a human shield around him.

"Are you going to hide away or face me like a man?" Juan goaded.

Renato made no move to walk out into the vulnerable space in front of the house. Instead, he tilted his head back and shouted upward.

"So, it *is* you? You're the head of the Castillos? And you didn't even have the balls to own up to it when you strolled into my warehouse downtown. Have you always been a coward?" Renato challenged.

Juan replied immediately, annoyance in his tone. "Not a coward, just smarter than you. I wanted to see your operation, and I did. Interesting stuff. Maybe we'll keep some elements when we take over from you. The days of the De Sanctis Mafia's rule are over."

"Is that right?" Renato prodded.

I could hear Giada murmuring in the earpiece and wondered what the hell she was saying.

"I don't care if you think I'm a coward. Soon, you'll be dead, and your city will be mine," Juan called.

"And what makes you so sure of that?" Renato asked, his tone an uninterested drawl.

Renato's nonchalance was clearly irritating Juan if the way his voice kept growing higher and higher was any indication.

"Because I'm not alone in my endeavors. You've pissed off the wrong people, De Sanctis, and now you'll understand the danger of that."

"The wrong people, or the wrong person? You're talking about

Commissioner Reynolds, right? This house is in his family, isn't it? He's really going to hate what you've done with the place."

"He wants you gone, and he wants me to do it. Win-win for me."

"Hmm, maybe. But you can't get to me here without risking yourself."

"True, maybe not, but we won't stop. If I don't get you today, then we'll never stop hunting you, or *her*. One day soon, we'll get to her."

Renato was silent for a long moment and then looked down at me. "I can't risk that," he told me quietly. He set me carefully down on the ground and avoided my hands when I tried to reach for him.

"What are we going to do? They've got the higher ground, we need a miracle," I muttered senselessly, fear paralyzing every part of me except my mouth.

Juan shouted down at us, "Or do you not care if your woman dies?"

"If she dies, I don't care about living," Ren said in a near whisper, his eyes fixed on mine. "Because I won't live without her."

There was a faraway sound in the air, like beating wings, growing closer and closer, but Renato held all my attention.

He cupped my cheek. "Keep reading *The Prince*, little nurse. It will help you lead the family. And I have to change my answer from the chapel, when you asked me if I'd ever been in love." He kissed me. "The answer is yes. You are the first, and last, woman I'll ever love."

"What the hell?!" I latched on to Renato's vest and refused to let go. "You can't go out there." Sonny's hands clamped down on my shoulders, pinning me in place.

Renato ran a hand over my matted, dirty hair and pressed a kiss to my forehead. "'Never was anything great achieved without great danger.' I have to go with Machiavelli on that one."

The sound in the distance grew closer. Help on the way? How would they get in here without being blown apart?

Renato pried my hands from his vest, and I swayed into Sonny. His grip didn't allow me even an inch to fight against. He wasn't going to let me go with Ren. My husband took two steps away from me, his gaze fixed on me.

"Very well, Castillo! I surrender," Renato shouted, his voice carrying over everything else. He took another step back.

I cried out, reaching out for him, but he shook his head at me.

"Don't even think about it, little nurse. Trust me." Then he turned and distracted everyone by walking out onto the battlefield that lay in front of the house, his hands rising slowly.

Everyone froze. A panicked cry left me as I watched him walk into the line of fire, drawing all attention, making himself a target.

"The mighty Renato De Sanctis, putting his own head on the chopping block instead of his wife's. How romantic," Juan sneered.

Renato stared up at the balcony. His gaze never wavered. *What was he doing?* He was going to get himself killed.

Then the noise overhead was upon us, and all hell broke loose.

Juan raised his gun and took a shot at Renato. I screamed at the sight of the bullet connecting with his gut. He fell to one knee. Absolute terror gave me strength I'd never known before, and I stomped hard on Sonny's foot and used the moment of his distraction to break free. I ran toward Renato.

Suddenly, the air around us came alive with bullets. Light shone down over the dark gardens, illuminating the place where Juan stood on the balcony with the human shield of his men.

Precise shots boomed, cracks of noise ripping through the early morning. The shield of men fell, and Juan was right after. The back of his head blew out, and then he disappeared from view.

The helicopter hovered for a moment, and I covered my eyes

and looked up, blinking in the bright lights. I glimpsed Elio sitting with his legs over the side and the sniper rifle in hand. Then I ran toward Renato again.

De Sanctis men swarmed out of their covered hiding places and ran down the remaining cartel members who were making a break for it. The sound of fighting filled the air again, but it didn't matter. Nothing mattered except the figure in black lying on the white ground. I dropped to my knees when I reached him and touched his face.

"Renato? Ren, can you hear me?" Tears splashed down my face. *Get a fucking grip, Charlie, you're a nurse. Save him.* "I won't let you die. I need you, so you're not allowed," I murmured furiously as I attempted to rip open his black vest and found it hard as hell.

I went searching for a knife to cut it off. I had to find the bullet hole and put pressure on it.

"You fucking wrecked my life and made me fall in love with you, and then you think you can just die on me? You evil, horrible bastard. I promised you my soul, and you have to be alive to claim it," I muttered, finally getting my hand under the vest and finding a hard, padded expanse of material. It felt vaguely familiar.

I stopped breathing, moving my hand under the vest over the smooth material beneath until I found it. A bullet encased in the hole it had ripped in the ceramic plate.

"You can't get rid of me *that* easily, *anima mia*. I'm afraid you're stuck with me."

I looked down and found him watching me. His voice sounded more like himself.

"You have a bulletproof vest on?!" I screeched at him.

"Of course I do. What's the point in waiting my whole life to meet you, just to die a few weeks later?"

I went to hit him, but somehow, I was just hugging him. His arms circled me, and he kissed the top of my head.

"You could have been shot in the head!" I protested.

"There are worse ways to die."

I thumped him, and my hand stung from hitting the bulletproof vest.

"Besides, most people, professional gangsters or not, are fucking terrible shots."

His grim humor made me smile, despite it all.

"Enough talking," he said and pulled me tighter into his arms.

My ribs hurt at the squeeze, but I didn't mutter a peep. It felt too good.

"Are you better now?" I asked, my voice muffled by his gear.

"Better?"

"You were different before . . . scary."

"I'm scary all the time, Charlie, it's just you who doesn't see it."

"Do you really love me?"

"Do you think I offer myself up for target practice for just anyone?"

I swallowed and leaned up on an elbow.

"I might love you, too," I admitted quietly.

He laughed and then winced. "Oh, I know."

"You know?"

"I knew when you destroyed that little bug and told the cops to fuck off."

"You heard that?"

"Of course I heard that. I've never been prouder." He kissed my forehead.

The helicopter had landed a little distance off, and Elio strode toward us over the bloodied snow, another man beside him. His companion was pale and tattooed, with the hardened air of a very dangerous man.

"How did you find me?" I wondered.

The De Sanctis men cleaned up around us. They seemed to be

under instructions not to leave any survivors. That was a terrifying thought, and yet it wasn't my choice or responsibility. It was my husband's.

"I started with this, and it brought us pretty close."

Renato reached into his pocket, rooting around until he found what he was looking for. Then he wrapped my Da's rosary around my wrist. New tears filled my eyes.

"You put a tracker on my sister?" I wasn't mad. Maybe I should have been, but I wasn't. His high-handed, controlling tendencies had saved the day. We lived in his world now. New rules applied.

"Of course I did. She's family."

I wet my lips and attempted my best pronunciation. "*La famiglia prima di tutto?*"

His smile was broad and real. "*Brava, anima mia*. Now, let me take you home."

38

RENATO

Charlotte sat obediently on the seat in the bathroom where I'd left her a few minutes ago.

We were at home, having put down every single Castillo Cartel member, including their cowardly leader. Kirill Chernov had come through, with a helicopter, no less. I'd owe the *Bratva* a favor down the line, but he was family of a sort. The Russians might be unpredictable psychopaths for the most part, but he was also family. *La famiglia prima di tutto.*

I'd taken Charlie and my men away before Kirill and his Russians had executed the survivors. I'd lost three men in the fight, and that weighed heavily on my conscience, as did the state of my wife. We'd stopped by the hospital on the way home, where she'd been checked for a concussion. She had bruised ribs, cuts, and contusions, but thankfully, not much more. The doctor had wanted to keep her in regardless, but Charlotte had insisted on going home. She wanted her own bathroom and bed, and I wasn't going to argue with that. Not when she was so muted. A muted Charlie just wasn't right.

My blood boiled to look at her. Her face was purple along one side with bruises, her lips cut and swollen, and she had one hell of a black eye. Her wrists bled, marked by handcuffs, and she was sore all over, like she'd been beaten. I hadn't seen beneath her dirty clothes yet.

Just the fact that they'd treated her with so little respect, forcing her to sit in those dirty clothes, made me want to dig the fuckers up and dismember them all over again. Unfortunately, that was a pleasure you couldn't experience more than once.

I stepped into the bathroom. Charlotte jumped. More anger flooded through me. My wife was afraid in her own home, because of those men.

Because of Commissioner Reynolds. He'd get what was coming to him, and soon.

"Let's get you cleaned up," I told her briskly.

Her gaze skittered from mine.

"I can do it myself," she murmured, embarrassment staining her cheeks.

"I know you can, but I want you to let me." I crouched in front of her and put my hands on her knees. "I don't want you to disappear on me or go where I can't follow."

She chewed her lip and then grimaced as she hit a cut with her teeth.

"Let me take care of you, Charlie."

She swallowed hard. I could see how it cost her to be vulnerable like this, and then how bravely she faced it. No one was as brave as my wife.

She squared her shoulders. "Okay. Fine. If you insist."

"I do." I removed her socks first and then her sweater and camisole.

Her side had bruising across the ribs, and she jerked when I lightly touched the purple skin there.

I moved to her jeans next. She made a muffled, embarrassed

sound when I tugged off the dirty, dried-up denim. Once it was off, I dropped it straight in the trash can, along with her panties, and turned the shower on. The air filled with steam. Her hair was knotted with tangles. I picked up the brush beside the mirror and slowly ran it through.

Her eyes closed as I worked, the brush tugging her scalp, and she leaned back against me. Lucy had fallen asleep with Carmella sitting by her bed. Sleep would do the girl well. Shock comes slowly and then in waves. Charlie was still soldiering on. She didn't know how to give up.

"Okay, in the shower with you." I set the brush down and guided her into the hot, steaming glass stall.

She stood under the spray for a moment, letting it soak her through. I was already barefoot, in just a T-shirt and loose pants. I stepped under the spray to help her.

Washing her hair was easy. Soaping her body was difficult. Despite the bruises and cuts, touching the slopes of her belly and curves of her hips and ass made me hard as hell. I felt an inappropriate and undeniable need to fill this woman up. I wanted to sink deep inside her and reassure myself that she was here, in my arms, alive and well. She didn't complain about how the soap must have stung. She didn't complain about anything.

"Turn," I instructed gruffly.

Her tight curves and wet skin were tormenting me. The bruises and cuts filled me with fury. I washed her carefully, like she was spun glass. She held on to me, staring at my chest.

"You're all wet." Her voice wasn't as tired as I'd thought it would be.

"I don't care."

She looked up at me and pressed up on her toes and kissed me softly.

“I can’t get it all out of my mind,” she murmured. “I want to forget.”

She was so beautiful and precious, standing there in the rain falling from the shower. I’d nearly lost her.

I cupped her face gently and kissed her, careful of her lip, and moved my lips downward. She leaned against the heated wall and watched me as I knelt at her feet, my T-shirt and pants soaked through, my gaze fixed on her eyes. I could read her desires there, just like mine. *Make me forget.*

“Leave that to me, *bambina*.”

39

CHARLIE

The next day, I got up early, ready to go to my classes.

I needed to take my mind off the last forty-eight hours, and there was no better cure for a low mood than being busy.

I'd half expected Renato to argue with me about that when I headed downstairs, backpack in hand, and announced I was going out—bruised ribs, black-and-blue jaw and all. Sonny had jumped out of his chair, looking worried, and Carmella had immediately disagreed.

Renato had only nodded, a smile playing on his lips. He was completely unsurprised by my stubborn refusal to let the whole thing interfere with my life.

"Answer my calls, and don't leave Sonny's side."

"I won't."

"Good girl," he said with a smirk that sent heat flushing through me.

This man could turn me on and distract me completely with one well-placed comment.

His hands gripped my hips, and I had to wrench myself away and then fight the urge to go back.

"What are you doing today?" I asked him as he walked me out to the car.

"Meeting my attorney, and then later, an old friend. I'll be home for dinner, though." He leaned in and pressed a kiss to my cheek. "Be on my place mat, pantyless, legs spread, in time for me to come home and eat."

Just like that, my wicked husband sat me in the back seat of the car and shut the door.

I was still blushing by the time Sonny got into the driver's seat.

We drove to campus. Snow had fallen, and everything looked fresh and new. I groaned as I pushed myself out of the car.

"You should have stayed home for the rest of the week, Mrs. D.," Sonny complained, coming around the car to take my arm.

"And do what? Cry in my pillow while I fall behind right before exams?"

He tutted. "The boss was right."

"About what?"

"Your big brass balls."

I laughed, and it hurt my ribs. Maybe Sonny was right, and I should've been taking it easy. Maybe I should have stayed in the hospital overnight, but I was loath to see any more people I knew. I didn't want anyone to ask me what had happened. I had no idea what I'd say. They say medical professionals make the worst patients, and it was true in my case. However, if I got worse instead of better over the next few days, I'd go back. I'd have to make myself, or my husband would do that for me.

"I hope Doctor Dan isn't presenting," I mumbled to myself as we walked along the hall.

"Oh, I'm sure he isn't. Didn't you hear?" Sonny mused. "He had an accident; lost half his front teeth and needs reconstructive surgery."

"Wait, what?" I stopped and stared up at Sonny.

He didn't even twitch. "Damn shame."

"Did he really have an accident?"

Sonny shrugged. "Having an accident isn't so uncommon. People have them every day. Leaving the house puts you at risk for one. Hell, staying at home does, too."

"And hitting on a mob boss's wife might make it even more likely, right?" I stopped on the threshold of the class and glared at Sonny.

He simply smirked. "Your words, Mrs. D., not mine. I'll be out here when you're done."

After class, I stopped at the coffee shop before going home. I really did love the seasonal hot chocolate from the place on campus, and I was past caring if that made me a basic bitch. Besides, I wanted a moment alone to think before I headed back to Casa Nera. I had a message from Lucy on my phone that had made me so excited, I couldn't stop reading it.

Maybe culinary school, what do you think?

It was a tiny step in the right direction. A real direction for Lucy's future. Most important was all that it didn't say. Choosing to move forward with her life meant accepting our new reality. It made me hopeful she'd turned a corner. Maybe we could put the guilt and resentments, the regrets of a lifetime, behind us, and finally move on.

I finished my hot chocolate and headed back to Sonny, who was reading the soccer pages from the Italian newspaper that was delivered to Casa Nera every morning.

"Ready to go?"

My ribs ached, I was tired and could have slept for a week, but I also felt oddly content, like the storm had finally passed.

I had barely nodded when the voice behind me sent me spinning around.

"Mrs. De Sanctis, you're a hard woman to find lately."

Detective Vane was flushed, like she was gearing up for a fight. Whitely stood behind her, solemn-faced.

Sonny immediately pushed between the detectives and me. "What business do you have harassing Mrs. De Sanctis?"

"Official business, if you'll excuse us," Detective Vane said, slapping a piece of paper against Sonny's chest.

He plucked it out of her hand and opened it.

"*Vaffanculo,*" he snarled, which I didn't take as good news.

"What is it?"

"It's a warrant for your arrest," Detective Vane said triumphantly. "Charlotte De Sanctis, you are being charged with actions connected to obstruction of justice including but not limited to destroying or concealing evidence, providing false information, and witness tampering. You have the right to remain silent . . ."

The rest of my rights faded away as Detective Vane cuffed me, taking great pleasure in the task.

Sonny was already on the phone, speaking in rapid-fire Italian. He took it from his ear and put it on speakerphone before the detectives could haul me out of earshot.

"*Bambina,* don't say a word. I'll meet you at the station." Renato growled across the space.

And then we were walking through the hall and down the stairs toward a waiting cop car.

"Your first of many perp walks, married to that criminal who you chose to side with, Charlie," Detective Vane muttered in my ear. "Isn't it embarrassing?"

I took a deep breath and steadied my nerves, raised my chin, and shrugged.

My composure lasted until I was handcuffed to a table in the interrogation room. Detectives Vane and Whitely left me to sweat for a while. It felt like my entire life flashed before my eyes. All the trouble I'd been avoiding for a decade had caught up with me. All those nights in the group home when I'd been the lookout, the kid too scared to sneak out the broken window on the second floor, and so instead had stayed behind, guarding the door. The one who'd stayed on the beach while my nursing friends had skinny-dipped at the shore after passing some hard exams.

The purse watcher. The wallflower. The rule follower. Now, my life had gone completely off the rails, so what had all that worry and sacrifice even been for? A wasted effort. I could have been sneaking out, skinny-dipping, and breaking the rules my entire life. I'd ended up in the same place, anyway.

"Miss Burke, we didn't keep you waiting too long, did we?" Whitely asked as they came in and locked the door behind them.

"It's Mrs. De Sanctis, and it's fine."

"Hmm, Mrs. De Sanctis." Detective Vane sat across from me and smiled. "How are you doing, Charlie?"

I shrugged. "Good. You?"

"Oh, I'm great. You look a little beat up there. Piss your husband off, did you?"

A bitter laugh left me at her hard tone. "If I had, I'm sure your warm and supportive manner would really set me at ease. Are you like this with real domestic violence victims, or just people you're trying to intimidate?"

Detective Vane glared at me. "I don't like weak women, Mrs. De Sanctis, and I don't like people who don't take help when it's offered to them."

"I don't need your help. The only people who are victimizing me are you two."

Whitely stepped forward, placed a folder on the table, and flipped it open. A white van sat at the corner of a photograph inside, and a row of body bags lined the ground in front. I recognized it immediately. It was the same setting as the shootout, and I could bet those bodies were the Castillo Cartel.

"Why are you showing me this?"

"Does it look familiar?"

"I think it's a scene from a movie, right? I just can't remember which one."

Detective Vane chuckled. "This is really how you're going to play it? Don't you know you've got serious charges against you? You could do time."

Do time? The only way I could do time was if they could pin something on Renato, and I believed in my husband far more than I believed in these clowns.

I didn't answer, deciding that was the best strategy from now on.

"I'm showing you this to make you aware of how dangerous the man you married is. He could hurt you and your sister."

I held my tongue and stared Whitely down. Their words had no power over me.

"Charlotte, we can still help you. We know Renato was involved last night. Have you ever heard the name Kirill Chernov? He and his brother are two of the most dangerous criminals to ever hit the East Coast. The only one more dangerous is your husband."

A hard knock broke Whitely's concentration, and he muttered as he got up and went to the door.

"I hope I'm not interrupting anything? Since I haven't had a call from my client, and you're already questioning her, there has to be some mix-up in communication, right?"

The newcomer's smooth confidence muffled the tension rising in me. He'd called me his client. This had to be Renato's attorney.

He stalked into the room, drawing all eyes. He didn't seem like any attorney I'd ever seen. He looked like a thug in a bespoke suit, and it worked for him. A buzz cut, neck and knuckle tattoos, and a suit that had probably cost more than my annual waitressing salary, custom-made to fit his huge hulking shoulders.

"Charlotte, I'm Ronan Black, a close friend and adviser of your husband."

"You mean his *consigliere,* don't you, Black? Just call a spade a spade," Detective Vane spat, clearly annoyed that the attorney had arrived so quickly.

Ronan didn't bother looking at her. All his attention was on me. "I'm here to represent you and get this misunderstanding cleared up as quickly as possible." He shook my hand, gently, despite the fact that his huge, tattooed hand was twice the size of mine. He sat beside me and set his briefcase on the floor. "Have you been offered a drink?"

I shook my head. His sudden concern and warmth was making me feel like crying, after the cold threats of the detectives. After the last few days I'd had, my reserves were running low.

Ronan chuckled. "My, my, we're just breaking all the rules today, aren't we, Detectives? We wouldn't want coercion charges on top of everything else I'm going to throw at you."

Detective Vane scoffed as Whitely went to get water. "Throw whatever you want at us, the law is on our side."

Ronan raised an eyebrow. "Are you a lawyer as well as a detective, Dolores? How interesting. Well, let's get this circus started. What have you got? Ask your questions." He turned to look at the two-way glass. "And just so we're clear, I'd like to request confirmation that this interview is being recorded."

A voice spoke over a loudspeaker. "I can confirm that."

"Excellent. Go on then, show us what you've got," Ronan said, arrogance dripping from every word.

Every single thing he said was designed to piss the detectives off, and it was working. I couldn't stand him already and had never been so relieved that someone was on my side, and not the other.

"We have reason to believe that your client knowingly revealed the position of a judge-approved listening device placed in a suspect's home, to aid them in concealing their crimes and providing false information," Detective Vane began.

"What does that mean?" I exclaimed.

Ronan smirked. "It means everything they heard on the bug was a lie, deliberately designed to lead them in circles. There's no proof my client revealed said device to her husband. Also, I would like to see the warrant for the device. Probable cause is such a tricky thing to get signed off on."

Whitely flushed. "We'll get it to you."

"I'd like to see it now, thank you very much," Ronan said and flicked his hand in a dismissive gesture.

"You're a real piece of work, Black, or should I say O'Connor? Birds of a feather flock together, I suppose. Italians, Irish, Russians . . . you're all scum."

"Actually, the full expression is 'Birds of a feather flock together—until the cat comes,' and Dolores," Ronan leaned in, "you're no cat. Keep it professional, or we'll have a problem."

Whitely reappeared and slapped a paper on the table before Ronan. He took his time picking it up and reading it.

"Judge Winfred Ellens. Oh, dear, that's a terrible coincidence for you. Have you not seen the news?" Ronan took his phone out of his pocket and pulled up a web page. He read aloud. "Judge Ellens has admitted to over ten counts of misconduct, including accepting bribes, coercion, witness intimidation, and colluding to pervert the course of justice. I hope you had someone upstanding to back up your request for this warrant?" He checked a field on the paper. "Commissioner Reynolds?" He chuckled warmly. "I'd say you might be in a spot of trouble over this. Don't tell me Judge Ellens also issued the warrant for my client's arrest? I'd like to see that as well, while we're here."

"What did you and that monster De Sanctis do? Did you intimidate them? Threaten them?"

Ronan rolled his eyes. "Judge not, lest ye be judged, Detective Vane. I'm very interested in how you've been treating my client here for the last few weeks."

She swallowed hard, her gaze darting around the room. She focused on me. "Charlotte, we can help you. I know you think we can't, but we can, you just need to tell us what he's done, and everything will change for you."

She had no idea that was the opposite of what I wanted. At that moment, a knock sounded on the door, and a harried-looking man peered in.

"Detectives, a word."

Detectives Vane and Whitely left me alone with Ronan.

"What happens now?"

"That was their chief. Given the serious evidence that's come to light about Judge Ellens, all his active cases, investigations, warrants, and the like will be suspended. We will push to leave right now, and in a few days, I'll make sure it's all dropped. It's over, Charlotte, this time for good. Judge Ellens has already stated that he accepted bribes in your specific case, so they have nothing to hold you on while it's investigated."

"I can't believe it's so easy to just walk away from an arrest warrant."

Ronan grinned. "It's not so easy, I'm just that good. Though, I suppose I should give your husband his due, as well as Giada."

"Meaning?"

Ronan nodded toward the glass, subtly reminding me of the recording. Right.

"Meaning they never stopped believing in you," he said with a wink. Code, surely, to cover our conversation.

I found myself smiling back.

A minute later, the detectives returned and uncuffed me. Detective Vane was so angry she couldn't meet my eyes.

"Now, I suppose an apology to my client is in order, and then we'll see ourselves out," Ronan said, straightening his cuffs and peering down imperiously at both cops. He was an extremely tall and burly man.

"Get lost, Black."

"A pleasure as always, Dolores. And if I may say, you're looking a little stressed. Maybe try yoga, it's great for tension relief."

With that, Ronan ushered me out of the room and along to Processing, where I collected my bag.

The next thing I knew, we were in the waiting room, and Renato was striding toward me. He pulled me into a hard hug, and I couldn't breathe anything except his warm scent. It was better than oxygen to a person suffocating.

"Are you all right?"

"I think you cracked another rib, but apart from that, fine," I teased him.

He immediately leaned back to survey me. "*Cristo*, you're never leaving Casa Nera again," he muttered.

"But I'm going to be working soon," I reminded him.

A muscle tensed in his jaw. "I'll build a hospital on the property."

I laughed and leaned into him.

"Are you all right?" he asked again.

"Yes, I am, except I feel like everyone knows more than me, and I hate that."

He pressed a kiss to my forehead. "Let's go home, and I'll catch you up."

40

RENATO

THREE HOURS EARLIER

Commissioner Reynolds lived at the top of a high-rise apartment block in Trenton. It was ideal, actually, like the gods were smiling down on me and approving my revenge, not that anything could have stopped me.

He lay on the concrete rooftop, sweating through his wrinkled dress shirt.

"I didn't have anything to do with any of it, why would I go against you, De Sanctis?"

"Haven't you seen some of those online challenges people make videos about? Some people are just too dumb to understand when something will result in certain death. You thought your little bit of power and pathetic reputation as a public figure would protect you. It's a mistake you can only make once, I'm afraid."

He groaned, staring at the sky. "I should have known those Castillo fuckers were all talk. 'We can take out Renato, just give us a chance.' Right." He turned a miserable expression on me. "None of this would have happened if you hadn't cut me off. You limit my funds and collect all kinds of crap on me, but you forget how much I have to pay to people to keep the things you do quiet."

"Not my problem. Did you see the news about your buddy, Judge Ellens?"

Reynolds swallowed hard. He'd seen. He had to have known he was next.

"I can still help you. You'll need a new judge to look the other way. You'll need someone to keep the detectives out of your business."

"Maybe so, but it won't be you." I nodded to Elio.

He had tied Reynolds's feet together with rope and anchored that around a cinder block. I took the bottle of lighter fluid I usually used to burn my gloves and dumped it liberally all over Reynolds and the rope.

"What are you doing? Renato, we can talk about this! I worked for your father."

"I don't care. I don't care about anything except that you involved *her*." The bruising on Charlotte's jaw filled my head, and fury burned through me.

I jerked my head to Elio, who dragged the length of rope, pulling Reynolds near the edge of the roof.

"She's fine, though! She's alive."

"This was going to be your outcome from the second you decided that she and her sister could be used in your small-minded games. Even if all she'd lost was a single eyelash, you'd still die just like this." I flicked my hand at my *sottocapo*.

Elio pushed Reynolds over the edge. He screamed and then jerked. The cinder block dragged closer to the edge but held.

Reynolds cried with fear now, pleading for his life, no doubt shitting himself with panic. I should have recorded it. He was wriggling like a worm on a hook, thirteen flights up.

Instead, I took my lighter from my pocket and held the flame to the rope. It went up quickly, roaring into a blaze as it traveled along the rope, right toward the man dangling headfirst over the precipice. His screams were music to my ears. I savored them for a long moment before turning to my second.

"Let's go. I want to be home when Charlotte gets back from class."

I nodded to the security camera in the corner. Giada was already on it, splicing out the footage, the master of her digital domain.

41

CHARLIE

"So, Commissioner Reynolds was deliberately encouraging Whitely's and Vane's underhanded techniques, just to make things difficult for you?" I wondered aloud. We were sitting in his office in a large leather wingback chair. Technically, Renato was sitting in the chair, and I was cradled in his lap.

"Mm-hmm. They didn't have a legal leg to stand on, pushing you to spy for them, trying to arrest Lucy and then you. Lucy's ridiculous arrest was simply a chance to get her out of Casa Nera. Reynolds needed the Castillo Cartel to clean up his mess, and they just wanted a shot at me, and revenge, of course, for what happened to the kid. The one who started all of this."

"How did they know Lucy would sneak out?"

"They didn't. I guess that was just a bonus. They probably planned on 'holding up' Vane and Whitely and stealing her from them. Her wandering out alone, and then you following, was too good to be true."

I shivered. "What happens now?"

"With Judge Ellens going to jail, and Commissioner Reynolds's unfortunate suicide?"

I snorted. "He set himself on fire and jumped off the roof to commit suicide?"

"Stranger things have happened."

I raised an eyebrow at him.

He grinned. "Well, you didn't hear it from me, but when the cops investigate, they are going to find very concerning images on his computer. It only makes sense that he killed himself before it was found."

"Images?" I thought of the way Giada had been cackling all afternoon. "Does the resident IT guy have anything to do with this?"

Renato smirked and cut his eyes to the potted plant on the corner of his desk. "I don't know what you're talking about, Mrs. De Sanctis," he said in a raised voice, as if acting up for the bug. "All charges against you and your sister have been dropped. All records of anything connected to you have disappeared. You have a clean slate, and Lucy as well."

I let out a long breath. "She wants to go to culinary school, you know, maybe."

Renato nodded. "I know. Carmella has been making a case for it. I wonder how she'd like Florence in the springtime. Or Le Cordon Bleu. Paris in March is lovely. We could tour the museums when we visit." He thought for a moment. "Switzerland is respectable, too."

I twisted on his lap and kissed him hard. "Thank you," I murmured against his lips.

"For?"

"For the first time in my life, I'm not alone," I admitted quietly.

Sure, I'd always had Lucy, but it was a different kind of feeling when you were caring for someone else. You could still feel alone, burdened by responsibilities that were growing too heavy to share.

"Then I should thank you, too, little nurse." Renato smiled and pushed my hair back from my face.

He leaned in and kissed my neck, his lips pressing against the pulse point that he'd first licked back at the charity benefit. The first time someone had rattled the walls of shame and repressed desire I'd built around myself.

"I prayed, you know?" I whispered.

He made a noise of appreciation against my skin.

"I prayed that you would come for me, and you did. I prayed you would save Lucy, and you did."

He continued his hot path up to my ear, while the words that had been brewing inside me slipped out.

"When I was thirteen, I prayed my Da would come back, and he never did."

Ren paused. "He was dead, *anima mia*."

Something about his dry humor took the sting out of the memory. "Thanks, genius. I know that. I knew it then, too, though it took a while to sink in. After that, I prayed that me and Lucy could be safe and happy again. It took thirteen years for that prayer to come true, but I think it has now." I threaded my hands through his hair. "Every prayer, every struggling step I took brought me closer to you. I think those childish, desperate prayers were answered."

Ren had reached the chain of the St. Anthony medal.

"Does that mean you aren't lost anymore?"

I shook my head slowly. A lazy smile spread over his lips, and he kissed me softly.

"You know, if this conversation is about to turn into denying me the soul you promised, we're going to have a problem."

I laughed. Renato De Sanctis, playful? No one would believe it.

"Oh really? How can we fix this dilemma?"

"You'll have to give me something else in return, it's only fair."

Renato flexed his hips against me, his cock lying in a hard line up my cleft, and it made me gasp.

I wriggled in his arms, wishing it was inside me instead of just tantalizingly close.

I reached down between us and stroked him through his pants. He grunted, a mutter leaving him at my touch. Having a man like Ren groaning under your touch was a new kind of power I was addicted to wielding.

"What did you have in mind?" I teased, my thoughts already heading into the gutter. I felt no shame in wanting this man. He was my husband. There was nothing wrong with wanting glorious, filthy fucking in general. It was something I was working on believing, one orgasm at a time. Maybe sexual healing was really a thing.

"As the one getting stiffed on the contract, I demand the right to choose the substitute," Renato murmured in my ear. "Keep your soul. I'll take your heart."

That's already yours.

I paused, overwhelmed for a second by this man. I'd never expected a lot for myself in life. Just surviving and supporting Lucy had been like achieving a goal set down for me by my Da every single day. But there was more to life than just surviving, and it was okay to want more. Tears threatened to fall again. I had rarely cried in a decade, but the last month had been intense. I'd cried, laughed, and fumed. I'd fought and hurt and screamed. I'd felt everything after years of feeling nothing at all.

"Too much?" Ren mused softly.

I'd left him hanging.

I shook my head and twisted to place a light kiss on his lips. "My cup runneth over," I whispered.

He smiled against my mouth, and then his hand joined mine, and he freed himself, dipping his hips so his length sprang free.

He guided it to me. When his hand moved up my thigh, pushing my knee-length skirt up and out of the way, he froze as his fingers met the soft curls on my mound.

"Wife, are you walking around here without panties on? What did I tell you about covering this fucking dream of a body for all eyes but mine?"

I sat forward and gripped his base, slipping it just inside me. He growled softly as I sank down on his length, facing away from him, my feet braced on the floor. He tugged my skirt out of the way so he could watch his cock disappearing inside me.

"You told me there'd be consequences if I broke your little rules," I reminded him and rolled my hips with him buried deep inside me. "I want to know what they are."

His hand landed on my lower back and guided me forward.

"You destroy me," he said thickly, just before his hand landed hard on my ass cheek, sending a curl of delicious heat racing through me.

He matched the other side as I ground myself on his length, enjoying every depraved moment.

"Now, bounce on me, *bambina,* until I come, then I want you to keep all that cum inside your cunt. Waste a single drop, and I'll have to refill you."

"You know it's a few weeks until I can even try to get pregnant, right?"

"Practice makes perfect, little nurse."

Epilogue: Six Months Later

CHARLIE

Graduation from nursing school at my age wasn't really a big deal, or so I told myself a hundred times as I waited in the spring sunshine for my family to arrive. Most other mature students had just had their diploma mailed to them. I'd suggested that to Ren, and he'd tutted in that infuriating way he did when he knew I was lying about something.

"You'll go and collect your diploma in person, and I'll be there to watch you, even if it's just waiting in line at the admin office," he'd said firmly, so here I was.

The other graduates around me were all younger, and I was pretty sure none of them were pregnant.

You couldn't really make out my bump yet. I was only four months along, and it was my first pregnancy, so I wasn't showing too much.

"Here they are," Sonny murmured to me.

I swiveled around in my seat. Yep, I had a bodyguard at graduation. I was that strange, untouchable student giving off secret princess vibes, and I was okay with that. I was sure Lucy would have it even worse in Florence when she started culinary school in a few weeks.

The small quad was full of chairs and parents and well-wishers. Pink-blossomed trees enclosed the space, and the sky was light blue.

Into that pastel palette, a spear of darkness appeared.

The De Sanctis family entered the quad, Ren's men spreading out to check the safety of the area. All in black, they didn't exactly fit in. Renato stalked down the central aisle, Elio at his shoulder, Giada on the other side, and Carmella and Lucy trailing behind them. Something clutched my throat at the sight of all the people who had become so dear to me, showing up here to support me.

Renato scanned for me, drawing eyes from the rest of the audience as he walked through the crowd like a king visiting his serfs. It parted naturally for him. He looked deadly, and more handsome than anyone had a right to. His eyes met mine, and the slight tension on his face faded. He smiled at me, inclining his head in a nod.

Good girl, little nurse. You've done so well. I could still hear the words he'd whispered in my ear last week when I'd told him I was pregnant, right in the middle of sex.

The Italians sat, looking like the rebel cool kids at school who everyone else wanted to be. The music started, and the ceremony began.

When my name was called, I took my diploma, and loud whistles filled the air. My ragtag group of family had all stood and were clapping so loudly, it should have been embarrassing. Giada led the charge, of course. Even the De Sanctis men, many of whom I knew by name now, having treated their various cuts and wounds, clapped loudly from the sidelines.

I didn't blush or rush away. *I deserved this.*

I raised my diploma in celebration, then took my damn time leaving the stage.

Epilogue: 14 Months Later

RENATO

I entered the bedroom and heard Charlotte sighing from the en suite bathroom. I'd been on a business trip to Las Vegas, and every single night I'd been away from my wife and twin daughters had been torture. I had a new measure on pain, now that I had my own family. Not being within arm's reach of my girls felt like a new and dangerously effective torture technique.

My girls.

The twins were nine months old, and Charlotte had proved to be exactly the mother I'd expected her to be. If anything, she'd grown more fearless, more loyal. A woman confident in her own power.

What a fucking turn-on.

The bathroom door was ajar. I watched as my wife paced back and forth on the marble tile. She was only wearing underwear, her beautiful body a testament to how much our lives had changed. Her belly was softer, her hips had stretch marks, and her breasts . . . I had no words to explain my obsession with her tits since she'd been pregnant. Her body bore the marks of my ownership. The evidence that we were bound together forever, and she'd never been more beautiful.

Right now, however, she cursed like a sailor and stared at herself in the mirror over the sink.

I knew she was alone, because I'd already stopped in on the girls. They were sleeping in the nursery while Carmella knitted in the corner, happily. The housekeeper had waited decades to have children in the house again. She was truly content.

Charlotte straightened up, and I finally saw her chest. She had her nursing bra open on both sides, and her perfect tits were swollen and full-looking. The sight was a kick of desire in the cock. I had no idea why nursing bras weren't generally regarded as an erotic item, given how much the sight of my wife in one turned me on. Maybe it was also the fact that her body was feeding my babies, too. It was primitive and hot as fuck, and I didn't question it.

"Come on, Charlie. You can do this," Charlotte said to her reflection, with no idea that her little pep talk was being witnessed.

I still loved to watch my wife while she was unaware. Sleeping, feeding the twins, from a distance while waiting for her.

I was about to speak and let her know she had an audience, when she leaned over the sink and grabbed her breasts. My words died as desire clutched my throat. She leaned over the sink and massaged the heavy globes, pulling at the nipples.

My self-control snapped, and I stepped into the room.

"I know I've been gone for two nights, but you're encroaching on my territory, and you know De Sanctis men take that seriously," I said to her.

She spun around and clamped an arm across her chest. "You're home early!"

"I couldn't wait." I took two long steps, and then she was in my arms. "Now, tell me what you were doing, and go into detail."

She blushed faintly. My little nurse still blushed over the most innocent things. She had a filthy mind, and I loved it.

"The twins are dropping feeds, and I have so much damn supply . . . it hurts," she confessed.

I took her by the hips and guided her to the counter, turning her again so she faced the mirror. I carefully pulled her long hair back over her shoulders, out of the way, and cupped her full breasts.

"Do you need help, little nurse?" I asked, reaching easily around her petite figure to wash my hands, slowly and methodically in the sink before her.

She nodded, her teeth sinking into her bottom lip. I dried my hands and then I was on her. I couldn't have waited another second. She stilled as I cupped her aching tits. I indulged in caressing them for a second, hefting their weight, brushing across the huge, dark nipples.

She shifted against me, arching her back so her ass pressed into my cock, already standing at attention from the moment I'd spied her in the bathroom pacing.

"Is this what you need?" My fingers latched on to her nipples and tugged, perfectly emulating the motion the twins made when they fed.

Charlotte nodded, leaning a little more over the sink. White beaded from the end of a hard bud.

"They just feel so full, like I'm going to burst." She sighed, her eyes fluttering shut as the first jet of milk released. "Tomorrow, I need to get a pump or something. Stockpile this milk in the freezer, maybe," she rambled, always organized and thinking ahead.

The other breast let down quickly after the first. She took a relieved breath. I hated the thought of her aching or uncomfortable. My eyes were drawn to the sight of her full tits releasing streams of milk. Dribbles of white ran across my tattooed knuckles, her skin wet and shining in the lights of the vanity.

Fuck, I was hard as hell. I was milking my wife, for her own comfort, and it had made me harder than I'd ever been.

It seemed like I wasn't the only one.

I met Charlotte's gaze in the mirror. Her eyes were hazy and lost in pleasure. I kneaded and caressed her hanging tits, eliciting more pleasure than milk now, the flow ebbing and then stopping. The sweet smell of it rose into the air. I rocked my hard cock against her backside, and she purposefully ground on me.

"Keep going like that, *bambina*, and you're going to get fucked over this sink, right here, right now," I warned.

She smirked and wriggled her hips against me. "Keep going like what?" Her voice was full of calculated innocence.

This woman was an endless delight.

It took a second to undo my fly and pull myself out. My hand was wet with her milk, and I rubbed it up and down the length of my cock to coat it and make me slippery for her, before I pressed to her entrance. Her panties pushed aside easily. Inside her was hot and wet. I sank in, imprinting kisses along her shoulders. Now, I felt like I was truly back from my trip. Right here, balls-deep in the woman I loved, my wife, I was home.

"If you're looking to play, *bambina*, just ask." I pumped into her, gripping handfuls of her ass to hold her in place.

She braced her hands on the counter to press back against me.

I fucked her hard until she panted my name. Before she came, I pulled her back against me, her hips flexing in an arch, and grabbed her throat. My other hand, still sticky and wet with milk, went into her sweet mouth, gagging her the way she liked it. I fit all four fingers in there and gripped her jaw, just like I had that first night in La Leonora, when I'd first discovered there was more to my good little nurse than met the eye.

She whimpered, her pussy only getting wetter at my control of her mouth. Her tongue caressed my fingers, and her pulse fluttered wildly under my fingers as she climbed higher and higher.

She imploded around me, clenching down on my pistoning cock relentlessly and nearly locking me in place. Her spasming muscles milked me, pulling cum from my balls with unstoppable intensity. I came hard, buried deep.

Later, when my heart stopped pounding and my cock slipped from her tight channel, I simply held her in my arms, watching her reflection. I enjoyed how her earlier frustration was gone, and her stunning features were soft and calm. My hand was still around her throat, just like she liked it, and now it tangled in the necklace she still wore. St. Anthony. The saint of lost things, and people.

"I was thinking of changing this necklace," Charlotte murmured, gazing at me in the mirror.

"It's a good idea. After all, you're not lost anymore, *bambina*, and you never will be again."

She grinned at me, a ray of pure fucking sunshine beaming right onto my unworthy face. In the end, she was the deity I'd serve until my last breath. My hope and salvation. My higher power. Happiness for me was, and always would be, the sight of her smile.

"Because you found me, and you're keeping me," she finished for me. My ritual prayer to my goddess. "Until death parts us," she whispered quietly.

I grinned against her skin, pressing a sweet kiss to her soft forehead. "Not even then, if I have anything to say about it. I told you I'm keeping you and I always keep my word."

ACKNOWLEDGMENTS

I want to take a moment to thank all those who made this book possible. My amazing cover designer, Angela; my editors, Emmy and Lauren; and my alpha reader, Katarina. Without you guys, Renato and Charlie wouldn't exist. I also want to thank my master marketer, my husband; my family for their support; and my Madrid 20 books ladies.

You know who you are.

xx

WELCOME TO MILA'S WORLD

Join my newsletter for deleted scenes, polls, and character inspiration at milakane.com.

PHOTO: JOANNA SILVESTRI

MILA KANE is a previously independent bestselling author. She is obsessed with cats, coffee, and antiheroes just the right side of insane. She writes dark and dirty romance with the alpha-holes of your most filthy nightmares. She writes only SAFE stories, and no matter how dark and twisted the story might be, there will always be a happily-ever-after guarantee. She lives with her husband in Scotland.

milakane.com
IG: @milakanebooks
Facebook: @MilaKanewrites
TikTok: @milakanebooks

ABOUT THE TYPE

This book was set in Jenson, one of the earliest print typefaces. After hearing of the invention of printing in 1458, Charles VII of France sent coin engraver Nicolas Jenson (c. 1420–80) to study this new art. Not long afterward, Jenson started a new career in Venice in letter-founding and printing. In 1471, Jenson was the first to present the form and proportion of this roman font that bears his name.

More than five centuries later, Robert Slimbach, developing fonts for the Adobe Originals program, created Adobe Jenson based on Nicolas Jenson's Venetian Renaissance typeface. It is a dignified font with graceful and balanced strokes.